# MCNEIL

# McNeil

### R. W. POWERS

iUniverse, Inc.
Bloomington

# McNeil

iUniverse books may be ordered through booksellers or by contacting:

iUniverse
1663 Liberty Drive
Bloomington, IN 47403
www.iuniverse.com
1-800-Authors (1-800-288-4677)

ISBN: 978-1-4620-1268-8 (sc)
ISBN: 978-1-4620-1269-5 (dj)
ISBN: 978-1-4620-1270-1 (ebk)

Library of Congress Control Number: 2011906648

Printed in the United States of America
iUniverse rev. date: 05/25/2011

The question on every soldier's mind is, especially if they have been brought up as Christians, there a special provision in the Sixth Commandment for those who have to go to war. There is no turning the other cheek when one is fighting for one's life.

To the many veterans who did not return home.

# MCNEIL

## DAI ICHI BUILDING
## TOKYO JAPAN

**Chapter 1**
**21 Apr 1950**

The sealed canvas dispatch bag marked 'MILITARY DISPATCH' was loaded on a C-47 in Washington, D.C. along with a ton of mail for the long trip to Tokyo Japan. When the canvas bag arrived at the SCAP (Supreme Commander, Allied Powers) message center at the Dai Ichi building in Tokyo it was opened and the contents sorted. A large manila envelope was immediately sent upstairs since it was sealed and marked for the Chief of Staff, SCAP.

Major General J. T. Jones, SCAP Chief of Staff, accepted the envelope, as he had done with so many others, and opened it. Even generals got their hands dirty with the cut back in personnel. There was a stack of messages plus another sealed manila envelope inside the large envelope. He set the small sealed envelope aside and sorted the stack of messages into two stacks. One stack required action such as reprint and distribution to the responsible commanders. The second stack should go in the trash can was his thinking, since they were non-informational with no action required. General Jones thought some chair warmer in the pentagon probably drafted those messages to justify his position.

He quickly scanned the second stack of messages, initialed each, and then marked them for file. The first stack of messages he read more carefully, initialed each, then attached a routing slip for reading by the concerned departments before they were filed.

It took General Jones two hours to complete the task and when the last message was in his OUT basket he reached for the sealed envelope he had saved for last. He noticed, as he opened the envelope, that there were no security markings on it, or on the single folded sheet of paper inside. As he read the contents of the message his eye brows rose in surprise. He reread the message to make sure he understood it. He stood up and checked his appearance, when he was satisfied he made his way to the office of SCAP.

He knocked on the door and entered when he heard the word 'Enter' called out. General Jones opened the door then stopped unsure of what to do when he saw the SCAP had a visitor. "Good morning sir. Sorry to interrupt," he said apologizing, "I wasn't aware you had company. I can come back later sir."

"That's ok Joe. Come on in," said the SCAP (Supreme Commander Allied Powers), General Douglas MacArthur from behind his massive desk. General MacArthur, as usual, was dressed in his washed smooth khaki shirt and trousers. He was a tall thin man and his trade mark sun glasses and corn cob pipe lay on the desk in easy reach. He had a small dark cigar between his fingers. "I'm sure you know General Walker."

"Yes sir. Good morning general."

"Good morning general," replied General Walker. Lieutenant General Walton H. Walker commanded the 8th Army in Korea. His middle name was Harris and his nick name was Johnnie bestowed on him for his love of Johnnie Walker Scotch. He was born in Belton Texas in 1889 and graduated from West Point in 1912. General Walker was a stocky man, with a second nick name of Bull Dog because of his short stature and never smiling face. He was very short of speech and not popular with the troops because of his mission first and troop comfort second attitude.

"I do believe Joe has official confirmation of the subject we were discussing," said General MacArthur putting the cigar in an ash tray and reaching for the message in General Jones hand.

General MacArthur quickly read the message then reached across the desk to pass it to General Walker. "Yes, the rumors we heard are now official. Joe, make sure General Walker has a copy of the message before he departs and get a copy to all subordinate unit commanders."

19 April 1950
Wash D C
SEDEF

CLASSIFICATION SENSITIVE
IFO: CHIEFS OF STAFF, PENTAGON
GREETINGS FROM THE SEDEF.

FOR IMMEDIATE ACTION.

1. PEACE IS UPON US AND FOR THAT WE ARE THANKFUL.

2. THE REDUCTION OF MILITARY FORCES, ARMY, MARINE, AIR FORCE, NAVY, AND COAST GUARD, WILL BE THROUGH ATTRITION AND WILL START IMMEDIATELY.

3. FORT POLK, LA, IS CLOSED. ALL OTHER BASIC TRAINING COMMANDS HAS BEEN ORDERED TO REDUCE TRAINING CYCLES TO ONE HALF.

4. OCS (Officer Candidate School) WILL BE REDUCED TO ONE CLASS PER YEAR PER COMMAND.

5. ALL NEW EQUIPMENT PURCHASES HAVE BEEN CANCELLED OR PUT ON HOLD.

6. REPLACEMENT PARTS WILL BE PURCHASED ON A PRIORITY, AS NEEDED, BASIS.

7. COMMANDERS AT ALL LEVELS WILL ENCOURAGE EXTENSION OF CURRENT ASSIGNMENTS, OVER SEAS AND CONUS, TO CURTAIL TRANSPORTATION MOVEMENT EXPENSES.

8. OPERATION OF AIR, GROUND, AND WATER VEHICLES WILL BE ON A PRIORITY BASIS.

9. MANAGEMENT OF CURRENT ASSETS IS A COMMAND RESPONSIBILITY.

FOR THE SEDEF
RALPH T. LIME
BRIG. GEN. USA

"Yes sir," replied General Jones.

General Walker handed him the single page message and he left the SCAP office. "Well Walton," said the SCAP after the door was closed, "seems we have some more belt tightening to do."

"It seems so sir but my belt is in the last hole now. If I do anymore tighten then I'll have to make a new hole."

"Orders are orders, regardless of how insane they seem to us. This office and all commands will comply with that order."

"I Understand Sir. Do you have anything else for me General?"

"Not at this time, but my door is always open."

Lieutenant General Walton H. Walker, commander of the Eighth United States Army in Korea, left the SCAP office wondering how he was going to manage an army, Eighth Army, on the provisions and equipment equal to that of a division.

Since many of the men in his command were not combat trained he was in the process of getting them up graded. Now with further cut back in personnel and equipment his job would be doubly hard.

As he got into the staff car which would take him out to the airfield where a plane waited to fly him back to South Korea he had another thought. With the cutback in fuel and equipment, transportation for generals will soon be by space available on milk runs. That's not very flattering for a general officer.

# MCNEIL

## SOUTH KOREA
## HILL 715

**Chapter 2**
**10 Aug 1950**

The wind whistled through the cracks in the rocks. Thunder rumbled and lightening flashed and five minutes later big drops of rain started to fall. Three hours ago the sky was clear and full of twinkling stars with a quarter Moon rising over the Yellow sea. Sudden storms were typical this time of year on the Asian land mass. Sometimes one would last all day or night but most times a few hours were the limit.

The thunder rumbled and shook the ground and the lightening flashed at regular intervals sometimes lighting up the cave through the small cracks and air vents.

A man yawned, stretched, and then sat up on the rock shelf where he had his bed laid out. The storm didn't bother him now since he had grown use to sudden violet storms that lashed at the island and pounded the hill with the cave at its peak.

The man was use to sleeping in short stretches and the storm was welcomed for three reasons; one, the rain would erase all tracks of a human presence on the island. Two, he would be able to build a fire to cook a hot meal. With the wind and rain any smoke would be dissipated. Most important, the rain would leave plenty of fresh water for both drinking and bathing.

He started the preparations. Everything was placed in the cave so he could put his hands on it in the dark. First he lit a small lantern, lowered the chimney over the flame so the gusting breeze wouldn't blow it out, then he set a shield over the lantern to direct the light downward.

When he was ordered to, and brought to the island, it was on a dark night. He scouted the island for the next two days getting familiar with every rock, tree, and brush. The island he was on, and he assumed the others were the same, was wind swept with a few short knurled trees and little underbrush. The island was mostly barren with wind swept rocks. When he discovered the

5

cave at the top of the center and tallest hill he knew that would be his base of operations. The cave had two openings, one facing east and the other facing west. Two entrances and two exits meant an escape route if needed plus the two openings would provide cross ventilation.

He had to make more than one trip up the hill on the narrow winding path before he got all his gear, which included a bulky radio, into the cave. His first job was to camouflage both cave openings.

Planning ahead for the unknown he had assumed he might have to pitch a pup tent to sleep in so he brought both halves with him. By using the cave as his operation center and sleeping area he had no need for the tent halves. He used the tent halves to cover the cave openings. Anchoring them in rock cracks by pounding in wooden sticks he proceeding to apply mud and dirt to make the canvas look as if it was part of the rocks. He made several trips up and down the hill checking on his work until he was satisfied the openings couldn't be seen at a distance.

There was a hundred to one chance that the lantern light could be seen from outside the cave but he was a cautious man and preferred to not take chances. He always placed the lantern on the dirt floor. He had been through this routine many times so he knew exactly what to do. It was only one in the morning he noticed looking at his watch and he had no idea how long the storm would last. He started a small fire in a stone lined pit on the cave floor using dry twigs he had gathered earlier. He put water in a pot and placed it over the fire. Searching through his supply of 3 in 1 rations he selected what he wanted to eat. Maybe not what he really wanted but he had to eat what was available. He selected a can of beef stew this morning. Opening the can he dumped the contents into another pan and set it over the fire. By the time he had that accomplished the water in the first pot was boiling so he dumped in a measured amount of coffee grounds.

Moving both pots away from the fire but still near enough to keep the contents warm he picked up his soap and razor and went to the rear corner of the cave where a trickle of water started coming down a rock chute. He went about washing and shaving.

The day he moved into the cave he discovered the cistern above the cave, a hollowed out rock that could hold about fifty gallons of water. The overflow from the cistern fell into the cave. Over the years the runoff had cut a shallow trench in the cave floor which allowed the excess water to exit the cave and flow downhill or soak into the ground, depending on the amount of rain fall.

When he discovered the half full cistern it had trash and bird droppings in it. He cleaned it out then stretched a camouflage net over it to keep the birds out. He wasn't depriving the birds of water because he discovered other cisterns on the hill. Under the camouflage net was a perfect place to erect the radio antenna so it wouldn't be seen.

The rain storms, though sometimes violet, were a blessing to him. It was the only time he had water for a bath and to wash his clothes, plus he could have coffee and a hot meal without worrying about the smoke from the small fire being seen.

The harsh living conditions plus the primitive method of washing his clothes had caused his uniforms to deteriorate rapidity. Pockets were the first items to go so he cut them off. As the uniforms deteriorated further he cut off the pants legs and removed the shirt sleeves.. He was down to two sets of cutoffs now with a week to go until, hopefully, he would be replaced. He held back one complete uniform and a change of underwear which he was saving for the day he would leave the island. He didn't feel it would be in good taste to report back to his unit in cutoffs.

After he washed himself he washed out a set of clothes, wrung them out, and hung them on a parachute cord he rigged from one wall of the cave to the other. With the water still running he decided his hair was a bit too long so he lathered up his head and shaved it. He dried off and dressed in a clean set of cutoffs.

He poured out a cup of coffee then started eating the warm beef stew. He knew the smell of coffee and cooking food would rise to the top of the cave and out through the cracks and be dissipated by the wind. There was no chance that anyone near the island could smell the food or see the smoke with the storm raging outside.

When he was able to anticipate an approaching storm he would normally cook up a good size bird or some fish. He baked them in hot coals using an old Indian method he had learned about years ago.

Fish, crabs and lobsters were plentiful around the island. Crabs and lobsters he trapped using twig traps he built. He speared fish with a homemade spear, a pointed stick, or picked them up by hand in a small lagoon where the tide left them after it receded. Sea birds of several types used the island for roosting and nesting. Sometimes he was even able to have fresh bird eggs.

A small crossbow fashioned from local wood and short shafts with fire hardened points were used to kill the birds of choice when the time was right.

The method of cooking the fish and birds were relative simple. The head, and entrails, were removed from the fish, and the head, legs and entrails were cut from the birds. After each was washed it was packed in a ball of clay. The ball of clay was then buried in a bed of hot coals for a period of time. When it was ready one simply hit the fire hardened clay ball with a rock until it shattered. The skin and feathers stuck to the clay when it fell away and left a perfectly cooked bird or fish. All one needed was some seasoning. The best thing was that the bird or fish could be left in the clay ball for a couple of days after it was cooked. With no air getting to the meat it would keep.

Fresh hot food was a welcome change from the 3 in 1 rations. Bread was a rarity, he had it only when the supply boat came, and most times he made do with the crackers from the 3 in 1 rations.

He was on the island as an OP (observation post), LP (listening post), and a sort of a coast watcher. His unit was on a bit of land, a peninsular, surrounded on three sides by water with the fourth side the 38th parallel facing the North Koreans. His job was vital as it was explained to him. Observe and report any and all activity on and around the islands. Maybe the locals had names for the islands but the military only gave them numbers in relation to the height of each one. His island was designated as hill 715.

Since his unit was under strength, as was most all units in Korea at this time, he had the lone duty of keeping watch over all the islands, and he had no idea how many there were. It would have been much simpler to do the job with more men but manpower was not available.

If the North Koreans could get in position on any of the islands, especially the one he was on, they could set up enough artillery to pin his unit down while the North Koreans attacked across the 38th parallel. If enough long range artillery could be set up on any of the islands more units could be bombarded on the mainland. He could see where it was vital that the islands did not fall into the hands of the North Koreans.

More than once the North Koreans tried to move onto the islands during the past two months. From his high vantage point he was able to determine their intended landing site and call it in. In twenty minutes planes appeared and bombed and strafed until no one was left alive. If it happened on his island, by now he was beginning to think of hill 715 as his island, he could walk down and get an assessment. If it happened on one of the other islands he would paddle to it on the raft he made from bamboo. He would then check the damage and call in a BDA, (bomb damage assessment).

The first time the North Koreans tried to invade his island there were twenty of them in full combat gear with a couple of small artillery pieces. They came in two boats. He was able to judge their destination while they were still off shore and called it in. The planes came over just as the boats touched shore. There was little left of the men and equipment when the planes departed.

He was never one to let anything go to waste so after he called in his first BDA he selected four undamaged rifles plus ammo and put them in his cave. Two rifles inside at each opening. He figured if he was ever attacked he would, with four rifles plus his M1 and a forty five caliber pistol, plus sufficient ammo, take a lot of the attackers with him before he was overrun.

The thought was constantly on his mind that if the Air force did not react quickly enough, if an attack occurred, he may not survive. But he was a soldier and he was doing what he was ordered to do. As he went about taking the best rifles he discovered a couple of pistols on what must have been officers. Once he collected the weapons and cleaned them he realized he knew the make and caliber of them. Something he had learned and retained during a weapons identification class back at Fort Benning Georgia.

All the weapons, rifles and pistols, were 7.62 calibers and were Russian made. On each side of the automatic pistol barrels were stamped a star and the top was stamped 7.62 RUSSE. The rifles had the same thing on them plus the word TOKAREV was stamped on the side of the barrel. Does that mean the Russians are active in the war, or are they just backing the North Koreans with weapons, he wondered. He decided to get a pistol and a rifle back to Battalion S-2 along with all the papers taken from the North Koreans pockets. Let the so called experts do the interpretation and make the decisions.

After each bombing he went through the pockets of the dead men, plus their packs, and removed all papers, wallets and maps. Then he tore a shoulder patch from a uniform. Touching dead men with blood and gore all over them wasn't a pleasant thing to do but he felt it was worth it. Everything he collected was bagged and held until he had a chance to get it back to battalion S-2 for analysis.

He had discovered black flesh eating ants on the island. He knew they were flesh eaters because he watched them attack a crab and eat it until there wasn't anything left but the shell. He came up with an idea to discourage any more trespassers on the island, his island. There were only three accessible sites for boats to land on the island. To each of the three sites he lugged a dead North Koreans. He sat them down with their backs against a tree and facing the water and tied them in place. He left a trail of food from the ant hills to the bodies and let nature take its course. The skeletons were a deterrent to any more attempted landings on his island.

He did feel a bit of remorse using a human as he did but, he was a soldier with a mission to accomplish. The powers to be called this uprising in Korea a Police action but people were getting killed, and that's what happens in a war.

Though the mission responsibility thrust upon him was a twenty four hour duty it was a lonely vigil. After completing the Army daily Dozen exercise twice a day plus other necessary chores he still had time to reminisce, about the past, about family and friends.

He was living at home, working part time plus attending college, when his father was killed by a job related accident during his first year of college. The loss of her husband hit his mother hard and she started to crawl into a bottle. Somehow, with her grief and drinking, she was still able to hold a job. He had a brother and sister, both married with their own lives and interests. The last time he saw or spoke to either of them was at his father's funeral. They had no idea where he was or that he had been drafted. He did tell his mother when he had to leave in April that he would be going away for a while. She just nodded her head and said, "That's nice," and turned back to the TV. He had no idea if she understood him or not.

With what little money he made plus what his mother brought home, plus the insurance from his father's death he and his mother was able to maintain the house and pay his tuition.

After the end of his third year of college, he was going for a degree in Political Science, the money was running low so he decided to lay out a semester and work full time to accumulate some extra money.

What he forgot was the draft. A month after he dropped out of college he received a letter from his friends and neighbors, he was drafted into the Army.

He knew that with three years of college and four years of R O T C he could apply for a commission but that would mean four to five years of service rather than the two years because he was drafted. He chose to keep quiet and do the two years as an enlisted man.

Twice during the time, before Korea, personnel had checked his records and twice he had been called in and asked about taking a commission. Each time he refused; better two years rather than four or five was his answer.

Because of all the R O T C training during high school and college he had prior knowledge of military procedures and training requirements. He put that knowledge to work. He attended both basic and advanced training at Fort Benning Georgia and placed first which earned him a promotion to Private First Class. In hopes that he could remain at Fort Benning for his two year tour he volunteered for both Airborne and Ranger training since the training was conducted at Fort Benning. Because of the schools and the waiting time between schools plus leave taken he had used up better than eight months of his two years. Because of the schools and his education he made Corporal in seven months. He was checking for other schools he could attend that would keep him at Fort Benning when he received orders for Korea.

He was assigned to 1st Battalion, 5th Infantry Division (un-mechanized), Baker Company, 3rd Platoon, 3rd Squad. The mission of the 1st Battalion was to advise the 17th R O K Battalion and provide backup to defend and hold the Ongjin Peninsular from a possible North Korean invasion.

The units, from the Division down, were understaffed, undermanned, and under supplied. All the units operated in a very relaxed mode. After a week at the company his analysis was that most of the men were National

Guard getting active duty training. Officers were fresh out of school getting practical experience. Corporal Charley R. McNeil not wanting to make waves and draw attention fell into the relaxed routine of the unit. Two things really stood out in his mind. One was he came here expecting it to be a peaceful assignment and he would be home in a year, but a war happened. The other thing was that one day he was a corporal and the next he was a 1st Lieutenant. A week after he pinned on the silver bar of a 1st Lieutenant he was sent to the island.

# McNeil

## Inchon South Korea

**Chapter 3**
**Apr 1950**

It was a hot humid day when the tug boats pushed the USS Bounder, an old troop ship, to the docks of the port city of Inchon South Korea. Corporal Charlie M. McNeil and several hundred other men lined the port side rail of the troop ship to watch the docking operation. While they observed the operation an odor drifted across the dock and onto the troop ship causing the men to wrinkle their nose. The odor that assaulted the nostrils of the arriving men smelled like a hundred outhouses with their doors open on a hot day. The men were to find out that the thing about an outhouse was somewhat true. Even though there were open sewers that provided the constant odor, the Koreans used human excrement to fertilize their rice paddies, and other crops. It was definitely an odor that took some time to get used to, if getting used to it was possible.

"Smells like shit doesn't it?" spoke a buck sergeant who had walked up beside McNeil. McNeil knew Sergeant Nettles from playing several games of poker with him, and others, during the long ocean crossing. Sergeant Nettles was a short slender man who had an opinion about everything. "Get used to it because the smell will not go away," Sergeant Nettles said as he leaned on the rail beside McNeil.

Before McNeil could form an answer the ship's PA blared. "All troops to the second deck portside, bag and baggage for departure."

McNeil went below and retrieved his packed bags. He located the correct deck and door and got in line with the other three hundred men and exited the troop ship. McNeil and the other men were loaded on trucks and trucked from the port to a holding company to await assignment. Camp Able was about a mile from the dock and most of the road was dirt. The city of Inchon could be seen off to their left as the trucks passed dikes with small brown, shirtless, men working knee deep in muddy water. Few trees could be seen along the way.

Corporal McNeil and many other men remained with the replacement company at Camp Able, which was nothing but tent city, for almost a week while records, that were previously checked, were rechecked. Medical records were rechecked to assure that everyone had the required vaccinations. Finance records were checked and each man paid up-to-date with MPC (Military Pay Script) funny money. They were required to turn in all their green backs for the funny money. Personnel records were checked to assure each man was qualified for the M O S, (Military Occupation Specialty), he was assigned. Clothing records were checked, up dated, and field gear was issued, less weapons.

Even though Corporal McNeil was technically a noncommissioned officer, an N C O, he did not have enough rank to be billeted with the other N C O's. Yet he had too much rank to be put in the enlisted quarters. The problem was solved when he and several others of similar rank were moved into private rooms with canvas dividers in the enlisted tent. Even though Sergeant Nettles was somewhere in the camp McNeil didn't make contact with him and for that he was thankful. It wasn't that he was antisocial he just wasn't in the mood to listen to more bragging.

There is always griping and complaining among the lower ranks but the biggest grip most of the time was that they were restricted to Camp Able. Being in a foreign country they were anxious to get out and mingle with the natives, read women. That was not to happen until they reached their assigned units, they were told.

Camp Able did offer some forms of entertainment. There were movies each night, shown outside, weather permitting. There was an adequately stocked P X, (Post Exchange) plus a beer hall, both in wooden buildings, of which many of the men occupied and proceeded to acquire a headache for the following morning. Fighting was constant among the men and the MP'S were kept busy.

Corporal McNeil took everything with a grain of salt. He looked at the five days spent in the replacement company as just five more days closer to the time of his release from the Army. He looked at the one week leave before departure from the States plus the long sea voyage the same way. Just so much time knocked off his remaining time in the Army.

He didn't waste his money gambling in the many poker games nor did he participate in any of the constant on going bull sessions. After a bath and a change of clothes that first day he located the PX where he bought some toilet articles he thought he might need later. He purchased a current copy of the local military newspaper, the Stars and Stripes, to see what was happening in Korea. He added several paperback books for leisure reading. On a shelf he found a dusty hard back book which caught his interest, a book on Political

Science, his college major. McNeil was not an addicted smoker but he did enjoy a good cigar occasionally. When he located his favorite brand of cigars, Romeo y Julietas, he added three boxes to his basket. Since he wasn't sure of what would be available where he was going he wanted to be as well prepared as he could. He paid for the purchases with M P C, (Military Pay Script), funny money as everyone called it. There were no coins; all denominations were paper of different colors.

He returned to his room with his purchases, undressed and lay down on his cot to read and smoke a cigar.

He did enjoy a cold beer now and again so he went to the N C O club a few evenings before the heavy drinking started. There he heard talk, from the old timers that supported most of what he had read about Korea after he had received his orders. The nick name given to Korea was Frozen Chosen. During the winter months it was very cold and windy with plenty of snow and ice. When the temperature rose a few degrees one put up with mud created when the snow melted.

Korea was an assignment no one asked for. It was the place where Reserve and National Guard troops did their activity duty time. Korea was a place where N C O's were sent for their last year or so before retiring in their current rank because few if any got promoted in Frozen Chosen.

Korea was an assignment no officer wanted from Generals on down the rank structure. Young Lieutenants were sent to Korea fresh from O C S, or other schools, to get basic experience in command. Captains and up were sent here because they had not performed up to standards, or they had stepped on the wrong toes. Most officers would be asked to resign or retire after completing a Korean tour of duty.

There are always exceptions to most rules and somewhere in Korea are a few good officers who know and perform their duties well, but with little chance of promotion.

## 11 Apr 1950

Every day men were loaded on trucks and sent out from Camp Able. This morning, the sixth day here for Corporal McNeil, his name was called out to load up and ship out. There were three 6x6 trucks leaving this morning and McNeil and nineteen other men boarded the last truck with their bags. The trip took all day since the trucks made several stops at different units to drop off men and supplies. Most of the trip was over rough dirt roads between rice paddies and small forests of trees. The houses visible from the road were constructed of mud and straw. Darkness was approaching when the truck pulled into the area where the 5th Infantry Division (un-mechanized) was camped. It was tent city. Tents were erected on what looked to be about fifty acres of land.

The Division had to know men were coming in but when Corporal McNeil and the four men with him entered the Headquarters tent it was deserted except for a young PFC clerk. He took their orders and records and had each man sign in. He then issued each man a set of bed linen, escorted them to a tent where they were supposed to make up a bed. He pointed out the showers and mess tent then told them to be at headquarters immediately after breakfast, which was at zero five hundred hours. With that bit of information imparted he left Corporal McNeil and the men to themselves.

Corporal McNeil was a trained Infantry man and he believed in the old adage, eat when there is food and sleep when you can. He dropped his bags on the unmade cot, put a cigar in his pocket, and located the mess hall. They were still servicing so he loaded up a tray, filled a cup with coffee, and sat down at a vacate table. This would be his second hot meal today. For lunch a cold roast beef sandwich and a can of coke was handed to the remaining men on the truck.

He cleaned his tray of food and drained his cup. After depositing the tray in the proscribed place he refilled his cup and sat back down. He lit the cigar and enjoyed the leisure moment. There were a few scruffy looking privates loitering in the mess tent, probably delaying going on a late night detail. The only other people were a couple of N C O's at a corner table drinking coffee, smoking, and talking. No officers, they probably had their own mess tent. No one paid attention to the lone corporal and McNeil had no desire to get in a conversation with anyone.

After smoking the cigar and finishing his third cup of coffee McNeil found his way back to the designated tent and made up his bed. With his shaving kit, towel, and clean clothes, he went to locate the shower tent. Later as he got into bed, just before the lights went out, his last thought was, one more day closer.

Corporal McNeil and the four privates spent all the next day processing. Again their records were checked, their field gear was inventoried to assure they had everything they should have. Weapons were issued this time, less ammo.

The M-1 Garand rifle was a very familiar weapon to Corporal McNeil. He had fired it many times. It was a heavy awkward rifle but very accurate when properly zeroed. It would operate even when it was dirty yet it was one of the easiest weapons to maintain and keep clean.

The first thing McNeil did when he received the rifle was to look at the serial number and start memorizing it. He went back to his tent and disassembled the rifle and cleaned and checked each part. He coated each part with a light coat of oil before he reassembled it and checked the action.

Orders were handed out two days later assigning Corporal McNeil and two of the privates to the 1st Battalion of the 5th Infantry Division. They were told to be packed and ready to depart at 04:00 hours the next morning. After an early breakfast the three men were loaded on a truck which was already loaded with supplies. After traveling east for about five miles the truck stopped and backed up. It was still too dark to make out any land features but the smell of water was on the air, salt water. There was a boat in the water with a couple of dim lights showing, the boat is commonly called an M-boat, or mike boat, and the ramp was down. As soon as the cargo from the truck was loaded along with McNeil and the two men plus their bags the boat ramp was raised and the boat eased away from the shore.

The mike-boat, though a Navy boat, was manned by two Army men and even though it was powered by a large diesel engine it was very quiet as it moved across the water. The inside of the mike boat was large enough that a large truck would fit inside but today there were only stacks of cargo and three men.

Even though the crack of dawn was still several minutes away there was enough light that men and a truck could be seen on shore when the mike-boat slowed and lowered the ramp at the shore line. Not having access to a map Corporal McNeil could only assume they had crossed a river or maybe a bay.

Corporal McNeil and the two privates were invited to help remove the cargo from the mike-boat and load it on the waiting truck. There were cases of food, ammo, other regularly used supplies plus a couple bags of mail.

After a short ride the truck stopped in the 1st Battalion area where several tents were set up among the trees. Since there were no facilities for transit personnel, the men were informed; they were quickly processed and assigned to companies. One private was assigned to Able Company, the other to Dog Company, Corporal McNeil to Baker Company. They and their bags were again loaded on a truck and they were on their way again.

McNeil stepped from the truck in the Baker company area and looked the set up over with a critical eye, a military eye. There were more tents erected for Baker Company than there were for the 1st Battalion. All the tents were set up in the wrong place. Why, he asked himself, was not terrain and concealment utilized? The sixteen tents were perfectly lined up in two rows facing an open area which would be called a company street or formation area. Another thing his critical eye had noticed was how close to one another the tents were erected. Even with the sides rolled up there would be little air flow in the tents. One artillery or mortar round would take out most of the company. Just to the rear of where the tents were set up was a wooded area that would have provided shade and some concealment, but it wasn't used.

A small sign in front of one of the tents proclaimed that to be the

Baker Company Orderly Room. A staff sergeant stepped out of the tent and stretched and yarned, then noticed McNeil with his bags. "Corporal McNeil I presume?" he asked as he walked the few steps and extended his hand. "I'm Sergeant Sampson the acting first sergeant, welcome to Baker Company."

McNeil took the offered hand and just nodded his head. Sergeant Sampson wasn't to impressive. He was a bit on the short side with thinning brown hair and his uniform was wrinkled as if he had slept in it

"We got word to expect you but not when," continued SSgt. Sampson as he motioned for McNeil to enter the tent, "if you will sign in and give me a copy of your orders we'll get you settled in."

After McNeil handed over several copies of his orders SSgt. Sampson continued, "our commanding officer, 1st Lt Richards, isn't here to meet you but he did inform me to assign you to 3rd Platoon, 3rd Squad. Gordon," he called out to a private sitting behind a field desk on the opposite side of the tent, "Locate Sgt Dill for me."

"Yes Sergeant," replied Private Gordon as he put his hat on and left the tent.

While waiting for Sgt Dill McNeil had a chance to look around the tent. It wasn't too impressive. A couple of battered field desks, a couple of chairs, a table with radios on it, and two file cabinets were the extent of the furniture. There was a piece of canvas stretched between two tent poles as a room divider. He couldn't see what was behind the canvas.

Pfc Gordon returned followed by a tall lanky Sgt Dill, what is called a buck Sergeant, a three striper. He had a thin narrow face and short cut brown hair.

"You sent for me sergeant?" he asked as he entered the tent.

"I did. Meet Corporal McNeil."

"Glad to meet you Corporal McNeil."

"Corporal McNeil just reported in. Lt. Richards desires he be assigned to 3rd Platoon 3rd squad. Get him settled in."

"Sure. Follow me Corporal McNeil." McNeil picked up a couple of his bags but was having trouble with the third. "Here, let me help you with the bags," offered Sgt Dill as he picked up one and left the tent. McNeil followed. When they left the tent Sgt Dill started explaining the setup of the company area.

"I'm the NCO for all four platoons," said Sgt Dill as he continued walking. Just what is going on here wondered McNeil; an E-6 as first sergeant, a first Lieutenant as company commander, and an E-5 for a platoon sergeant?

"As you can see there are eight tents on each side of the company street," continued Sgt Dill. "Lt. Richards wanted everything even so he had us setting up extra tents so both sides of the street would have the same number of tents. As you know we just left the orderly room. The first tent west of it is where support personnel sleep, cooks, motor pool, and orderly room people. Then there's supply and their storage tent. The last tent is for officers, make that officer. East of the orderly room is the mess hall, the kitchen, and the kitchen storage tent. On the other side of the street is where the men live. Two tents are assigned to each platoon. 3rd platoon has tent five and six, you will be in tent six. Showers and outhouses are out back of the squad tents. As you can see each tent is numbered. Tiny!" called out Sgt Dill when he stopped in front of tent six.

From somewhere at the rear of the tent a voice answered, "Yes sergeant?"

A second later a body filled the tent opening. The tent opening was so low most man had to duck to go through it but this man had to bend at his waist to get through the opening. The man would probably weigh around two hundred and fifty pounds and he was at least six foot tall. No fat, just a big man. Now McNeil was no slouch, he stood five eleven and weighed one eighty. The name tag on the man's uniform read Brockman and he wore PFC stripes (Private First Class) on his shirt sleeve. PFC Brockman, though a big man, was soft spoken. His dark hair was cut close and his uniform wasn't wrinkled as SSgt Sampson's was.

"Tiny," said Sgt Dill, "I told you that if you didn't shape up you would be replaced, well meet your replacement, Corporal McNeil."

"I don't mind sergeant. Glad to have you with us Corporal McNeil," he said and reached out a hand that swallowed McNeil's. His grip was firm but he didn't squeeze McNeil's hand and for that he was glad.

"You don't live up to your nick name PFC Brockman." There were chuckles from men inside of the tent.

"That nick name Tiny was bestowed on me a long time ago and it seems to follow me. I don't mind."

"Tiny has been acting squad leader," explained Sgt Dill, "and is also your B A R (Browning automatic rifle) man. He has done a good job. Listen, we'll talk later. Right now I'm in a hot poker game and I'm down ten. I need to get back and try to recoup some of my loss. Tiny, get McNeil settled in for me."

"I'll take care of him sergeant. Your cot is over here," said Tiny after Sgt Dill departed and they entered the tent, Tiny helping McNeil with his bags. "I shuffled everyone so you could have the first cot. Mine is next to yours. I have already picked up your bedding."

The first thing that caught McNeil's eye was the lack of cots in the tent. There should have been fourteen, seven on each side. There were only five cots on the side where Tiny indicated he was to sleep, and only four on the other side. It seems there is a personnel shortage here, was his thinking.

While they worked to get McNeil's gear squared away they talked, rather Tiny talked, giving McNeil what information he possessed. McNeil wasn't one to form close friendships but he began to like the big man.

"PFC Brockman,--

"Please," interrupted Tiny, "call me Tiny."

"Ok Tiny. You seem to be an agreeable, easy going fellow, do you ever get mad?" McNeil asked the question because he feared he may have problems with Tiny if he was temperamental.

"Not too often," replied PFC Brockman with a twinkle in his soft grey eyes. Tiny was wondering why this man was asking such questions of him.

Even though PFC Brockman (Tiny as he said to call him) was a big man he didn't seem to be intimidating. He was a pleasant easy going man.

"I'm glad to hear that. Since you prefer to be called Tiny call me Charley, when we're alone that is."

"Ok Charley," replied Tiny smiling as he fished a key from his pocket and unlocked a rifle rack that stood in the middle of the tent. "Let's lock up your weapon then it's time for chow. The other men are on details so I'll introduce them later. Now, since you are the 3rd squad leader and the ranking man in the tent the gun rack key is yours," said Tiny locking the gun rack and holding the key out to McNeil.

When they had food and drink they sat together in the mess tent and talked some more. "Sprechen sie Dutsche?"

"What? What did you say?" asked Tiny.

"Your name sounds German," said McNeil as he tasted the unappetizing looking meat on his tray. "I asked you if you speak the language."

"I'm from German descendants, my grandparents came over from Germany many years ago," replied Tiny, "but I don't speak the language

McNeil's friend, and study mate, at college was German and McNeil became quite proficient in the language since they sometimes studied and talked in German.

"I know a couple of words but not enough to recognize what you asked me," added Tiny.

"I see," replied McNeil as he took a sip of the strong coffee.

"You obviously speak German even though your name sounds more Irish than German?"

"In deed it does. I'm a product of Irish descendants. In answer to your question, I had a German friend in college and he taught me to speak the language quiet well."

"In one year?" asked an amazed Tiny.

"Fortunately I made it for three years before I dropped out and the draft caught me."

"I see," replied Tiny taking a sip of his coffee. "Your accent leaves me to believe you are from a Southern state."

"Close, I'm from Kentucky. How about you? Where are you from?"

"Pennsylvania. Many Germans settled in the area around Harrisburg Pennsylvania because the climate and terrain was so much like their native Germany. We're called Pennsylvania Dutch."

"How much longer are you here for Tiny?"

"Six more months then back to college."

"The draft got you did it?"

"Yes. I had to drop out after the first year to earn enough money for the second year. I forgot about the draft until one day I received my invitation letter."

"We have more in common than you realize Tiny. Basically the same thing happened to me. My friends and neighbors decided I should serve my time in the military after I dropped out of college for a semester to work and earn some money. The Army wanted me to see some of the world."

"Some world we're seeing, huh?" replied a somewhat bitter Tiny.

"Always look on the bright side of things Tiny. We could be somewhere where shots are being fired in anger."

"Yeah, I guess. Well, in six months they can have this frozen chosen. I'm out of here."

"Well, unfortunately, I have a year to go here."

"I see the airborne and ranger patch on your shirt sleeve. What prompted you to go to these particular schools?" asked Tiny.

"At the time it seemed the right thing to do. The time spent in the two schools, plus basic and advanced Infantry training, kept me in the states for a total of eight months. While I was looking around for more schools to attend I was ordered over here."

"I heard we were getting a new corporal," spoke a voice behind McNeil and he turned to see who had spoken.

Tiny did the introduction. "Corporal Johnson, meet Corporal McNeil. Corporal Johnson has the second platoon."

"Glad to meet you Corporal McNeil and welcome to our little paradise," greeted Corporal Johnson shaking McNeil's hand.

"Thank you Corporal Johnson but paradise I haven't seen yet."

"Call me Bob," said Corporal Johnson, "and paradise or not is what one makes of an assignment. I've got to run but we'll get together soon and swap stories."

"Sure, and again thanks Bob," replied McNeil setting back down. How many corporals are assigned here?" asked McNeil of Tiny.

"Just you two," replied Tiny.

That evening, before the evening meal, McNeil had a chance to meet the other three men who comprised the third squad of third platoon. Each was a private fresh out of advanced Infantry training and with less than a year in service. Tiny did the introductions when the men were gathered around. "Men, meet our new squad leader, Corporal McNeil. He's from Kentucky and fresh from some of the best schools offered at Fort Benning. Private Dennison is from Ohio."

"Glad to meet you Dennison," said McNeil shaking the man's hand. PVT Dennison looked far too young to be in the Army but then so did the other two men. PVT Dennison was a short man with sandy short cut hair and blue eyes.

PVT Antony, though young, was just the opposite of PVT Dennison. He was muscular and was almost as tall as McNeil. He had black hair and dark piercing eyes. He was obviously of Italian heritage. He was from New Jersey. "Glad to meet you Antony," said McNeil shaking his hand.

PVT Welting was the antithetical of the other two. He was of average height, brown hair and brown eyes. Where the other two were quite PVT Welting was talkative, animated. He only had a high school education but he tried to pass himself off as a highly educated man. He had one of those none descript faces that wouldn't stand out in a crowd. Pvt Welting was from Idaho. "So, you're the epitaph of a well-trained Infantry man Corporal McNeil," he said reaching for McNeil's hand.

McNeil didn't take the hand. "An epitaph is what one finds written on a tomb stone and I haven't reached that stage yet PVT Welting, said McNeil. "If you chose to use big words my advice is to know the meaning of them. The word you should have used is epitome. And yes, I'm the epitome of the well trained Infantry man so don't try to bull shit me. We'll be getting together soon but now I suppose each of you have duties to perform."

As the three walked away talking to themselves McNeil turned to Tiny who had stood by without speaking once he introduced the men. "Who is in charge of the fourth squad Tiny?"

"PFC Odell has the fourth squad."

McNeil wondered just what he had gotten himself into. First Lieutenants commanding companies, E-6's acting as first sergeants, a buck sergeant in charge of all the platoons. I wonder what other surprises are in store for me."

## 19 Apr 1950

Corporal McNeil soon fell into the relaxed routine which was quite a contrast to what he had left in the states. It was almost like not being in the military. The company had one informal formation each morning for accountability and detail assignment. Most of the time there was little to do but laze around, read, or sleep. After three days of not seeing the company commander McNeil asked Tiny about him.

"Lt. Richards is a young officer not long out of O C S and he spends most of his time at battalion brown nosing and trying to rack up points."

"No X O?"

"Lt Richards is the only officer assigned. SSgt. Sampson runs the company most of the time."

When McNeil came from the landing and the battalion he noticed several villages with grass covered shacks on plots of land. There were rice paddies near the houses and obviously other crop beside rice was grown because he could see something green growing. As on the mainland he saw few trees and what he saw were small stunted ones of a variety he had never seen.

During the few days he was in the company he had a chance to look around some and did notice the ravine about a hundred yards north of the company area. It looked as if the ditch was dug and the dirt thrown up on the side forming a high bank. Off in the distance he could see some low hills and trees with some of the rice paddies in between.

When the mike-boat arrived there was cold beer. Due to the heat the beer had to be used fast or the cans would swell up and burst. For entertainment a movie was shown at battalion once a week, if one could be obtained. Other than reading, playing cards, and the occasional movie there was little else for entertainment. McNeil had been assigned a week and no word was passed to him of what was expected of him. Of course he had heard the rumors and speculations but nothing official. He decided it was time for some straight answers and he headed for the orderly room.

"Good morning Sergeant Sampson," he greeted as he stepped into the tent.

"Good morning to you Corporal McNeil."

"If you can spare me a minute or two of your time Sergeant Sampson I have some questions."

"Certainly Corporal McNeil, what's on your mind?"

"I'm quite confused right now."

"Confused?"

"Mind you I'm not complaining about this assignment but it would be nice to know what the assignment is."

"Were you not briefed in Inchon, at the 5th Infantry Division; or even Battalion?"

"I have not been briefed anywhere by anyone on anything."

"Good Lord. I knew things were fouled up but not that bad," said Sergeant Sampson getting up from his chair and motioning for McNeil to follow as he went behind the canvas in the rear of the tent which was designated as Lt. Richards office, he was told, "I'll impart to you what I know," he said as he went behind another battered field desk where a full sheet of plywood leaned against a tent post with a large map of the area tacked to it, "let's start with the command structure. You have met our commander, Lt. Richards?"

"I have heard the name but as yet haven't had the pleasure."

"Seams more than one thing has slipped through the cracks around here. I'll try and set up a meeting as soon as he returns. Now, Colonel Layton is the 5th Division Commander. Lieutenant Colonel Winters is the 1st Battalion Commander. Now this is where things become confused and screwed up. We are assigned to a military unit for pay, rations, and accountability only. Our mission and reason for being here is as advisors. We are designated as advisors to the ROK troops. You know what the acronym ROK means?"

"I'm afraid not."

"ROK is Republic Of Korea troops. K-Mag is Korean Military Advisor Group to which we are attached. Until a month ago K-Mag was commanded by a Brigadier General. Since his departure a Colonel Reaper is the commander.

"Over K-Mag is Eight Army Commanded by Lieutenant General Walton. Even though General Douglas MacArthur is the Japan Occupation Force Commander he is the ranking general in the area and all the above falls under his command."

"Now, if you are thoroughly confused by all that let me confuse you even more by showing you where we are and what we do, or what we are tasked to do. We are here," he said pointing to a spot on the map, "on what is called the Ongjin Peninsula. There are only two ways off the peninsula. One can cross the thirty eight parallel into North Korea or one can depart here in a boat. Since we are surrounded on three sides by water and we're forbidden to cross the 38th parallel, does that make this place an island?" He didn't wait for a comment from McNeil as he pointed to the symbol on the map that was the designation for a company. "We are here. Able company is to our right, Charlie and Dog Companies are to our left, west. The 1st Battalion is set up about a mile to our rear.

"The thirty eight parallel, which is the dividing line between North and South Korea, extends across the peninsula about four miles to our front, north of us. The 17th ROK Division is to our front and they patrol the thirty eight parallel. The 17th is a division in name only because their strength is less than one of our full battalions. Not only are they under strength but their commander releases the men on a rotational basic to go to their homes to plant and or to harvest crops. At any given time there are no more than a hundred to a hundred and fifty ROK troops on the line."

"What, in your opinion," McNeil asked Sergeant Sampson, "would happen if the North Koreans decided they wanted to own this piece of real estate?"

"They will get it. There are enough North Korean troops to walk over the 17th ROK as if it wasn't there. We'll have a choice of fighting or swimming. I believe lots of swimming will be going on."

"What a boondoggle," commented McNeil.

"I agree," said Sergeant Sampson, "let's hope this peninsula is undesirable land."

It was five days later that Lt. Richards found time in his so called busy schedule, battalion briefings he said, to meet and brief Corporal McNeil. It only took a few minutes for McNeil to categorize the young lieutenant. He was not tall, maybe five six, and looked to weigh about one thirty to one forty. He had shortcut brown hair and deep set brown eyes. He had a narrow sharp featured, unsmiling, face. He was the kind of man who used his rank, position, and a lot of bluff, probably to make up for his size. His briefing was short and far less informative than SSgt. Sampson's. Was it because he didn't know, or maybe he thought a petty corporal didn't need to know? Whatever the reason McNeil left the orderly room with even less confidence in command and the survivability of himself and the men if the North Koreans ever decided they wanted the Ongjin Peninsula.

That night after the generator was shut down McNeil lay on his bed in the dark and gave the situation some thought. He had a responsibility to the men assigned under him, regardless of the number. Being a captain in the ROTC with a full company to care for was a lot of responsibility but couldn't be compared to the active army. He was a corporal now, and a squad leader. He made the decision that he would do everything in his power, the limited power of a corporal, to assure his men were taken care of and properly trained. McNeil had met the other NCO's, which were few in number, in the company. SSgt. Sampson was the acting first sergeant. There were two more E-6 N C O's; one was SSgt Anderson, the supply sergeant. He was a trim man with short cut blond hair and piercing blue eyes and high cheekbones. He was well versed in his job and he and McNeil hit it off the first time they met.

The other E-6 NCO was SSgt Leeks the mess sergeant. He was the type of man that couldn't get along with anyone. He always seemed to be grumpy. As are most mess sergeants he was overweight. His uniform never seemed to be complete and what he wore was always dirty with food stains. In addition to being overweight his hair, streaked with grey, was worn longer than the regulations allowed.

There were two E-5 Sergeants. One was Sgt Dill, who he had met earlier, who was tall and rail thin with short black hair. He was designated as the company platoon sergeant. He wasn't an aggressive man but rather waited to be told what to do.

Sgt Hicks, the other E-5 sergeant, was the company medic. He was well versed in his job and handled sick call each morning passing out medicine and treating the sick and slightly injured. He was a stocky man and wore his dark hair cut close and had sad looking brown eyes. Sgt Hicks was like the family doctor and listened to the complaints of the men with passion.

There was one other corporal beside McNeil, Corporal Johnson who he had also met earlier, was in charge of the second platoon. Even though neither SSgt. Sampson nor Lt. Richards had said anything McNeil knew it was common practice that the ranking man was in charge. Since he seemed to be the ranking man he gradually took over the third platoon with no complaints from the three PFC squad leaders or acting PFC platoon leaders.

He had been giving the situation a lot of thought and the conclusion he came to was that something had to be done, changes had to be made. Even though there was no war all military men should be in some state of readiness. They were in a foreign country so anything could happen at any time. McNeil certainly didn't want to make waves and alter the relaxed mode of the company but on the other hand he knew certain things should be taking place. One evening he looked over to where Tiny was laying on his cot reading. "Tiny, how often are those weapons cleaned and checked?"

"There is no schedule Charley," replied Tiny lowering his book, "but I have only cleaned mine once since I've been here."

Corporal Johnson entered the tent as Tiny and McNeil were talking. Corporal Johnson was not a serious individual but rather a happy-go-lucky man. He seemed to always be smiling with a twinkle in his blue eyes. He was stocky and wore his black hair cut close for easy maintenance. Corporal Johnson was a resident of Virginia. "How do we know the weapons are not rusty or clogged up with dirt or insects," continued McNeil as Corporal Johnson sat down on Tiny's cot to listen. "How do we know they will function if needed?"

"I just do what I'm told and no one has ever said to clean weapons."

"Did something come up during your meeting with our esteemed leader that we should be aware of?" asked Corporal Johnson.

"No. It's just proper military procedure for a good 11B Infantry man to make sure his assigned weapon is clean and operational. What about drills and alerts?"

"You have to be kidding McNeil. Nobody wants to rock the boat or be reminded that they are still in the army any more than absolutely necessary," replied Corporal Johnson.

"I'm a firm believer, Corporal Johnson, in the boy scout motto, Always Be Prepared. If you prepare yourself, your men, and your equipment, then you can perform the mission without wasting time playing catch up. Tiny," said McNeil turning back to the big PFC, "where is the ammo stored, here or at battalion?"

"It's here. Under lock and key, sandbags and concertina wire."

"As of now, make that tomorrow, we, the third platoon, will break down, clean, check, and oil our weapons. We'll start doing that about once a week. Pass the word Tiny and I'll make it official at the morning formation."

"Are you sure you didn't find out something from your meeting with Lt. Richards?" asked Corporal Johnson very seriously.

"I got more information from SSgt. Sampson than Lt. Richards which isn't saying much. The reason we are going to clean our weapons is because of the Boy Scout motto."

"You're the boss Charley. I'll get the word out to the guys," said Tiny as he picked up his book and continued reading.

The next morning, a Wednesday, McNeil spoke to Sgt Dill in the mess tent. "Have you any idea why Lt Richards assigned me to the third squad?"

"No Idea why do you ask?"

"We have a situation that isn't in accordance with the rank structure. You have a PFC in charge of a platoon while I'm merely a squad leader."

"Not I but Lt Richards. I wasn't consulted on your assignment."

"Then I'm informing you that as of this morning I'll be taking over the third platoon."

"I think you should speak with SSgt Sampson before you do that," replied Sgt Dill looking around hoping to spot SSgt Sampson to ask his opinion.

Just about how I had him pegged thought McNeil, no balls Dill. "You are the designated sergeant in charge so it's your duty to inform SSgt Sampson that an improper assignment has been corrected."

Sgt Dill stood and watched as McNeil walked out of the mess tent. He made a decision since he had no desire to make waves and bring attention to himself. I'll wait and see what SSgt Sampson says when he sees the change this morning.

When the company was formed McNeil motioned for Tiny to move over and take his place as he left the third squad and went to the front of the third platoon. He stopped in front PFC Ballinger who held the platoon leader position. "PFC Ballinger, I'll be taking over the third platoon," McNeil informed him, you will have the first squad." PFC Ballinger, a young and inexperienced PFC, was glad to relinquish his position. He had been thrust into that position because there was no one else to take it, he was the ranking PFC, that is until Tiny was assigned to the company but no changes were made.

SSgt Sampson noticed that McNeil was in front of the platoon rather than in his assigned position but he decided to not comment on it. Since Lt Richards assigned him I'll wait and see what he says when he finds out, was his decision.

The company was called to attention, SSgt Sampson got a head count, then passed out the details before he released the company. McNeil did an about face and faced the men of third platoon who were still standing at attention. He waited until the other platoons were dismissed before he spoke. "I'm sure by now most all of you know who I am but for those who don't I'm Corporal McNeil and as you just saw I'm now in charge of the third platoon. PFC Ballinger, since your squad has the most men pick one for the morning detail. We'll start rotating the details by squad. What you will do now is return to your tents and clean up your area of responsibility. In thirty minutes each of you will report to tent six with your assigned weapon. Dismissed."

The four men of the third squad started grumbling when Tiny passed the word to them about cleaning their weapons but they did as told. There was lots of grumbling after McNeil released the men of the third platoon. They resented the fact that McNeil reminded them that they were still in the Army.

When all the men had gathered in tent six McNeil got their attention and spoke to them again. "Until such time as I'm relieved I will be in charge of the third platoon. Two things I will not tolerate; failure to follow orders and being out of uniform. When PFC Brockman, who is the ranking man under me, passes out instructions consider them coming from me. The current squad leaders will remain as is for now. I know you don't wish to be reminded but we are still in the U.S. Army. The U.S. Army trains for a war while hoping one will never happen. Two items we'll accomplish here today; first is making sure your assigned weapons are cleaned and serviceable. Your weapon is a piece of military equipment of which you have signed for. If it becomes corroded and unserviceable you are responsible and may be required to pay for a neglected piece of equipment. The second item is for you men to get to know each other. If a war happens, and we certainly hope that doesn't happen, your buddy, your pal, your friend, will be the one guarding your back. Speak to and learn something of the men assigned with you. Later on we'll get into platoon and squad responsibility in case of war. Right now break down those weapons and clean them. I'll be moving around so if you have questions ask them of me."

There was no pressure and no hurry as the men found positions on the beds and on the ground and started cleaning weapons and talking. They learned about each other and their families and told a lot of jokes.

Never could all men be pleased so some grumbled but they did as instructed. It became a ritual that every Wednesday evening after the noon meal the men of third platoon gathered in tent six with their weapons and cleaned them. McNeil began instructing his men on basic platoon and squad tactics in time of war.

Sergeant Sampson began noticing the men gathering every Wednesday evening, and was curious about it but said nothing. One day he spoke to Sergeant Dill about it in the mess tent. "I have a couple of questions Sgt Dill, first, why is McNeil now the third platoon NCO rather that where Lt Richards assigned him. Did you move him?"

"I had nothing to do with it but I feel he is justified in making the move himself."

"Oh. And why is that?"

"It's not proper to have a PFC in charge of a corporal."

"What do you think will happen when Lt Richards finds out about this change?"

"I say let's wait and see."

"You do know it will come back on me when he finds out about it?"

"You are the man in charge but I still think it's justifiable."

"Then we'll play the wait and see game. Have you any idea why the third platoon men gather in tent six every Wednesday?" SSgt Sampson was afraid there might be excessive drinking or maybe the men were gambling.

"They gather and clean weapons."

"Is the weapons cleaning thing your idea?"

"I wish I could take credit for it but it was McNeil's idea."

"I never thought I would see the day in the Army when men cleaned weapons without being ordered to."

"Corporal McNeil has the ability to get the men to do chores they dislike without giving orders. But these weapons cleaning sessions have turned into training classes."

"Oh? And just what else goes on?"

"The men get acquainted. I mean really get to know each other. They talk about their problems, their home life, their hopes and dreams.

"How do you know so much about this sergeant Dill?"

"I listened outside the tent one day and heard McNeil explaining squad and platoon responsibility in a combat situation."

"So, you are not involved in these sessions?"

"Not me. I have all the training I need plus I don't believe I'll ever have to use what training I have. In three more months I'll kiss this place goodbye."

Acting first Sergeant Sampson was a bit disappointed to find out that what was going on was on the up and up. He was also disappointed that he hadn't thought of the idea himself to keep the men occupied in their free time. But if it wasn't on the training schedule he wasn't going to make waves.

One day, three weeks after the weapon cleaning session was established, McNeil asked Tiny to accompany him and show him where the third platoon's assigned fighting positions were located. "Have there been any alerts since you have been here Tiny?" McNeil asked as they walked.

"A few."

"Ammo ever been passed out?"

"Never. It stays locked up."

"What is the procedure when an alert is called?"

"We get dressed, grab our field gear and weapons and head for our assigned fighting position. There we wait for the all clear."

"What do you think would happen if an alert was called and ammo was needed?"

"There would be a whole lot of confusion."

"This is it," said Tiny when he stopping at the eight to ten foot rise in the ground. "Third platoons area of responsibility is from this stake to that other one down there, about twelve hundred feet."

"What about the other platoons?"

"Fourth is to our left and first and second is to our right. Each platoon has about the same distance of responsibility."

McNeil looked the area over with a critical eye and could immediately see areas that would cause problems in inclement weather. The eight to ten foot rise of dirt was caused by a trench being dug sometime in the past and the dirt piled up. It's possible that run off water dug a shallow trench and the farmers dug it deeper to hold water for the rice paddies. No attempt was made to improve the defense position, which is to dig fighting positions or remove any vegetation that blocked the view of a gunner. There was no specific spot for a man to come to so how did a man find his assigned area in the dark? With mud, rain, snow, or frozen ground, the men would have a hard time getting up on, or staying on, the slope.

McNeil climbed to the top of the berm and walked it from one stake to the other. Weeds and grass covered most of the berm but didn't block the view. He looked to the front and could see there would be a good field of fire for about a half mile or more then there was another rise in the ground about a mile away plus other obstructions, trees and brush. Several diked rice paddies were scattered to his front but none were being worked now. A couple of mortar tubes and a well-placed machine gun could pin down an entire company he surmised. If the other three companies are as under strength as Baker Company, and there is no reason to believe otherwise, then there will be large gaps in the line of defense. From what I see here, if the North Koreans ever decide they want this piece of South Korea they will probably get it.

"What do you think he is doing Corporal Johnson?" asked Tiny as they waited and watched McNeil walk the ridge of the berm. Corporal Johnson had walked out to the berm to see what was going on.

"I suppose he is checking out the area of defense. He must have had a lot of good training in that ranger school."

"He is a nice easy going guy, isn't he?"

"That's true, and he can instill confidence in others."

"He acts more like an officer than an enlisted man," commented Tiny as they continued to watch McNeil walk the berm.

"Tiny," said McNeil when he slid down off the berm, "Tomorrow morning at zero nine hundred notify the men that it's my desire that they all gathered here, with their entrenching tools, at our assigned position. If any trouble arises let me know."

There are always a few men who want to grumble and fuss but most of the men seemed to want some direction. When the men gathered the next morning McNeil spoke to them about what was going to happen and why. All the men had the basic knowledge but as of late no leader. Now they had one. McNeil gave refresher classes on Infantry tactics and preparing proper fighting positions then put the men to work. He paced off the area and marked each position then assigned men to prepare it. He put Tiny as near the middle as he could so the BAR would cover the most area. Since there were other duties to perform it took the men a week to complete the job to McNeil's satisfaction.

Corporal Johnson stopped by the third day to see how the work was progressing. He also thought it was a good idea to prepare fighting positions and asked McNeil to instruct his platoon.

# MCNEIL

## SOUTH KOREA
## ONGJIN PENINSULA

## Chapter 4
## 22 June 1950

It was a Wednesday morning and Lieutenant Richards was making what he liked to call his monthly drive around inspection of his area of responsibility. Even though it was supposed to be a monthly inspection it had been more than three months since he made the last one.

1st Lieutenant Lonny Brice Richards the third felt there were great things in store for him in the future, maybe even stars, after twenty years, or less. He tried to picture himself with the shiny stars of a general on his shoulders. Being a company commander as a 1st Lieutenant would look good on his records.

His father, Lonny B. Richards, senior, had only achieved the enlisted rank of sergeant E-6 before retirement. His brother, Lonny D. Richards the second, had enlisted as a private and was now somewhere in Europe and was up to the rank of a corporal. Lonny Brice Richards the third decided he wanted to do better than his father and brother so he did the required two years of college, two years of business was the easiest, then he applied for and was approved for Officer Candidate School after basic training.

Second Lieutenant Richards, fresh from OCS, was assigned as XO (Executive Officer) to a basic training company at Fort Jackson South Carolina. Captain Tuttle was the commanding officer.

To this day Lt. Lonny B. Richards the third couldn't understand why Capt. Tuttle had him sent to Korea. Lt. Richards who had a friend in S-1 who told him that Capt. Tuttle had requested newly promoted 1st Lt. Richards be given an overseas tour, preferably to Korea.

Didn't I give my all to Capt. Tuttle? I put in twelve and sometimes sixteen hour days trying to make sure the recruits were properly trained, that is when I wasn't involved with my XO duty. I was always beside Capt. Tuttle, or behind him, to keep him straight on issues and didn't I correct several letters

31

he drafted and made them read more forcefully? Why would he won't to get rid of a good XO?

I feel sure I'll get a good assignment when I leave here, thought Lt. Richards as he continued to drive around the area, because I have made myself useful and made friends in battalion. I have helped where I could by applying my expertise. I have glad handed, back slapped, and lost money in poker games when I deliberately dropped out even though I had a winning hand.

That Capt. Wells, the S-1, is a twerp who shouldn't be in such a high position. He can't even play a good game of poker, much less win unless I let him. Maybe all I have done will bear fruit though. I do remember Capt. Wells said he would take care of me at rotation time. Maybe, since I will have completed all my required command time, both XO and CO, my abilities will be recognized and I will get a staff position. A promotion to Captain sounds nice.

One thing I know for sure is that as soon as I reach the states I'll change the way I sign my name. Everybody signs using their first name, middle initial, and last name. I'm going to be different and maybe people will be impressed when they see my signature as 1st Lt. Infantry, L. Brice Richards 111.

Hell, I could even handle Capt. Wells job right now, S-1, of battalion. Wouldn't that be something; a Lieutenant giving advice to a colonel? A lieutenant issuing orders and making sure the commanders carry them out. "What the hell!" said Lt Richards aloud as he suddenly stopped the jeep at Baker Company's defense line.

"Just what is going on here?" Again he said it aloud as he exited the jeep for a close look. The entire company, for lack of something better to do, had joined in and transformed the pile of sand, a berm, into secure fox holes and comfortable firing positions under the guidance of McNeil and Johnson.

I did not authorize this, thought Lt. Richards as he stood with his hands on his hips, defacing the Korean land but I will find out who did and have his ass.

The air was heavy and moist with dark clouds looming in the distance when Lt. Richards stopped the jeep in front of Baker Company Command Post. As he went through the tent opening, jerking his cap off, he said rather loudly, "Sergeant Sampson, my office now," then he stomped on back to his area.

Something seems to have put a bur under his saddle, thought Sergeant Sampson as he got up to follow Lt. Richards.

Pfc Gordon turned his head so Sergeant Sampson couldn't see the smile on his face. I hope he gets his ass chewed out, thought PFC Gordon. He and many other men had little, if any, respect for Sergeant Sampson.

"Yes sir?" asked Sergeant Sampson as he stood before the field desk Lt. Richards had just taken a seat behind.

"I just completed my monthly area inspection and do you know what I found?"

A month is thirty days, thought Sergeant Sampson, and everyone knows it's been ninety days since your last inspection. "No sir I don't," replied Sergeant Sampson after hesitating a moment to try and think of anything that may have changed around the area.

"You are the acting first sergeant and the top enlisted man and you should be aware of everything that goes on around here so you can keep me informed. Are you remiss in your duties sergeant?"

You little shit, thought Sergeant Sampson. If you were present here rather than brown nosing at battalion I might be able to keep you informed. So what have you found that has you upset? I can't think of a thing out of the ordinary. "Sir, if I knew what you were referring to I could better answer you."

What a dolt I have been saddled with, thought Lt. Richards as he shook his head. "I'm referring to the Baker Company area of responsibility, more specifically the designated defense line. Can you tell me why it's been altered?"

"'I' haven't given anyone permission to change the defense line in any way sir."

"So you don't know what's going on. Get Sergeant Dill in here and let's see if he can enlighten me."

"Yes sir." He was mad as he left Lt Richards and motioned for PFC Gordon to go. He knew the men up front could hear everything said through the thin canvas. Pfc Gordon grabbed his hat and left with a smile still on his face.

"It took PFC Gordon five minutes to locate Sergeant Dill and for both of them to get back to the CP. "PFC Gordon said you needed me Sergeant Sampson. What's going on?"

"Report to the CO," was all Sergeant Sampson said.

"Sir, Sergeant Dill reporting as ordered," said Dill when he entered, what Lt. Richards like to call his office, and stopped in front of the field desk and rendered a hand salute.

"At ease," said Lt. Richards after he returned the salute, "I have been trying to ascertain from Sergeant Sampson exactly what is going on in Baker Company. To be more exact, the alteration of the defense line. Can you enlighten me?"

"Not much sir."

"Just what does that mean, not much? Either you know what's going on or you don't. Might I assume both you and Sergeant Sampson, two NCO's in a responsible position, are derelict in your duties?"

Sergeant Dill thought about the question a few seconds. I know a lot of the men have been spending time on the defense line with Corporal McNeil leading them. Do I plead ignorance and let the ass chewing continue, or do I give up McNeil? I should have gone to the line to see what they were doing but it's too late for hind sight.

"I asked you a question sergeant." spoke an impatient Lieutenant Richards.

"Yes sir you did. I must plead ignorance to what was done to the defense line but Corporal McNeil may have an answer for you." Sergeant Dill had decided to give up Corporal McNeil rather than take the blame for something he knew nothing about.

"Who is this Corporal McNeil? Sergeant Sampson!" he called out. Lt. Richards was in his element now.

"Yes sir?" asked Sergeant Sampson as he stepped behind the canvas.

"Sergeant Dill tells me a Corporal McNeil may have some answers for me. Just who is this Corporal McNeil? Is he assigned to Baker Company? If so why don't I know him?"

You shit head, thought Sergeant Sampson, if you spent more time around the company you might know him. "He was assigned to us back in April sir. You met and briefed him about a week after he arrived."

"I don't recall briefing a Corporal McNeil. Well, get him in here and let's see if he can shed some light on this. You two wait outside until the corporal gets here then I'll see all three of you."

Sergeant Sampson, with a wave of his hand sent PFC Gordon on his way to locate Corporal McNeil.

While they waited Sergeant Dill whispered to Sergeant Sampson, "Shouldn't we let Corporal McNeil know what's going on?"

"I'm not going to get between a corporal and that----that----lieutenant in there. Besides, I'm not real sure just what is going on."

Corporal McNeil entered the CP a few minutes later followed by PFC Gordon who went to his seat in front of the radio to watch and listen to the final outcome of this circus. Would Corporal McNeil admit blame and end this or would he lie about his part and pass the blame? Who could he pass the blame to?

McNeil, following his rule of always being prepared, had taken the time to straighten his uniform and dust his boots off before entering the CP. Sergeant Sampson just waved his hand and pointed toward the lieutenant's alcove. When McNeil went that way without asking questions Sergeant Sampson and Sgt Dill followed him.

McNeil marched up to the desk, rendered a salute, "Sir, Corporal McNeil reporting to the Commanding Officer as ordered." Since he was at the position of attention he could only sense that Sampson and Dill were on each side of him. Just what in the hell is going on, he wondered.

"At ease," said Lt. Richards after he returned the salute. "Corporal McNeil, I have been informed that you may be able to shed some light on a problem I have?"

"If it's the lieutenant's request and I'm able I will do so gladly."

"During my area inspection I discovered alterations to Baker Company's defense line. Do you know anything about that?"

"Yes sir I do."

"If you had said you had no knowledge of the alterations my next step would be to call a private in here for some answers," spoke Lt. Richards as he looked at each of the sergeants. McNeil caught the insinuation of incompetence and he also sensed that for some reason the lieutenant was mad, why, he wasn't sure. "But, since you seem to know what's going on around here, appraise me."

"Sir, it's the responsibility of any leader to evaluate and provide training for the men assigned under him. I was assigned as squad leader to third squad of third platoon. Being the ranking man the leadership of the entire platoon fell to me. I determined the men were bored, lacked training, and out of shape. I taught them proper tactics and proper defense procedures. The unimproved defense line provided a solution for two of the problems, boredom and lack of exercise. I taught the men, and supervised them, in the making of a proper defense line with excellent firing positions. The other platoons joined in the work because of boredom."

"You, a corporal, decided all that?" asked Lt. Richards who was now trying very hard to control his anger.

"A Corporal with a responsibility to the men assigned to him. Yes sir."

"You did all that without keeping either Sergeant Sampson or Sgt Dill informed? None of what you did was according to the published training schedule."

"I readily admit I was derelict in not using the chain of command and not going by the training schedule Sir. But I was not derelict in my duties as a platoon sergeant."

"Corporal McNeil, what you are derelict in is failure to comply with company policy, which came down through battalion from division. Could it be that you weren't properly briefed upon arrival at Baker Company? Or could it be you were properly briefed and it didn't register? Is it possible you were aware of the company policy and decided to ignore it? Regardless of your reason you did violate a company policy of which I have a copy in front of me.

"Paragraph five so states," said Lt. Richards as he started to read it out loud. THERE WILL BE NO DEFACING OF THE KOREAN COUNTRY SIDE OTHER THAN HOLES FOR BURN PITS AND LATRINES. THESE HOLES, AFTER USE AND PROPER TREATMENT, WILL BE COVERED OVER. "Now is that clear to everyone?"

There were three "yes sirs," in unison.

"Now," said Lt. Richards just as rain started beating on the tent, "I was going to say you will repair the damage to the defense berm now, but I'll change that to immediately after this storm passes. Corporal McNeil you will form up all the men involved in the policy violation and march them, with entrenching tools, to the defense line where you will instruct them to return the berm to the original shape. Report the accomplishment of the task to Sergeant Dill who will assure himself the task is done properly. He will report that fact to Sergeant Sampson. Sergeant Sampson will personally inspect the work and when he is satisfied he will report to me. I will make the final inspection. Have I made those instructions too complicated?"

"No Sir," answered the three in unison.

"Corporal McNeil," said Lt. Richards, "while you are repairing the berm, and until it's completed to my satisfaction, I will be deciding if further punishment is deemed necessary. You three are dismissed."

The three men came to attention, saluted, did an about face, then left the office. McNeil, not wanting to get into a discussion or hear any false excuses dashed from the C P into pouring rain and ran to his tent.

After McNeil left, Sergeant Sampson whispered to Sergeant Dill, "You keep an eye on Corporal McNeil because I don't want anymore surprises like this."

When McNeil entered tent six he took off his damp shirt and hung it up to dry. He wiped the mud off his boots before he took them off and put them under his cot. Corporal Johnson had been spending time in the tent now that he had gotten to know McNeil and he was laying on a cot reading. He had heard PFC Gordon tell McNeil the Co wanted to see him. "Trouble Charley?" asked Johnson as he watched McNeil clean his boots.

"The lieutenant's feathers are ruffled a bit. Nothing serious," replied McNeil as he tore the paper from a cigar and lit it. He picked up his book and lay down to get some reading done.

Corporal Johnson shrugged his shoulders and went back to his reading.

I'm sure most of the company will know of the minor violation of a company policy by Corporal McNeil, by noon tomorrow, or sooner, so there is no need for me to elaborate on it now, though McNeil. The key word here is 'minor' and if the CO wants to make something big out of this I'll request a Summery Court Martial at battalion. I know the rules and the UCMJ (Uniform Code of Military Justice) as well as, if not better, than Lt Richards. What I don't really need is a conviction, no matter how minor, on my military records which may hinder my chance of a political service job with the government.

Deciding if further punishment is warranted is a ploy I used many times as a ROTC company commander. It's a way to unnerve individuals and keep them on their toes. I can't believe the lieutenant will proceed any further after the berm is repaired. But who knows. Sgt Dill, when he should have been supporting me has been avoiding me. I'll just have to wait and see.

It continued to rain the rest of the day, that night, and for the next two days. The men ventured out of the tents only to eat and use the latrine. During this time of none activity the rumor mill was operating at full force.

Saturday, as McNeil lay on his cot reading his book, Corporal Johnson and Tiny entered the tent, removed their ponchos and shook the water from them. The two looked at each other with a mutual understanding and both sat on Tiny's cot. "Charley," said Johnson to get his attention, "we've heard a rumor that Lt Richards may Court Martial you. Is there anything to it?"

"I'm not up on the latest rumors," answered McNeil as he continued to read.

"We heard it's because of the work we did on the defense line," said Tiny.

"If that ass hole of a lieutenant tries to---"

"Hold it Bob," said McNeil closing his book, "rumors do not always indicate a truth and one should never refer to those appointed over him as an anal orifice."

"Be that as it may," said Tiny, "if Lt. Richards tries to stick it to you the entire company will back you. It will be interesting to see how the little lieutenant handles that."

"One should never listen to rumors and one should never make plans until one knows the objective," said McNeil very calmly as he puffed on his cigar, "and if the entire company acts together against Lt. Richards he may call it mutiny."

"I never thought of it that way," said Tiny.

"You don't seem too worried," said Corporal Johnson.

"What have I to be worried about, rumors?"

The rain did slack off to a drizzle late Saturday evening. After eating and as McNeil prepared himself for bed he resigned himself to the fact that he would have to perform the task he was ordered to do on Sunday, that is, if it didn't start raining again.

## 25 June 1950

He was in the bottom of a small boat floating on a silk smooth lake with not a breath of wind to ripple the sparkling water. His arms were wrapped around the warm body of a beautiful blond. He was kissing her neck when suddenly thunder boomed and the boat rocked. Not now, he muttered. Please don't rain now. Two more loud booms and the boat rocked again. Slowly, the dream of the blond and the boat faded away as McNeil, hugging his pillow, became semi awake. Several more booms in the distance and the ground trembled. Rain, he thought in his half asleep mind. Well at least we won't have to worry about rebuilding the berm today.

The booming noise that his sleepy state of mind mistook for thunder came in rapid succession, both to the front and rear of Baker Company. McNeil suddenly sat up in bed shaking his head to clear away the cobwebs of sleep. A mortar round burst a couple of hundred feet to the rear of the tent. Now McNeil's mind recognized the booming noise as artillery and mortar. He could also hear, faintly, the pop of small arms fire.

He sat on the edge of his bed disbelieving what he was hearing. Two more mortar rounds exploded closer to the tent and he could hear shrapnel peppering the tent. No alert had been sounded yet but McNeil didn't need anyone to tell him what was happening. He jumped from his bed and kicked Tiny's bed and shouted. "Roll out Tiny and shake the others. We're under attack."

As he spoke he was getting dressed by feel. From habit he always laid out his clothes and boots where he could put his hands on them, in case there was no light, as now.

"What is it Charley?" asked Tiny as he started fumbling with his clothes. Three mortar rounds burst close enough to shower the tent with shrapnel again and this time several holes appeared in the top.

"We are under attack. Move it Tiny and shake up the other guys."

As McNeil strapped on his field gear and set the helmet on his head there were multiple booms both north and south.

"What's going on," muttered one of the men as Tiny shook his bed to wake him.

"We are under attack," McNeil shouted again, "wake those other men and grab your field gear and weapon and run to the ammo dump," said McNeil as he unlocked the weapons rack, by feel, and picked up his rifle. He checked his watch and noted that it was 05:00 hours.

"Tiny, get all the men to the ammo dump. I'll be ready for you when you arrive," he said as he went out of the tent leaving the preparation of the men to Tiny. Outside he could see men running around in their white under wear. Some were muttering to themselves and some just standing looking. Most were looking and pointing toward the fireworks that lit up the sky. McNeil yelled at them as he ran by them just as a mortar round burst close to one of the tents which finally convinced the men that this was the real thing. Suddenly there was a rush of men in several directions at once.

McNeil knew in which direction from the company the ammo dump was located but he had never visited it. It was placed west and to the rear of the company. There were no lights to guide him and he stumbled several times on the uneven ground. The only light was from an exploding mortar round and it didn't last long.

When McNeil finally arrived at the ammo dump he found about what he expected. By feel he found the gate was chained and held with a pad lock. He looked around but no one was rushing his way with a key, nor was any of the men headed his way, that he could see. The word, 'I had a war and no one came,' was running through his mind when he heard the whistle of incoming artillery rounds. He fell to the ground as he was trained to do. His helmet, the chin strap was not fastened, rolled from his head and when the round fell and exploded the ground shook under him. He felt a sting on his left arm and felt something warm. Then a sharp pain told him he had been hit by shrapnel.

He felt fear but not for himself. The overriding fear for the men, his men, left no time to fear for himself. Time was slowly running out. He knew that a mortar and or artillery barrage was normally preceded by a ground assault. He had to hurry. The men had to hurry. Everyone had to hurry.

McNeil felt of his arm and found a tear in his sleeve. He felt blood but the wound was small, though a bit painful. He decided to use a handkerchief on the small wound and save his first aid bandage. It may be needed later.

After he tied the handkerchief on his arm he felt around and located his helmet, and this time he fastened the chin strap. He picked up his weapon and again looked to see if anyone was headed for the ammo dump.

# MCNEIL

## SOUTH KOREA
## ONGJIN PENINSULA

**Chapter 5**
**25 June 1950**

There was only a hand full of American troops in South Korea, a few thousand, a peace keeping force. They were poorly equipped and trained and no one was ready for what happened. No one believed the North Koreans would attempt a border crossing. There was no intelligence to give anyone a clue as to what would happen that Sunday morning.

Most of the men could probably tell you just what they were doing at 05:00 hundred hours that Sunday morning but most of them would say they were sleeping with a bad hangover.

That was the case of Lt Richards, commander of Baker Company of the 1st Battalion. There had been a so called staff meeting, who ever heard of a staff meeting on a Saturday night, which soon turned into a poker game and bottles were passed around. Lt. Richards felt he had too much to drink to drive the distance back through the woods to his own company so he found a cot at battalion. Ssg Sampson was left in charge of Baker Company.

The company ammo dump consisted of a tent enclosed with several coils of concertina wire. Access was through a rickety gate made of barbed wire and boards. Time was running out so with no one coming his way McNeil used the butt of his heavy M-1 to smash open the gate lock. It took several tries before the lock shattered and fell to the ground. He jerked the gate open and went to the ammo tent thinking that if a mortar round hit the ammo tent small pieces of him would be scattered over a large area. He pushed that thought from his mind because he knew it was imperative that the ammo be passed out as quickly as possible so the men could get to the defense line and be ready for the ground assault sure to follow the mortar and artillery attack.

There were no lights in the small tent so McNeil flicked his zippo lighter on to get a feel of where and how the ammo was stored. Someone had the good sense to store the ammo by caliber. McNeil took two cans of Cal. 30. Ball. Clipped ammo at a time and set them at the tent opening. When he located the clipped BAR ammo he set two cans of that on the opposite side of the tent opening. He broke open a case of grenades and set them outside. Just as he finished Tiny came rushing up and called out, "Charley!" he shouted.

"Those two cans on the right is your ammo Tiny. Grab a couple of grenades and head for the line. I'll send the other men up as soon as they have ammo."

"Right boss," replied Tiny as he picked up both cans of ammo in one hand as if they only weighed an ounce or two, "the other men are right behind me," he said as he grabbed a couple of grenades and started running for the line.

The artillery and mortar rounds were still falling and getting closer when McNeil passed ammo and grenades to the last man of the third platoon and left the ammo dump. Corporal Johnson arrived so McNeil turned over the ammo dispensing to him. Some of the artillery rounds were whistling overhead and falling far to the rear and McNeil knew the only target worth firing on back there was battalion headquarters and the way the sky was lit up he knew they were taking a pounding.

Several more mortar rounds fell into Baker Company area as McNeil ran to his position on the line. After he loaded his M-1 he peeked over the berm and couldn't believe what he saw. There was a dark mass, almost a formation, of men walking toward his platoon's position. They were walking and firing, like one saw in the pictures of civil war battles, rather than using terrain for concealment and firing positions. The other men of B-Co were laying down a field of fire when he lifted his M-1 and started firing into the mass of humanity which was just dark moving shapes. As he fired his thoughts were that if so many men coming at his platoon's position were spread out they could easily overrun and surround the company.

The firing increased as more and more men came on line. The mass of North Koreans started splitting left and right, that is those that had not fallen or turned and ran in the opposite direction. It was obvious a surprise attack was planned but the surprise was thwarted. As the mass of North Koreans spread left and right they came under the fire of the other platoons. The effectiveness of the sudden frontal assault was lost as more and more of the North Koreans fell or started to withdraw. The remaining men fell back to the security of the low ridge where they continued firing on Baker Company.

Artillery and mortar rounds were still whistling overhead and were now dropping into the company area. Small arms fire had tapered off now that most of the targets were concealed. A few low cries for medic could be heard along the line. The adrenal rush of a few minutes ago eased off as McNeil used the lull to step back and walk the line to check on his men. He spoke to each man and gave encouragement. As he neared the last position of his platoon, which joined the fourth platoon, he couldn't see a man in the position. His first thought was that the man was missing; next he thought the man may be killed or wounded. As McNeil got closer he could hear someone sobbing but still couldn't see anyone. When he eased into the firing position he could barely make out the form of a man huddled in the bottom of the hole.

"Are you hurt soldier," he asked because at the moment he couldn't remember the name of the man he had assigned to the position. When there was no answer he kneeled down to check on the man.

He could still hear the man sobbing but no answer to his question. "What's your name soldier?" he asked grabbing the man by the shoulder.

"I'm,----Private Hall—sir," the man finally answered between sobs."

"I asked if you are hurt Private Hall?"

"No—No."

"Then what is your problem? And don't sir me, I'm Corporal McNeil."

"I—I—I'm—scared—Corporal."

"So are all of us."

"You don't —seem—scared."

"That's because you can't see me."

"All—the noise,---the bullets. I—I'm—scared I—I--- might get killed."

"I guess so."

"W—what?"

"I'm agreeing with you, you might get killed. We all might get killed."

"But—I—I—don't want—to—die."

"Neither does anyone else but unless you stand up and use that weapon to kill those who would kill you some of us may die."

There was still sporadic gunfire up and down the line so McNeil stood up, as he talked, to look over the berm to check on the action.

"Bu—but—,"

"No buts private Hall. It's a fact that there are those out there whose one desire is to kill you. To prevent that from happening you have to stand up and kill them first. Now, come on, get up," said McNeil helping the man to stand.

As he helped the private up and brushed some of the dirt off his shirt he saw, out of the corner of his eye, a shadow of movement as a body eased in behind a bush. "Stand up now and get that weapon ready. Wipe your eyes and look for the enemy that wishes you dead."

"I—I—don't—know if I—can do —it," said the private wiping his eyes with his shirt sleeve.

"Sure you can. See that bush about 200 feet straight out from you?"

"I—I—see it."

"Aim about the center of it and fire two rounds into it."

"But—it's—just a bush."

"Trust me. Humor me. Aim at the bush and fire two rounds into it."

"Ok," said Private Hall as he wiped his eyes again. He raised the M-1, took aim on the indicated bush. He fired two quick rounds into it. There was a yell and a figure rose up and fell over the bush. "Damn," said Pvt Hall in a very surprised voice, "I did it."

"Yes you did," replied McNeil, "you just eliminated one of those who would kill you. Now keep that weapon pointed that way, keep your eyes open, and eliminate more of them."

"Thanks----thank you corporal."

"Don't mention it and I won't either. Just stay alert now. It'll be daylight soon."

McNeil eased himself out of the position and made his way back to his own position. He wondered just how many others were like Pvt Hall.

The artillery had let up some but a few rounds were still whistling overhead. It was starting to get light now and one could see several of Baker Company's tents ripped to shreds. There were still faint cries for a medic from the line. No NCO's or officer had appeared on the line yet. Where is Sergeant Dill? Where is Sergeant Sampson? Where is the lieutenant, the man in charge, who knows so much, wondered McNeil?

# McNeil

## Ongjin Peninsula
## South Korea

**Chapter 6**
**25 June 1950**

The Commander, Lieutenant Colonel Titus W. Winters, of the 1/5 Infantry Division (UNMECHANIZED) felt secure in his belief that with the ROK 17th Infantry Regiment, although with the strength of maybe a battalion, on line at the 38th Parallel and with the four companies of the 1st Battalion, even though at only 65% strength, on line across the Ongjin Peninsula, the battalion was safe, or at least would have ample warning of any border crossing or saber rattling from the North Koreans.

Before assuming command of the 1st battalion he had been briefed on how important the Ongjin Peninsula was, both strategically and economically. The peninsula was strategically important to the American Military, the ROK Military, and to the North Koreans. Ownership of the peninsula was mentioned several times at the North and South Korean peace talks before Korea was divided by the 38th parallel. The peninsula would be of great economic value to those people north of the 38th parallel, if they could obtain it, for the additional food source to feed their millions of people.

Ltc. Winters asked a question, to himself. If the Ongjin Peninsula is such a valuable piece of real estate, as he had been told, why is the security of the peninsula vested in a ROK Regiment with less manpower than a battalion and commanded by a Colonel? Why is an under strength American Army Battalion the backup unit for the under strength ROK Regiment?

He didn't voice his concern and ask those questions out loud because one does not obtain the rank of Lieutenant Colonel, nor can one expect to progress higher in rank, by questioning those appointed over him. One goes where one is told to go and does what one is told to do and keeps his mouth shut.

Ltc. Winters, after assuming command of the 1/5th Infantry Battalion, decided to satisfy his curiosity about this piece of real estate and took the time to tour the peninsula from coast to coast and up to the 38th parallel. He met and dined with the ROK 17th Infantry Regiment commander, Colonel Haun. He found the colonel to be a very easy going and likable man who acted more like a civilian in uniform rather than a career officer. Ltc Winters filed that bit of information away as just one more glitch in the security of the peninsula.

During his tour he found the peninsula to be fertile land, a few low hills and several streams, which produced large quantities of rice and other vegetables. On his tour he passed through several villages, farm communities, where the people were working their rice paddies and gardens. Up near the 38th parallel he came across a little used grass landing strip that could maybe handle a small plane. He found no large docking facilities anywhere along the coasts, just small rickety docks used by local fishermen. Nowhere did he find any kind of industry on the peninsula. He found the peninsula and the people to be very tranquil.

Two months after Ltc. Winters assumed command of the 1/5th Infantry Battalion a sealed envelope reached his desk. It was stamped SECRET and addressed to him personally. Inside the envelope he found a quarter inch thick booklet titled; **Inter Service Contingency plan for American Military Forces in South Korea.** The long title was shortened to; **K.C.P** (Korean Contingency Plan).

When Ltc. Winters started reading the K.C.P. He certainly knew right away that the document had been drafted by some rear echelon chair warmer who didn't have anything better to do and obviously had never taken the time to visit units in South Korea. This fact was further reinforced when he came to ANNEX-1, K.C.P, for the Ongjin Peninsula.

**If hostile forces attempt an attack on the Ongjin Peninsula the commander of American forces, on the peninsula, backed by the ROK military, will make an all-out effort to thwart the attackers. The American Military Forces on the Ongjin Peninsula will be reinforced within twenty four to forty eight hours after hostile action begins. In the event of extreme hostile action American Forces will be evacuated within same time frame.**

Ltc. Winters almost laughed out loud when he read the K.C.P. he certainly had not found an airport nor any suitable docking facilities on the peninsula. Reinforced, evacuated, how? By the single seat L-5 plane? That would take forever evacuating or reinforcing one man at a time, beside that the only suitable landing strip is up near the 38th parallel which will be in enemy hands if we are attacked. What kind of rescue plan did the man have in mind?

To pluck those left alive out of the water as they swam for the mainland. He finished reading the K.C.P, initialed it and passed it on to his S-2 for filing in a safe.

The only good thing generated by the K.C.P. was that the basic load of battalion ammo was doubled, and four machine guns and fifty M-1 rifles were added to the inventory. The down side when the ammo and extra weapons arrived was that it took extra manpower to store and maintain them. Manpower that was already stretched to the limit.

Ltc. Winters, like other commanders, was reveling in the glory of WW 11, if one could see glory in war. The general conscious was that no country would rise up against the mighty American Military, the nation that had the balls to use the Atomic bomb not once but twice. It was also believed that with the best intelligence service of any nation any saber rattling from across the 38th parallel would be reported in time for all commanders to prepare their commands for battle.

Ltc. Winters was so steadfast in his belief that the North Koreans would never cross the 38th parallel, and that he would have advance warning if it did happen, that he operated his battalion as if it were garrison duty.

Weapons and ammo was secured under lock and key. Field gear and helmets were never worn and was kept packed away in duffel bags. No fox holes were dug which may alter the Korean landscape, per letter of instruction from Division. No fighting positions were ever designated or prepared. No sandbag bunkers were built and no sandbags were laid up around the closely erected tents. Work hours were from seven to five with Saturday evenings and Sundays off.

There was no R & R (Rest and Recreation) for those unlucky enough to be stationed on the peninsula. Sometimes Officers and NCO's were able to get to Division, which was on the mainland, on business. The mike-boat was the only means of transportation to the mainland. Going from one military unit to another certainly didn't qualify as R & R. Recreation for the troops as a morale booster was very important to Ltc. Winters. Outdoor movies were shown, weather permitting and availability of film. Three tents were set up as clubs for the ranks, Officers, NCO's and enlisted men. Poker games were allowed as long as no money was visible, poker chips only.

Even though there was a two beer limit per man per day drink rule in effect in Korea Ltc. Winters decided it did not apply to his battalion. He allowed his people to drink all they wanted, if it was available. Ltc. Winters knew some of his people were having bottles of whisky sent over on the supply boat but he had to look the other way since he was doing the same thing. The recreation at the battalion was open to anyone in the companies that is if they had time and could find transportation.

To further ease the strain of his overworked people Ltc. Winters curtailed the use of OD (Officer of the Day) and CQ (Charge of Quarters). Since the only communication link between division and battalion and battalion and the companies was radio, a radio operator was on duty twenty fours a day. It was impossible to put phone lines in the water to division and Ltc. Winters didn't want to mar the country side by laying phone lines to the companies. Since there was no phones to ring at all hours of the day and night and with the only transportation to the mainland the Mike-boat there was no chance of unexpected visitors.

The men of the 1st battalion fell asleep around midnight Saturday night. The generators at battalion were not shut down at 22 hundred hours as was required at the companies but ran until midnight. Many went to sleep that Saturday night, 24 June 1950, with alcohol dulled minds. Some went to sleep out of shear boredom.

There was no traffic on the radio so the young man, PFC Willis, who was unfortunate enough to have the duty fell asleep in his chair shortly after midnight.

There were a total of three men in the entire 1st Battalion Headquarters who had ever heard shots fired in anger. Like the majority of military personnel the others came aboard after or during the final days of WW 11.

Lieutenant Colonel Titus W. Winters, Commanding, was a ruddy faced man with a few grey hairs showing in his short cut dark hair. He was of average height but over weight enough that he had to struggle to fasten his pants lately. He was a first Lieutenant during the last year of WW 11. He was awarded the purple heart, for a minor wound, plus a bronze star with 'V' for Valor for his actions in France just before V-day.

Major Jerry T. McCall, the 1st battalion executive officer, was a barrel chested man with red, short cut hair. He heard shots fired in anger during the last two months of WW 11 as a second lieutenant. Most of his time was spent as part of the Army of Occupation in Europe.

Sergeant Major Tim S. Callings had short cut blond hair and brown eyes. He was tall and thin and was very easy going in his duties as Battalion Sergeant Major. He saw action with the famous 9th Infantry Division as a staff sergeant. He heard several shots fired in anger.

The first artillery round that impacted in a grove of trees several hundred feet to the right of battalion tent city had little effect on the sleeping men. The trees absorbed most of the shrapnel and explosive force so little damage was done to any equipment or tents. There had been so many thunder storms lately that each man had grown use to the rumble of thunder and had contributed the noise to yet another storm. The three men who had heard shots fired in anger recognized the distinct difference between the sound of thunder and exploding artillery rounds and the sound was forever etched in their memories. Even though the noise woke them and they recognized the sound their sleepy minds kept telling them it was impossible. It took three more artillery rounds, this time closer, to convince them that they weren't dreaming, and urged them to action.

Another barrage of artillery rounds burst closer and shrapnel ripped through the tops of tents where men slept. Up until now they thought they were hearing thunder, but now they knew it was something different. The next barrage of artillery shook the ground and those men who had not gotten up were thrown from their cots onto the dirt floor of the tent.

There was pandemonium and confusion in tent city as more rounds impacted and men started running around in all stages of dress yelling orders that were never obeyed. LTC. Winters made it to his command tent just as the duty man was getting up off the ground shaking his head and wondering what had happened. His first thought was an earthquake had happened. His sleep was interrupted when the noise caused him to jerk and his chair tipped over backwards.

"Are you ok son?" asked Col. Winters when he saw PFC Willis getting up off the ground. When the generators were shut down at night a gas lantern was lit for light in the command tent.

"I'm ok Sir," replied the shaken man, "do you know what caused this Sir?"

"It appears, for some unknown reason, we are under attack. Shut down that radio and move control to my jeep. Get the jeep into the trees east of here."

"Yes sir," replied PFC Willis as he quickly shut off the radio, located his hat and left the tent on the run.

A few more artillery rounds burst and several minutes later Col. Winters had rounded up enough officers to carry out his orders. He knew the artillery was bracketing the battalion area and seldom did two rounds fall in the same spot. He wanted everyone clear of the tents and in the grove of trees where the first round had impacted.

Sergeant Major Callings entered the tent as PFC Willis ran out. Ltc. Winters told his SGM to get the men in field gear with weapons and ammo and into the grove of trees where he had sent his jeep. "Have the radio operator get Division on the radio and I'll have a message ready. Maj. Hall, get me a status report," said Col. Winters as soon as he reached his jeep. He quickly began writing out a short message using his flashlight to see by. More artillery rounds landed and exploded and screams of pain could be heard.

"I have division commo sir," said the PFC.

"Send this message in the clear. No time to encode it. 1/5 Battalion and subordinate units under heavy attack. No status at this time."

"Yes sir," replied PFC Willis as he reached for the message.

Col. Winters barely heard him as he watched his people come straggling into the grove of trees, few with helmet or field gear. They dropped down on the ground and just sat.

Three minutes later the first call came in on the radio. With no surprise to anyone it was Lt Richards of Baker Company. Col. Winters knew Lt. Richards had gotten up early this morning and left to return to his company.

"Baker six to Raider six. Baker six to Raider six. Come in raider six."

"Go Baker six," said PFC Willis.

"Baker Company under heavy ground and mortar attack at this time."

"Roger?"

"Need ammo, supplies, and personnel."

"Raider Commo understands requirements. Do you have a casualties list?"

"Negative at this time."

"Stand by Baker six."

Virtually the same information came from Able, Charlie, and Dog companies. No casualty numbers from anyone yet. Col. Winters was in that frustrated situation that all commanders dread, lack of information. He had units on the line, under attack, and his only link to them was a radio. He wanted so much to be there, or raise the units on the radio and demand information. But he knew there were some frightened young men on the line and for him to rush up there would serve no purpose. To demand information they may not have at this time would be a waste of time. The radio channel had to be kept open. He had to have faith that information would be passed as soon as the commanders had it. That artillery has to be shut down, was his thoughts. What has happened to the 17thROK? Did they get rolled over?

Ltc. Winters tore the wrapper off a cigar and jammed it in his mouth. He thought about how blue stallion commo wasn't surprised at his report when they acknowledged receiving it and from what they said he had to assume that this attack wasn't isolated to the peninsula. Seems we were all wrong and the North Koreans did have the balls to mount an attack. Suddenly something long forgotten popped into his mind, the long forgotten K.C.P (Korean Contingency Plan).

When Ltc. Winters read the plan months ago he laughed at it as just one more paper some chair warmer had drafted but now he was recalling ANNEX -1 of the K.C.P, specifically paragraph 5.

5. **Due to the unique Geographic's of the Ongjin Peninsula special considerations are made for the American troops stationed there.**

**The Commander, or ranking officer, of the American troops on**

the Ongjin Peninsula is here by afforded the authority to declare an emergency (Code Red) if a situation ever exists where the loss of control of the Ongjin Peninsula is imminent.

The Commander, or ranking officer is authorized to by-pass the normal chain of command and request assistance. It is extremely important that the Ongjin Peninsula remain a part of South Korea.

When paragraph 5 of the K.C.P. is evoked and A Code Red situation is declared any commander called upon by the commander, or ranking officer, of the forces on the Ongjin Peninsula will render immediate assistance. Reports of K.C.P annex -1, paragraph 5,activation will be made by requester and provided through normal chain of commands.

"Son," said Ltc. Winters to PFC Willis open up your little book and connect me with Blue Ten Six." The little book he spoke of was a listing of all commands in Korea, their call signs and radio frequencies. It was classified secret and hanging on a chain around PFC Willis' neck. By rights it should be locked up in a safe but there it would do little good since it was passed from one radio operator to another and was in constant use.

Pfc Willis who had been squatting down beside the jeep reached up and dialed in the frequency once he located it in the book. "Raider six for Blue Ten six. Come in Blue Ten six."

Blue ten was the Air Force Control Center, established by 5th Air Force that controlled all flights over the South Korean land mass.

"Blue ten commo. Go Raider Six commo."

It was a very frustrating conversation with the Air Force with very little assurance of help. Battles were raging all along the 38th Parallel and all available planes were in the air, Col. Winters was told.

Since he wasn't getting anywhere with a normal request he decided it was time to step it up. "This is Raider Six, commander of forces on the Ongjin Peninsula. Get this to Blue Ten Six. I am evoking a Code RED situation. Raider Six standing by."

"This is Blue Ten Six," another voice was heard on the radio five seconds later, "I understand you are declaring a Code Red?"

"A Code Red has been declared."

"What can the Air Force do for you?"

Ltc. Winters explained the situation to Blue Ten Six and about all he was promised was that some of planes already in the air would be diverted his way.

The artillery was still pounding the battalion area when the sky started to lighten up in the east. The next call on the radio was from Able Company with a status and casualty report. "Able six to Raider six. Able six to Raider six."

"Go able six."

"Need ammo and personnel. 2 KIA, 4 WIA."

"Roger able stand- by."

"Baker six to Raider six."

"Go Baker six."

"Need ammo and personnel. Repelled heavy ground force. Under mortar attack. 3 KIA, 6 WIA. Planes strafing and bombing near 38thParallel."

"Roger Baker six. Good copy. Stand by." Ltc. Winters was writing as fast as the information came in.

The reports were about the same from the other two companies. "I have the Battalion casualty report sir," spoke Maj. McCall interrupting Col. Winters' chain of thought.

"Add it to the company's reports and give me a total." A minute later Maj. McCall handed Col Winters a penciled copy of the total casualty report.

|         | KIA | | | WIA | | | WIA | | EVAC |
|---------|-----|------|-----|-----|-----|-----|-----|-----|-----|
|         | Off | NCO | EM | OFF | NCO | EM | OFF | NCO | EM |
| BN      | 1   | 2   | 8  | 1   | 1   | 4  | 1   | 1   | 1  |
| Able    | 0   | 0   | 2  | 1   | 1   | 5  | 0   | 1   | 2  |
| Baker   | 0   | 1   | 4  | 0   | 0   | 7  | 0   | 0   | 3  |
| Charlie | 1   | 0   | 2  | 0   | 1   | 4  | 0   | 1   | 1  |
| Dog     | 1   | 1   | 5  | 0   | 0   | 6  | 0   | 0   | 3  |
| Total   | 3   | 4   | 21 | 2   | 3   | 26 | 1   | 3   | 10 |

"That doesn't look too good Jerry," spoke Col. Winters after he saw the final figures. Twenty eight people had been killed and forty five wounded, some serious enough to be evacuated.

"It doesn't Sir but there's little we can do at this time."

Col. Winters suddenly looked up from the casualty list he had been studying, and turned his head left and right. "I do believe the artillery is easing up some Jerry."

"It would seem so Sir."

"Tiger two nine to Raider Six. Tiger two nine to Raider six."

"Go tiger two nine," answered PFC Willis.

"Be advised, twenty artillery pieces destroyed. No activity at ROK 17th.

Heavy concentration of ground forces moving your direction. Tiger two nine is bingo and headed home."

"Roger and thank you Tiger two nine. Raider radio standing by."

"That's somewhat of a relief and at least we know a little of what's happening."

"What do you think happened to the 17th?" asked Maj. McCall.

"I think they were rolled over, eliminated. But that's another problem. Right now we have our people to think about."

Now that Col. Winters had eye witness information of the, so called, battle field situation he formulated a plan and began giving rapid fire instructions. First order went to his radio operator. "Notify each company to expect a heavy ground assault."

"On it sir," replied PFC Willis as he turned back to his radio.

"Four?"

"Right here sir."

"Load a truck with ammo, all we can spare, and rations, and distribute it to the four companies. I need that done two hours ago. Check with me before you depart."

"Yes sir."

"Two."

"Here sir."

"It's far more important that we have people on the line and since there's little intelligence coming in, round up your people and send them with the supply truck. How many do you have?"

"I have five Sir."

"Send one man to each company plus two to Dog who was hardest hit. Dog has been doing ok without an officer so far but I want an officer there now, you are elected Captain Berg. You are far more valuable there than here right now."

"Yes sir. I understand."

"Sir," called out the radio operator, "Baker said to revise the casualty report. They just lost Lt. Richards."

"Damn," was all Col. Winters said. A minute later he spoke again. "Raise Division and give our status and casualty report and request any assistance they can provide. The Mike boat will be needed to evacuate casualties and it's hoped there will be supplies on it.

"Yes sir."

"Captain Stevens?"

"Yes Sir?"

"Gear up and catch the supply truck. You are now Baker Company commander. Take your people, and any non-essential personnel, with you and distribute them among the companies. Sergeant Major do you have an equipment status for me?" asked Col. Winters without waiting for an acknowledgment from Capt. Stevens.

"Yes sir. Cook tent ok but mess hall tent unserviceable. Dispensary tent serviceable, supply tent useable, barely. We have one GP large and one GP medium serviceable. Generator seems to be serviceable but that will have to be checked out. All vehicles came through ok but lots of small equipment destroyed or damaged."

"That means convenience and comfort will be at a minimum. Gather what men you can find, to include cooks and medics. Tear down what tentage is useable and set up operations in among those trees behind that low hill."

"I'm on the way sir."

"Major McCall, you and Capt. Wells, and Capt. Kilgore when he returns, now comprise the battalion staff. Lend a hand and let's get operational."

"Sir," called out the radio operator when there was a lull in Col. Winter's instructions.

"Go ahead."

"Division says they and other units were hit also. No replacements available. Mike boat due here in three hours with limited amount of ammo and rations. They will not accept a status and casualty report in the open. We are to have KIA bagged and tagged and ready for the boat. Division requests your presence with the battalion status and casualty report."

"Thank you son," said Col. Winters to the young radio operator. This is a hell of a time for me to be absence from my command, thought Col. Winters. But then I should have known better than to try to send status reports in the clear. That's my fault. Well, the situation seems to be well in hand here and there isn't much more I can do. Maj. McCall will have to take charge until I return.

"Sir," spoke Capt. Kilgore, breaking into Col Winters thoughts, "the ammo and rations are ready. You did say to check with you before I departed."

"Time is critical. No time to delay at the companies. Drop off the supplies and pick up the KIA's. The boat will be docking in three hours. Your sergeant can get our KIA's ready while you are gone. Your shop will be picking up more ammo and rations from the boat. Get it distributed also."

"Yes sir."

"Jerry," called Ltc Winters to stop Maj. McCall before he got too far away, "who was the officer we lost?"

"The young lieutenant who just arrived last week, Lt Aspen."

Ltc Colonel Winters looked at Maj. McCall with a raised eye brow and made a motion with his hand for more information. He couldn't remember a Lt. Aspen.

"He was that young blonde haired lieutenant who we were getting ready to send to Charley Company. He was only here a few days."

Ltc Colonel Winters remembered the man now and he just hung his head and shook it. "Would you write the letter for me Jerry?"

"I'll take care of it sir," replied Maj. McCall.

Now, thought Ltc. Winters after his moment of silent grief, everything seems to be under control. He had started to take a drink from his flask earlier but an unexpected artillery round had landed nearby which caused him to forget the drink. Now he opened the flask, looked around to make sure no one was looking his way, uttered a silent prayer, and drank to those who had fallen this day.

# MCNEIL

## ONGJIN PENINSULA
## SOUTH KOREA

## Chapter 7
## 25 June 1950

The curtain of darkness was slowly being peeled back as the eastern sky started showing some light. The big orange orb would be rising up over the Sea of Japan shortly causing an increase in the already warm temperature. There were no clouds for the sun to hide behind.

The front that had passed on through yesterday had dropped enough rain to cool the temperature and cleanse the air but now the smell of battle, dead men and gun powder, floated across the land. The serene Ongjin Peninsula had been suddenly replaced by confusion, death, and fear.

After the bombardment for several hours, the quietness was almost painful to the ears. Several minutes ago the men had watched as three planes appeared to the north, at first no one was sure if they were friend or foe, and started bombing and strafing. The planes were too far away to hear the guns but the dull thud of exploding bombs could be heard and soon dark smoke rose up from several places along the 38th Parallel. Suddenly there was no more artillery whistling overhead and exploding to their rear. With the artillery quiet the mortar rounds falling on and around Baker Company started tapering off. "That sucker, that mortar tube, has to go," decided McNeil. One of the machine guns had been silenced by Tiny's BAR and now there was only sporadic small arms fire.

For the first time since the attack started Lt. Richards made his way to the line from the grove of trees where his jeep with the radio was located. He met up with SSgt Sampson behind 3rd squad's location. McNeil's first thought upon seeing the small Lieutenant this morning was that he looked like forty miles of bad road.

McNeil had just returned from checking on his platoon. He found the men doing better than he expected. Fear was evident and he took the time to give each man a few encouraging words. "What are you doing off the line

Corporal?" asked Lt. Richards in a rather loud, high pitched voice, "and don't you know to salute an officer?"

"Yes sir, but I would think that custom should be eliminated on the M L R (Main Line of Resistance) during a time of hostile action."

"You think? I'll make that decision. I asked what you were doing off the line?"

"Checking on my men sir," he answered calmly.

McNeil's first assessment of Lt. Richards was correct. His eyes were red and his movements were jerky. He had his web gear on but not hooked up and it flopped around every time the Lieutenant moved. His fatigue jacket was buttoned up wrong and he wore the steel helmet without a liner.

"You stay on the line and me and the Sergeant will check on the men," he said turning to SSgt. Sampson. "Make sure all the men are on line and alert because we are about to be attacked again."

McNeil noticed he didn't ask how the men were or if they needed food or water, just keep them on the line and awake.

"And another thing," continued a frightened Lt. Richards, "I've been informed the ammo dump lock was broken. Find out who did it and I will personally court martial the one responsible."

"Sir," spoke SSgt. Sampson, "the man with the ammo dump key, PFC Jett, was killed by mortar shrapnel. We needed that ammo."

"There's no excuse for destroying government property."

"Sir, to solve the so called crime and save some of SSgt. Sampson's valuable time," spoke McNeil, "I broke the lock and issued the ammo."

LT. Richards jerked around, walked to where McNeil stood in the firing position, and stood as close as he could get. "You, Corporal, have been a nuisance since your arrival. I know all about the curriculum you established which wasn't authorized by any training schedule. I intend to take care of both problems as soon as the situation allows," said Lt. Richards straightening up to his full short height and placing his hands on his hips. It was supposed to be an intimidating posture but Lt Richards, in his anger, failed to call McNeil to attention. McNeil was not intimidated by the little lieutenant.

Before Lt. Richards could get another word out a small red hole appeared in his forehead. A second later the sound of a fired weapon could be heard. Lt. Richards, with a surprised look on his face, simply folded up and dropped to the ground, sliding down the incline. His helmet came loose and rolled to the feet of SSgt. Sampson who stood frozen in place. When McNeil realized Lt. Richards had been shot he ducked down in his firing position and watched the lieutenant fall. He called out, "Tiny!"

"On him boss," came a reply just before the B A R opened up ripping off rounds. In the distance shredded leaves and a few twigs fell from a tree. Next a scream was heard, and a body fell from the tree.

McNeil was wondering why the lieutenant was shot and not him since they were standing so close together. The answer came when he looked down and saw the helmet at SSgt. Sampson's feet. The white Lieutenant bar worked as a bull's eye for a sniper. SSgt. Sampson, who was still staring at the body of Lt. Richards, had not moved. Finally he shook his head and looked up at McNeil. "I guess by God there won't be a court martial now. The little shit got what he deserved."

"He was just a scared young man, like so many others," said McNeil very calmly.

"Yeah. Lt. Richards caught the bullet, as he shit his pants, while chewing on the ass of a soldier. Sound about right?"

"One should never speak ill of the dead sergeant, since they can't defend themselves." McNeil had also pegged SSgt. Sampson soon after his arrival in Baker Company. Probably got his stripes by being in the right place at the right time. Certainly not very educated and lacked both tact and couth, **A fool is a fool unto himself until he opens his mouth, then he is a fool to everyone,** but, he was the NCO in charge.

"How about reporting his demise as; Lieutenant Richards was felled by sniper fire while giving moral support to his men, "

"Hold that thought," interrupted SSgt. Sampson, "here's a pen and paper," he said holding out both to McNeil, "you write it up. He was threatening to court martial you and was just now chewing your ass so I can't see why you would want to glorify him."

"Everyone has somebody somewhere Sergeant, a girl friend, wife, certainly a mother or father, or both. His stupidity should not be a shadow on their grief. I'll write it up and sign it," he replied as he started writing very fast. "Do you know why the lieutenant came to the line?"

"Yeah. He just got a call from Battalion. There is another mass of North Koreans headed our way."

"Then might I suggest, Sergeant Sampson, that you have someone distribute the rest of the ammo to the line. Have the medic's remove the lieutenant," said McNeil passing the completed and signed statement and pen back to Sergeant Sampson, "also, it would be nice if the cooks could see their way clear in getting hot coffee and a cold sandwich to the men on the line."

"Ammo is already being distributed and I see the medic's headed this way. I had not thought about food but hot coffee is a good idea. I'll call in the lieutenant's demise then talk to the mess sergeant."

The stretcher was placed beside the Lieutenant's body as one medic dropped to his knees and started checking for a pulse. He straightened up and shook his head no. "Bag and tag him Sgt. Hicks," spoke SSgt. Sampson who was still there, "a battalion truck is on the way with ammo and rations. They will be picking up KIA's."

"Right Sergeant. But first I need to check out that arm," said Sgt. Hicks pointing to McNeil's bandaged arm that he had long forgotten about.

"Damn, I didn't catch that," said SSgt. Sampson. "Didn't you feel anything Corporal McNeil?"

"That's why there is a bandage on it. But I suppose my adrenalin high blocked any pain and I forgot all about it. I'm sure there are far more serious wounds for you to attend Sgt. Hicks."

"Not at the moment." he replied as he started helping McNeil to get out of his web gear and shirt. "You have a small slice in your underarm," declared Sgt. Hicks, "I'll clean it, apply some ointment and a bandage and you'll be ok."

After he finished and helped McNeil get into his shirt he spoke, "That will get you a purple heart Corporal McNeil."

"Yes. That and a dime will get me a cup of coffee, anywhere but here it seems."

"I'm on the way," said SSgt. Sampson remembering what he was supposed to do.

"How about the other wounded men Sgt. Hicks?" asked McNeil as he got his web gear back on.

"They have been taken care of and are secure."

"Are they mobile? By that I mean any wounds serious enough to prevent them from firing a weapon?"

"Most are mobile except one with a leg wound. Why do you ask?"

"With the mortar rounds dropping back there," he said pointing to the tents, "I should think they would be more secure here on line with us. I know we could use all the help we can get."

"I see your point. I'll see what can be done."

## 25 June 1950

A 3/4 ton truck, a weapons carrier, appeared at the MLR soon after Sgt. Hicks left and the cooks started passing out coffee and sandwiches to every man on line.

Everything was quite until about midmorning when there was a sudden increase in mortar rounds falling in or near the company area which signaled trouble. Soon after the increase of mortar rounds another attack started. Everyone on line was too busy to notice that a battalion truck had arrived with ammo and rations, and several men. The bagged and tagged bodies were loaded and the truck quickly departed.

The morning attack, the second one, on Baker Company defense line was beaten back. The North Koreans, who dared attack in broad daylight, did so at a great loss of human lives because, again, they did not use terrain and concealment, but continued to attack in mass. Three more men of Baker Company were wounded with one more KIA.

McNeil was bent over concentrating on removing some carbon from his weapon receiver. A movement to his right caused him to look up and he saw an unfamiliar figure ease up to the line about ten feet to his right. The man crawled up the side of the berm them lay down and looked over the top with his binoculars. There were railroad tracks on the man's collar, a captain. The man must have sensed someone was staring at him because he turned his head and spoke, "How is it going corporal?"

"I could think of better places to be right now sir and if we don't get more men and ammo we may all be where we don't want to be."

"Everything that can be done is being done. Col. Winters is stripping battalion headquarters and putting the men on line. Ammo and supplies were just dropped off along with some men plus me. I'm Captain Stevens, formally battalion S-3, now Baker Company Commander. And you are?"

"Corporal McNeil Sir, third platoon NCO."

"From what I hear, and see, you guys are doing a bang up job. I see almost wall to wall bodies out there. If only that mortar was silenced we, you men, would have some peace and quiet. Hang in there Corporal and I'll see about getting some ammo and maybe food to you." With that Capt. Stevens slid off the berm and moved on down the line, checking the situation, giving encouragement to the men, but never criticizing anyone.

## 25 June 1950

After Capt. Stevens left McNeil did some thinking. But, that's the purpose of it, the mortar. I would do the same if I was in the position of the North Koreans. Yes, that mortar fire is definitely working on the nerves of the men and preventing them much needed rest. But, I'm not with the North Koreans, and like the captain said, if only that mortar was silenced. As he continued looking over the berm he formed a plan in his mind.

There was only sporadic firing, harassing fire, the rest of the day. Just before dark McNeil left his position and moved down the line. He made contact with Corporal Johnson and together with Tiny they had a conference.

"Guys, our new Co is in agreement with me. That mortar must go," he proceeded to explain his plan to them.

"That's crazy Charley," protested Tiny, "you could be killed."

"A lot of men may be killed, and no one will get any rest, until that tube is silenced."

"And you are going to do it all by yourself?" asked Corporal Johnson.

"I'll do it with your help, from the line. As soon as those guys on the tube get tired of pounding the company area they may turn it onto us. I'm going to do this because I, as well as many other men need some sleep."

"What can we do to help?" asked Corporal Johnson.

"Either of you familiar with the number pass word system?"

"I've only heard of it," replied Corporal Johnson.

"I've never heard of it. What's it about?" asked Tiny.

"Tonight the prime number will be nine," McNeil went on to explain. "If I say three what would be the counter number?"

"I have no idea," said Tiny shaking his head.

"Would it be six?" asked Corporal Johnson.

"Correct. Whichever number you hear you repeat a number added to it that equals the prime number."

"Ok, I got it, I think. If I hear five I answer four," said Tiny.

"Correct. Corporal Johnson, can you arrange to be here in my place for a few hours after dark? That way you can command both platoons. Also each of you let the men know what's going on because I would rather not be shot by friendly fire."

McNeil spent the time before dark looking over the terrain until he formed a mental map. He memorized the location of every tree, rock, and brush. He could see a ravine, probably made from years of water runoff, that zigzagged for about three or four hundred yards between the rice paddies and toward the low hill where the mortar rounds seemed to be coming from.

He took off his helmet and put on his soft cap. With no camouflage paint available he wet some mud, using water from his canteen, and smeared it over his face and hands to cut any glare. The M-1 was much too heavy to carry, plus he didn't want to be tempted to shoot it and give himself away, so he left it with Tiny, but took his bayonet. After the sun set and darkness fell McNeil gave himself one last check, made sure Johnson and Tiny were ready, then eased over the berm and crawled to the beginning of the ravine.

McNeil was unequally qualified for the mission he delegated to himself. He had done this very same thing during ranger training, more than once. When his hair wasn't cut so close, as it was now, one could tell it was brown, which matched his light brown eyes. He stood five eleven and there was no fat on his one hundred and eighty pounds of weight. Sixteen weeks of Infantry training, three weeks of Airborne school, and eight weeks of ranger training had melted the fat away, built up toned muscles, and prepared him for just what he was about to do tonight.

As hard as they tried to watch his progress, Tiny and Johnson lost sight of McNeil when he entered the ravine. All they could do now was to wait and keep alert, and hope he returned safely. "What do we do if someone comes by and asked for Charley?" asked Tiny.

"He must have gone to take a crap," replied Johnson. "You do know that man has a set of large balls."

"He does. I could never do what he's doing now. I have never seen him nervous or shook up, even in the middle of a fire fight. He's like a rock," added Tiny, "didn't even realize he was wounded this morning. Like a rock he is."

"He didn't even know he was wounded? He got his purple heart then. The Rock? That's a good nick name for him," commented Corporal Johnson.

McNeil crawled along the bottom of the ravine, sometimes it was deep enough that he could get to his feet and bend over and still remain hidden. He marked his progress and position by the dark shapes of the trees and bushes he had memorized the position of earlier. The further he went the stronger he could smell the odors of the battlefield, the coppery odor of blood and the unmistakable smell of human excrement. A few minutes later he came upon the body of a North Korean in the bottom of the ravine. He froze in place as cold chills moved up and down his spine.

It was so dark he couldn't tell if the North Korean was dead or alive. After a few seconds and he didn't hear any movement he poked the body with the bayonet. There was no movement. He reached and touched the body to be sure and found it cold. The dead body was blocking his way and would have to be moved. The odor of excrement was so strong that McNeil almost gagged. He had to turn his head away from the body and breathe deeply. He held his breath and quickly, and by feel, took the weapon, an AK-47, the ammo for the weapon, three grenades, then after going through the pockets of the man and finding nothing he rolled the body up and out of the ravine. Then and only then did he allow himself a deep breath. The items he found were much too heavy to take alone so he stacked them at the side of the ravine, then placed the rifle across the bottom of the ravine to mark the spot so he wouldn't miss the items upon his return trip.

He came upon two more bodies of men who had either been killed in the ravine or crawled into it to die. McNeil stripped them of their gear and marked the spot with one of the AK-47's. He did keep three of the grenades this time plus one of the rifles and ammo for it. At first he had feared the ravine may be mined but after finding the bodies in it he knew it wasn't.

When he came even with the low mound of dirt, visible from his fighting position, he raised up to see if anyone was using it to hide behind. He couldn't hear any noise or see any light. It was so dark there could have been a company of North Koreans camped there and he couldn't see them. Where are all the men, he wondered. Have they retreated? If so to where? Earlier today it seemed there were more than a company of men shooting at Baker Company, now there was nobody to be found, alive that is.

It was eerie quite, no sound except for the chirping of crickets and the buzzing of mosquitos, which was a good sign that no one other human was present. McNeil hesitated and started to wonder just what he had gotten into. Did he have fear? Yes, but he allowed his fear to work for him. He wondered what would happen if he didn't return from this foray? Who would the blame for this unauthorized scouting expedition fall on? He turned to look behind him but there was nothing to see, the darkness was complete. I could just turn around and return to the MLR, he thought, but then the mission I set out on wouldn't be completed. That mortar must be located and destroyed or captured and there is no one else in the unit trained for this kind of work. If I don't do it then it won't get done.

McNeil realized he would have little cover, except the cover of darkness, for about a hundred yards, until he reached the low hill which was his goal. There was no turning back, he had come this far and he was committed. He took a deep breath and eased over the low mound of dirt then regained his feet and moved slowly forward.

He reached the sloop of the low hill without incident and slowly crawled up to the top of it. After peering over the top and seeing nothing and he couldn't detect any sound, he started easing down the far side on his stomach. He became more cautious now. He was deep into enemy territory with no back up. He was on his own and the slightest error in judgment could cost him his life, or he could be captured.

When he reached the bottom of the hill, still on his stomach, he stopped again to look and listen. Dark clouds moved across the sky and blotted out what little light the few stars provided. A few drops of rain fell. Off to his right he heard a pinging sound, a metal to metal sound. A second later he heard the familiar sound, whoosh, as a mortar round was launched. He knew he had reached his goal. As he moved slowly toward where he had heard the first sound he heard another sound, people talking in low voices. As he got closer he could see a flickering light, a small fire was lit. It was decision time and he quickly made it. He had come out here to either mark the location of the mortar so it could be taken out by some means, or maybe taken out his way. He knew the approximate location of the tube but what he didn't know was how many men were in the immediate area.

McNeil started low crawling toward the noise and flickering light. The glow of the fire grew brighter as he neared it. He eased up behind a bush to look the situation over.

He saw five, of what he guessed to be North Koreans, sitting in a circle around the small fire. They were talking and eating; occasionally one would reach over and dip food from a pot heated by the fire. All five men were facing the fire so McNeil knew their night vision was shot and they wouldn't see him even if they looked his way. He could see their bed rolls were laid out with their weapons on them. The men didn't seem to be in any hurry nor were they worried about an attack. The question on McNeil's mind was what were they doing here? He couldn't see a mortar tube. Were they the relief men for the tube crew? Were they ammo bearers who would be leaving the area soon? Were there others out there somewhere? How far back is their ammo point established?

He chided himself. Stop worrying about the unknown and find some answers. He eased back from the bush and started moving toward where he figured the mortar tube would be set up. He knew he was near the mortar tube when he suddenly heard a rustle, cloth on cloth, then a whisper. Hugging the ground McNeil slowly moved his head back and forth until he could see the silhouette of the mortar tube against the dark sky. How many men are here, he wondered as he stopped about thirty feet from the tube?

Suddenly, as if in answer to his question, the dark clouds parted for three seconds and revealed two men sitting at the rear of the tube. A stack of mortar rounds were a few feet to the right. The cloud opening closed and full darkness returned again. A match flared and McNeil could see that each man lit a cigarette from the match before it was extinguished but the glowing end of the cigarettes defined the location of the two men. He slowly retreated until he figured he was at a safe distance from the tube. He did some thinking.

I can lob a grenade at the tube and take out the two men but that would surly damage the tube of which I have plans for. If I do that I will have the other five men to contend with. The thought that other men may be near worried him some. If I'm able to take out the five men, ammo bearers, with a grenade, then what about the two at the tube? After giving the situation more thought he settled on a plan. Hopefully his plan would work. If it didn't work he would be caught in the middle of a fire fight, and if he couldn't find a hole to crawl into his ass was grass.

He placed the rifle against a bush where he could find it easily. Taking two of the three grenades, one in each hand, he placed himself in position. A grenade only makes two sounds; a ping when the handle is released and the grenade arms itself and the explosion a few seconds later when it explodes. He had been taught that two was better. Never take a chance that one grenade, or bullet, could get the job done. He was hoping the unexpected noise would cause the two men at the tube to freeze. He was ready now and there wasn't anything else to do but act.

He pulled the pins from both grenades, tossed one then immediately tossed the other at where the five men were camped. As soon as the second grenade left his hand he reached for the rifle and at the first explosion he fired a clip of ammo at the two men at the tube. He heard the second grenade explode as the last round left the rifle. He quickly changed magazines then moved several feet from his current position and lay waiting and listening. As the noise and echo of the exploding grenades and rifle fire faded an eerie silence once again settled over the area, broken only by the moans of a dying man.

After waiting what he estimated to be five minutes and hearing no sound of advancing men or rifle fire McNeil decided he was safe for a short while. At least until someone came to investigate the rifle fire. He crawled toward the camp site, no fire glow to guide on now, just glowing embers scattered around. The grenades had done their job and he found five bodies. After making sure each was dead, or mortally wounded, he went and checked on the two men at the tube. No one was left alive.

During his ranger training he was taught to always carry a water proof bag in his back pack. One could serve many purposes, to keep ammo, weapons, and clothes dry while fording rivers or streams. It could be used as a floating device to ease the strain of a long swim. When filled with air it served as a pillow. This night it served an additional purpose.

McNeil moved from man to man and removed grenades, ammo, and any food he found, and there were tins of it but probably unidentifiably because of the strange language. He found several sealed bamboo tubes of cooked rice. Everything he found, to include the rifles went into the bag. He emptied the pockets of each man, wallets, letters, and maps, and added the contents to his bag. He even managed to rip off a shoulder patch from one men's shirt sleeve. He took two of the bed rolls and tied each end together then zipped up one side and placed the bag inside the tied together bedrolls. He went through the pockets of the two men at the tube and adding what he found there to the bag. He disassembled the tube and added it and its plate to his tied bed roll plus two cases of mortar rounds then zipped up the other side. He took another bed roll and used it as a harness to drape over his shoulder and tie it to his so called sled. It was a heavy load but it would serve two purposes. First, there was far too much equipment for him to carry but he could pull it stuffed inside the tied up bed roll. Second, by dragging it behind him all his tracks would be erased. Even though there would be a strange groove in the ground for someone to see.

It was a struggle to get himself and the gear up and over the low hill. He had to stop and catch his breath before he continued on. As he started his return trip he stopped at each spot he had marked earlier and added what he left there to his bundle. The odor of the battlefield was once again in the air as he dropped down into the trench. His one problem now was to get back without getting shot by his people.

It was midnight, or a bit after when McNeil finally got his load down into the ravine and up the other end and stopped at the berm where he had marked a spot with a stick. After catching his breath he whispered, "Two".

"Oh shit," said a voice he recognized as Tiny.

"Wrong answer Tiny," he said trying to keep from laughing.

"Seven," whispered Corporal Johnson.

"Correct. Now the both of you reach over the top and grab this strap and pull," said McNeil holding the strap up until he felt hands take it. He then crawled over the berm.

"Damn Charley, I'm glad to see you back," said Tiny helping McNeil to his feet, "when we heard the grenades and rifle fire we thought you had bought the farm."

"As you can see, thoughts of my demise are greatly exaggerated. But, I have to wonder about you guys. If I were the enemy I could have dropped grenades over the berm and taken all of you out. Weren't any of you watching and listening?"

"We were but I didn't see or hear you," replied Corporal Johnson.

"Hell Charley, its pitch black out there," answered Tiny, "we couldn't see anything."

"Remember what just happened and keep it as food for thought. I could have been the enemy. Plus, Tiny, I do believe you have forgotten your education. I hear a lot of cuss words lately."

"Sorry about that Charley. I do forget sometimes."

"What do you have here that's so heavy?" asked Corporal Johnson.

"The mortar tube that was keeping us awake will now be turned against the enemy. It'll be quite for a while until, and if, they bring in another one."

"You took it from them?" asked Tiny very surprised.

"Yes, along with enough rounds to harass them for awhile. After you two distribute those weapons and ammo, Tiny, to our men, and Johnson to your men, as far as they will go. I'll give them some instructions come daylight. Clean out a flat place and set up the tube. Try not to change the settings. While you do that I'll grab some shut eye."

McNeil lay down in his fire pit and closed his mind to everything and slept for two hours. He woke up feeling refreshed. Tired and a bit sore, but refreshed. The first thing he did was drink a full canteen of water. Next he opened some of the tins of Korean food and ate some with rice. Corporal Johnson stopped by as he finished eating. "How are things going Bob?"

"Good so far."

"Keep your men alert because I believe we can expect another attack about daylight, or just before. I don't believe Capt. Stevens has much tactical experience even though he seems to care for the men. SSgt. Sampson is acting like a lost soul. Have you seen Sgt. Dill lately?"

"Come to think of it I haven't."

"He must have bought it earlier. Which means you and I have double duty now. I'll cover the third and fourth platoons and you take the second and first platoons. Stop by and speak with the men and let them know they are not alone. You seem to have some training and a cool head. It's up to us to try and save this rag tag band of men. Is the mortar set up?"

"As per your instructions."

"Good. We need to pass out some of these grenades I brought back plus there is some food here. The food is ok, except, unless one can read Korean, it is unknown what is in the tins. The rice is excellent. While you and Tiny distribute the items I'll instruct the men on the AK-47. Where is Tiny by the way?"

"I just saw him down the line. He should be back here in a minute."

"Pass the instructions on to him, if you would."

When McNeil returned to his position after explaining to the men how to load and fire the AK-47 he found Tiny waiting for him. "Tiny, I know this is putting a burden on you but I need your assistance."

"Talk to me boss."

"Pass on these instructions to the man on your left and to the right of me. Have them pass it on to the next man. No one is to open fire or toss a grenade until they hear your B A R. Got it?"

"Got it boss and I'm on my way."

Just before dawn the dull sound of mortars exploding could be heard left and right of Baker Company area, but none fell on or around Baker Company. McNeil picked up his AK-47 and left his position to go to where Tiny was. As he passed the captured mortar he looked at it and was satisfied with where Johnson had set it up. "You see anything Tiny?" he asked as he came up behind Tiny.

"Nothing yet boss."

"They will be coming, and soon. Don't stare; keep your eyes moving back and forth."

"Yeah, boss, I'm beginning to see some movement now."

"Wait until they get closer, about a hundred and fifty feet, then fire. I'm leaving you now," said McNeil as he stepped back and went to his position. He met up with Johnson. "Where is that man you said could handle the mortar?"

"I'll get him," answered Johnson as he left running.

McNeil waited until the man came then he explained just what he wanted. He had high hopes of bracketing the North Koreans with both heavy rifle fire in front and mortar rounds in their rear.

Suddenly the quiet of the night was shattered by the sound of Tiny's B A R, followed by the distinctive sound of several AK-47's plus M-1's firing. McNeil added his fire power to the fighting. Several mortar rounds could be heard exploding but this time it was behind the advancing enemy troops rather than on Baker company men. Cries of anguish and pain could be heard out on the battle field and now with enough light one could see confusion as the North Koreans ran first one way then the other. They couldn't advance nor retreat. When the light rain stopped and the dark clouds drifted away a quarter Moon gave enough light that McNeil could see a few men retreating.

The rifle fire was tapering off when McNeil went to the man manning the mortar and had him walk some rounds up to and over the low hill. When he went back to his position to look over the battle field three figures appeared beside him. "What's going on Corporal?" asked Capt. Stevens.

"Not much now sir; we just stopped an attack of better than two hundred North Koreans."

"And you did it quickly. I barely got dressed before the firing stopped."

McNeil felt a dull ache on the left side of his head. He raised his hand up to massage his head when he felt a sharp pain in his shoulder. When his fingers touched his head above the right ear it felt wet. He moved his fingers around and found a small gash. Suddenly, what Capt. Stevens had just said sunk in and all thoughts of pain left him. Just barely got dressed, the captain had said. These three, plus probably the cooks and medics, were able to undress and sleep in comfort while the men on the line has had no rest or sleep in better than twenty four hours. McNeil's temper flared but he managed to control it.

Something else he had noticed before but it just now registered. Moon light twinkled off shinny captain bars plus the rank had been painted on his helmet in white the same as Lt. Richards. Both were like a sign pointing to an officer; a target for any enemy sniper. The radio operator with a radio strapped on his back with the antenna whipping in the air only added to the sign that not only was it an officer but one in command. McNeil just shook his head rather than speak. No wonder there was is such a high officer attrition rate. They are continuing to operate by the book as if they were in State side duty rather that in a combat situation. It's not my place to correct a captain he thought as the pain hit him again.

"Are you alright corporal?" asked SSgt. Sampson when he saw McNeil cringe.

"Just a scratch sergeant but if you could see your way clear to getting the medic's out of bed there may be some men on the line hurt more serious. A cup of hot coffee would be very welcome by the men also, if the cooks ever wake up."

"Why are you being so bitter corporal?" asked SSgt. Sampson.

"Me bitter; perish the thought? This should be taken to battalion," said McNeil picking up the water proof bag and handing it to Capt. Stevens.

"What is it?" asked Capt. Stevens taking the bag.

"The bag contains information from dead North Koreans. There is plenty more out there if you can get anyone to go get it." Capt. Stevens moved closer to the berm so he could look where McNeil indicated.

"You have been out there corporal?" asked a bewildered Capt. Stevens

"You again," interrupted Sgt. Hicks as he started checking McNeil using a filtered flashlight.

"I forgot to duck again."

Capt. Stevens passed the bag to SSgt. Sampson who along with the radio operator moved away when Sgt. Hicks went to work on McNeil. Capt. Stevens stayed and watched while Sgt. Hicks cleaned and bandaged McNeil's wounds.

"There's just a small gash above your ear. Looks like it has bled a lot which is good. A bit of cleaning and a small bandage and you'll be ok."

"When you finish with the head better take a look at my left shoulder."

"Another one?"

"I'm afraid so."

"Another gash," said Sgt. Hicks after he helped McNeil removed his shirt and checked the wound. As he went about cleaning and bandaging it he spoke. "The question now, since this will get you two more purple hearts for a total of three, will it cost thirty cents for a cup of coffee or can you get three for a dime each?"

"Right now I would gladly give a dollar for one cup of hot coffee."

"I'll see about getting one sent up to you," spoke Sgt. Hicks as he finished dressing McNeil's wounds. A shot was heard and a body fell against McNeil. One quick look told him who it was.

"Tiny!" McNeil yelled out.

The only answer was the ripping sound of a B A R spitting out bullets. "That SOB won't shoot anyone else," yelled Tiny.

"Damn, another officer bit the dust," declared Sgt. Hicks after he felt for but couldn't find a pulse on Capt. Stevens.

McNeil finished buttoning his shirt. He looked to see both SSgt. Sampson and the radio operator hugging the ground. "SSgt. Sampson," called out McNeil. When there was no answer he called louder. "Sergeant Sampson!"

"Ye—yeah—w—what is–it?"

"When you feel you can move would you see about water and food for the men on the line? A hot cup of coffee would be well received."

"You are worried about food at a time like this?" he was finally able to say.

"The reason you people back there are alive is because of the efforts of the men on line. Someone has to think of them."

"I'll—I'll check into it," he finally said as he got up and brushed himself off.

"Pfc Gordon," called McNeil when he could make out the name tag of the radio operator.

"Yes Corporal."

"Would you be so kind and refrain from appearing on the line with that radio. The antenna acts like a magnet for bullets."

"I believe you Corporal. I'm getting away from here and find a hole to crawl into."

SSgt. Sampson suddenly stopped, turned back to McNeil, and pointed to where the mortar tube was placed. "Since I haven't heard a mortar round fall since midnight would it be safe to assuming that is the reason?"

"That would be a safe assumption."

"I won't even ask how."

"That suits me. Might I suggest that you get that bag to battalion then notify them of the current situation?"

"I believe I am capable of handling my job. I don't need a corporal to tell me what needs to be done," snapped SSgt. Sampson as he stomped off followed by Pfc Gordon.

"Damn," said Tiny. "Sorry about that explicative," said Tiny pointing to McNeil's head, "I didn't know you were hit again."

"I didn't either but its minor. Now that we have enough light let me show you how to clean and care for an AK-47. You can pass it on to the others."

Sgt. Hicks showed up about that time with a hot cup of coffee and a couple of APC's, Army aspirins.

McNeil started to speak but Sgt. Hicks held up his hand, " before you ask, yes there is coffee and food coming for the other men."

"Thank you ever so much Sgt. Hicks and I'm sure the men will be forever grateful."

# MCNEIL

## 5TH INF DIV HQ

**Chapter 8**
**25 June 1950**

Lieutenant Colonel Winters left Major McCall in charge of the battalion. He did so reluctantly. This was combat, even though no one had declared it so yet, and he was the commander who should be with his command.

He got into his jeep which was followed by two ambulances carrying the more serious wounded which would be transported to division where better medical personnel were available. Two 6x6's, one loaded with bagged bodies and one with several men to help with the ammo and supplies coming in made up the small convey headed for the beach head where they would meet the mike boat.

There were several vehicles waiting when the mike boat docked on the mainland. The first one was two ambulance backed up to the edge of the water with the doors open with another ambulance waiting. Those were here to take charge of the wounded men. The bodies of dead men would be placed inside the third ambulances so they wouldn't be seen as they were transported to Graves Registration. There was a 6x6 supply truck loaded with ammo and supplies for the return trip. There were three jeeps, two with pedestal mounted machine guns and manned by MP's. Each MP was dressed in full combat gear.

An MP stepped aboard the mike boat, after the wounded men were removed, saluted, then spoke, "Colonel Winters sir?"

"Yes," replied Ltc. Winters after he returned the salute.

"I have transportation waiting for you if you will follow me," said the MP Sergeant turning and leaving the boat without waiting to see if Ltc. Winters was following. Ltc. Winters picked up his bag and left the boat.

The jeep the MP stopped at bore the number '6' indicating it belonged to the division commander, Blue Stallion, Colonel Layton. Ltc. Winters dropped his bag in the rear and took the right seat. As soon as the MP started the jeep, the other jeeps were started. One MP drove and one manned the machine guns in the lead and rear jeep. "Been having some trouble around here?" Ltc. Winters asked the MP driver.

"An occasional ambush sir," replied the MP then he concentrated on driving without offering any more information. Ltc. Winters noticed that the jeeps moved at a fast pace.

They passed a burnt hulk of a bullet ridden jeep in the ditch then a bit further on Ltc. Winters could see a cratered field where many artillery rounds had exploded.

A battle, or, battles took place along here and this is almost the rear of division. I can't help but wonder how the North Koreans got this far past the battalions.

The convoy of jeeps slowed as they came around a corner and there in front of them was a concertina wire fence with a barrier across the road. On the left side was a sandbagged bunker with a machine gun and the barrel was following the jeep. The barricade and the machine gun was manned by armed MP's. The sign hung on the barricade read; *STOP FOR INSPECTION*, and that's what he jeeps did. As soon as the three jeeps stopped and was recognized the barricade was lifted and the jeep convoy proceeded.

There were shell holes beside the road inside the compound and it was easy to see where the road had been repaired. Several tents had been destroyed and they were piled away from the main tent area. War does not discriminate, thought Ltc. Winters, it reaches out and touches the just and the unjust alike.

When the jeep convey stopped in front of a new looking General Purpose Large tent with a sign indicating this was the **5th DIVISION HQ** Ltc. Winters knew that many changes had taken place since his last visit to division. The new larger tents were erected to the side of the median of the division and away from the congested area. There were four more of the large tents, two on each side of the Headquarters tent, side by side with space between them and sandbags stacked four foot high around each tent. Each tent clearly marked with a sign, **S-1, S-2, S-3,** and **S-4.** Looking between two of the tents Ltc. Winters could see a rather large sandbag bunker, half underground, with several antennas sprouting from the roof. That is Division communications center or Blue Stallion commo.

The word Ltc. Winters had been trying to think of since he left the mike boat suddenly came to him, Professionalism. He had seen it when the MP came aboard the boat, again at the check point, and now at the division headquarters. Ltc. Winters wasn't jealous; he was too professional for that

When the jeeps stopped in front of the Division HQ tent Ltc. Winters stepped out, thanked the MP, and picked up his bag. "Good morning Titus," called a voice he recognized. Colonel Layton stood just inside the tent with his Chief of Staff, Colonel MacMasters.

"Good morning sir."

"You remember Colonel MacMasters?"

"Yes sir I do. How are you sir?"

"Very well Colonel and thank you for asking."

"Nice set up you have here Walter."

"We make do. Come on inside Titus. How was your trip?"

"Smooth."

"How are you?"

"I've seen better times Walter but I can't seem to remember when."

"It's rough all over right now Titus. No one saw this coming and we are ill prepared for war."

"I couldn't agree with you more on that subject Walter, but, are we at war?"

"That's a toss-up right now. Eighth Army says it's a scrimmage, a border crossing. No one wants to call it a war. But we old soldiers know it as war."

"A scrimmage, confused fighting, I can agree with. But a war by any other name is still a war."

"Well come on in. I need to talk with you before the staff meeting gets started."

"A Staff meeting? I don't remember hearing about a staff meeting."

"I couldn't give out too much information over the radio Titus. How about some coffee laced with good scotch?" Col. MacMasters was forgotten so he left the two old friends and went to his office where he had a pile of work to catch up on.

"Now you are talking my language," Ltc. Winters said as he followed Col. Layton into the tent.

Col. Layton led Titus back into the big tent to an area enclosed with tentage. Over the door was a sign that read; Commander, 5thInfantry Division, Colonel Layton. Inside the ground was covered with carpet and there was a desk and swivel chair behind it. A couch and two more easy chairs sat at the side of the room with a coffee table in front of them..

"Nice. Very nice. Nice set up Walter," said Titus.

"You are referring to the new tents?"

"Actually everything I see."

"Have a seat Titus," said Col .Layton as he went to the desk and used his intercom to call for a pot of coffee. Removing two cigars from his desk drawer he sat down, handing a cigar to Titus. They went through the process of lighting the cigars while waiting for the coffee. When the coffee was delivered Col. Layton filled two cups then removed a bottle of twelve year old scotch from his desk drawer and poured a liberal amount into each cup. "Like old times huh Titus?"

"Does bring back memories," answered Titus as he took a puff on the cigar and tasted his coffee.

The two had served together many times and knew each other for years.

"Now, about those tents Titus. When the quartermaster people in Inchon realized the warehouses might be overrun by the fast moving North Koreans they were willing to give us anything just to empty the warehouses. There are more of the tents if you want some Titus?"

"GP Large tents are much too big for me. GP mediums would certainly be nice."

"Have your S-4 send a list of what you need to my S-4. See how easy that was?"

You are too agreeable Walter, there must be something you want or need and you are trying to butter me up. New tents, Cuban cigars, and good scotch, I wonder what is next.

"Titus, if you feel your XO can handle the battalion I want you to stay overnight."

"Major McCall is a good man. He can handle the battalion."

"I'm glad to hear you say that Titus but you won't like what I'm about to say."

"You are going to take my XO? Walter, I need more men on the Peninsula not less. I have stripped the battalion to send officers and men to the Companies and I'm still short. Enlisted men I need yesterday to fill vacancies. Tell me, when I can expect some replacements?"

"I can't Titus. You have to look at the big picture. I know you, as does other units all over Korea, need men. When the North Koreans crossed the 38th Parallel they advanced between the 2nd and 3rd Battalions. 2nd Battalion lost half its men plus the XO and four officers. 3rd Battalion was hit even harder. They lost the Co, Xo, and five officers, plus twenty enlisted men. 4th battalion fared much better but there is no XO there. Right now I have a young, inexperienced, captain as Co of 3nd battalion."

"I had no idea Walter."

"You couldn't have Titus."

"If you need Major McCall you can have him."

"I'm glad you agree with me Titus. When you depart you can take the orders back with you. For now let's get off the dire military situation. I took the liberty of ordering food so we can eat and talk here. After the staff meeting we will retire to my quarters and work on that bottle of excellent scotch. No sooner had Col. Layton got the words out of his mouth that a voice called out and Col. Layton asked him to enter. Two cooks entered each carrying a covered tray. They placed them on the coffee table then left the room.

"Let's dig in before it gets cold," said Col. Layton moving his chair closer to the coffee table. "Pardon my manners Titus but I didn't ask about your family. How are Sally and the children?"

"My wife, being a good military wife, tells me everything is fine back home except that she misses me. Both kids are away in college and I hear from them maybe once a month or when they need money. How about your family Walter? How is that good looking Italian wife of yours, Marie, and your daughter?"

"Like you said, they seem to be fine and miss me as much as I miss them. Connie has about a year to go before she has her teacher's certificate. I hear she has met a young man and Marie tells me they seem serious."

"You could be Grandpa Walter in a short while then."

"Don't remind me. I've been thinking about just that lately."

They ate and talked until the food was finished then when the trays were taken away Walter poured more coffee but no more scotch. The staff meeting was scheduled to start in ten minutes and he didn't want either of them smelling of booze.

"Walter, per the K.C.P instructions I called a Code Red this morning. I have the written report with me."

"Was it that bad on the peninsula Titus?"

"Artillery up near or across the 38th parallel was devastating the Battalion so I called the Air Force for assistance. They responded and did an excellent job of silencing it. They also reported that the 17th ROK was no more."

"I'm not sure how 8th Army will react to the using of a Code Red but give your report to the S-2 at the meeting. He'll pass it on. So we have lost our buffer on the 38th parallel. I'll have to report that fact to 8thArmy."

"Back up there Walter. What do you mean, how they will react? They wrote the K.C.P and I used it. If it's not supposed to be used tell them to rescind it."

"Don't get yourself all worked up Titus. I'm sure you did the right thing. We'll just wait and see how 8th Army reacts to the report. Right now we need to get to that meeting."

It was a sad looking staff that called attention and stood up when Col. Layton entered the meeting room followed by Ltc. Winters. Col. Layton called 'at ease' and everyone sat down. Ltc. Winters sat next to Col. Layton.

One item of news, told to Ltc. Winters before he departed division, was history making news but it would be a while before it was heard on the peninsula. Seldom did the Stars and Stripes, the military newspaper, reach the Peninsula. On July 8 1950 the newly formed United Nations, to replace the League of Nations, unanimously approved President Truman's request that General Douglas MacArthur be named Commander in Chief of all

United Nations Forces in Korea which consisted of, U. S. , South Korean, British, Canadian, Australian, Colombia, and India medical units. General MacArthur designated himself SCAP, (Supreme Commander Allied Power), and established his headquarters in the Dai Ichi Building in Tokyo Japan.

If, Ltc. Winters wondered, there are so many different Countries stationed in South Korea where are they located, and where are the men? We could certainly use some extra men about now.

Of the thirty eight enlisted men who were reported KIA or wounded and evacuated by Ltc. Winters Col. Layton was able to replace thirty of them. So there were thirty men, young enlisted men but no officers, who boarded the Mike boat early this morning with Ltc. Winters. He would have liked to have more but he would settle for what he could get. The boat was already loaded with men and supplies and ready to depart when the division jeep dropped Ltc. Winters off at the beach. As soon as he was on board the ramp was raised and the mike boat moved away from shore.

The early morning breeze felt good to his throbbing head this morning. He had drank far too much last night after the staff meeting and his head was throbbing. Drinking was something he knew he had been doing too much of lately and he had to start thinking about cutting back.

He had come to division with hopes of some of his problems being solved but instead more were heaped on him. It was a dreary picture that the staff meeting produced yesterday. The S-2, Major Kimball, had the most to say. It was a sad situation he explained to the men gathered there. There had been no warning that the North Koreans were ready to cross the 38th parallel. They were still fighting and trying to take over both Inchon and Seoul. Plus a large force was moving toward Pusan. If the North Korean's could take over both ports it would cripple the American military supply lines. He passed out the new SOI (Signal Operating Instructions) for a combat situation. Ltc. Winters had five copies of the classified document with him.

The 17th ROK was no more, of that Ltc. Winters was aware of already. Now his command had the entire Ongjin Peninsula, from the 38th parallel to the water, to defend. Plus now he had to put a man, an officer, on one of the islands off the end of the Ongjin Peninsula to act as a lookout, a Coast watcher. And to top it all off he was losing his XO.

There was no relief for the personnel shortage said the S-1. It will take three to six months for the pipe line of men to start moving again.

Supplies have been promised and the ships are on the way, arrival date unknown, reported the S-4.

There was little the S-3 could do without more information and that was slow arriving.

It was a commander's nightmare. 1st Battalion strength should have been

20 officers and 650 enlisted men, now he had to operate with five officers, including his self, and he was short 230 enlisted men. He, as well as the other battalion commanders, was told to do with what they had.

The only bright spot, if it could be called that, was that General MacArthur had given his permission for division commander to promote from within. About all that would do was to assure each unit had a leader, a man in charge, but it would also use some of the current assets.

Ltc. Winters had been promised one of the next officers to arrive at division, no date or time. He also had been handed copies of five sets of records of qualified enlisted men to pin battle field commissions on. He had to make the decision. Two he declined right off as undesirable. Three he would take another look at. One he felt sure would make an excellent officer but he, after reading the file, knew he had some convincing to do of the individual. But he had an ace in the hole to help convince the man to pin on the bars of a second lieutenant.

This morning, before he departed Division, he had been given the word that Capt. Stevens was now listed as KIA. Will it never end?

His head was starting to clear up some but he wished he had a drink right now.

Maybe when he arrived at battalion he could grab a quick one to clear his mind.

During the trip across the water Ltc. Winters looked the thirty men over. Most are young but there are a few older ones, but not much older. Some of the older ones may have some time in the service but the young ones look like they were dropped off by a school bus. These are the last of the men from the holding center, Walter had said. How quickly will these young men learn the rules of warfare and how many will become just a memory on the 1st Battalion rolls? Maybe they just look young to you Titus, he chided himself. It doesn't seem that long ago when you were just a scared young man. Yeah, and back then I had others to carry the burden of responsibility and make the hard decisions, like these men, now I'm the one in the hot seat.

As the mike boat neared the beach he could see a truck and a jeep waiting. Maj. McCall was there with his packed bags as he had been told to be by an earlier radio message. "Good morning sir," said Maj. McCall when Ltc. Winters stepped off the mike boat, "glad to have you back."

"You may not think so when you find out what's going to happen," spoke Ltc. Winters searching for the orders in his attaché case, "Jerry you have been reassigned for the good of the Division."

"I thought I was doing a good job here sir?"

"You are Jerry and I'll make sure that is indicated in your records. The decision has been made and the boat is waiting. My guess is that you will get a Battalion. That should get you a promotion."

"No chance I could remain here sir?"

"No there isn't. Here are you orders and good luck Jerry," Ltc. Winters said shaking Maj. McCall's hand.

Sergeant Major Callings met Ltc. Winters as he got out of the jeep in the new Battalion area. "How was the trip colonel?"

"The trip was fine but the information was lousy. Get this to the radio operator," he said handing over a copy of the new SOI, "and this order to S-1. I brought back thirty men. Get them to the companies now."

"I see we're losing Major McCall," said SGM Callings after he scanned the order.

"Make that, we have lost him. He's on the mike boat as we speak. Where is my tent set up? I need to freshen up before I have a meeting."

"Right this way sir." said SGM Callings.

Ltc. Winters located his bottle of good scotch, opened it, and without using a glass took a couple of healthy gulps. He recapped the bottle and looked at the contents. Less than half full and he only had one more bottle plus a half full bottle in his desk. Good thing I thought to bring back a couple of bottles and some of those good cigars. At one time he shared his scotch with other officers but now he hoarded it. With the slowdown of supplies he had no idea when he could replenish his supply. He felt somewhat better after the drink so he splashed some water on his face, dried off, picked up his attache case, and went back to what was left of his battalion.

"Sergeant Major Callings," he said as he entered the command tent, "three things I need done immediately. Get these SOI's distributed, one to each of the Companies. Have the jeep driver pick up a Corporal McNeil at Baker Company and deliver him here. Notify Capt. Wells to join me, and you also when you finish."

"Yes sir I'll get right on it."

Ltc. Winters filled a cup with coffee then went to his, what served as his bleak office. He sat down heavily and opened his attache case to remove the papers inside. As he sat and waited he sipped the coffee and remembered what Walter had said to him just before he departed, "Best of luck Titus and watch your six."

Up until his trip to division his only thoughts were of his battalion, the 1st Battalion and its problems. But he found out there were other units in far worse shape than the 1st battalion was. But then there is always someone in worse shape.

His thoughts were interrupted by the arrival of Capt. Wells. "Good Morning Sir."

"Good Morning Capt. Wells. We're waiting for the Sergeant Major. Get some coffee if you need it?"

"I'm fine sir," he replied as he took a seat in front of the desk.

A couple minutes later SGM Callings arrived and took a seat. "The SOI's are on the way along with the new men Sir."

"We have new men?" asked Capt. Wells.

"Yes sir, thirty of them. The orders and Company assignments are on your desk."

"Well that's a bit of good news."

"Let's get into this and get it over because I'm sure each of you has plenty of work to take care of. First, read this," he said passing an official looking document to Capt. Wells, "when you finish pass it to the Sergeant Major."

"That should lower the already low morale of the men when they hear about it," said Capt. Wells after he read the paper and handed it SGM Callings.

"The up-side is we won't be losing any more men to transfers," said Ltc. Winters.

What the document said, and it was an order from the Commander in Chief of the Armed Forces of America, Harry S. Truman, was as of this date no one, enlisted or officer, of any branch of the military would be released from active duty for the duration of the North Korean situation plus six months.

"When will you pass out the sad news sir?" asked SGM Callings as he laid the document back on the desk.

"Capt. Wells will get the information out to the company officers who will brief their men. Next item; We, I, have permission to promote from within for mission accomplishment. That bit of information is not to leave this tent.. My first promotion is to Capt. Wells. You are now Major Wells. Here are the orders. Congratulations Major."

"I—I'm very surprised, yet pleased," stammered Maj. Wells.

"Other than a few more dollars in your pocket, which is the only good part of it, you will now take on more responsibility. You are, as of now, my XO, plus the S-1, S-2, S-3, and S-4. You will wear many hats until we get some relief, such as more men. The Sergeant major will give you a hand. Now let's get into the really bad news. There are no large numbers of replacements due in for three to six months. There will be few supplies, other than ammo and food, for a long while. Promises have been made but that's about all. I realize we can't fight a battle with promises but the word is; do what we can with what we have.

"It has been confirmed that the 17th ROK no longer exists. The 1st Battalion now has the defense of the entire Peninsula. Plus, I, or we, have to send an officer to the islands off the southern tip of the peninsular to be a coast watcher."

"That's almost ridicules," said newly promoted Maj. Wells, "how can anyone expect us to expand our area of responsibility without increasing our troop strength?"

"It may sound ridicules but be that as it may. We either perform the assigned mission to the best of our ability with what resources we have or follow the demise of the 17th ROK. The other three Battalions are in far worse shape than we are. What I need from each of you is a can do attitude, not complaints and excuses. If there is anyone else in the Battalion we can turn lose do so. I can't see having men here when it is far more important to have them on line. The three of us will remain here plus the radio operator. The radio operator will be relieved by us and he will double up as a driver. Keep a couple of supply men, one medic, the mess Sergeant and two cooks. Does anyone have any questions?"

"One sir," spoke Maj. Wells, "where do we get a commander for Baker Company?"

"I'm working on that now. Is there anything else?"

"Yes sir," said Maj. Wells, "a bag of captured documents plus some other items were sent up from Baker Company for us to look at."

"How did Baker Company come into possession of captured documents?" asked Ltc. Winters.

"I was told a Corporal; a Ranger qualified Corporal, ventured out on the battlefield at night and collected them from dead North Korean soldiers."

"Might I guess the name of this man is Corporal McNeil?"

"I believe that is the name given me sir."

"Well, we don't have anyone who speaks Korean here so get the documents on the next boat to Division S-2. Carry out my orders and get them done fast. Has that man arrived that I requested Sergeant Major?"

"I'll have to check sir."

The Sergeant Major came back and reported that the jeep had not returned yet. Ltc. Winters decided he would have time to get to his tent for a quick shot of scotch plus pick up some of those good cigars from his dwindling supply. He needed a drink and possibility a drink would be called for to help convince this Corporal McNeil to accept a commission. Desperate situations required desperate measures.

When he returned to the command tent Ltc. Winters decided he should have another drink while he waited. Two turned into three. He sat down at his desk to get started on the stack of papers that had accumulated during his absence.

His mind really wasn't on the task at hand. The strange ending to the message that had been receive at division had him wondering what it could have meant: **the mortar that fired on Baker now fires back,** courtesy of a Corporal. He set that aside for a while as his mind turned to the possible trouble the other three Battalions could be in if and when the North Koreans advance was turned. The three Battalions would be fighting a battle on two fronts, or rather they would be in the middle of the advancing and retreating North Koreans. Well, I have enough to worry about right here rather than dwelling on others problems.

## 26 June 1950

McNeil was on the line checking out his weapon. He made sure all the men who had the AK-47 were checked out on it and knew how to clean it.

The men on the line had not had a break in over thirty six hours now. So without seeking permission McNeil took it on himself to give them some relief. He allowed every other man on the line a two hour break, after they had cleaned their weapons, to return to the company area to locate what they could of their personnel gear, grab a bath, some hot food, write a letter or read. As the men returned he rotated the other men. When his turn came he found very little of his gear worth keeping. He did find his cigars, a couple of books, and some uniforms that weren't torn up by shrapnel. After his bath and some food and coffee he wrote a letter to his mother then returned to the line.

While he kept half the men on watch he had the others breaking down and cleaning Ak-47 rifles and improving their firing position. In situations like this he knew he had to keep them busy. He made it a point to check on Pvt Hall several times to make sure he wouldn't have any adverse reactions to his scare two nights ago. The man seemed to be ok now.

McNeil had just reassembled his M-1 and checked to make sure it operated ok when he saw SSgt. Simpson headed his way. He stepped out of his firing position and waited.

"I knew your exploits wouldn't go unnoticed too long McNeil. Grab you gear, the Battalion jeep is waiting for you. It seems you have come to the attention of the Colonel. He wishes to speak with you."

Having relayed the order to McNeil SSgt. Sampson turned and walked away with a smile on his face.

Ltc. Winters finally got his mind of the tactical situation and back on the mound of paper work. He was in deep thought when he sensed that someone was trying to get his attention. He looked up.

"Sorry to disturb you sir but I was told to report to the Battalion commander and there was no one out here to announce me," said McNeil.

"You have the right place and you are?"

McNeil leaned his weapon against a table, marched into the area designated as the commanders office, stopped three feet from the desk, rendered a salute; Sir, Corporal Charley R. McNeil reporting to the Battalion Commander as ordered."

"Stand at ease Corporal McNeil," said Ltc. Winters after he returned the salute. In fact since there's only the two of us let's be informal. Have a seat."

"Sir?" asked McNeil with raised eyebrows.

"Sit down. Relax. Would the Corporal care for a cup of coffee?"

"Yes sir," replied McNeil as he sat down, "a hot cup of coffee would be most appreciated," said the condemned man, thought McNeil. Word of my exploits must have reached Battalion and in a few minutes he will lower the boom on me.

Ltc. Winters left and soon returned with two china cups of hot coffee. He handed one to McNeil and sat back down behind his desk with the other one. "Thank you very much sir," said McNeil.

"Would the Corporal be opposed to stepping that up with a shot of good scotch?"

"The Corporal would love it sir, but I'm still on duty."

"In garrison duty where duty hours are clearly defined a good soldier does not take liberation until he is off duty. Here we find ourselves in a unique situation in that our duty hours are twenty four hours a day. If one indulges one must do so at a convenient time. You do indulge don't you corporal?"

"I have been known to tip a few sir." just where is this conversation going wondered McNeil.

"Good, I have just declared this to be the proper time for a drink."

"Do I see twelve year old scotch in that bottle Colonel?"

"If my eyes are not deceiving me I believe that is what the label reads."

"Since the Colonel has been gracious enough to declare this the cocktail hour I would be most grateful for a splash of scotch in my coffee sir."

After Ltc. Winters poured scotch into each cup he put the bottle away then took two of his special Cuban cigars, Romeo y Juliet's, from his desk. "Would the corporal care for a cigar?"

"I would be profoundly grateful for a good cigar Colonel Sir."

After each went through the process of lightening the cigar then tasted the coffee, the Colonel spoke. "I have heard of, shall we say, some of you unorthodox actions Corporal." With no officer available in Baker Company to answer questions Ltc. Winter was curious as to why the documents had been collected and why did a man risk his life to collect them.

Here it comes, thought McNeil. I knew all this generosity was leading up to something. I'll either lose a stripe, get an ass chewing, or a word to the wise. "I was hoping what I did would go unnoticed sir."

"A good Commander always knows what is going on in his command. What prompted you to take such risks?"

"Necessity Sir."

"Explain."

"When one can, one must utilize all resources. When one can use the enemy's food and supplies one eases the burden of one's own supply system."

"You have read Sun Tzu?"

"Yes sir. The art of war was required reading in ROTC."

"As you can tell I'm full of questions today corporal."

"I noticed sir."

"For instance; I read a message while at division that originated from here, but the last part of it stumps me. Can you explain what this means; **the mortar that fired on Baker** now fires on the enemy?"

"Yes sir I can. The North Koreans set up a mortar out front of Baker Company, and each of the other companies as well, which prevented the men from getting rest. At an opportune time I relieved them of the mortar plus a couple cases of rounds. We turned the tube on them."

An enterprising young man, thought Ltc. Winters. I can't help but wonder why the other companies allow the mortars to still operate. "I have an opinion but I'm curious to hear yours in reference to the high attrition rate of officers."

"Do I have permission to speak freely sir?"

"By all means."

"To answer your question Sir; lack of experience."

"Expand on that please."

"Officers are operating by the book as if they were still in school."

"I see. Please continue?"

"Shiny insignia with their rank painted on their helmets acts as a bull's eye. A radio operator with an antenna whipping in the air dogging the heels of an officer marks him as a target also. An officer is someone a sniper loves to eliminate."

"I see. My theory was along those lines but I didn't get past young and experienced."

"Yes sir. Inexperienced means never having heard a shot fired in anger."

"You corporal have heard those shots fired in anger. If memory serves me correctly I believe your blood was drawn twice?"

"Close sir. Make that three times. I can never seem to remember to duck."

"Yes, well, let's move on to another subject. I had an opportunity to read your records so I'm curious as to why you turned down a commission?"

"I was drafted sir."

"I'm aware of that fact but that doesn't explain why you declined a commission."

"My one desire is to complete my military obligation and get back to college, as soon as I can, and complete my masters. I laid out one semester to earn some money and the draft caught me. So here I am with a year left in service."

"Expound on that so this old Colonel can comprehend."

"Sir, the draft is for two years of service of which, as I said, I have completed half of it. If I had accepted a commission I would have been extended on active duty for four to five years."

"And that's the only reason for you not accepting a commission?"

"Yes sir, the time factor."

"I see. If a situation existed that would prevent you being discharged in one year would you consider accepting a commission?"

"Sir, I have heard rumors that General MacArthur has stated that we will be home by Christmas."

"I never listen to rumors Corporal, only facts. I have heard that rumor, but which Christmas did he mean?"

"Sir, does a situation exist where I, and others, may not be discharged on time?"

"You are answering questions with questions Corporal."

"Sorry about that sir."

"In answer to your question a situation does exist. Here read this," said Ltc. Winters passing over the message from the Commander in Chief.

McNeil read it, shook his head, and then passed it back.

"Comments?" asked Col. Winters.

"Sir, If, and I emphasize the word 'IF', I accepted a commission and General MacArthur is proven right, then I will have cut my own throat, so to speak. I would have to stay on active duty far beyond my current discharge date."

"One thing you are forgetting Corporal. An enlisted man must serve his full time but an officer has the option of resigning his commission. But, of course, as you just read, no one, officer or enlisted, leaves the service until six months after this situation with the North Koreans gets solved. How long that will take no one knows."

"If I was offered a commission, and if I accepted, I don't believe I will be sent back to the states to attend OCS."

"Correct. Due to the current situation, and due to the shortage of officers, I have been given permission to award Battle Field Commissions to deserving individuals."

"I see. If I agree to accept a commission what would you have me doing sir?"

"As you are aware Baker Company needs a commander and I have no more officers and none are due in."

"So I would take command of Baker Company?"

"Yes, for a short while."

"Could you explain that sir?"

"It's a classified matter of which I'm not at liberty to discuss with a Corporal. However, I could discuss it with an officer, of which I'm in dire need of, provided he had the correct security clearance."

"How long do I have to think this over sir?"

"About five minutes."

"Would it be possible to have another shot of that excellent scotch while I do some thinking?"

"I believe we can squeeze another one or two out of the bottle."

I do believe I am being led by the nose here, thought McNeil, after he had more scotch and sat back to think. I do believe the Colonel is right. If I do accept a commission that will mean more money I can save toward my next year or so of college, plus I can send mom a bit more. Better to spend the time remaining on active duty as an officer plus, as he said, I would be able to resign a commission at any time after this mess is over. The question is can I handle the duties of an officer on active duty? This isn't ROTC where mistakes can be forgiven and chalked up to a learning experience. This is war where mistakes can get myself, or others, killed. Am I experienced enough to accept this promotion and carry out the duties required of an officer on active duty? I feel I'm just as capable, if not more so, than the late Lt Richards, if I can stay alive. If officers are needed so desperately that authority has been granted to promote enlisted men to officers why should I accept a lowly 2ndlieutenant's bar? I sound as if I have agreed to the Colonel's proposal, but then I guess I have. I wonder just how serious Colonel Winters is since field commissions have not been handed out since WW2.

"Sir," spoke McNeil after a bit of thinking, "I realize there is a shortage of officers and I don't care to exploit a situation, but, if I'm to accept a commission then I would rather it be as a 1st Lieutenant as opposed to a 2nd Lieutenant, the low man on the totem pole, a butter bar. If, as you say, and I have no reason to not believe you, that you have the authority to award battle field commissions, and for the exigency of the service, I would accept an active duty commission as a 1st Lieutenant."

"You have this old colonel over a barrel in his time of need Corporal. But, since I haven't been given specific instructions I believe I can comply with your request."

"You are most kind sir."

"Thank you. Now with that settled would you remove those stripes and pin on this crossed rifle and silver bars?" he said laying them out on his desk. He had thought far enough ahead to bring back from division several sets of officer insignia plus some enlisted chevrons.

"No sir."

"What? Correct me if I'm wrong but didn't I just hear you say you would accept a commission?"

"You heard correctly sir. But, I don't want this to be just a temporary promotion. I don't wish to accept the responsibility of an officer only to be reduced back to an enlisted man when qualified officers are assigned. I'll pin on the rank and accept the responsibility only after I have official orders and the officers oath has been administrated."

Ltc. Winters hesitated a moment, then he got up from his seat. "Corporal, just outside there, to your left is a table with a coffee pot on it. Would you refill our cups while I round up the S-1?"

Ltc. Winters returned a few minutes later followed by SGM Callings and Maj. Wells. "These two men comprise the battalion staff, plus several enlisted men," he said introducing Corporal McNeil to them. "The Corporal, who is well qualified, has agreed to accept a commission. Will you Major Wells get the paper work started and cut orders and both of you witness the officer's oath as I administer it?"

"Be glad to sir and congratulations Corporal McNeil," said both men as they left the room to get started.

"Now if you are satisfied that everything is on the up and up will you pin on those bars so we can get started here. Time is of the essence."

McNeil, after hearing that the Battalion staff was only two officers finally realized this wasn't a game. He was needed as an officer, and now, but for what wasn't explained to him just yet. I do have to wonder just what I may have gotten myself into here, he thought as he took off his shirt and started removing the corporal stripes using his pocket knife to cut the thread holding them to his shirt sleeve. "It will be my honor to accept a commission sir."

After McNeil pinned on the silver 1stLieutenant bars Ltc. Winters spoke, "now with that settled, and while we wait for the paper work would you step over here to the map? I'll work on a clearance for you."

"That shouldn't be too hard sir. I was cleared for top secret in ROTC which should be reflected on my records."

"I'll have it checked out. Give me your thoughts on the so called big picture."

The big map was full of military symbols and unit designations and McNeil was aware of what each meant. After he studied the map a moment he spoke. "No unit should try and fight a battle on two fronts and what I see here is a wide open back door. No unit can hope to win on even one front with its rear exposed."

"More Sun Tsu I believe?"

"Yes sir. But what I said applies, not only to us here on the Peninsula but to the entire 5th Division and other units."

"How will the situation effect the Division?" asked Ltc. Winters just to see how much military knowledge Corporal McNeil had picked up in R O T C.

"When 8th Army gets its act together, and it has to be soon, and starts pushing the North Koreans back to the north the Division will be fighting both advancing and retreating North Koreans. Also if the North Koreans can get enough artillery on those islands off the coast here," he said pointing to the group of islands, "they, the 5th Division and other units, will be bombarded with artillery fire. We here on the Peninsula will have to battle the North Koreans to our front plus be under artillery fire while doing so. Not a very good situation to be in sir."

"I suppose you have a solution?" asked Ltc Winters amazed that an enlisted man had picked up on an adverse military situation that no commander should find himself in.

"To prevent the North Koreans from utilizing the islands we must occupy them first, but with what and whom?"

Very good, thought Ltc. Winters. I can't help but wonder why I, and other so called experts, didn't catch all that sooner and take action? I only hope we are not too late. "What you say is all true Corporal, no make that Lieutenant. I have orders from division to secure those islands. You seem to have the grasp of the situation so you are selected to accomplish just that. When we are finished here you will go back and take over Baker Company until such time as we have approval for the island occupation. While you wait come up with a list of what you think you will need, in the way of supplies and equipment, to accomplish the mission."

"This mission is for only one man sir?" asked McNeil wondering just how one man was expected to accomplish a mission that should be given to a squad of men.

"As you should know by now there is a man power shortage. It'll have to be a one man mission."

"I suppose one man with binoculars and a radio could pretty much cover all the islands if he established himself on the tallest one. But, how is one man to defend all the islands?"

"I have been told to expect support from the Air Force since the islands are critical and since there is a shortage of ground forces."

"Air strikes huh? That could work sir."

"Ah, that was fast," said Ltc. Winters as he saw both Maj. Wells and SGM Callings enter the room. Maj. Wells went to the desk and laid out a stack of paper work. "If the corporal, excuse me, the Lieutenant, will take a seat and sign where indicated we can have you official in a short time. We'll have to wait on the Department of the Army for your new serial number."

McNeil sat down and started signing his name. He signed until his hand hurt. Then with witnesses Ltc. Winters administered the officer's oath to his new officer, 1st Lieutenant Charley R. McNeil. "If you two will get cups we'll have a toast to Lt McNeil's promotion?"

After a toast was given and congratulations added, Maj. Wells and SGM Callings excused themselves. "That makes it official Lt. McNeil. Now with the mission started we need a mission name."

"Let's keep it simple sir. How about the LOP MISSION. LOP for Listen and Observation post."

"I'll go along with that. LOP mission it is. I'll see about getting you a copy of the new SOI for the mission."

"If you don't mind sir, my taking a copy of an SOI to the island might be dangerous. And besides, if it's a new one you can bet it'll be decoded real fast once it's used, which would put me in danger."

"Danger! In what way?"

"If the North Koreans were smart enough to plan and execute battle plans without us, the U S Army, hearing about them then I'm sure they have the means to listen in on our radio transmissions. It wouldn't take them long to break the new S O I and learn what we are up to. With no means of leaving the islands my ass would be up a creek. Excuse my language sir."

"I have heard worse. So what is the solution?"

"While on military maneuvers we in the ROTC came to the conclusion that our plans were know ahead of time. Some enterprising person had broken the SOI we were using. We came up with a simple number code that has never been broken. One uses random numbers rather than the coded four letter word groups of the SOI. The four letter word groups are hard to comprise plus sometimes they are misunderstood or misread."

"You want to change an established military system to an unknown system? How hard will this be to learn?"

"It's really very simple sir. I'll get with the radio operator and teach him the system. Once he receives a message from me he can put it in the proper SOI code for re-transmitting. Since I'll be just one man out there I have no compulsion to being located and overrun. As I said before sir, I believe we should throw away the book and adopt ourselves, and our tactics, to the fast changing situation. Using the number code I spoke of I can get out an entire message in a tenth of the time it takes using the current SOI. That in itself prevents triangulation of a transmitter."

"Make it so then Lt. McNeil. Now, as I said before, the first order of business is for you to get to Baker Company and take command. Second, work on that number code with the radio operator. Third, get a list of supplies and equipment to me as quick as you can since we have no idea when division will give the go ahead. If you don't have anything else for me I have much work to attend to. "

"One more question sir. If I can find qualified men will you offer them a commission also? Also how about promoting some qualified enlisted men. I know for a fact that PFC's are platoon leaders in Baker Company and the situation may exist in the other companies. With my promotion there will be a gap in the chain of command."

"I'll take your recommendations one at a time but I reserve the right to final decision. See the Sergeant Major about some enlisted strips but don't hand them out too freely."

"I understood sir and thank you for everything." McNeil stepped back and rendered a salute. When it was returned he did an about face and left the room. He found the Sergeant Major after roaming around a while. "Sergeant Major Callings," he said, "I have been authorized by Ltc. Winters to offer some promotions to enlisted men. May I assume that you have some extra stripes?"

"You can and I do. What did you have in mind, in the way of strips?"

"Several PFC's, a couple of Corporal's, and one Buck Sergeant should do it. Also would you be so kind and have the radio operator call Baker Company and tell them to send a jeep to fetch their new Company Commander?"

"I believe we can handle that," replied the sergeant major as he handed McNeil several sets of enlisted strips. "How do those new bars feel?"

"They got real heavy shortly after I pinned them on."

"I'm sure the load will lighten quickly. Now let me see about a ride for you."

1st Lieutenant McNeil stepped outside the big tent to await his ride. He found a shade tree to stand under. He looked back at the small collection of tents that comprised 1st Battalion headquarters. Not too impressive but then there wasn't enough men to maintain much more than the few tents set up. He also remembered that when he came through here the 1/5th Battalion was set up in the open space where now he could see piles of damaged tents and other equipment. Now they were set up under some trees. Better location but not near good enough.

When the jeep from Baker Company stopped in front of the big tent McNeil walked from the shade tree and got in before the driver could shut the engine off. Pfc Gordon looked at his passenger then did a double take. "I'll be da----"

"Hold the expletive language Pfc Gordon," interrupted McNeil, "and don't spare the horses getting us to the Company."

"Yes sir," replied Gordon as he put the jeep in gear and drove away from Battalion. Boy, is someone going to be surprised, was his thought.

"If you had thought to salute me PFC Gordon you would have been a dollar richer but now you have lost your chance," McNeil said to Gordon.

Neither spoke again until PFC Gordon stopped the jeep in front of the tent that represented Baker Company orderly room. McNeil stepped out and turned to Pfc Gordon. "Might I assume you are still the radio operator?"

"Yes sir."

"Good. From now on you will wear more than one hat of which we'll discuss later. My first order to you is; never get near me with that radio and never take it on the line. Keep it in the tent or the company area. If I get a call take a message then locate me, minus the radio. Are we clear on that?"

"I understand sir."

"Then park the jeep and resume your duties."

1st Lt. McNeil took a look around at the company he was about to assume command of. Once it was a neat company but now damaged equipment and shredded tents were everywhere. He walked on into the command tent to find SSgt. Sampson bent over some papers. The dirt floor did not echo footsteps. Sergeant Sampson looked up when he realized someone was in front of him and his face registered surprise. "Corporal, if this is some kind of joke I'm not amused," he said when he saw the silver bars on McNeil's collar, "my advice is for you to shred those bars because I'm expecting the new Company Commander at any time now."

"I assure you this is no joke and I am the new Commander Sergeant Sampson. I believe proper military curtsey dictates that you come to attention and welcome your new Commander."

McNeil stood patiently waiting while SSgt. Sampson glared at him. He is wearing the rank so I will have to go alone with this crap, thought SSgt. Sampson, but if I find out he's pulling a fast one I'll have his ass. He slowly stood up and saluted. "Sir, I'm 1st SSgt. Sampson and welcome to Baker Company."

"Let's be precise here Sergeant Sampson. I believe you are the acting 1st Sergeant."

"My mistake Sir. The acting 1st Sergeant welcomes the new commander."

"Thank you very much SSgt. Sampson," said McNeil returning the salute.

"Are you, McNeil, also an acting Lieutenant?"

"Duly commissioned with orders," McNeil replied placing a copy of the orders on the desk for Sergeant Sampson to see.

McNeil looked around to see the clerk PVT Rogers and PFC Gordon standing at attention, PFC Gordon with a big grin on his face. "At ease," McNeil called out. "PFC Gordon wipe that grin off you face."

"PVT Rogers. Are you able to compose the order for me to take command?"

"Yes sir."

"Good. Three copies should do it."

"Now, pencil and paper Sergeant Sampson, for you, because I'm about to issue some direct orders. If any of my orders are disobeyed the man who disobeys them will lose a strip on the spot. I should think you would want to write that down."

"Yeah, ok," replied SSgt. Sampson as he looked for and found a pencil and paper in his desk.

"The correct response is, Yes Sir. I shouldn't have to explain that to you plus you are setting a bad example for the men."

"Yes Sir. I will take notes sir," replied SSgt. Sampson not at all pleased with what was taking place.

"Good. Next order; and this will be done before dark because I expect coffee for the men this evening. Have the cook tent struck and reset to our rear in that opening between the trees."

"That can't be done in such a short time, Sir," he finally added.

"Sergeant, the last two words in American is I CAN. If the tent isn't moved and ready so there is food and coffee by meal time I'll find a mess sergeant who can comply with orders and a 1st Sergeant who can issue them. Please pass that on.

"Next order; there will be no fire in that cook tent during the hours of darkness. There will be no matches struck, nor lighters lite, in the company area or on the defense line after dark. Any man with the habit will smoke in a tent where the light can't be seen."

"Sir," interrupted SSgt. Sampson, "how can we have coffee in the morning if no fires can be lit?"

"I enjoy a hot cup of coffee in the early morning as well as anyone but in my opinion It's far more important to be alive than have coffee. Next order; pass the word that unless there is action on the M L R the squad leaders will give their men a two hour break. During daylight they can rotate the two hour break. That will give the men time for a shower, to eat hot food, write a letter, read or catch up on some much needed sleep. Am I going too fast for you SSgt. Sampson?"

"I've got it Lt. McNeil," then he remembered to add 'Sir'. "But I think you are wrong."

"Your disagreement is duly noted but my orders will be carried out for the safety of the company and more importantly for the safety of the men. Without them you and I would not be needed here. Keep that in mind. While you are passing out those orders tell Pfc Brockman to report to me."

SSgt. Sampson got up slowly shaking his head. He did remember to take his rifle and helmet with him. McNeil went to the back of the command tent and saw two cots made up with sheets, pillows, and a blanket. He almost lost his temper until he remembered his new position. He couldn't afford to lose his cool at this time. Instead he propped his rifle against a post, picked up a cot, walked to the front of the tent and threw it out the tent opening. The second one followed. He ripped down the tentage that had divided the tent giving the previous commander some privacy. He did leave the battered field desk and chair. PVT Rogers and PFC Gordon sat and watched without saying a word.

"What the hell," yelled out a voice outside the tent, "then SSgt. Sampson entered. "What is going on here?"

"Just a little house cleaning sergeant," said McNeil very calmly.

"Lieutenant, are you aware that those two cots are mine and yours?"

"Where do PVT Rogers and PFC Gordon sleep?"

"This is VIP tent, sir. They sleep in one of the other tents."

"Sergeant, PFC Gordon and PVT Rogers, as is everyone else, are vital to this companies operation. As of now, you and I, and the other NCO's will take no comforts exceeding the comforts of the lowest private."

"Bu—but—where will I sleep?" sputtered SSgt. Sampson.

"Where does the lowest ranking man sleep sergeant?" asked McNeil as he got out of his field gear.

"I guess in his fighting position."

"You guess?" I suppose you have never checked the defense line at night, have you?"

"I wasn't required to, Sir," he added.

"As of now you are. Starting tonight you will gear up just like the men and spend half the night on the line checking the men to make sure they are awake and alert. You have a choice of shifts, evening to midnight or midnight to morning. I'll take the other half. Are my orders being carried out?"

"Reluctantly sir," said SSgt. Sampson as he removed his gear and sat down. He wasn't used to all this activity and passing out orders.

"I would suggest you encourage them to speed up because the men, and I, expect coffee this evening. My first order still stands. Is PFC Brockman on the way?"

"I got word to him sir."

"Good. Now I need the last five days morning reports. When you locate those for me you should go check on the progress of the tent moving."

McNeil walked over to where PVT Rogers was typing. "Are you good at what you do, PVT Rogers?" he asked the man.

"I suppose so sir. I like to think I am. Here is that order you asked for." he said laying the three copies on his desk. McNeil read then signed them.

"Now, type a set of orders for a promotion, three copies effective today; PVT Rogers to be promoted to PFC Rogers, effective today."

"Yes sir," replied PVT Rogers with a big smile on his face as he fed more paper into his typewriter.

"Now that I have your attention, you two will work together. PFC Gordon, you will spread your bed under the table holding the radios. That way you will always be near them. PFC Rogers, make your bed over there in the corner so you will be handy in case PFC Gordon has to leave here. Do you have any questions?"

"No sir," they both replied in unison.

McNeil went back to his desk and sat down to go over the morning reports so he would have an idea of just how many men he had and of what rank. He was on the fourth day when he heard Tiny enter the tent. "Well I'll be damn," he said coming closer to where McNeil sat. "I heard it but I couldn't believe it."

"PFC Brockman, I'm sure I passed the word that you were to report to your Commanding Officer, not use cuss words."

"Yes sir. Sorry sir." Tiny had no idea just what was going on but he did come to attention, saluted, and reported in the proscribed manner. "Sir, PFC Brockman reporting to the Company Commander."

McNeil waited a full minute before returning the salute. "Stand at ease PFC Brockman. How are things on the line?"

"Very well sir."

"Are you having trouble with the men?"

"Not much sir."

"Tiny," said McNeil, "come around here and sit down." There was a seat at the side of the desk.

"What you see is for real. I am a duly appointed 1st Lieutenant regular Army, and I have just signed the order stating that I am the Commander of Baker Company. I have to treat each man equally. I expect you to use proper military courtesy from now on. Do you have any questions so far?"

"I have one. How long did you get extended by accepting that commission?"

"There is something I haven't passed out yet. You will be the first to know and I expect you to keep in under your hat for now. Our Commander in Chief has seen fit to extend all members of all military services for the duration of the Korean conflict plus six months."

"Does that mean I won't be leaving here as soon as I expected to?"

"That's exactly what it means. Now, if you desire I can get a bar for you if you want it."

"I'm not sure I can handle being an officer, Sir." He added

"You handle yourself well so I don't see where you will have a problem being an officer."

"A lot of responsibility rests on the shoulder of an officer Charley. How long do I have to think about it?"

"About as long as I did, five minutes."

"I realize we are short of officers but I just don't think I can handle the responsibility. I hope you are not disappointed Charley?"

"No, I'm not. Some men can and some men can't. I respect your decision Tiny. Think you could handle a small promotion?"

"How small?"

"I'm authorized to promote to fill positions within the company. I need someone to handle the platoons. I thought maybe you could handle, say a sergeants rank, a three stripper."

"I guess I could handle that Charley."

"Good. You will take charge of the third and fourth platoons. I'll see if Corporal Johnson has someone to take the first and second platoons."

"What about Corporal Johnson? Can't he handle those two platoons?"

"I'll know more after I speak with him. Here are your strips. Get them sewn on as quickly as you can. Orders will be ready shortly."

"PFC Rogers," McNeil called out.

"Yes sir."

"When you finish cutting your orders cut a set for PFC Brockman. He will be Sgt E-5 Brockman as of today."

"Yes Sir."

"If you don't have any more questions Tiny please tell Johnson to report to me. Pick up you orders in about an hour."

"No questions Charley, and good luck."

"The same to you Sgt Brockman."

Apparently Tiny had met up with Johnson and briefed him on what to expect because when he entered the tent a few minutes later he went straight to where McNeil sat, stood at attention and reported in the proper military way. "At ease Corporal Johnson," said McNeil. "You must be curious but I see you are not asking questions."

"I got most of the answers from Tiny but I thought you and Tiny were so anxious to get out of the Army?

"Read this and make no comments," said McNeil passing him the order that extended everyone on active duty.

"That will make some people very unhappy," said Corporal Johnson after he read it and passed it back.

"Not you?"

"I had already decided to make a career of the army and I re-enlisted for three more years. So, no, it doesn't bother me. What does bother me is, will we survive this Korean situation?"

"We have so far and if we continue to be alert and keep our heads down I believe we will. The Army can't leave us hanging here too much longer without sending in more men. We must believe that Bob."

"How did that happen so fast?" he asked pointing to the silver bars on McNeil's collar.

"It was fast, but as you know officers are desperately needed and that is the reason I wanted to see you. How would you feel about pinning on the rank of a 2nd lieutenant?"

"Hold on a minute Charley. Who doesn't talk and dream about becoming an officer because each thinks he can do a better job than those appointed over him, but, there is a big difference between idle talk and reality."

"So, you don't want to become an officer because you don't think you can handle the responsibility, is that it?"

"Stop putting words in my mouth Charley. Where is this conversation going anyway?"

"There is a shortage of officers in Korea. Colonel Winters has been given the authority to award battle field commission to qualified individuals. I am asking you if you would consider accepting a commission."

"That's quite a jump isn't it, from Corporal to Lieutenant?"

"That's exactly what happened to me but stranger things have happened and stranger things will happen again. You said you have decided to make a career of the Army so why not serve your time as an officer?"

"But I have no experience along those lines; I can barely make it as a Corporal. It sounds good but what if I fall on my face?"

"Don't let the fear of the unknown hold you back Bob. You just continue as you have been with a platoon, except it will be with a Company."

"Would I stay here if I accepted a commission?"

"You will more than likely be sent to either Charley or Dog Company. Charley Company doesn't have an officer so that would be my guess. There is a good 1st Sergeant there to show you the way. Let him know you are inexperienced and need help. Don't try to pull the wool over his eyes because he has been around and will know immediately. It's always best to be honest and up front. But if you do decide to accept a commission, I will highly recommend, due to inexperience, that you be allowed to remain here until I leave then take over Baker Company. I need an answer from you Bob."

"Leave! Where are you going Charley?"

"That's Classified. All I can say is I will be departing here soon and be gone for an unknown length of time."

"Will we be allowed to keep the rank when all this is over?"

"Good question but I don't believe anyone will have the answer to that at this time. But, by serving as an officer in combat on your records will look good for future promotions even if you aren't allowed to keep the rank after Korea."

"Then I suppose I will give it a shot. What do I do?"

"First you get cleaned up and ready to go to Battalion first thing in the morning. You report to the Battalion Commander, Ltc Winters, for an interview. He will have been briefed as to why you are there. I will take some time later today and brief you on what to expect. Now with that settled, I need your replacement. Who do you recommend?"

"Tomorrow! That's fast."

"Time is of the essence Bob. I only had five minutes to make the decision myself."

Tiny returned, after Corporal Johnson left, to pick up his orders and brought the name for Bob's replacement so PFC Rogers was kept busy typing orders. With that taken care of McNeil decided it was time for him to make an appearance in the Company area.

He walked the line stopping at each position and speaking with the men. Those who knew him offered congratulations and those who didn't greeted him with "hello sir".

Lt. McNeil was now seeing the company through the eyes of a commander, the man responsible for the lives of men. After the line tour he went to where the cook tent was being set up. There was grumbling but the job was getting done. Change never comes easy and many men had doubts of the orders they had received, especially form someone who was an enlisted man this morning. Next McNeil located the supply tent and the supply sergeant, SSgt. Anderson, a man he had not met yet.

"May I be of assistance Lieutenant?" asked the tall slender Sergeant.

"You may, but first I would like to compliment you. I'm glad to see you and your men, or man, are not taking comforts beyond the men on the line."

"Thank you for the compliment Sir. When I saw those cots come flying out of the CP tent I thought I would get ahead of you and get rid of ours."

"Good thinking. Do you have an adequate supply of forms to report combat damaged equipment?"

"I do sir and I was wondering when someone would get around to thinking about it."

"Tomorrow. I'll have SSgt. Sampson get you some men to help. Get it done as quickly as possible then burn the damaged equipment."

"Burn it sir?"

"Burn it. That's an unsightly mess out there. Clean it up."

"Yes sir."

"One last item; when and if there is an attack get yourself and who ever, just how many men do you have?"

"Just one sir."

"You and he get your rifles and get to the line. We can use ever able bodied man up there."

"Will do sir."

"No fires or lights of any kind after dark."

"Yes sir."

McNeil went back to the cook tent where he could smell the aroma of coffee perking. He had his canteen cup in his hand as he entered the tent. It was taken from him and filled with coffee by one of the cooks. Nothing was said. Now that the tent was erected everyone was busy getting the evening meal ready.

McNeil stood back sipping his coffee and waiting for the men to get food first. When there was a lull in the food line he stepped up, took a tray, and filled it with food. Taking the tray and his coffee he put it on the hood of a nearby jeep. About the time he finished eating he saw SSgt. Sampson enter the cook tent. It was a known fact that few, if anyone, could get along with SSgt. Leeks, the mess sergeant. McNeil watched as the two men had a heated discussion then SSgt. Sampson pointed toward where McNeil stood.

Staff Sergeant, E-6, Leeks was a bit old for his rank and he had just over fourteen years of military service. His big mouth and overbearing attitude had caused him the chance for a promotion and got him transferred to Korea.

SSgt. Leeks looked toward McNeil, jerked his apron off and tossed it on a counter, and came stomping toward where McNeil stood sipping his coffee. McNeil watched the man come toward him. I know everybody tries to stay out of SSgt. Leeks way to keep from riling him. I am also aware of how SSgt. Sampson avoids him. In my position I don't have much of a choice. I have to face him now and set him straight without losing my temper. SSgt. Leeks had food stains on his pants and one pants leg was partially out of his boot. He wore no jacket and the, once white, T-shirt was filthy. The cap on his head was lopsided. He didn't look clean enough to be handling food and he was not dressed properly to speak to an officer. He certainly wasn't setting a good example for the lower ranks.

One of the young cooks nudged his buddy, "there goes old Sarge to chew up another young officer."

"Yeah, and he sure knows how to do it. Let's watch."

Other men had stopped what they were doing to see the outcome of the encounter.

"Lieutenant, I want to talk--, said SSgt. Leeks in a deep voice he used to shake up other men but he was interrupted before he could finish.

"Good day SSgt. Leeks. That was a fine meal you turned out for the men," said McNeil in a calm voice.

"What? Oh. Yeah. I always turn out good food. Now—"

"And the coffee is excellent also." again McNeil interrupted him before he could finish what he wanted to say.

"My coffee is always the best but----"

"You are out of uniform Sergeant Leeks."

"I've been working. Now----"

"Do you know anything about military courtesy Sergeant Leeks?"

"What? Yes I do. But----"

"SSgt. Leeks, you are an NCO and I shouldn't have to tell you this but it seems to have slipped your mind. You are not only out of uniform but not once have you shown proper military courtesy to an officer. I have received no salute and I haven't heard the word 'sir' once." Having pointed out the error of his ways McNeil stepped closer until he was in SSgt. Leeks face. "This is a direct order Sergeant Leeks. You will get into a proper clean uniform and report to me in the proscribed manner in the CP. I'll give you twenty minutes before I prefer charges for insubordination. If you understand say, 'yes sir'?"

"Yes sir," SSgt. Leeks finally said.

"Twenty minutes," said McNeil. Then he turned and took his tray to the cook tent.

Sergeant Leeks stood there for a full minute trying to figure out what had just happened. That gruff attitude has always scared people, especially that SSgt. Sampson, and I get my way and they stay off my back. The way that kid lieutenant kept interrupting me threw me off. Yeah, that's what it was. The way he complimented my cooking then chewed on me really threw me off. Well, I guess I better change and see what's on his mind. Then I'll tell him a thing or two about how to run this company.

"What are you guys looking at?" asked Sergeant Leeks when he got back to the cook tent and noticed the cooks looking at him. "Get busy. The meal isn't over yet. Right now I have to change and confer with the Lieutenant."

"I would have never predicted the outcome that way. I thought that old Sarge would have chewed him up and spit him out," said SSgt. Sampson in a low voice.

"I think he just got a thorn stuck in his mouth," replied Corporal Johnson who had heard the remark.

"SSgt. Sampson looked to see who had made the remark then he quickly moved away.

McNeil wanted an after dinner cigar but he decided to wait. Instead he pulled the U.C.M.J. book (Uniform Code of Military Justice) from the desk drawer and opened it on the desk top. He had checked his watch so he knew when the time would be up for SSgt. Leeks. To pass the time he opened the book to the section dealing with **INSUBORDINATION TO OFFICERS.** While he read he gave some thought as to what he would say to SSgt. Leeks, that is, if the man made it on time.

When SSgt. Leeks entered the CP far more subdued that he was a few minutes ago, two minutes before his time was up, he was in a clean uniform although it was a bit wrinkled. He marched up to the desk and reported in the proscribed manner. McNeil left him holding the salute a full minute while he checked the uniform over. After he returned the salute he left SSgt. Leeks standing at attention while he proceeded to reacquaint SSgt. Leeks with the duties of an NCO, proper dress, and military courtesy, and what was expected of him while assigned to Baker Company. McNeil summarized the previous ass chewing in a loud voice so anyone near could hear. "If you ever fail to use proper military courtesy to me or anyone else I promise you will be a Buck Sergeant immediately. If I ever see, or hear, of you being out of uniform again the same thing will happen. Maybe it hasn't sunk in yet SSgt. Leeks but we are in a war time situation which means the penalty for misconduct is much harsher than normal. You have a rebellious attitude that could get you sent to prison for a long stretch.

"You will change your attitude and become a more positive influence to those men out there. I don't have time to concentrate on one inept person when I've got over a hundred men to worry about. If you had failed to report to me on time you would have left here minus a stripe. I hope our talk today will bear fruit Sergeant Leeks, but to make sure that incident out there isn't forgotten there will be a written reprimand placed in your records. I'll remove it when you prove to me that you can handle the responsibility of the rank on your sleeve. Do you understand what I have said Sergeant Leeks?"

"Yes sir, I understand," replied a very much somber Leeks.

"Good. From now on I expect you and your men to be part of this unit, not a group of individuals. I expect everyone to bear arms and support the men on the line."

"But sir, we are cooks not infantry men."

"You were trained as infantry men first. If the North Koreans break through our line of defense you won't be either. I doubt very seriously the enemy will consider you a noncombatant. I hope you are getting the picture Sergeant Leeks. You have work to do and you are dismissed.

SSgt. Leeks, who was still standing at attention, replied, "Yes sir," saluted then did a very smart about face and left. McNeil striped the paper from a cigar and lit it. Even though it's wrong to critique a man in hearing distance of his subordinates I hope there were enough men within hearing distance of what was said here to pass the word.

McNeil knew there were mixed feelings among the men of Baker Company. Some hated him for his sudden and seemingly irrelevant orders where others, who knew him, could see the relevancy of them. If the men relieved their stress by hatred maybe it would be for the better. At least they would have someone to lay blame on. The men would surely be very upset tomorrow when they heard about the extension of military duty.

Change never comes easy and many had doubts, especially the cooks, of the orders they received.

In most cases a ground assault is preceded by an artillery or heavy mortar bombardment. About midnight mortar rounds started falling behind the lines but no ground attack followed. Before the captured mortar tube could silence the incoming mortar rounds three rounds fell in the company area. One hit an already damaged tent, one fell into an open area, and the other one fell where the cook tent stood just ten hours before. That caused several men to change their minds and believe that maybe the new Lieutenant knew what he was doing.

When McNeil came off the line at first light he could smell coffee. As he came to the cook tent he was greeted more warmly than yesterday. SSgt. Leeks greeted him, took his cup and filled it for him. McNeil stood there watching the men get the warm food and smoked a cigar as he drank the coffee. He watched SSgt. Leeks and his people cleaning up the used pots and pans and other utensils used for cooking. Since there were no men to send him to help wash the trays and silverware each man used, it was a burden for the cooks. He had a thought. Every man is issued a mess kit to include silverware plus a canteen cup for water or whatever they drink, why are we using all those food trays? The trays, silverware, and china cups takes up a lot of the cooks time keeping them clean and storage is at a premium. Why not turn in all the luxury items and ease the burden on the cooks? I'll discuss it with Sergeant Anderson. But first I'll feel out Sergeant Leeks.

"SSgt Leeks," called McNeil when he saw Leeks pass by, would you be opposed to getting rid of those trays and cups so as to free up some of your time?"

"I have made that request before sir but nothing has ever been done about it."

"I'll get back to you on that," said McNeil as he finished his coffee and walked to the company CP tent.

You will get back to me on that, yeah, that's what they all say, thought Sergeant Leeks. "Why are you guys goofing off?" yelled Sergeant Leeks when he saw his men looking his way and not working, "we have food to serve. Get with it."

SSgt. Sampson was just coming awake when McNeil stepped inside the tent. "You did such a splendid job of carrying out my orders yesterday I have decided to issue more orders Sergeant. Please get your pencil and paper."

"Don't I have time for coffee first, sir?" he finally added.

"Most of the men have already had their coffee. If you were up earlier you would have already had your coffee and been ready for work. Here is a message that you should get out to all men. It's a message from our Commander and Chief that no one will like but nothing can be done about it. Next, have some men give SSgt Anderson a hand, and rotate them every hour. He will be recording and burning destroyed equipment."

"Sir, you can't burn government equipment."

"The equipment is mine since I signed for it. Right now it is useless and it must be destroyed and reported as such. Save any large pieces of undamaged tentage for future use. SSgt. Anderson will handle the paper work. Pass the word for all men to gather up useful gear, personal or military, and pack it in a duffle bag. The bags will be stored on a truck. Any military gear or equipment not in use will also be stored on a truck. If we have to move we won't have time to pack so do it ahead of time. Be prepared.

"I'll need today's morning report as soon as it is finished. I'll be taking it to Battalion along with Corporal Johnson. We shouldn't be gone more than an hour or two."

"The morning report isn't normally finished this early Sir, maybe in a couple of hours. And may I ask where are all those promotions coming from?"

"As the Commander the orders are from me Sergeant. I have been given the authority and permission to promote as needed."

"I have the morning report ready sir," spoke PFC Rogers handing it to McNeil. Along with a stack of orders that had been generated. Sergeant Sampson just stared, then turned and walked away.

"PFC Gordon," called out McNeil.

"Yes sir."

"Get the jeep ready. Round up Corporal Johnson. And let's get on the road to Battalion."

"On the way sir," he said as he gathered his gear and went out the tent door.

When they reached Battalion it was quiet. No one stirred. And the big Battalion Command tent was empty when the three entered it. Fresh coffee was on the table beside the commanders' area so McNeil filled a cup and motioned for Bob and PFC Gordon to do the same. They had finished half a cup before Ltc. Winters came into the tent. "Good morning Lieutenant McNeil, Corporal, Private. I see the coffee is ready and you three found it. To what do I owe the honor of your visit today?"

"Good morning sir. May I have a moment of your time?"

"Come on into my office." McNeil followed him in and waited until he sat down behind his desk.

"Sir, this is in reference to our discussion yesterday about qualified men for a commission. I have one with me. He's a good knowledgeable man but a little reluctant to accept a commission. I feel he would make a good officer and if it's possible, and if you agree with me, could you see fit to assign him to Baker Company until I leave. I'll have him ready to take command by that time."

"I did say I would make the final decision."

"Yes sir you did. Sorry if I sound pushy."

"Do you have that list of supplies and equipment I asked for?"

"Right here sir," said McNeil handing over several sheets of paper. I have one more item I would like to discuss with you sir."

"What is it?"

"Luxury items on the TOE sir. We are an un-mechanized unit, not enough vehicles to move what equipment we really need much less luxury items. Would the Colonel consider a request to turn in such items that are not essential to the current mission?"

"Such as?"

"Cots. Food trays, silverware and china cups, just to name a few items Sir."

"Let me give that some thought."

"Unless you have something for me sir I will send in Corporal Johnson then spend some time with your radio operator?"

"Nothing further here Lieutenant. Go ahead."

McNeil located the radio operator, a PFC Willis, and proceeded to explain to him what he wanted. The code he wanted to use was a simple one that would be hard to break because it was just random numbers that represented certain actions.

After McNeil explained the simply number code which consisted of 21 items they started writing out messages and practicing. "I will always start a message with the number one. That tells you I am free and ok. If I start a message with 17 shut down your radio immediately because I have been captured. Let me give you a sample message PFC Willis. Say you hear the numbers from me, 1- 20-18-15. Read that for me."

"That means you are transmitting freely to this base and there is no activity. Out."

"Correct. See how simple that is. Let's try one a bit more complicated. I-20-19-4-3 north beach 345- 13 now-14 1600-15. Now read that back to me."

"Let's see, you are free and transmitting to base that there is activity of 10 to 50 men on north beach of hill 345. Need air strike today at 16oo hours. Out."

"I do believe you have it PFC Willis. If need be we can add more numbers but I believe what we have will do for now. Study that number code and be ready because we don't know when Division will kick off this mission. By the way it's called LOP Mission."

"Yes sir I was briefed on that."

McNeil had time for another cup of coffee and to light a cigar before Corporal Johnson came from Ltc. Winters office with a big grin on his face and wearing the gold bars of a 2nd Lieutenant. He was now 2ndLieutenant Robert Johnson, Bob to those who knew him well. "Congratulations Bob," said McNeil, "I see you made it."

"I did but I still don't believe it. I know if I had stayed in there much longer answering questions I would be drunk the way the Colonel passes out those shots of scotch."

"He does like to wet down a promotion, doesn't he. But as I said Bob, don't worry. You'll be ok. Just follow my lead. Right now we need to get back to Baker Company and see how things are progressing."

Black smoke marked the location of Baker Company. It spiraled up until a breeze spread it out over the area. It worried McNeil some, because it marked the exact location of the company, but it was a job that had to be done and he felt it was better to do it now rather than at night.

There was a bustling of activity at Baker Company as men went about dragging damaged tents and other items to the roaring fire. "No time to relax Bob," said McNeil when the jeep stopped in front of the CP, "you get with SSgt. Anderson and see that all the damaged equipment is burnt. Then we need two of the GP medium tents set up as sleeping quarters just past the cook tent. I'll check with you later."

"Christ," SSgt. Sampson said when McNeil entered the tent and handed him the order for Corporal Johnson's promotion, "they will pin bars on anybody."

"Only on those recommended," said McNeil as he went to his desk to check on any paper work that might have accumulated, "the Colonel does the selecting."

"Maybe if I make a trip to Battalion I can get promoted?"

"You have my permission to try SSgt. Sampson but only after all my orders have been complied with."

McNeil had five days to work with 2nd Lt. Johnson to prepare him for the duties of an officer and to take command of a company. During the five days there were several short fire fights but no one was seriously injured. They were getting better at keeping their heads down. Several mortar rounds fell and exploded in the area where the tents once stood but no more were damaged. The burn pile was hit twice scattering ashes so McNeil knew the fire and smoke had been marked for aiming points by the North Koreans. That in itself made the men more aware of his order of no lights or fires after dark.

He had a chance to speak to Sergeant Anderson about his idea and asked him to start preparing a list of such luxury items the unit could do without.

McNeil read the probing attacks and few mortar rounds dropped in the area as possibly a prelude to a bigger attack which could come at any time. He briefed the men in charge as to his thinking and he walked the line talking to the men and making sure they were alert and ready.

"If it doesn't happen then we have alerted the men for nothing," said Lt. Johnson.

"On the other hand, if it does happen then we have prepared them," answered McNeil.

The once laid back Baker Company with the strength of ninety should be one hundred and forty, slowly turned into a combat unit. The training was realistic and the men had been baptized by bullets and mortar and many had seen men killed or wounded. With the new order from the President they knew they would have to fight or die because no one would be leaving the Peninsula for home, alive.

Even though the order of no discharges had lowered the morale some it quickly picked up after several promotions were made and there was always hot food and coffee available. People were starting to pull together rather than work as individuals. There were still those men who complained, but that was nothing new.

On the fifth day after Corporal Johnson was promoted to 2nd Lieutenant McNeil had him on the line explaining some of the finer points of observing the enemy action when PFC Gordon came running to him with a message. "There will be no answer," spoke McNeil after he read it. The message simply said; LOP Mission approved. Report to Battalion. "Is SSgt. Sampson in the CP?"

"No sir. I saw him at the cook tent."

"Locate him and tell him his presence is needed at the CP."

"What is it Charley?" asked Bob as they left the line and headed for the CP.

"The order for my departure just arrived Bob."

"So soon Charley?"

"Time really flies when one is having fun doesn't it Bob?"

"I agree that times flies but I don't see any one having fun."

SSgt. Sampson entered the CP tent right behind them. "You two come back here with me," said McNeil as he shed his gear and sat down. When he was sure they were close enough to hear him he spoke. "SSgt. Sampson, have PFC Rogers cut orders for Lt. Johnson to assume command of Baker Company."

"Why? I mean you are still here."

"Please get the order started and I'll explain as much as I can."

"Now, said McNeil when SSgt. Sampson returned, I have been selected to head a classified mission and I'll be leaving here as soon as I brief you two."

"Where are you going sir and will you be returning," asked SSgt. Sampson who had gotten use to Lt. McNeil now and valued his military way of thinking.

"I have no answers for you. In my absence, and until and unless, another officer is assigned I hope you, SSgt. Sampson, will give your support to Lt. Johnson as you have given it to me. I leave this rag-tag band of good men in the capable hands of you two. SSgt. Sampson I have said about all I'm allowed to say and I need to have a private word with Lt. Johnson. Would you see about getting my bag from the storage truck and loading it on the jeep?"

Nothing more was said until SSgt. Sampson departed then Lt. Johnson spoke. "Christ Charley. Things are moving too fast. I've barely gotten use to the weight of these bars and now I'm to be the Commander of a combat unit."

"Now isn't he time to worry Bob, have faith and everything will work out for you. Just don't ever show uncertainty or fear in front of the men."

"Charley I don't have your calm nerves and cool confidence. I don't have the bold flair for command that you have. Do you know some of the men call you the 'ROCK'?"

"Calm down Bob. Yes, I've heard the nick name but I have no idea why I'm called that."

"You are called the rock because you always seem, never nervous or scared."

"Let me tell you I have been scared many times but I let that fear work for me rather than let it take control. As I said, never let the men think that you are scared or in doubt. Always take time to calm down and think before making a decision or issuing orders. Take care of the men first and rely on the NCO's. Don't try to imitate me, or any other officer for that matter. Develop your own ways to command. I've got to get out of here but one last item. In that desk is several sets of enlisted stripes. Pass them out to deserving men but not all at once, spread the promotions out. It will help to boost the morale of the men."

"Will we see each other again Charley?" asked Lt. Johnson.

"That's up to the man upstairs, and I don't mean General MacArthur or the President."

"Bags in the Jeep and Gordon is standing by," said SSgt. Sampson upon his return.

"Thank you Sergeant. Take care of the men, Sergeant and Lieutenant, and best of luck. Never hesitate to seek counsel when in doubt." McNeil shook their hands and went outside the tent.

"I don't know where he's going or how long he'll be gone but I sure as hell wish he was still here," spoke Lt Johnson as he watched Lt McNeil depart the area.

"I know what you mean," added SSgt Sampson, "I've sort of gotten used to his ways and having him around."

When McNeil arrived at Battalion he was met by the Sergeant Major and led to where stacks of supplies and equipment were laid out on a table. Apparently SGM Callings and Maj. Wells had been briefed in on the mission. McNeil inventoried and checked everything out then bagged it. After he ate with the Colonel, his bags were loaded, and he donned his field gear. After a final briefing he was trucked to the beach where he was to meet the mike boat. It was after dark when it finally nosed up to the beach.

"Lieutenant," Ltc. Winters said, he had decided to accompany him to the landing site, "I don't have to tell you how important this mission is. Do it and do it right."

"Yes sir. I will," said McNeil as he turned and walked away.

Apparently the mike boat operator had been briefed on the mission because no questions were asked and as soon as McNeil and his gear was loaded the boat ramp was raised and the boat eased silently away from shore and headed out on the water. An hour later McNeil could hear the engine slow down and then he felt the boat touch shore. He started moving his gear ashore and as soon as the last bag was off the boat it moved away from shore and disappeared in the night. He was alone on a strange piece of land and it was dark. He had to find a place to settle down and wait for morning before he could explore the island and establish an OP.

# MCNEIL

## LOP MISSION

### Chapter 9
### 1 Oct 1950

McNeil noticed that the nights were getting longer and the temperature had dropped a few degrees. Today marked two months since he was dropped off on the island in the dark of night. Tonight he expected a radio call with the number 22 in it indicating his replacement was on the way. Only in the case of an emergency or enemy activity would the radio transmit during daylight hours. Normal traffic was between the hours of midnight and morning. Using the number code he had established there was no cause to worry about the North Koreans locating his position because the transmission time was far too short for any triangulation.

There had been no activity in and around the islands for the past week. McNeil had to wonder what was happening on the peninsula since his departure. The only news he had received was from an old copy of the Stars and Strips newspaper which had been dropped off by the mike boat. Why is there a sudden lull in the activity, he often wondered.

Since he had been deposited on the island, other than the North Koreans who wanted a piece of the island, he had not spoken to a sole, except on the radio, nor seen another human except for the men who operated the mike boat and they were just shapes in the dark and spoke in whispers. No mail had been sent to the island so he wondered just how his mother was doing, not that she answered any of his letters, at least so far. The one thing he never lost sight of was his plans for the future; getting a discharge and returning to college to complete a Masters in Political Science. If this sudden North Koreans uprising had not occurred he could have been home next April, or before; in time to register for the summer semester. Now there was so much uncertainly.

The one thing he had plenty of on the island was time, time to think. He had been thinking a lot about the dream he was having the night before this madness happened. He was in a boat holding the warm body of a blond hair girl, someone he felt he knew from his past but couldn't put a name to her. He finally remembered who she was. It seemed such a long time ago that he was in high school yet it was only a few years. She was a cheer leader, a very pretty girl with long blond hair which she almost always kept tied back with a ribbon. Samatha was her name, Sam she was called. As did other boys McNeil's eyes were drawn to her as she and the other girls went through their cheer leading routine in a short skirt and her hair whipping around. She was known as the untouchable because she refused to date. She only smiled and spoke to me once so why did I have a dream about her, McNeil wondered.

Remembering her now brought back memories of other things, like the reason he never had extra money or the time to date and socialize like other students. When he was a junior in highschool his brother Kenneth was a senior and dating a bouncy dark hair girl named Janice. He often brought her home to meet the McNeil clan. McNeal's sister, Katherine, never seemed to be around with so many school activities and dating to keep her busy.

Brother Ken was the sort of fellow who looked down his nose at those less fortunate than he was and he was forever talking about someone, always in the negative. How it happened he had no idea but he and Ken lost the warm feelings brothers should share and Ken soon became very distant. Other than his mother and father, and several fellow students, he became friends with the only person who seemed to care about him, Ken's girl Janice. She was very friendly and easy to talk to. Once when Ken had her at the house, and he was busy in another room, Janice asked Charley why he didn't date and socialize. She even offered to fix him up with a date. Charley declined the offer without a chance of an explanation because Ken entered the room and saw the two talking and accused Charley of trying to make out with his girl. Ken's ego was bruised and no explanation offered by Charley or Janice satisfied him. Thinking back on the event McNeil thought that maybe that was the start of the wedge that separated the two.

Katherine had her nose in the air, so to speak, and she couldn't wait to divorce herself from the McNeil name. She got married soon after she graduated from high school, to a boy named Calvin Holland, and moved away and settled down in Bridgeport Kentucky where Calvin had family and a job waiting for him. Her visits back to the family in Duckers Kentucky and to the family home where she was born and raised grew less and less.

Janice became pregnant in her senior year of high school and it was well known who the father was since her and Ken was together constantly. Janice and Ken had to drop out of school, she because of her pregnancy, and Ken because he had to find work to support the two of them, soon to be three.

Ken or Katherine seldom called home and visited even less once they left. The only time the McNeil's were together was at the funeral for Mr. Robert Jon. McNeil who was killed in a job related accident.

Before Ken dropped out of school he always had an excuse as to why he couldn't take care of the chores around the house so they fell to the youngest, Charley. Now McNeil always knew what he wanted and he started working toward that goal in high school. He wanted to study Political Science and Military History in hopes of working for the government someday. To better understand the military part of it he joined the R O T C and stayed with it in college. So with all the studying he had even less time to spend at home with his mother. She soon developed the E N S, (Empty Nest Syndrome) and slowly crawled into a bottle. Somehow she managed to hold down a job which was her only outside contact with the world.

He met and became good friends with a German exchange student, Herman, and they spent time together studying. Most times they conversed in German after Herman taught enough of the language to Charley. He realized then he had a flair for languages. With the insurance money and some part time work Charley was able to stay in college but the money started running low so he laid out a semester to earn enough money to get back in college. The draft caught him. When he told his mother he had to go away she didn't ask when or how long he would be gone. All she said was "that's nice. Be careful."

Why now after all this time am I thinking about the past? Things have happened that no one has control over and the past cannot be relived. Get on with your life Charley and forget the past. I know I'm remiss in not writing to anyone but the only address I know is Mom's and if I wrote to her she would just toss the letter on the counter. For her, time has no meaning. To her I'm still in school and will be home soon.

In anticipation of his replacement arriving McNeil, well before dark, had cleaned up the cave which had been his home for two months, and packed the few items he would be carrying back with him.

It was two in the morning when he heard the radio crackle. He had not slept much in his anticipation and he was instantly by the radio to copy down the message. In the numbers he copied there was the 22 he had hoped for. It gave a three as the time for the boat to arrive.

McNeil dressed in his last and best uniform, picked up the two bags, and walked out of the cave to meet the boat. He had been sitting by the shore in the dark waiting when he heard the low muted sound of the boat engine as it neared shore. Suddenly the boat started moving away from shore. McNeil stood up and called out but the only answer he heard was his name being called. "Lt. McNeil!"

"Yeah, I'm over here. Why is the boat leaving without me?" he asked the unseen man.

"Sorry about that but it was a last minute change. It was thought that I would need a briefing before you departed."

"And who is speaking?" he still couldn't see anyone but he had the location by the sound of the voice.

"I'm Lt. Calloway, your replacement. Where are you?"

McNeil eased up beside the man and spoke making the man jump. "Right here. I should have anticipated the delay, but how much of a delay will it be?"

"Twenty four hours."

"How much gear do you have?"

"Just the one bag."

"Then grab my hand, no lights, and walk behind me. One misstep and you'll slide off a cliff. I'll lead you to your home away from home."

When they reached the cave, which McNeil thought he had seen the last of, there was a strong west wind blowing so he thought it would be ok to light a small fire. He put the pot on the fire and started coffee. While they drank coffee McNeil started his briefing which would not be completed until he could take Lt. Calloway around the island come morning.

McNeil showed Lt. Calloway where his traps were and how he could trap birds, crabs and fish, to supplement his food supply. He answered many questions all that day and when night started to fall they went back to the cave for food. After midnight McNeil allowed Lt. Calloway to make the nightly radio transmission to make sure he had the procedure correctly. There was a code 16 before he could shut down the radio. Code 16 meant stand by.

The message McNeil most wanted came over the radio. The boat would pick him up at two. He had left his bags of gear hidden at the shore so after shaking the hand of Lt. Calloway and wishing him luck he started down the hill to wait for the boat. It was, as last night, very dark when the boat eased up to shore. This time McNeil gave it no chance to leave without him, he was ready with his bags in hand. As soon as the ramp was lowered he jumped on and the boat started to ease away from the shore of the island. The next stop would be the peninsula.

When the mike boat stopped again McNeil stepped off with his bags and stood waiting but he couldn't see anyone or anything. He was about to think he had been forgotten when a voice called out to him. "Is that you Lt. McNeil?" after the man spoke McNeil looked in the direction of the voice and could just make out the outline of a jeep.

"Yes it is," he answered as he walked to the jeep and placed his bags in the rear of it, "and who are you?"

"I'm PVT Denton. PFC Willis wanted to fetch you but he couldn't leave the radio."

"Thank you ever so much PVT Denton," said McNeil as he got in the jeep.

Pvt Denton turned on the black out lights and moved away from the shore. Apparently he had made the trip enough during daylight hours that he knew the way because he made the trip without incident.

## 2 Oct 1950

Being dark there wasn't much to see when the jeep stopped and McNeil got out taking his bags. He followed PVT Denton who moved a tent flap aside and he could see some light inside. He followed PVT Denton inside to where dim lantern light had him blinking his eyes that were used to darkness. Ltc. Winters, Maj. Wells, and SGM Callings were waiting to greet him. "Welcome back Lt. McNeil," said each man as his hand was shook. "What have we here?" asked Ltc. Winters as he pointed to the bag McNeil still held.

"Thank you Col. Winters and this is some items I felt division S-2 might be interested in sir," replied McNeil.

"You don't look none the worse for wear," commented SGM Callings. McNeil had actually gained two pounds and he sported a tan.

"Attending luaus and fighting off hoards of naked women kept me fit."

"You do have a vivid imagination don't you Lt. McNeil," spoke Maj. Wells.

"Would you care for a cup of coffee, laced with something a bit stronger, while we go over the contents of the bag? Put the bag on the table there."

"Coffee sounds great and a step up would be fine. I haven't tasted good scotch since I left here," said McNeil putting the bag on the indicated table and dumping the contents.

"You wouldn't turn down a good cigar to go with the coffee, would you?"

"That would be most appreciated sir. I would kill for a good cigar, excuse my language. I ran out three days ago."

"Did I see you limp just now," asked SGM Callings, "would that be from the wound you radioed about?" Two weeks ago when McNeil had gone out to check on a bombing and strafing result for a BDA he was wounded in the thigh by a North Korean who had pretended to be dead. He finished off the man, then limped back to the cave and applied first aid to the wound which was a through and through wound. The wound was slow in healing and gave him a bit of pain sometimes. He learned a valuable lesson that day, never take anything for granted.

"The same Sergeant Major but it's almost healed now," answered McNeil as he sat down and lit the cigar then tasted the coffee. There was much more than just a shot of scotch in it, more like two shots, but he had no complaints.

"After you have had a hot bath and a change of clothes we'll let the medics decide the state of healing," said SGM Callings.

"A hot bath and a change of clothes does sound good but these rags I'm wearing is all that is left of my uniforms. The harsh climate and stone washing did a number on the clothes plus the rough walking conditions were hard on boots."

"Sergeant Major see about getting an issue of clothes for Lt. McNeil, to include boots and underwear."

"Yes sir. I'll get right on it." There were bags of clothes left by the deceased and wounded men who would not be returning to the 1/5th.

McNeil did notice that Ltc. Winters looked as if he had aged several years. There were bags under his eyes and his pants and shirt hung loose on him. McNeil smoked and sipped the coffee and answered questions while Maj. Wells wrote everything down. When they got around to examining the weapons, Maj. Wells commented on them. "These appear to be Russian made weapons."

"They are sir. Based on what I saw when Baker Company was attacked, plus these weapons, leads me to believe the Russians are supplying arms and instructing tactics to the North Koreans."

"Better get this bagged along with the other papers and get it on the next boat to division S-2." said Ltc. Winters.

"If we are through here sir I'll take care of Lt. McNeil?" asked SGM Callings.

"For now I would say we are through, there may be more questions later though. We'll get this statement typed up along with the radio log and you can check it over then sign it Lt. McNeil."

"Right this way," said SGM Callings as he led McNeil to the rear of the tent where a cot was set up with a stack of uniforms, two pair of boots, underwear and socks laid out on it.

"When you are ready I'll show you where the shower is. When you finish bathing a medic will be waiting to check that wound, your fourth I believe?"

"I lost count but that sounds about right. One of these days I'll learn to duck." He wasn't about to relate the stupid incident that got him wounded.

McNeil picked up a towel, along with a shaving kit that had been provided then followed SGM Callings out of the tent and to a shower enclosed with canvas. There were no lights so he had to bath by feel and do the same while shaving. He could have stayed under the warm water much longer but he knew there were people waiting for him.

He wrapped a towel around himself and dropped his well-worn uniform into a trash can on his way back to the tent. A man was waiting for him in the dimly lit tent whom he surmised was the medic. "I'm Corporal McFadden sir, the medic," spoke the man, "and if you are Lt. McNeil you are the man I'm looking for. I understand you have a spot that isn't healing well," said the corporal switching on a flash light.

"I'm Lt. McNeil and you are at the right place," he said removing the towel so the medic could get a better look at the gunshot wound in his left thigh.

"It appears to be healing nicely but there is some infection in one corner. I suppose it's tender."

"Just a bit."

"It looks as if it would be. Some antibiotics should take of the infection and help the healing along. Unless the pants irritate it I would rather not bandage it."

"No problem so far."

"Good. Take every pill in this bottle according to the instructions and I advise you to see a medic in three days."

"Sergeant Major," said Corporal McFadden, "in my opinion the Lieutenant will live to fight another day."

"I'm sure that bit of news thrills the Lieutenant to no end, about fighting I mean. But thank you for your time and opinion Corporal McFadden. Get that wrote up and I'll relay the results to the Colonel."

"Now," said SGM Callings after the medic departed, "I'll wait out there until you get dressed then we can go to the mess hall where steak and eggs await you."

After getting dressed McNeil followed the Sergeant Major out the rear of the tent along a short path to the mess hall. Inside there were lights where the cooks were working and one light lit up a table where Ltc. Winters and Major Wells, having finished eating, sat talking and drinking coffee. The Sergeant Major sat down and motioned for McNeil to do the same. There was a pitcher of hot coffee on the table and without hesitating McNeil poured himself a cup. "I must say, you look somewhat refreshed," said Ltc. Winters.

"I feel much better sir."

"How would you like your steak and eggs sir?" asked a man who had walked up behind McNeil.

He started to say on a plate but thought better of it. "I could probably eat the steak raw but medium steak and over medium on the eggs."

"I thought that you might need some protein after eating C-rations for two months," said Ltc. Winters.

"I have eaten so much, clams, oysters, fish, crabs, and lobsters that a steak sounds real good right now."

"Wait a minute. Did I hear you say crabs and lobster?" asked Maj. Wells.

"They are plentiful around the islands. If I could have had a fire every day I could have eaten them every day."

"What I wouldn't give for a large plate of steamed crab legs. Colonel, may I be the next relief man to the island?"

"I'm afraid not. I need you here."

It's funny how when man has one thing he want's something else. McNeil would have gladly traded lobsters for a steak and here those who had steak wanted lobster.

A steaming plate of steak with three eggs was set before McNeil along with a plate of bread and butter. He refilled his cup then started cutting the steak and buttering the bread. He savored every bite of the steak and eggs, plus several pieces of buttered bread. He washed it all down with three cups of coffee.

When he pushed his empty plate away Ltc. Winters commented, "Lieutenant, I'm certainly glad I don't have to foot the bill to feed you. How about another cigar to top off that meal?"

"That would be my pleasure sir."

When they were through with their coffee they got up and McNeil followed them back to the big tent. "The statement and radio log should be typed up by now so let's go up front and check on it," said Maj. Wells.

The statement was ready and when McNeil sat down and read over it the only thing he could find wrong was a couple of events were out of sequence. But he felt it wasn't important enough to warrant having it retyped. Only he would know that small error. He signed the statement.

"With that accomplished Lieutenant you should get some sleep," said Ltc. Winters, "you know where your bed is set up."

"Yes sir I do." McNeil said goodnight to everyone then went to his cot thinking he wouldn't be able to sleep but after he got undressed and crawled between the two clean sheets he drifted off as soon as his head hit the pillow.

Four hours later he awoke to find himself in a strange place. Daylight was seeping through openings in the tent and everything looked different. It took him a moment to shake the sleep from his mind and remember he was no longer in the cave on the island but in the 1/5 Battalion CP. He listened but he couldn't hear any gun fire. He slowly got up, picked up the clean uniform and a towel then went out back where he took a shower to clear the cobwebs. After getting dressed he located the mess tent and since it had only been a short while since he ate he asked for only coffee and toast.

After eating he went back to the C P tent and packed up all the uniforms then made up the bed. Since he had not heard or seen anyone this morning he went up front to find out what was expected of him. He found a pot of coffee on the long table they had used last night, make that early this morning, so he figured someone was up and about. He poured a cup and waited. No one had showed up by the time he finished the cup of coffee so he set the cup down and went forward in the tent to where he remembered the colonel's office was.

McNeil stopped outside what represented the Commanders office and there sat Ltc. Winters behind his desk working on some papers. Has he even been to bed, wondered McNeil, because the colonel was still dressed in what looked to be the same wrinkled uniform he wore earlier. When the Colonel didn't look up McNeil went on into the room. Ltc. Winters noticed the movement and looked up. "Good morning Lieutenant did you sleep well?"

"Good morning to you sir, and yes I did. I slept like a baby."

"Good. As soon as Maj. Wells shows up he has something for you. Right now let me brief you on the current situation, which hasn't changes too much since you left. Come on over to the big map." said Ltc. Winters getting up from his chair.

McNeil had thought that with the LOP Mission up and running he might not be needed anymore, as an officer. Certainly they have enough officers by now to command the Companies. I could operate as a 1st Sergeant ok. But, if I'm to be briefed on the current military situation then it's possible I'll remain on active duty as a Lieutenant. Surely the colonel wouldn't be briefing an enlisted man, or someone who is to be an enlisted man.

As Ltc. Winters talked McNeil realized the situation in Korea wasn't much better now than it was when he left. "The North Koreans are still roaming all over the South Korean mainland robbing, killing, and disrupting power and communications," spoke Ltc Winters. "General MacArthur wants to send troops across the 38th parallel but the Chinese, who are supporting the North Koreans along with the Russians, warns that they will attack if American troops cross the border. General MacArthur doesn't believe them and is sending troops across the 38th parallel starting tomorrow. All the troops will be under the command of General Walton Walker for the drive to the Yalu. We won't know the results of the push for a few days.

"Now that the commanders have decided to start doing something several things have happened since you left. Inchon port and the city has been taken back along with Kimpo airport. Pusan has been retaken and a perimeter has been established around the city. Some of the same units have retaken Seoul. Right now the UN forces are getting geared up to start pushing the North Koreans toward to 38th Parallel.

"I feel man power is the reason for the delay. I heard some units from

Hawaii were shipped in but nothing official on that yet. I do know that some of the closed training bases in the states have been reopened and they will be doubling their output of trained men. Replacement men and equipment is still slow in arriving. Most often we get three men for every two body bags we send back to Division. Officers are still scarce. We are not the only units hurting, the same situating still exists all over Korea.

"Intelligence, yes intelligence," repeated Col. Winters when he saw McNeil raise his eyebrows in question. "Intelligence tells us that the North Koreans are massing their men plus reserves and if that is so we can expect to get hit hard in the near future. We will be far better off than some units on the mainland who will be doing battle on two fronts when the big push starts. At least we have our back door secured and only have to worry about our front. We can't fight very long on promises of men and equipment and that's all I have, promises.

"As I said before, the Companies aren't in much better shape than they were two months ago. As I also mentioned, we have been receiving replacements on a ratio of three men for every two K I A. This tells me that somehow the pipeline of replacement men may be working. We did get two officers, a Captain Downs who commands Able Company and a Lt. Calloway whom I believe you met?"

"Yes sir I had the pleasure."

"With the few replacement personnel the companies are holding at around 60% strength and so far we have been able to hold the line."

"Are the companies still at the same location sir," asked McNeil as he studied the map.

"Yes they are. The line of defense that is currently established is in a good location and I don't have any commanders with enough experience to move a unit and establish new defense lines."

"Are there any villages between our lines and the 38th parallel sir?"

"Several abandoned villages. It seems the South Koreans got the word of the invasion before us and decided they didn't want to be caught here on the Peninsula. Why those particular questions Lt. McNeil?"

"Well sir, we have been reacting rather than acting, defense rather than offence. It's possible that if the North Koreans are amassing their men, and without the 17th ROK at the 38t Parallel, they could have already crossed the line and are using the abandoned villages as a forward base of operations."

"Hmm. Something to think about. I'll pass that along to division S-2."

"Another thing sir is that the units, Companies and the Battalion, have been in one place so long the North Koreans artillery will have pin pointed their exact locations by now and they can rain artillery and mortar on us. If I was planning a ground attack that's the way I would do it."

"Are you suggesting something Lieutenant?"

"See that low ridge about a mile out front of the Companies sir?"

"I see it. When I first arrived on the peninsula I toured it and as I remember it extends all the way across the Peninsula."

"In the past the North Koreans have been able to use that as their defense position. From there they can mount ground attacks on the companies, and in fact that is where the mortar was that cost Baker Company so much grief and equipment loss. With your permission sir I would suggest that the companies be moved up to that ridge."

"As I said Lieutenant, I have no one with the experience to make such a move."

"I have moved units before sir. Full R O T C units. Might I suggest a late evening move, just before dark, after some reconnoitering. It should be a coordinated move of all four companies."

"Let me think about that for a few days."

"Yes sir. I know the odor of decaying bodies on the battlefield was bad before I left. I can't imagine what it's like now."

"Bad. I can tell you it's bad. The odor really takes some getting used to."

"All the more reason to make a move sir. Since the Battalion has been in this location a while may I suggest you think about moving it sir?"

"We're far behind the lines so right now I don't feel we are in too much danger of an attack. We'll remain here. Maybe with winter coming on the stench of decaying bodies won't be so bad."

"Speaking of winter sir, if we must keep the LOP Mission operational provisions will have to be made for the cold weather. A man can't keep a fire burning for warmth."

"I'll pass that along to division also. You have anything else?"

"Nothing more except, where am I to be assigned Sir?"

"I'm short one commander. Would you care to have a company again?"

"That would be my pleasure sir."

"I'll give you a choice. Charlie Company needs a commander. You can have it or go back to Baker Company. If you select Baker Company I'll have that young lieutenant—what's his name?"

"Are you thinking about Lt. Johnson sir?"

"Yes, Lt. Johnson. I can transfer him to Charlie Company. I'll leave it up to you."

"If it's not too much of an imposition sir I would like very much to return to Baker Company."

"I anticipated that you would say that. Orders transferring Lt. Johnson have already been cut."

"Sorry I'm late," said Major Wells as he entered the room.

"Have you the orders?" asked Ltc. Winters.

"Right here sir."

"Explain everything to Lt. McNeil." said Ltc. Winters taking his seat behind the desk.

"Here are the orders transferring Lt. Johnson from Baker Company to Charlie Company and ordering you to command Baker Company. There are six copies so take all of them with you. Now----"

"Sir," interrupted McNeil, "there is an error here. These orders read Captain McNeil."

"I was about to get to that. When the order for your battle field commission reached the Department of the Army they researched your records. What they found was that you had better than four years of ROTC training, plus three years of college, and that you held the rank of Captain in the ROTC. Orders came back making you a Regular Army Captain on active duty. They also assigned you a serial number, 0-637813, which is on your orders. So the orders are correct. Notice your date of rank is one day after you were made lieutenant which gives you two months' time in grade."

"Sorry for the interruption sir," McNeil apologized, surprised that the Army was so observant.

"Pin this on," said Ltc. Winters sliding a captain's insignia across the desk to him, "and leave the lieutenant's bars here. While you pin on the insignia I have something else for you. That request you made before your departure about turning in luxury equipment. I spoke to Division S-4 and they left it up to each battalion. If I give you the ok where would we store it? Have you given that any thought?"

"Yes sir I have. Battalion has several 6x6's with no drivers and no one to maintain them. I thought about using one, or more, to store the items on and park it here at Battalion. That would make use of idle equipment sir."

"Let me talk it over with Maj. Wells and get back to you on that. Anything else?"

"Nothing I can think of sir. I would like to speak with the Sergeant Major before I leave though."

"Go then. Congratulations and good luck Captain McNeil."

"Thank you sir," replied McNeil standing up and saluting the Colonel.

"What can I do for you Captain McNeil?" asked SGM Callings when they were out of the colonel's office, "and by the way, congratulations on the promotion."

"Thank you Sergeant Major. It was a surprise to me. Actually I have three things; first, the radio operators, like most everyone else, has been doing multiple duty and doing it well. They put in some long hours with no complaints. Before I left I promised PFC Gordon a promotion. Is it possible at this time to offer him a promotion?"

"I was thinking along those lines the other day. They have been doing a fine job, all of them. They carry a big load and a lot of responsibility for a mere PFC. I might have a set of corporal stripes here somewhere," he said, "I'll have them for you before you leave."

"Next item is me. I haven't been paid in over two months."

"There is a change in pay procedures since you left. Since there is no place for the men to use money other than to purchase necessary personal items, each man, officer or enlisted, is paid a partial pay of twenty dollars a month. The balance is held at finance until a man is transferred. I'll speak with finance and see about getting you some money."

"Along that same line I need some personal items now, such as razor blades and shoe polish."

"As soon as we finish here we'll get it for you."

"Last item; I'm aware that NCO's have a means of getting things done so would you tell me how I can get, say three, boxes of those good Cuban Cigars the Colonel smokes and a couple bottles of that good scotch?"

"I believe I can make some arrangements for you."

"How much will it cost me?"

"Wait until I get what you want then we can deduct it from your pay."

"Fair enough; I know I said three things but there is one more. Would you ask PFC Willis to call Baker Company and have then send the jeep to pick up an officer?"

"Just pick up an officer, No name?"

"It's probably best to do it that way. By the way, how much of the original crew is still at Baker Company? "

"As you heard Lt. Johnson is still there as well as most of the NCO's. Baker Company lost a man two days ago but we do have some replacements for you. You wouldn't mind taking them with you would you?"

"Not at all Sergeant Major. By the way, is SSgt. Sampson still around?"

"No he isn't. He was reported MIA. Seems he went out on the battlefield to recover some equipment and never returned. We have to assume he was captured."

"That's not only a shame but stupidity on his part."

"Could be that he was emulating his former commander," said Sergeant Major Callings looking at McNeil with a raised eyebrow. "Well let's get those personal items you want."

He had no comment to the possibility that others may be emulating his past actions. The past is hard to change, but he would have to make sure that in the future he didn't do anything to give others ideas that would put them in danger.

"Unless one is already assigned I'll need a 1st sergeant."

"No 1st sergeant has been assigned and still none due in. We still have to make do with what we have."

"Do you have some stripes, say Master Sergeant stripes?"

"I might come up with a set of E-7 stripes but not E-8."

After McNeil had purchased what he needed and had several sets of strips he decided to wait outside for his ride. "My profound thanks for everything Sergeant Major," he said shaking the Sergeant's hand.

McNeil stepped outside the big tent, dropped his bag and proceeded to light a cigar he managed to hang on to when Ltc. Winters was passing them out. SGM Callings, when McNeil mentioned he would like to have some of those cigars, just happened to have four in his desk that had been given to him by the Colonel. He didn't smoke. Suddenly he heard the word, "attention," called. He looked where the sound came from and saw ten privates, in fresh new uniforms, standing at attention in the shade of a tree. McNeil removed the unlit cigar from his mouth and said, "As you were men."

As McNeil approached the men they became nervous at seeing a Captain and a couple started to assume the position of attention. McNeil held up his hand and spoke, "always obey your last order. I'm Captain McNeil, Commander of Baker Company, how many of you are assigned to it?"

Two men held up their hands. "There will be a vehicle here shortly to pick me up so you can ride with me. I suppose transportation has been arranged for you other men. Welcome to the Ongjin Peninsula of South Korea."

McNeil left them and went back to the side of the big tent where he lit the cigar and waited. He didn't have to wait long before he saw the familiar jeep of Baker Company arrive. PFC Gordon drove it and when Gordon saw who he was picking up he jumped out of the jeep and saluted. "Welcome home sir."

McNeil returned the salute. "This time that salute earns you no money but we can't have a mere private driving a Captain around. Get these sewn on as soon as we get to the company Corporal Gordon," said McNeil handing him the set of Corporal stripes.

"Yes sir," replied, now Corporal Gordon, as he started to get back in the jeep.

"Before you do that Corporal Gordon," said McNeil dropping his bag in the jeep, "two of those men over there will be going with us. Get them loaded."

## 3 Oct 1950

What once was a smooth ride, if one could call a man- made dirt road a smooth ride, from 1/5th Battalion area to Baker Company area was now a matter of bouncing over pot holes and driving around craters where artillery rounds had impacted. Several trees had been blown down across the road which had to be traversed. It was obvious the battle for control of the Ongjin Peninsula was still going on.

When the jeep stopped in front of the Baker Company CP McNeil stepped out and turned to the two men who were out and retrieving their bags. "You two wait over there and someone will be with you shortly. Corporal Gordon get those stripes sewn on before you do anything else. I'll have the orders cut and waiting. Leave the jeep here because there will be a need for it shortly. Who has been ram-rodding this outfit in my absence?"

"Tiny sir," answered Corporal Gordon. Then he caught what he just said and changed it, "I mean Sgt Brockman sir."

I have a feeling everyone will know I have returned in a few short minutes, McNeil thought as he headed for the CP tent. Sgt Brockman, Tiny, looked as big as ever bent over the small field desk concentration on some papers. He apparently didn't realize he had a visitor until he heard a familiar voice. "Seems military courtesy has deteriorated in my absence."

"I'll be an SOB," said Tiny jumping up and almost turning the field desk over, "you are back. Is that Captain bars I see on your collar?"

"Correct on all accounts except that I don't believe you are an SOB."

"A slip of the tongue at my excitement at seeing you Captain sir. Welcome back to Baker Company sir."

"Thank you very much Tiny it's good to be back. But let's get down to business. I need several things done at once."

"Just like old times sir. Always something going on when you are around. Not that Lt. Johnson hasn't been ok, Just that I prefer you in charge."

"For that head swelling comment Tiny you can remove those Sgt stripes and sew on these stripes," said McNeil handing him the set of Sergeant First Class stripes. "I see we still have PFC Rodgers."

"Yes sir and welcome back," PFC Rodgers said with a big smile.

"In this order PFC Rodgers; I'll need orders for me to assume command of Baker Company, orders to promote PFC Gordon to Corporal, orders to promote Sgt Brockman to Sergeant First Class and to assume duties as acting 1st Sergeant of Baker Company. Get started on those and I'm sure there will be a need for more orders shortly. Tiny" he said turning back to the big man who was still holding the sergeant stripes in his hand, "there are two new men outside who need to be processed. Where is your esteemed leader?"

"He was on the line the last I heard, shall I get him? By the way, I'm not sure if I should thank you for the promotion or not. I've been struggling here since we lost SSgt. Sampson. No one else wanted the job so I sort of unofficially took over."

"Since I didn't hear anything in the negative at Battalion I must assume you have been doing a good job. Change never comes easy Tiny. But, right now you have more important things to do than run errands. Lt. Johnson will get the word, I'm sure. Now to work people. By the way Tiny, you need to find a replacement for yourself on the line."

"I have a good man who has been doing my job since I came in here."

"Promote him then. Give him your stripes."

"Don't you want to speak with him first?"

"I shouldn't have to second guess my 1st Sergeant. If I have to do that then I don't need him."

McNeil had just finished signing his order to assume command when Lt. Johnson came through the tent door. "I heard it but I didn't believe it," said Bob reaching for McNeil's hand, "and a Captain also. Congratulations Charley and welcome back."

"Thank you very much Bob."

"From that tan and healthy look one would think you have spent time on a tropical Island."

"Any rumors to that idea are just that, rumors."

"I see, well, we'll drop that subject. But it is good to have you back, or you just visiting?"

"I'm back Bob. I just signed the order to assume command of the Company."

"Great. It'll be like old times again."

"I don't think so Bob, you will be leaving."

"Leaving? Have I been relieved?"

"Relieved of duty with Baker Company to assume Command of Charlie Company. I brought the orders with me."

"I'm not too sure about this Charley. I was just getting use to being in charge of Baker Company, now this?"

"Step back here Bob," said McNeil moving to the rear of the tent where they would have a bit of privacy. "Looks like you have done a good job here so I'm sure you will do the same at Charley Company. I was just briefed so I'll pass it on. The North Koreans are starting to amass their reserves. We could get hit hard anytime now. You need to get to Charley Company, assess the situation, and get them ready. No time to waste."

"Damn. Will it ever end?"

"Only when we cause it to end."

"I was hoping we would have time to sit down and talk, over a drink."

"Water or coffee Bob?"

"Yeah, you are right. We haven't had beer in weeks."

"Bob, I'm only a short drive away and even closer by radio. If you need help ask. Battalion isn't that far away either."

"Yeah, well, I guess I asked for it. Orders are orders so I guess I best get packed."

"One other item Bob but keep it quiet until its official. I feel sure all the companies will soon be moving, forward. Get your unit packed and ready, as much as you can without disrupting operations. "

"Might I assume that we won't have a buffer of South Korean ROK troops at the 38th Parallel anymore, huh?"

"No comment on that Bob. See me before you leave."

Tiny was holding the orders for the two new men when McNeil went back up front. "An 11B and a supply man, where do you want them assigned?" he asked McNeil.

"Where they are needed, after you brief them on what is expected of them."

"I suppose one to SSgt. Anderson and one to the line, second platoon to be exact."

"Make it so. Meanwhile I'll be taking a tour of the Company."

McNeil noticed several changes, changes for the better. Instead of the small water trailer there was now a thousand gallon water truck. Not unlike a fuel truck. More than one shower station was set up at the rear of the sleep area. The small water trailer had been replaced with a fuel trailer. Everywhere he went someone remembered him and welcomed him back to the unit. He saw three new looking GP medium tents set up behind the cook tent with signs indicating one was for the medics and supply. When he entered the supply/medic tent he found Sgt Hicks taking the temperature of a man lying on a cot. To the rear he saw SSgt. Anderson busy at his desk.

"How are things going SSgt. Anderson," spoke McNeil startling the man who was engrossed in his work.

"Sorry sir, great day, Captain McNeil? Are you back with us sir?"

"I am as of this morning. How are you progressing with our idea?"

"You mean about turning in luxury items? I have a long list but we should go over it sir."

"You go over it with the other NCO's and I'll approve what you decide. I have a feeling the idea will get approval soon. I'll check with you later SSgt. Anderson."

McNeil stopped by the cook tent and even though SSgt. Leeks seemed much more subdued he didn't seem too happy to see McNeil back. His uniform was clean and complete and he was very polite with his greeting. "Sergeant Leeks, in reference to what I spoke to you about a couple of months ago, turning in the excessive luxury items, see Sergeant Anderson about it when you have the time."

"Yes sir," Sergeant Leeks replied with a surprised look on his face.

Before McNeil toured the defense line he tucked his collar points, with his rank on them, inside his shirt. Many of the men on the line remembered him and welcomed him back. Those who had no idea who he was simply said nothing. One man did comment on his collar being tucked in and asked why. "Rank has a bad habit of becoming a target for snipers," he told the young man.

Battalion gave approval for the turn in of luxury items and McNeil sent the supply people to battalion to pickup, not one but two of the unused 6x6's. One would be returned to Battalion loaded with nonessential items for storage and the other would be used for the cooks to store and move their equipment. One of Baker Company's 6x6 trucks was full of duffle bags. That left a jeep, a 3/4 weapons carrier, and a 6x6 for supply. If the forward move was approved Baker Company would be ready.

A couple of days after McNeil returned he stepped out of the CP tent one evening after dark to get some fresh air. He could smell coffee brewing and when he looked toward the cook tent he could see a blue flame under a pot. He was instantly pissed that someone had broken one of his rules and it could affect all the men in the company. He took several deep breaths to calm down then he pulled his pistol and put a round through the pot of coffee which drained out and extinguished the fire. As soon as the pistol fired there were shouts of sniper and incoming and a scramble of men in all directions. McNeil holstered the pistol and walked into the dark cook tent almost tripping over a prone figure. The man yelled out, "incoming, better get your ass down."

"There is no sniper fire, said McNeil, "get off that ground soldier. I did the shooting. Where is SSgt. Leeks?"

"He's back there somewhere," the man replied pointing as he got up and brushed himself off, but it was too dark for McNeil to see where he was pointing.

"SSgt. Leeks," called out McNeil.

"What's all that noise out here and who is calling me?" came a voice from the rear of the cook tent.

"Captain McNeil is calling and he requests your presence now."

"Damn, can't a man get some sleep around here? Who's calling for me?"

"I am Sergeant Leeks," spoke McNeil when he saw a figure approaching through the dark tent, "one of my golden rules has been broken. I suggest you find out who it was and set him straight."

"Is that you Captain McNeil?"

"It's me. Did you hear what I just said?"

"Something about a rule being broken."

"No fires after dark. I just found a fire going here that could have put this tent and possible the Company in danger. I'll expect you to report to me tomorrow with an answer as to what you have done about the incident. Let me appraise you of a fact you seem to have forgotten SSgt. Leeks. This is not garrison duty; we are not in the USA. We are in Korea in a war time situation. Different rules apply and disobeying orders is a serious offense in war time. Keep that in mind in the future."

Set up rules that are not to be broken; do not fail to punish any offenders. A quote from Sun Tzu that McNeil remembered well.

"What happened Charley?" asked Tiny when McNeil entered the CP through the blackout curtain. The only light in the tent came from a lantern on the field desk. After McNeil explained what happened Tiny said, "boy, that just makes these strips you bestowed on me feel awful heavy boss."

"You are a big man and a fine soldier Tiny, you can handle them."

"I just wish I felt the confidence you seem to have in me."

"What happened to the generators Tiny?"

"A new rule since you left. SSgt. Anderson's man who is in charge of the generator has orders to shut it down at the first sign of hostility. It'll be back up soon now that there is no danger."

Sure enough, two minutes later a shout was heard, 'all clear,' and the generator was started up and the lights came on.

After midnight while McNeil was taking his turn on the defense line a lone mortar tube, somewhere out front, started lobbing rounds. Little damage was done even though rounds fell behind Able, Baker and Charlie Companies. The mortar tube reminded McNeil of the tube that now sat on his defense line. There was no ammo for it but at least it wasn't lobbing rounds at him and his men. Suddenly the mortar lobbing rounds on Charlie Company went silent. There was still small arms fire but not too much of that. Just probing fire.

Two days later a Charley Company jeep stopped in front of Baker Company CP with a smiling Lt. Johnson in the right seat. "What brings you back here," asked McNeil as Bob got out of the jeep and walked to where McNeil stood waiting, "not that I'm not glad to see you?"

"Did you hear the sudden silence last night?"

"You mean the mortar? It didn't last long did it?"

"I took a page from your book Charley. I have a well-trained man in the unit and he and I did a bit of recon work last night. Charley Company now has its very own mortar tube. The North Koreans had just been re-supplied so we have some ammo. I brought you a couple of case's since I know you are out of ammo because I fired the last round."

"I'm sure we can put it to a good use. Thanks Bob.

"Peace and quiet shall rein over Baker and Charley companies once again."

"You got time for coffee Bob?"

"I would like to say yes but my merry band of men awaits their leader."

"You sound as if you are enjoying this command responsibility Bob?"

"It does seem to grow on you doesn't it?"

"Bob as you go about performing these unauthorized missions please keep in mind what happened to SSgt. Sampson. You are the commander and I can't tell you what to do, but don't take any unnecessary chances."

"I'll keep that in mind Charley and thanks for your concern."

"Let me give you a heads up Bob. As I said before, there is a strong possibility that the companies may be moving, forward that is. I can't say when but be prepared. Also you should think about storing some of that extra equipment. Charlie Company has to lighten their load."

"I got a message two days ago along that line. Something about storing unneeded equipment in unused vehicles. That what you're referring to Charley?"

"That's it. Baker Company has already stored all extra and luxury items."

"Well thanks for the heads up. I'll catch you later. Come visit." said Bob as he got back in the jeep and motioned to his driver to drive on.

"Was that Bob?" asked Tiny coming out of the CP.

"You just missed him. He brought us some ammo for the tube. Have someone from the line come and get it."

"I'll run it up to the line," said Tiny as he started to bend and pick up the two cases of mortar ammo.

"Tiny, you must start listening close to what I say. Have someone come and get the ammo. You are the man in charge now, not the laborer. Try and remember that."

"Sure boss," answered Tiny as he headed for the line.

See who is able to make rules clear and commands easy to follow so that people listen and obey. Another quote from Sun Tzu that McNeil remembered. A page from McNeil's book was that if one can't have manpower then one should have fire power.

Most every man on the line of Baker Company had an extra weapon with extra ammo, with extra grenades. All courtesy of some North Koreans who no longer had a need for them. Take advantage of what's at hand and make use of it was something he believed in. Live off the land as much as possible.

There were many other Sun Tzu rules of war fare and several other McNeil rules to follow.

He had good men and they were well trained, trained under fire and bloodied in battle. They had to be well trained if they were still alive. By getting rid of the fat, so to speak, the luxury and unused equipment, left more time for the men to do what they were trained to do, fight battles. Everything a good infantry man needed he carried on his back. This was an un-mechanized unit so the men moved on their feet, light loads made that so much easier.

When supplies came in and they were lucky enough to get beer McNeil allowed the men only one each and only when they came off the line. They still got their two hour breaks every four hours. That was their only time for relaxing and McNeil made sure there was always hot food and coffee, during daylight hours.

It was almost eerie quiet on the battle field the last few days. Few, if any, mortar rounds fell and there were only a few probing attacks by the North Koreans. No artillery and no planes overhead. The question was asked, "Is the war over," by those who still maintained their vigilance. The probing North Koreans never got close and the men saved their ammo by not returning fire.

McNeil knew the nightly probes were done to check out the effective reaction of the American troops. Something was being planned but there was no intelligence of what was being planned.. Just how long will it take the American Army to get off their ass and do something was on the mind of every man on the front line.

McNeil was a firm believer that a Commander should be visible. A leader should not alienate himself from the men he has been sworn to train, lead and protect. When he wasn't tied up with duties elsewhere one could find him on the defense line. He was once one of them and there was a special camaraderie between him and the old timers of Baker Company that few commanders ever experienced. Because he had been there he knew what it was to be on the line day and night. Even though camaraderie existed, respect for their commander existed in their words and actions.

Men who were assigned duty in Korea and told it would be an easy assignment but to not expect any promotions was suddenly thrust into a war. Since McNeil was promoted from the ranks from a corporal to a Captain and now their Commander, suddenly promotions were being passed out. This was a big morale booster for the men who had expected nothing. Another of their own, PFC Brockman, a squad leader, was now the company 1st Sergeant. At least once a month a deserving man was promoted in Baker Company.

The men had confidence that if they performed their duties they would be protected and cared for. The one thing they disliked and, couldn't understand, was when their luxury items, such as cots and clean sheets were suddenly taken away from them. They slept where they could find a place to lie down. They never voiced their complaints out loud, just to each other, because they knew that their commander, Captain McNeil, had a good reason for taking away such items, what it was escaped them. They did know that he slept on the ground as they did. He never ate before they did and he made sure the NCO's did the same. He never took privileges that weren't offered to his men first.

Even though McNeil was on the line most of last night he was back after eating and having his coffee. That was where Corporal Gordon found him after he had decoded a message. The message didn't make much sense to Corporal Gordon but it was addressed to Captain McNeil and he figured it would make sense to him.

"No reply," said McNeil when he read the short message. 'Bug out approved, Baker six to coordinate.'

# McNeil

## Ongjin Peninsula
## Relocation of Companies

**Chapter 10**
**12 Oct 1950**

McNeil entered the CP right behind Corporal Gordon. "Tiny?"

"Yes sir?" Tiny was use to calling McNeil Charley or Boss but not in front of the troops.

"There will be a meeting here in ten minutes; All NCO's."

"I'll round them up," said Tiny getting into his field gear and picking up the seventeen pound BAR as if it weighed no more than a BB gun.

"Still hanging onto that BAR Tiny? Wouldn't it be more beneficial to the men on the line?"

"They have one," answered Tiny as he went out the door.

And I'll not ask where the extra one came from, thought McNeil as he went to the big map. "When the NCO's arrive I want you, Corporal Gordon, outside at the front of the tent and you PFC Rodgers at the rear. Keep everyone out and away from the tent. What's to be discussed in here is classified."

The two men started to done their gear without asking questions. But it didn't stop Corporal Gordon from wondering if this had something to do with the strange message he had decoded earlier. What is a bug out? All he knew was that when something had to be done no grass grew under Captain McNeil's feet; unlike some commanders who sat around and delayed for days before acting.

When all the Company NCO's were present McNeil started what he felt would not be received very well. "I received a message today that approves a move for all four companies. There is no, if it can be done, it will be done, and done this day. As soon as I brief you I have to get to each of the companies and brief them because this will be a coordinated move with no loss of security. We'll be moving forward to this ridge which is about a mile in front of us. As you should know by now there are no more ROK troops between us and the 38thParallel. We must shoulder all security of the peninsula.

"We'll be packed up and moving out well before dark. Some of the tents and equipment can be loaded now but the cook tent and equipment plus the CP will be the last to be loaded. SSgt. Leeks, see SSgt. Anderson for a truck to load your gear and tent on. Serve the evening meal early then start breaking down and loading. By that time there should be some help for you. SSgt. Anderson, have the fuel trailer top off every tank then send it to battalion to be refilled, same with the water tanker. While you are at battalion pick up a 3/4 ton weapons carrier for Sgt hicks to use. We'll make this move with as little noise as possible. No racing of engines and grinding of gears. Sergeant Brockman will be in charge of the main element. I'll be moving on foot with the men."

"Do you think that's wise sir?" asked SSgt. Anderson, "I mean walking out front with the men."

"I think so. I have never understood the infantry motto, 'Follow me' when the instructions dictates that an officer should be the fourth or fifth man from the front. I'll be visible and with the men. You NCO's can handle everything back here. Remember, this is one unit, there are no individuals, work together to make this move as quickly and quietly as we can. We, the men on the line, will provide security and be on line when you arrive. Once you arrive get as much set up as possible before dark, the cook tent first then the CP."

"Why go to all this trouble just to move a mile?" asked SSgt. Leeks. "We have been here for over a year and it's a good place with lots of shade."

"I suppose now is a good time to bring each of you up-to-date on the situation, or as much of it as we know. As you stated before SSgt. Leeks you are not infantry, and I'm sure there are more of you who are not trained infantry men. How many snipers have been killed? Anyone?"

"I've taken out two," said Tiny.

"Two or three have been taken out but how many more were out there that didn't have a shot but went back to their units with information about us and our location? How much do we know about what happened to SSgt. Sampson? If he was captured you can bet he was interrogated. As you said, SSgt. Leeks we have been in one location a long time. Don't you think that by now the North Koreans know all there is to know about the 1/5st Battalion and the companies? With the main force of the North Koreans roaming all over the main land they have had to amass their reserves. Don't think that for one minute that just because their artillery was destroyed they don't have more and is moving it into place as we speak. Once they get geared up the American forces on the main land will be caught between the main forces of the retreating North Koreans and the advancing reserve forces crossing the 38th parallel. This peninsula is very important to the North Koreans, **politically**, because so far we have been able to hang on to it which makes them look bad. **Strategically,** if they could take the peninsula they could move in long rang artillery and pin down American troops on the main land. **Economically,** this is rich farm land which they would like to have to help feed their thousands of starving people. We have been charged with the task of keeping it out of their hands. So far we have been successful. That's the big picture. The little picture is for us to do everything we can to stay alive. Now if there are no more questions I have two day's work to get done in a few hours."

## 13 Oct 1950

So much information had to be passed out that McNeil thought it best if he visited each company and explained just what was to happen and why. Since Able Company was next door to him he headed east first. Charlie Company was no problem since Lt. Johnson had advance word on the bug out and he knew McNeil wouldn't steer him wrong. McNeil gave him final instructions then moved on to Dog Company.

Dog Company was commanded by a Lt. Hampton. He was a young and inexperienced 1st Lieutenant with his first chance at command. He was a tall slender man who was trying to grow a mustache, possibly to make him look older. He was not Infantry but Artillery so McNeil spent extra time with him to make sure he understood just what to do. Everything had to be timed so that no unit was left behind nor one alone on the new M L R (Main Line of Resistance).

The biggest problem arose when he introduced himself to Capt. Downs the Able Company commander. He was an older man and still a Captain with much more time in grade than McNeil. Capt. Downs felt a bit slighted that Ltc. Winters had not put him in charge of the move. It took a bit of talking for McNeil to smooth Capt. Downs ruffled feathers and convince him that the move was necessary regardless of who was in charge. To feel he had contributed something Capt. Downs made a change in McNeil's plans. McNeil wanted all the commanders to be with the advancing troops but Capt. Downs decided he would ride and lead his small convey of trucks and let his 1st Sergeant lead the troops. McNeil had to concede to that small change to make the man feel better.

As McNeil headed back to Baker Company that evening he worked out the messages and times to send them and handed them to Corporal Gordon to encode. When McNeil reached Baker Company every tent, except the cook tent and CP, was down and loaded and the trucks were lined up and ready.

After the evening meal everyone who could be spared pitched in and helped break down and load the cook tent.

McNeil, after checking with the men on the line to make sure they were ready, waited with Corporal Gordon for the time to pass. At exactly seventeen hundred hours Corporal Gordon keyed his radio and gave the signal to the other companies for the ground troops to move out. With McNeil leading and Corporal Gordon in the rear, McNeil still didn't want a radio with a tall antenna near him, the men of Baker Company eased over the berm and started walking on line to their new M L R.

At seventeen thirty hours Corporal Gordon, as instructed, keyed his radio and gave the signal to all units for the trucks to move out.

There was still enough daylight left, when the men reached their new M L R, for them to see and to start digging in on the mound of dirt that ran across the peninsula. McNeil left the platoon leaders to supervise the defense position preparations and went to meet the first vehicle, Tiny in the jeep. McNeil showed Tiny where each tent was to be erected then left him to direct that operation.

McNeil had instructed Tiny to gather up all the tin cans he could find before covering up the garbage pit. Tiny had no idea what the cans were for but he didn't question the order. He had two bags full of the old tin cans.

As the calls came in that the other companies were at the new M L R Corporal Gordon notified Raider commo of that fact.

McNeil took the two sacks of tin cans that Tiny had collected and with two of the platoon leaders helping him he went forward of the M L R and using string he showed the men how to tie the cans to bushes and rig trip strings with cans on them. Small stones were put into each can. A simple, but effective, early warning system that would let men know the enemy was close. The men on the line were instructed that if they heard the stones rattle to start throwing grenades, but only if they were sure the rattling was caused by something other than the wind.

The man Corporal Johnson had selected months ago as the mortar man, with help, got the mortar tube set up and aimed as best as he could. He would have to fire some rounds then adjust it. With the rule of no lights at night the only tent that got set up that evening was the cook tent and the CP. McNeil consented and allowed the stoves to be lit, as long as all tent flaps were down, so the men could have hot food and coffee.

There was a small grove of trees behind the M L R with brush growing around it that would provide concealment and a wind break. The other tents would be set up there at first light. The men on the line spent a rough night expecting the unexpected. To make it worse the weather was getting colder and a north wind was blowing in their faces.

The next morning as men started setting up the tents others went to find their stored duffle bags and brought out some winter clothes. They also brought out ponchos and shelter halves. To keep the cold off the men in the firing pit they rigged the shelter halves and ponchos over their positions so as to ward off some of the cold wind.

Well before noon the next day all the tents were erected and Baker Company was once again operational. As the other companies went operational they transmitted a coded signal to Baker Company and when Corporal Gordon had the message from all companies he transmitted the unit operational signal to Battalion.

The attack that McNeil predicted did not occur the night they moved nor did it happen the next night. The sudden move to a new location plus the stress of waiting for the unexpected was working on the men. McNeil knew he couldn't keep the men alert much longer without them losing some of their edge. He heard a lot of grumbling and arguments and tempers flared at the smallest thing. He knew he could stop the grumbling with harsh discipline but that would only aggravate the stressed out men. Best to let them work out their problems if it doesn't interfere with their alertness.

## 16 Oct 1950

The third night on the new MLR after the cold wind died down some the men on line could still hear the stones rattling in the tin cans. It had been such a long wait that they were not sure if they should toss grenades or wait. McNeil, as usual, was on the line and when he heard the stones rattling he didn't hesitate, he tossed a couple of grenades then started spraying the area with his M-1. That woke the men up to the fact this was again real and they started tossing grenades. It was just before midnight and suddenly the quiet was broken by exploding grenades and rifle fire. There were cries of the wounded, not Baker Company men, but the North Korean who had no idea they were walking into a trap.

The instructions given to the North Korean reserve force was to move silently up to the ridge and wait for the artillery and mortar fire to begin. After the mortar and artillery barrage was lifted they were to cross the ridge and attack the American troops.

When the stones in the tin cans started rattling they froze in place not knowing what to do. The first grenade exploded in their midst killing several and wounding more of them. They started running back until the first mortar round exploded. That really confused them. They had been told there was no danger in the area they were going to, now they were caught in a fire fight with nowhere to go. Soon the sound of exploding grenades and rifle fire could be heard in the areas of both Able and Charlie Companies.

After a couple of hours the noise died down and there was only sporadic rifle fire as the now alert men saw movement to their front. The North Korean reserves had been surprised at what they had been told would be lax and laze Americans. The blitz, so sudden and unexpected, cut the, not too well trained, North Korean reserve force in half.

Just before daylight the sound of artillery rounds whistling overhead could be heard. None fell on the new M L R but many fell and exploded where they had once camped, the previous M L R.

When it grew light enough one could see the rounds landing and stirring up clouds of dirt and dust when they exploded. Smoke from the many exploding shells hung over the area. Men could be heard muttering; shit, would you look at that; glad I'm not back there, we moved just in time.

McNeil watched as tons of North Korean artillery rounds fell and exploded on the old M L R and just behind it. He was thankful that Ltc. Winters had come through with permission for the move, just in time. He also knew that such a barrage of artillery was a prelude to a ground attack and if he wasn't mistaken the attackers had just been stopped, or held in place.

McNeil moved up and down the line urging the men to be on the alert just in case the devastated North Korean reserve force got up the nerve to attack again once the artillery was lifted. He came across SSgt. Leeks and his cooks, plus SSgt. Anderson and his men, on the line. Sgt Hicks and his helper was moving around taking care of the few men who had been wounded, nothing serious, and for that McNeil was thankful. As he moved along the line he kept a watch on where the artillery impacted and he noticed a heavy cloud of smoke coming from the area where 1/5st Battalion was camped.

McNeil left the line and ran back to the CP where Corporal Gordon monitored the radio since McNeil had banned him from the line with a radio. "Any traffic from Raider commo?" he asked as he entered the tent.

"Nothing sir. All quiet," answered Corporal Gordon from his position under the radio bench.

"See if you can raise them."

"Raider commo, Raider commo, Baker commo for Raider commo. Come in Raider commo." Corporal Gordon rechecked his radio frequency then tried again. Still nothing.

"Sir, No contact and there is a squeal on the radio every time I key the mick."

"Stand by that radio," said McNeil as he left the CP in search of Tiny. He had a sinking feeling as to why there was no radio contact with Raider commo after seeing the cloud of smoke hanging over the area. But, Raider six has a radio in his jeep so why isn't he answering?

"He located Tiny on the line. "Tiny, you are in charge here. Keep the men alert and expect the unexpected. I have no idea what those untrained North Koreans will do."

"Sure boss but where will you be?"

"As soon as the artillery is lifted I'm headed for Battalion."

"I'll get Gordon to go with you."

"Right now you need every man you can get. I'll drive myself."

"I would feel much better if Corporal Gordon was with you sir," replied Tiny with a pleading look on his face.

"I'll pick him up at the CP then," replied McNeil. I just might need an extra hand if what I think happened back there.

As McNeil and Corporal Gordon sat in the jeep waiting for the barrage to be lifted his mind was active as he had been trained to be. He analyzed potential problems and situations and stored the solutions in his mind for future use. Even though the men of Baker Company were soldiers he thought of them as his children since he was responsible for their health and safety. He often wondered if the commanders at higher levels thought of the men as he did, rather than just assets.

Suddenly the sounds of airplanes could be heard to McNeil's rear. He turned to look and could see several planes strafing and bombing in the area where he guessed the North Korean artillery was located. He wondered, since Raider Commo was not active, just who had requested the planes. Not important who but just the fact that they were there was what mattered. There were only a few scattered rifle shots on the line now and it wasn't long before the artillery fell silent. At McNeil's signal Corporal Gordon started the jeep and as they started moving McNeil wondered just why the North Korean reserve force did not attack again.

There would always be speculation on exactly what happened on the morning of 14 October 1950. Even though many aspects were known, the true facts would not be known for several years. Bits and pieces of information came from many sources, POW interrogations, captured documents and maps, classified lessons learned and command documents.

The day it happened, the heavy artillery bombardment, no one of the four companies of 1st battalion cared how it happened, they were just glad it didn't happen where they were dug in.

In good military planning artillery and mortar barrages precede a ground action. It's called softening up the objective. It would be years later that the reason for the failure of the North Korean reserve force to attack was known. What the exploding rounds really do is destroy, by blast, shrapnel, and fire, supplies, equipment, vehicles, and people. Big strong, combat experienced veterans cringe in fox holes or any ground depressions praying they won't become ground zero for an artillery round.

The ground trembles, explosions are ear shattering, and great mounds of sand and rock are thrown into the air to rain back down on the men. Anything combustible is set on fire. The bombardment area becomes a living hell for those caught in it. Fear, death, destruction, and psychological problems are the aftermath of a artillery barrage. Hours after an artillery barrage the smell of cordite, dust, and smoke lingers along with the unmistakable odor of death. It's possible that the North Korean Reserve forces was overcome with the grenade and mortar attack and were in hiding licking their wounds.

It would take an experienced officer to get them moving again.

# McNEIL

## ONGJIN PENINSULA
## 1/5 INFANTRY BATTALION LOST

**Chapter 11**
**16 Oct 1950**

When Corporal Gordon drove across the berm at the previous M L R as far as McNeil could see there were shell craters. Smoke and dust hung in the air and several small fires were burning where debris and small brush piles had caught fire. They had to dodge craters until they located the road to Battalion. Even then there were several craters, plus more trees were down across the road that they had to dodge. The pall of smoke, and dust that hung over the trees, guided them to the Battalion camp site.

When Corporal Gordon drove into the area where 1/5st Battalion once operated from McNeil stood up in the jeep for a better look and he was stunned. The destruction was complete except for the vehicles which someone had thought to move a short distance away from the tents. Not a tent was left standing and not a soul moved. It was eerie quiet. Dust and smoke hung in the air and the odor of cordite was still strong.

McNeil had no idea how long he stood and stared at the carnage. Finally he roused himself and got slowly out of the jeep. Never in his life had he seen such total destruction. "Let's get those fires out Gordon," called out McNeil, when he didn't hear an answer or notice any movement he called again louder to get Corporal Gordon's attention. Together they stomped on, threw dirt on, or beat the fires out with whatever was handy. As they worked to put out the small fires McNeil kept hoping to see people coming from the woods, but no one appeared. Where are all the battalion people?

As they started pulling some of the shredded canvas away there was an unusual odor in the air, the odor of burnt flesh. McNeil noticed that Gordon was getting a bit ashen face so he sent him on an errand to get him away from the site of carnage and destruction hoping a breath of fresh air might help. McNeil feared the man may pass out if he had to help search under the downed tents for bodies, or survivors. "Corporal Gordon," called out McNeil, "go to the vehicles and check each one out for damage. Start each one up to make sure it will run. Bring the command jeep back here."

"Yes sir. On the way sir," said a relieved Gordon.

McNeil started the grim task of searching under the downed tents for bodies even though he didn't feel there was much of a chance of finding any survivors. When he located a body he dragged it from the tent and laid it out near where the Battalion tent once stood. Each body he found was ripped apart by the exploding artillery rounds. He knew there should be ten bodies but he only had nine laid out in a row. After checking each of the bodies he determined that the one missing was the commo man, Corporal Willis. It was near the time for Corporal Gordon to return so McNeil took some sheets from the downed supply tent and covered the bodies. It made sense that the missing commo man would be under the downed CP tent so McNeil got down on his hands and knees and started crawling. The only light under the canvas came through shrapnel holes but it was enough for him to see his way around. As he neared the area where he knew the commo was set up he heard a low moan. Thank God, he said to himself, maybe at least one is alive.

Finally he located where the moan was coming from and he found Corporal Willis. The man was lying on his back with a broken chair under him and the big radio on top of him. McNeil could see blood on Willis' face and a big bruise. Willis was still moaning and trying to push the radio off himself. "Take it easy Willis," said McNeil softly, "I'm here to help you."

Once the big radio was off the man McNeil checked further but couldn't find any broken bones. "I can't see and I hurt. My head," Willis was finally able to say as he moved his hand to his head.

"Can you move your legs?"

"I'll try. Who are you?"

"I'm Captain McNeil. Now try to move your legs."

Corporal Willis was able to move his leg's which was a relief to McNeil. He feared the man's back may be broken. "My legs are ok but my back hurts and my head feels like it's about to burst open. What happened anyway?"

"First things first; your back hurts because you fell on a chair. Your head hurts because apparently the radio hit your head. I can see a small gash and a good size bump on your forehead."

"I still can't see. Is it still dark?" Then he remembered who he was talking to and added, "Sir".

"No it's not dark. You are under the downed CP tent. I'll take your hands and try to drag you out of here. If it hurts you too much call out."

"I still can't see you sir."

"That's alright, for now. Once I have you outside we'll be able to check you out further. McNeil struggled and finally got Willis clear of the downed tent. He then picked the man up and carried him to the Raider jeep where Gordon sat waiting. Willis was placed in the left seat. "Do you know Corporal Willis, Corporal Gordon?"

"Only by his voice on the radio sir."

"Use some water from your canteen and try to clean his face," said McNeil as he turned to the radio in his jeep. "Baker six for Baker commo. Come in Baker commo."

"Baker commo. Go Baker six."

"Get Baker five on the radio."

"Hold one sir."

McNeil didn't have to wait long before he heard a breathless voice on the radio, "Baker five here. Go ahead Baker six."

"All empty vehicles to Raider position in thirty. Drivers plus one. Send chief medic, chief supply, and chief cook also. Good copy?"

"Good copy." Tiny wondered just what was going on but he didn't want to tie up the radio with questions which he knew McNeil probably wouldn't answer anyway.

"Situation on line?"

"Quiet."

"Send status with chief supply."

"Status with chief supply. Got it."

"Baker six standing by."

"Baker commo standing by."

Corporal Gordon had washed most of the blood from Corporal Willis' face but the man was hurting and still couldn't see. McNeil decided to wait for the men to arrive before he did anything else. He could see where blood had soaked through the white sheets draped over the bodies but nothing could be done about that now.

The scene that greeted the Baker company convey twenty minutes later brought comments from thankful survivors; damn, would you look at that, shit, glad I wasn't here. Sgt Hicks jumped out of the ambulance with his medical bag, as soon as the convoy stopped, and headed to where he saw McNeil standing by a jeep. "Is he the only one sir?" Sgt Hicks asked pointing to Corporal Willis. He had seen the sheet covered bodies.

"Right. Check him out and give me your opinion. When you finish get started tagging and bagging."

When Tiny got an order he complied with it. The order said all vehicles and he sent all vehicles, to include the water truck. With Willis being taken care of McNeil went to where SSgt. Leeks had stopped his truck. The other drivers and men from Baker Company gathered around. "It's a bad situation men but you have seen death before. There is no time to stand around and gawk. Work needs to be done. SSgt. Leeks watch the shell craters and move your vehicle around to the cook tent. Strip away the canvas and salvage any useful equipment and rations. The same goes for you SSgt. Anderson. Start with the supply tent then go through all the others. Load your vehicles first then we'll bring up the Battalion vehicles. If you come across any water proof bags I'll need two or three of them. We'll also need nine ponchos for the bodies. You two, McNeil couldn't remember the names of the water truck drivers, fill that tanker then lend a hand here. You other men lend a hand where you can."

"Tiny said to give this to you Sir," said Sgt Anderson passing over a single hand written sheet of paper. McNeil folded it and put it in his pocket. By the time McNeil finished giving instructions Sgt Hicks had finished his examination of Corporal Willis. McNeil walked to the jeep. "What's your verdict Sgt Hicks?"

"Some back bruises, nothing broken, which will be sore for a while. His vision is clearing up some. I gave him some A P C (aspirin) and he said his headache was easing up some. That bump on his head, which I'll continue to monitor for a while, is causing the vision problem and headache. And," said Sgt Hicks winking at McNeil, "my opinion is that gash on his head was caused by a shell fragment which calls for a purple heart."

"If that's your opinion then so be it. Should Corporal Willis be evacuated as WIA or can you handle him here?"

"Unless he gets worse I can handle him."

"Thank you Doctor Hicks. Now you may proceed with your other duties."

"Corporal Gordon," said McNeil after Sgt Hicks walked away to begin the grim task of identifying the bodies, "get all these radios on the air. Call each company, less Baker, and get me a status report. Use the Raider call sign and write the information on this," he said handing him the report from Baker Company. "Corporal Willis, have you any idea where the S O I is?"

Willis felt for it which was normally on a chain around his neck. All he found was the chain. "I have no idea sir."

"Don't worry about it. How's the vision?"

"Still a bit blurry sir but the headache is easing up some."

"Stay where you are and help Corporal Gordon as much as you can."

"Am I----"he couldn't get the rest out but McNeil knew what he was trying to ask.

"You are the lucky one."

McNeil waited until all the units had reported their personnel status. It wasn't good. Counting Battalion there were 11 K I A. Of the 12 WIA 2 would have to be transferred to the division medical unit for treatment that wasn't available here. "Get Blue Stallion Commo on the radio. Tell them there is a priority message for Blue Stallion six from Baker Six."

Corporal Gordon left the Baker company jeep and got in the Battalion jeep to make the call. He wanted to keep the Baker jeep radio open for any local calls that might come in. Corporal Willis, even though he still couldn't see properly gave Gordon instructions and the frequency for Blue Stallion Commo.

While Corporal Gordon was setting up the radio McNeil was trying to figure out just how one went about telling a Division Commander that one of its units was lost, and without an S O I. It all had to be done in the clear and in as few words as possible..

"Raider commo for Blue Stallion commo. Come in Blue Stallion commo."

"Welcome back Raider commo. You have been off the air for two hours. What's the problem?"

"Priority message from Baker six for Blue Stallion six. Copy?"

"Blue Stallion six is unavailable. Blue Stallion commo will pass the message."

"Understood," replied Corporal Gordon and he passed the mick to McNeil.

"Baker six with a priority message for Blue Stallion six. Message is; the headquarters on the Ongjin Peninsula is no longer a viable unit. Copy?"

"Good copy Baker six. Stand by." while he waited for Blue Stallion commo McNeil took another look at the casualty figures. They were the same; nothing had changed since he read them five minutes ago.

"Baker six this is Blue Stallion six," came a different voice over the radio, "use an S O I and explain what is meant by 'non-viable'."

"S O I is lost. Ongjn Peninsula headquarters is non-viable due to artillery barrage. Copy?"

"Copy. Stand by." Colonel Layton, newly promoted to Brigadier General, held onto the mick as he sat back to analyze the information he had just received. Just who is this Baker Six? What did he mean when he said non-viable? He certainly doesn't sound like some young shook up shave tail. He's very calm indeed for a man reporting this kind of information. I need more information, answers. I wonder where Titus is. Someone handed General Layton a piece of paper with Baker Six Captain McNeil written on it.

"Baker six do you have a casualty report?"

"Roger that sir." Well, that's surprising, thought General Layton. Most men wouldn't have thought to acquire one. I wonder how he got it so fast.

"Do not transmit status. Send in dispatch. Status of Raider six?"

"K I A."

"Stand by." General Layton hung his head. Damn, he thought, another good friend lost on this God forsaken land. If raider six is K I A then maybe this Baker six, Captain McNeil, knows what he is talking about. He now recalled Titus talking about a very sharp, and very knowledgeable, young man he had commissioned and sent to the island to set up that L P? Could this Baker Six be the same man? Is this the man? He now remembered Titus sending in several award requests for a Captain McNeil.

"Baker six. Am I speaking to the man who spent some time on a tropical island recently?"

"That's a roger sir."

"Stand by." I don't have much choice and very little time, though General Layton as he made a decision. This, Captain McNeil, must be good if Titus thought so highly of him.

"Baker six I now have your name and rank. My orders are as followers. Negative on the non-viable situation. By V O C G you are now Raider six. Copy?"

"Baker six is now Raider six. Copy."

"Mainland units still under attack. Unable to send assistance. Do what you can with what you have. 1/5 will remain a viable unit. Maintain the integrity of the 1st. Copy?"

"Copy and understand sir."

"Copy of casualties and report of event is requested in dispatch. Transportation will be your location in two. Not to leave empty. Copy?"

"Copy and congratulations sir."

"Luck Raider six. Blue Stallion six out."

McNeil slowly handed the mick to Gordon without really seeing who took it. He stood deep in thought for several minutes. I was sent on this assignment expecting no promotion and being back in the states and out of the Army in a year. Now look what's happened. War has broken out. A war that's being called a Police Action, but a war by any other name is still a war. I have been extended on active duty with no known date of release. I've been promoted from a corporal in the trenches to a Battalion commander, all this in less than a year. What else could possibly happen?

At least now we have a general in charge of the Division rather than a colonel. But we have me, a captain, as both a Company and a Battalion commander. That's a stretch. What do I know about running a Battalion? I can't help but wonder what else is going on that we here on the peninsula don't know about. Are more men arriving? Is more equipment coming to Korea? When will we here on the peninsula get the personnel we, make that I, need to properly defend the peninsula?

How does one go about recreating a Battalion headquarters from nothing? Every unit, here and on the main land, is operating at about three quarter strength so where do I find the personnel to staff and operate a Battalion? I could establish a Battalion headquarters in name only and run it through Baker Company. No, that wouldn't work because General Layton said to maintain the integrity of the first. That means it has to operate as a separate unit. That's such an awesome load to drop on the shoulders of a young man. I certainly hope the Generals faith in me is not wasted. Oh well, those are problems I'll work on later. Right now I have priorities. Those few minutes of thinking gave McNeil time to assess the situation and decide on a course of action.

"Corporal Gordon," said McNeil turning back to the two men in the jeeps, "I believe Corporal Willis has recovered enough to handle the radios. Lend a hand to SSgt. Anderson."

"Corporal Willis you were privy to the orders I just received so you know what's going on. You are still Raider commo. Get on the radio and tell Abel, Charlie, and Dog companies to get their KIA and transportable wounded to Battalion at once." McNeil didn't wait for an acknowledgment but went to where Sgt Hicks was finishing tagging and wrapping the bodies in ponchos. He motioned for SSgt. Anderson to join them.

"Sgt Hicks, the KIA and serious wounded are on the way from the companies. Get these bodies loaded and when the others arrive get them all to the landing. The mike boat is due in shortly. You are in charge of that operation. Take a couple of men with you then return here. SSgt. Anderson, take a 6x6 and get to the landing to pick up supplies."

"Sir here are the water proof bags you wanted and the supply truck is loaded and I could use another one."

"Take what you need from the Battalion trucks but check with me before heading for the boat."

Without waiting for questions McNeil crawled under the Battalion CP tent and located some paper that wasn't torn up too bad. He used the hood of a jeep to write out the casualty list and composed a synopses of the event as well as he knew it. Since there wasn't time to get it typed up he wrote both reports out in block letters then signed them:

Charley R. McNeil
Captain Inf
Commanding

He added a PS: The S-2 safe was found but no one has the combination. I'm sending it to you so maybe someone at Division can open it.

He put both papers in an envelope, sealed it, and then wrote on the outside; From Raider Six to Blue Stallion Six. When SSgt. Anderson reported he was ready to roll McNeil handed the envelope to him with instructions to pass it to the boat operator. "Get some men and load the safe on the truck and make sure it gets on the mike boat."

With that done McNeil crawled back under the damaged tent and went about picking out what he figured he might need in the way of office supplies plus whatever else he thought he might need to operate a battalion. Since the file cabinets were too damaged to salvage and the contents shredded he passed them up. He did find a case of green hardback journals which he thought would do to enter daily staff reports and other useful information in. He found one undamaged typewriter. In the battered desk of the late Ltc. Winters he found several cigars which he stuffed in his pocket. He also found an envelope with several sets of officer brass in it. In the late Sergeant Major's destroyed desk he found enlisted rank. When he filled the three bags he took them outside and loaded them in his jeep, now Raider Six jeep. He went back under the tent one more time for a last check and found a full mail bag which must have just arrived because it wasn't opened yet. Nowhere did he find the S O I. He loaded the mail bag in the jeep. He lit one of the cigars as he tried to think of what he might be missing.

"Sir," said SSgt. Leeks, "I have everything I can find in the cook, mess, and supply tent loaded."

"Pull your truck out there," McNeil pointed to the road, "and park it then have the water truck park out there also. One other thing SSgt. Leeks, have your men go to where the battalion trucks are parked and move all of them on line. We'll be taking all of them with us."

As McNeil stood there smoking the cigar he felt he was missing something but he couldn't figure out just what it was. When the trucks started returning form the landing he had all loaded trucks put in line with the others. "Sir," spoke SSgt. Anderson when he returned from the landing, "this is for you," he said handing over a large manila envelope, "also there were ten young men on the boat for us."

"Put them to work for now. Their assignments will come later. SSgt. Anderson, have you found any serviceable tents yet?"

"None so far sir but I have another tent to go through."

"We'll need a couple of each, GP Medium and GP small."

"I'll check around sir."

McNeil had that feeling again that he was missing something. What really designates a Battalion, or any unit for that matter? Not just a bunch of tents. What am I missing here? He asked himself. It suddenly dawned on him. A unit is designated by its guidon.

In the US Army a guidon is a military standard that signifies the unit designation and Corp affiliation. It consists of a staff with the emblem of an eagle at the top.

The significance of the guidon is that it represents the unit and its commanding officer. When the commander is in the guidon is displayed. When the commander leaves for the day the guidon is taken down.

The guidon is a great source of pride for a unit plus the swallow tail flag at the top, dark blue with white unit numbers for Infantry, and any unit citations or war service or campaign streamers are attached below the flag.

I know I have seen one here at Battalion but where is it? It should be at the side of the tent opening but it isn't there. Maybe it was inside last night; he decided and went back under the downed tent looking for the Battalion guidon. He did not locate it. He went to where Corporal Wills sat in the jeep.

"How are you feeling Willis?"

"Much better sir. The headache is easing off some but my back still hurts."

"I know it will be rough on you but do you think you can drive this jeep?"

"I believe I can handle that sir."

"Wills, I have seen the battalion guidon many times outside the tent door but I can't find it. Do you have any idea where it might be?"

"The last I saw of it sir it was on the left side of the tent opening."

"I'll look again then."

McNeil found it under and in a roll of the damaged tent canvas. The pole was broken but the flag and streamers were ok with a few holes and a bit dirty. He rolled up the flag and streamers and put them in the jeep.

Once the NCO's reported to him that they had located and loaded everything worthwhile and all the trucks were lined up he called all the men together and spoke to them. "Men, you have just witnessed the destruction of a Battalion and the loss of some good men. Let's remove our helmets and bow our heads for a moment of silence to those lost to battle.

"What is left here, said McNeil a minute later after he put his helmet back on and looked around at the faces of the somber men, "must be burned to keep any bit of useful information out of the enemy's hands. Take the fuel cans from the jeeps and soak all the tentage. When that is done we'll lite it."

When all the tentage was sprinkled with gas McNeil gave another speech to the gathered men. "Even though you see a destroyed Battalion it will be reborn. Per orders of the Division Commanding General the 1/5th Battalion will once again fly the colors of a Battalion. I have been tasked with the rebuilding of it. Any help you can give me in that endeavor will be most appreciated. Many of you, as I must, will be asked to wear more than one hat. Each of you are combat veterans and I know you can shoulder the burden. Lite the fires please."

Every man stood and watched as the fires flared up and the remnants of what once was the 1/5 Infantry Battalion went up in flame. No one was anxious to move and McNeil didn't rush them. When he was sure everything had burned and the flame slowly died down, and he felt sure there was no danger of the fire spreading McNeil called out, "Mount up."

The convey of vehicles pulled out of what was once known as the Battalion area and headed for the road and to the new location of the yet to be reborn Battalion. McNeil led the convey in the Raider Six jeep and Corporal Willis brought up the rear. An extra driver was needed so Corporal Gordon drove a 6x6.

## 16 Oct 1950

There was an area about a hundred yards to the left rear of Baker Company that McNeil felt was the place to set up the new 1/5st Battalion Headquarters. There were a scattering of stunted trees with some underbrush which would provide some concealment plus block some of the cold wind. It was as close to the center of the four companies as he could get. He parked his jeep then directed the other vehicles in. "SSgt. Anderson, get everybody fed and back here as quick as they can make it. After the new men are fed turn them over to Sergeant Brockman. They can leave their bags on the truck for now. Corporal Gordon, take Baker Six jeep back to Sergeant Brockman. I won't be needing it."

McNeil relit the cigar that had gone out on the ride. He stood and watched as men, his men, went to the cook tent to eat the noon meal. He was near enough that he could also see, in the distance, some of Able Company's men moving around. Even though last night had been chilly the sun was up and shining and felt good. He judged that he had about twenty minutes before he would be able to get food so he opened the manila envelope that SSgt. Anderson had handed him earlier.

Inside he found a hand written message to him from General Layton. **Captain McNeil, Situation and circumstances permitting I will visit the Peninsula in three or four weeks. Exact day and time to be announced. Luck. Gen Layton.**

A month, that sure doesn't give me much time to establish the 1 /5st Infantry Battalion again, thought McNeil

He found three copies of an order dated today and signed by General Layton the gist of it was that his original order, V O C G, for Captain McNeil to be 1/5th Infantry Battalion Commander, was canceled and made official by Special Order number 223, dated today, the 16th of October 1950..

McNeil had hoped that General Layton would notice that Captain Downs, commander of Abel Company, was older, had more time in the service, and far more time in grade than he did. But with the order making his new position official he figured he would have trouble when Capt. Downs heard the news. And he couldn't blame him. Just one more burden to shoulder and one more hurdle to cross.

The last item in the envelope was ten sets of orders for the ten new men. With no staff the responsibility of getting the men assigned fell on McNeil. He went through each order and marked on the top where he wanted that man assigned. With that task completed he could see the line had thinned out some so he decided to eat.

Tiny was waiting for him at the cook tent and followed him after he got some food and coffee. "I heard what happened but tell me it isn't so. No, I know you can't do that. So what happens now boss?"

"What happens now Tiny is we all start wearing more than one hat. I have been designated, on orders, as the 1/5th Battalion Commander. I expect you to continue as you have been but as of now consider yourself the acting Battalion Sergeant Major." SSgt. Anderson came by before McNeil could finish with his instructions.

"SSgt. Anderson," said McNeil, "your work load will be getting much heavier now. First, get SSgt. Leeks to help you, break down the rations and get them to the other companies."

"Sir, there is about fifty cases of beer on the truck. What shall I do with that?"

"Load it on the ration truck, ten cases to each company. Have you ever considered becoming an officer SSgt. Anderson?"

"It never crossed my mind sir."

"Give it some thought. I need an S-4. If I recommended you, and if my recommendation was accepted, for lieutenant you would be transferred and made a company commander. I'm thinking along the line of a Warrant Officer. I need an answer from you by tomorrow."

"I'll give it some thought. Sir, where are the ten new men to be assigned?"

"Use them as needed for now. Tiny and I will get them assigned later today. We'll be setting up the battalion tents in the vicinity of the trucks but that will happen later today also. Right now get the rations broke down and distributed."

"Yes sir."

"Also there is a mail bag in my jeep. Would you, or have someone, bring it to Sergeant Brockman so he can get it distributed."

"I'll take care of it sir."

"Now Tiny, Since I have been ordered to be the 1/5st Infantry Battalion Commander, I will be wearing two hats, Battalion commander and Baker Company Commander. With your additional responsibility comes a promotion. Have Pfc Rodgers cut an order making you a Master Sergeant. Get these sewn on," said McNeil passing over a set of Master Sergeant stripes, "make sure PFC Rodgers cuts the order under the 1st Battalion heading and for my signature. Those ten new men SSgt. Anderson spoke of, I have their orders and where I want them assigned. We'll get the orders cut and take care of them later today. One of the new men is a clerk typist. Once PFC Rodgers is finished cutting orders have him cut a set of orders assigning himself to Battalion and you can have the new man. You'll have to train him but I know you can do it. As quickly as possible get Corporal Gordon to train the new man on radio procedures. Which reminds me, I'll need your S O I. Battalion's was destroyed. I want you to work in both the battalion and the company. I realize I'm throwing a lot at you Tiny but we don't have much time to spare. General Layton, this is not to be spread around, will be paying us a visit in about a month to check on the progress of the new battalion."

"As usual, when you are involved, things move in a hurry. Tell me about the battalion. I heard no one was left alive."

"The battalion and about eighty percent of its equipment was wiped out except for one man, Corporal Willis, who will continue as the battalion commo man. I hope I never have to witness such devastation again." He hung his head as memory of the devastation crossed his mind.

Those who saw the destruction of the battalion and loss of human life seemed to have matured overnight. Each was a different man. All the men started working together as a team and the work that had to be done got done without any grumbling. The tents were set up with a battalion medical station in one end of a GP Medium tent, operated by Sgt. Hicks, with a six bed hospital plus ambulance. McNeil had the stripes to promote Sgt Hicks to sergeant E-6 but he would have to wait until he could get the orders cut.

SSgt. Anderson set up and operated the supply and S-4 in the rear of the medic's tent. SSgt. Anderson made sure each company got its equal share of supplies as they came in. He also took over the vehicle maintenance using the two water truck operators. Later, he did consent to accepting the warrant rating pending approval of General Layton.

There were actually eleven people assigned to battalion by the time McNeil got it up and operating. Of the eleven only three were actually assigned where the others did double duty, Battalion and Baker Company. Someone made up a sign, crude but effective, to hang over the Battalion CP tent door; **1/5 Infantry BATTALION CP.** McNeil located a slim sapling to represent the Battalion guidon, with flag and streamers, attached. It stood just outside the CP door.

Once all the battalion tents were set up to McNeil's satisfaction he set out on a mission he really didn't want to undertake but he knew it had to be done. He, as the newly appointed Battalion Commander, visited each Company Commander to set the record straight and squelch any negative rumors. The first company he visited was as usual Charlie Company. When Lt. Johnson heard about the destruction he was very sad. But when he heard that his friend was now the Battalion Commander he perked up. "Hot shit," he said, "boy, are we coming up in the world."

"If you were under the gun, as I am, you wouldn't think it was hot shit," McNeil said. "I'm going to expect lots more from you than the late Ltc. Winters did. Cut out the cussing Bob. That's bad for the troops to hear their commander use cuss words. Normally people use cuss words as a substitute when they can't think of the proper word to use. When General Layton's visit is confirmed I expect each company commander to be on hand to greet him. Any questions?"

"As usual, we'll do our best Charley. Keep us informed."

The visit went well at Dog Company. Lt. Hampton, the commander, though young, seemed to have everything under control. McNeil had not met the lieutenant until he returned from the island so he assumed that the man was assigned while he was away. Lt. Hampton was apparently awed by rank because it was yes sir and no sir with no questions and no demands.

The only trouble McNeil ran into was at Able Company. Able Company was the only company that was commanded by a Captain. Captain Downs was a trim man in his late twenties, close to thirty. He had dark hair cut very close as did most men. In fact he was a very handsome young man with just a trace of a mustache. It was always easy for McNeil to characterize a person by his actions and mannerisms. If Captain Downs was married he didn't advertise that fact by wearing a wedding ring. He probably thought of himself as a ladies man. He sported a tan which he must work on daily. His movements were all very precise and very military like. He was a man steeped in his own self-importance, preparing himself for the day when he would pin on the rank of major.

When Capt. Downs heard the news about the loss of the battalion and that McNeil had been appointed Battalion Commander he was very distraught. Since he was the ranking man on the peninsula he had no one to complain to. His first words when McNeil introduced himself were; "You do know that I have more time in service and grade than you do Captain McNeil?"

"I certainly do."

"Then why did you accept the assignment?"

"I didn't ask for it, I was ordered to the assignment. When a general says do it I don't say no."

"Then I'm within my rights to file a grievance."

"You do have that right. You will have to draft your grievance, send it through channels, which means through me, and request an audience with the General. The situation may be that you can't be released from here to make the trip to division. Let me make it easy for you and save you some time. Weather and war time situation permitting, General Layton will be in this area in about a month. You will be notified once the visit is confirmed. All Company Commanders are requested to be on hand to greet the Division Commander. You may request an audience with the General at that time. You have done an excellent job with Able Company and I hope it continues. Now; let me say this to you Captain Down; I came here to Korea with one thought on my mind which was to put in my time and get back to college. I didn't order this war nor did I ask for what has been laid on me. Until I have been relieved of the responsibility I'll continue to do the job to the best of my abilities and I hope I have your corporation. That's all I have so if you have nothing further I have duties to perform." With that said McNeil turned and walked away. One man outranked the other but then the other man held a higher position. No salutes were exchanged.

No matter how smooth we want the road that we travel on there is always bumps and curves. With all the other problems put on the shoulders of McNeil one more was added; a disgruntled officer. Maybe he will protest my appointment and relieve me of this heavy burden, thought McNeil as he drove back to the new 1/5th Infantry Battalion area.

Later that same day Tiny came to McNeil in the battalion CP tent and presented him with two packages. "Sir, these were in the mail bag," he said handing them to McNeil who was at a table working on some papers. There were no desks in the new Battalion CP. It would have been nice to have them but none were available. Tables from the devastated battalion mess tent had been salvaged and were put to use.

After Tiny departed McNeil looked at the two packages. One was addressed to the late Ltc. Winters. If the contents were personal he would send it back to division. When McNeil opened it he found a bottle of scotch and two boxes of cigars. The items were not personal so he decided to hang on to them for future use. The other package addressed to him had the exact same thing in it. Then he remembered asking the late Battalion Sergeant Major about acquiring some good cigars and scotch for him. Apparently he came through but he would never know it.

McNeil took the scotch and cigars to his sleeping area and stowed them in a bag.

# MCNEIL

## ONGJIN PENINSULA
## NEW 1/5 BATTALION

**Chapter 12**
**15 Nov 1950**

The days following the 16 Oct disaster, the loss of a battalion, were hectic and nerve racking for McNeil. He caught himself nipping from the scotch bottle far too often. It made him realize that the unreal situation in Korea and the unrealistic demands placed on a commander was maybe the reason the late Ltc. Winters was slowly crawling into the scotch bottle.

When he was a squad leader or a platoon sergeant, there wasn't so much to be concerned about. Even as a company commander, though he had more responsibility than a platoon sergeant, it wasn't near a feverish pace as it was now. If he had a full battalion staff and a headquarters company to take some of the load off his shoulders it would be much better. Now, some things fell through the cracks. One important thing that had slipped his mind was the **L O P Mission.** One lone man, a young lieutenant, was on an island doing an important job that should have been done by a squad of men. McNeil, in trying to rebuild a battalion and take care of the problems of four companies, had forgotten the mission. He had to suppose that division and the mike boat were keeping the man supplied but; assumptions were not a responsibility of a commander. A commander should know. What reminded him of the **L O P Mission** was a late night radio call. PFC Rodgers was on duty and he had not been briefed on the L O P Mission and had no idea what to do when the call came in. He copied down the strange set of numbers then woke up McNeil to ask him what he should do.

When McNeil saw the numbers PFC Rodgers had copied down he knew instantly what they meant, he had the number code memorized. 'Enemy activity on the south beach of hill 427'. "I must apologize for not bringing you up to date on this PFC Rodgers but we'll remedy that oversight. Right now go wake Corporal Willis."

McNeil knew what the procedure was up to this point but he had no idea who to call with the information. It was a bit demoralizing when a commander had to ask a corporal what to do.

Corporal Wills read the number codes, took the S O I and quickly wrote out a message, located the correct frequency on the radio, then made the call that would have planes in the air and on the way to the islands in minutes.

"I have to apologize Willis because neither I nor Rodgers knew what to do. We'll remedy that come morning when you will brief both of us on the procedures."

"No problem sir." replied Willis as he rubbed his eyes and went back to his bed roll for more sleep.

There were still some attacks on the M L R but nothing serious. The attacks were more like probes to check the M L R defense for something bigger to come. It could be that another major artillery barrage was in the works.

McNeil knew it was important for him to stay in touch with the companies and talk with the commanders. He made it a point to visit each company, tour the M L R and speak with the men every two or three days, time permitting. Nothing more was said by Captain Downs about the awkward situation when McNeil visited Able Company and McNeil never brought it up again. He had not received any paper work from Captain Downs and had no idea if he had done it or still planned to register a grievance. It could be that he decided to bypass battalion and go straight to division. McNeil would have to wait for the General's visit to find out.

What Capt. Downs had decided to was wait and see. He knew an almost impossible task had been laid on the young captain and when he failed, and without assets he had to fail, and being more experienced I'll step in and do things right. Probably get my gold leaf before I leave here.

The morning of 15 Nov 1950 dawned with a layer of frost on the ground but the sun came up and warmed the air up some. Everything that could be done had been done to establish a viable battalion with its integrity intact. McNeil wasn't about to have overworked men running around painting trees and rocks in preparation for a general officers visit. First there wasn't any paint and there was no extra manpower for such foolishness. Besides, this was a combat zone. McNeil had complied with his orders. He had a battalion up and operating, maybe not on all eight cylinders but operational just the same.

Late that evening of 15 Nov 1950 a message was received: 'Blue Stallion and party of seven to arrive at eleven hundred hours 16 Nov 1950 with transportation'.

McNeil had expected the general and possibly one, but seven? Just who was coming with him?

"Get a message to each company commander; "be prepared to take lunch with General Layton 16 Nov at noon," McNeil told Corporal Willis, "and confirmation requested upon receipt of message."

One of the things that had happened without McNeil knowing about it was that a 3/4 ton weapons carrier had been turned into a patrol vehicle.

The two men assigned as water truck drivers and motor vehicles mechanics had decided to convert a vehicle. They took a weapons ring from one of the nonoperational 6x6 truck and mounted it on a 3/4 ton truck. One of the fifty caliber machine guns SSgt. Anderson had found at Battalion was mounted on the ring. The two men, both privates, PVT Jose Mendez and PVT Billy Joe Hatfield, were very enterprising young men. Once they had the weapons carrier set up PVT Hatfield decided it would be nice to have a radio on the vehicle. Since there were several extra radios salvaged from battalion Corporal Wills helped them mount one on the truck.

The unauthorized vehicle came to McNeil's attention last week when a radio message came in from Abel Company that two sampans was sighted on the water acting strangely. "Strange in what way," McNeil asked?

"They are circling off shore with no visible signs of any fishing gear."

"If they turn to shore blow them out of the water," was his answer.

The after action message read; "two sampans sunk with about forty bodies in the water."the last part of the message must have been hard for Captain Downs to say but he did transmit it. "Thanks for the assist."

What assist McNeil wondered. He had sent nobody so who assisted? That was when he found out about the modified vehicle. When McNeil looked the modified vehicle over he decided to let the two men keep it. They were not lax in their duties and the vehicle had proven itself.

"Since you two men have seen fit to modify a vehicle without permission you have just earned some extra duty." the two men, PVT Jose Mendez and Billy Joe Hatfield thought they were in deep trouble until McNeil explained what the extra duty consisted of. "Since you two seem to have so much extra time on your hands you will take this vehicle and patrol both the shore lines each day. Report anything that looks out of place." he couldn't have made two men happier if he had handed them a bottle of whisky.

The morning of 16 Nov 1950 McNeil, like the boy scouts, wanted to be prepared. The message read that the general's party would have their own transportation but, what did they bring with them. Normally when the mike boat arrives it brings supplies. McNeil decided to be on the safe side and take two jeeps, the 3/4 ton and a 6x6 truck.

When the mike boat touched shore at 11 hundred hours the sight that McNeil saw was unbelievable. Two waxed and shiny MP jeeps rolled off the boat with antennas whipping the air. A one star general's flag decorated the front bumper of the second jeep. The four MP's, two to a jeep, one standing up and manning a machine gun, wore gleaming white helmets. Not steel pots but just the helmet liners which would barely stop a BB much less a real bullet. The only thing McNeil could see that was done right, in his combat conscious mind, was that the officers who accompanied General Layton were not all in the same jeep, they were split up between the two jeeps. And there were two officers, one a full Colonel and a Captain. I suppose the Colonel is my replacement and General Layton came along to make the transfer official, thought McNeil. I will be much relieved; sad at the loss of command, but very relieved.

McNeil could see there were supplies on the boat so he motioned for the trucks to move to the boat. The jeeps stopped and General Layton stepped out. McNeil rendered a salute and reported; "Sir Captain McNeil reporting to the Commander. Welcome to the Ongjin Peninsula."

General Layton returned the salute. "Don't you mean the 1/5st Battalion Commander, Captain," he asked.

"I suppose sir, but it's hard to get use to the title."

"I would like for you to meet my Chief of Staff, Colonel MacMasters."

McNeil turned to the man who had just walked up, rendered a salute, "very nice to meet you sir." Well maybe this isn't my replacement after all, thought McNeil

"I've heard much about you captain so it's nice to finally put a face to the name," said Col MacMasters after returning the salute.

"We brought you another officer which I suppose you can find a use for. Captain Donohue."

"Any and all assets are most welcome sir. Welcome to the Ongjin Peninsula Captain Donohue."

"Thank you very much Captain McNeil."

"Shall we get this show on the road?" asked General Layton.

"If I may General," said McNeil, "before we move from here several things need to be altered. Those white MP helmets, that rank flag on the jeep, and those antennas, are a target for a sniper. Did you men bring any different head wear?" he asked the MP Lieutenant.

"No sir. The white helmet is standard wear for MP's."

"I'm sure it's ok in a secure area but not here on the peninsula. I prefer you go bare headed rather than be a target. Please remove the General's flag and tie down those antennas."

"But sir, we need to remain in communication with General Layton aboard," protested the MP Lieutenant.

"I have all the communication required."

"Do as he says," spoke General Layton, "I'm sure Captain McNeil knows what he is doing.

"Why isn't your rank displayed Captain McNeil?" asked Col Mac Masters.

"Too many officers have been killed by exposing their rank. I have no plans of joining them." As McNeil was answering the question the 3/4 ton weapons carrier came flying out of the woods and parked in front of the lead jeep. Both the driver and gunner wore big grins. PVT Hatfield was at the wheel and PVT Mendez was standing up in the weapons ring manning the fifty caliber gun.

"And what is that?" asked General Layton pointing to the strange vehicle.

"That sir will be our escort with both weapons and communications. That vehicle patrols the shore lines of the peninsula looking for anything out of the ordinary. Just a few days ago, I'm sure you saw the report Sir, it blew away a couple of sampans loaded with North Koreans who were trying to land behind us. It's hard enough fighting one front with limited assets much less having to fight two fronts."

"I believe I do remember reading that report," said General Layton, "and that subtle remark about assets didn't go unnoticed. Are we ready to move out Captain McNeil?"

"Let me bring my jeep up sir," said McNeil motioning to PFC Rodgers who was waiting a few yards to the rear.

"I believe I'll ride with Captain McNeil," said General Layton as he climbed in the Raider Six jeep and removed his helmet. McNeil, in the rear seat, motioned for PFC Rodgers to lead off behind the wasp, as PVT Billy Joe Hatfield called his creation. When asked why the name wasp, he replied, because it stings.

"Rank doesn't scare you does it Captain McNeil?" asked General Layton after they were on the move. The wasp led off and soon it was out of sight but occasionally it darted across the road and disappeared in the trees.

"I respect rank and the man wearing it, but no sir, "rank doesn't scare me."

A very quick and to the point answer, thought General Layton, I like that. "In your honest opinion, Captain McNeil, what caused the loss of the battalion? I mean other than the artillery."

"Sir, I don't care to speak ill of those who have passed on because they are unable to defend themselves but, I approached Ltc. Winters with the idea of moving the companies forward because I felt they had been in one location long enough that the North Korean artillery had their coordinates. The move saved them. At the same time I asked Ltc. Winters if he had considered moving the battalion. He declined to move it."

When they reached the berm where the companies had been set up, McNeil spoke, "Sir, this is where the companies M L R was. As you can see the area is tore up by artillery rounds."

"From what I'm seeing here I believe you were right, there wouldn't have been much left of the companies if they had stayed in place."

"Moving is something I would like to discuss with you later Sir, among other things, that is if you have time?"

"If that, 'among other things' is about men I can tell you that I had a hard time talking 8th Army out of Captain Donohue. There just aren't enough replacement personnel coming in, even though we have been promised some in the near future."

"Yes sir, I can understand the lack of personnel but didn't I hear that some units from Hawaii were being shipped in plus some National Guard units were being activated?"

"You heard correctly but those units are assigned to 8th Army to help drive the North Korean back and keep them from taking Seoul and Pusan. If any Guard units are activated they will come as a unit and be assigned where needed."

As the small convey continued moving toward the companies and battalion area the wasp kept up its surveillance and was seldom out of sight of the convey for long. The stink of dead bodies still floated in the air but the men on the peninsula had long ago gotten use to it. McNeil saw General Layton wrinkle up his nose at the odor as they passed through the old battle field.

When the four jeeps pulled up in front of the new 1/5st Infantry Battalion tents General Layton got out and was joined by Col. MacMasters. The MP's were self-conscious being without hats but they flanked the general with their rifles ready. General Layton stopped and studied the set up then spoke, "Mac, what is wrong with this picture?"

"Well everything seems to be in place but that's a poor excuse for a guidon staff plus I don't see the American flag displayed."

"My thoughts exactly. Make a note to get a proper staff and flag sent here."

The first place General Layton visited was the medic's. SSgt. Hicks stood up and reported. "At ease sergeant," spoke General Layton

"Sir," spoke McNeil, "SSgt. Hicks was Baker Company medic until I saw a greater need for him at battalion. Each company has a trained medic but SSgt. Hicks assists where he is needed in addition to operating the battalion hospital."

"No one being treated today SSgt. Hicks?" asked General Layton

"No sir."

"How many men on sick call today?"

"Only four men sir. All returned to duty."

Sfc Anderson was next. The general asked many questions which Sfc Anderson had ready answers for. "Sir," spoke McNeil, "Sfc Anderson, like many of us, wears more than one hat. In addition to operating the battalion supply he looks after the companies needs plus he handles ration distribution and oversees motor maintenance. He's also the acting Battalion S-4."

When General Layton walked into the Battalion CP tent Tiny was there and he called attention. The three men there stood up at attention. MSg Brockman the acting Battalion Sergeant Major plus Baker Company 1st sergeant, PFC Rodgers the Battalion clerk, and Corporal Willis the radio operator. "At ease men," said General Layton as he turned to McNeil, "this is your battalion staff?"

"Yes sir, plus the two men you saw driving the weapons carrier who are also the motor mechanics plus they make sure we have plenty of water. MSg Brockman is the acting Battalion Sergeant Major in addition to being the first Sergeant of Baker Company. PFC Rodgers and Corporal Willis work together and trade off duties. I also wear several hats. I'm still the commander of Baker Company plus the designated 1/5st Battalion commander. I also have the duties of S-1 - S-2 - and S-3. I assist Sfc Anderson with the duties of the S-4."

"Just exactly how many men are assigned to the battalion?" asked Col MacMasters.

"Including myself, nine sir."

"You manage an entire battalion and administer to four companies with the help of only nine people?" asked Col MacMasters.

"The extraordinary situation we find ourselves in calls for unconventional methods of operations to overcome the seemingly impossible tasks."

"All of you are spread pretty thin aren't you?" asked General Layton

"Yes sir but we get the job done."

"Does anyone here not wear more than one hat?"

"Most of us wear more than one hat. The mission comes first sir and everyone fills in where they are needed."

"I understand there was one survivor of the previous battalion?"

"Yes sir there is. Corporal Wills."

General Layton walked over and shook Corporal Willis' hand and spoke to him but not loud enough for the others to hear. Willis just nodded his head.

"The furnishings are sparse, no desks and no file cabinets. How do you keep track of day to day activities Capt. McNeil?" asked Col. MacMasters while General Layton was speaking to Willis.

"We were unable to salvage much from the heavy destruction to the battalion. The tables came from the mess tent and we keep up with daily activity by recording everything in these ledgers."

"I believe it's about time we sampled some food," said General Layton after speaking with Corporal Willis.

"Yes sir, right this way," said McNeil as he lead the general and party out of the tent. The Company Commanders were waiting outside so McNeil had to stop and introduce each to the general.

SSgt. Leeks had set up a table under a tree and he had set out silverware, coffee cups and a pitcher of hot coffee. "Sir," spoke McNeil, we are short-handed here so each man gets his own food. My policy is that no officer or NCO eats until all the men have eaten. They eat in shifts so some are always on the line. The first shift is finished so we can get in line. If you gentlemen will pick up a tray and follow me?"

With Captain Donohue and the MP Lieutenant there were eight officers seated at the two pushed together tables. More officers in one place than McNeil had seen since he arrived on the peninsula. As soon as the party sat down McNeil saw the wasp ease up to the M L R and get into position. No one else seemed to notice. This was leisure time and no business was discussed. General Layton told a couple of jokes and asked some personal questions of the men to put them at ease.

When everyone finished eating a couple of the cooks came over to take away the silverware and trays and to bring a fresh pot of coffee. The three enlisted MP's were eating a few feet away but with their eyes on the general. General Layton filled his cup with fresh coffee and as he started to take a sip he thought of something and leaned toward McNeil. The cup of coffee he was holding shattered and the General and Col MacMasters were splattered with coffee. Even though it was sudden and unexpected most of the men assigned to the peninsula were use to rifle fire. Those who were not dropped what they had in their hands and fell to the ground. As soon as the sound of the short fired reached the ears of the men the sound of the fifty caliber drowned out everything. When it went silent McNeil, who was still seated, Spoke, "the danger is past now. You men can stand up."

"Without a doubt I would say that bullet was aimed at me," said General Layton as he brushed coffee from his shirt.

"Those stars make a fine target sir," commented McNeil as he picked up his cup and took a sip. Everyone started to hide their rank insignia by emulating McNeil. He simply tucked his collar inside his shirt. "But not to worry sir that fifty took care of the sniper."

"Does that happen often?" asked Col MacMasters as he also brushed dirt from his shirt.

"Not as often as it once did. The two last Baker Company Commanders were hit by sniper fire."

"Sir," said McNeil when they finished eating and was walking back to the battalion CP, "may I ask a favor of you?"

"You may ask but I can't guarantee anything."

"Those two young men who drive the weapons carrier, one is from Porto Rico and the other is from the back woods of Alabama. It would mean a lot to them if you could see your way clear to promote them and shake their hands. They really deserve a promotion."

"I believe we can do that. Mac, get some orders cut for the promotion of those two men."

Col. MacMasters went straight to PFC Rodgers and they got started on the orders. "Sergeant Brockman," said McNeil, "round up Mendez and Billy Joe and get them in here fast."

"Yes sir," replied Tiny as he left the tent in a hurry.

"While we wait we have another promotion to consider. Where is Sergeant Anderson?"

McNeil motioned for Willis to go get him. "He'll be here shortly sir."

"Then while we wait for Sergeant Anderson we have another promotion to make. In this, Police Action, as the powers to be calls it, we have some unusual things taking place. In some cases where there aren't enough officers, NCO's are in command. The 1/5st Infantry Battalion and companies are lucky to have all officers commanding. One of those is a 2nd Lieutenant. Is he available?" The company commanders had entered the Battalion CP and stood at the rear of the group.

"Yes sir he is. Lt. Johnson, front and center, " called out McNeil.

"The orders please Mac, and you young man get those butter bars off and pin on these silver ones. I hear you have done an excellent job so keep up the good work. Congratulations. Lt. Johnson."

"Thank you very much sir," said Lt. Johnson as he stood with his mouth agape.

"You can close your mouth now Lt. Johnson and congratulations," said McNeil as Johnson stepped back.

"I see Sergeant Anderson has arrived so let's continue," said General Layton. "I have a request for you to be elevated to a Warrant Officer position Sergeant Anderson. How do you feel about that?"

"I feel that I have the experience and training to handle such a position. I'm ok with it sir," spoke Sfc Anderson who had moved forward and stood in front of General Layton.

"Mac, read the orders and let's move along. Just an abbreviated version will do."

When the orders were read and passed to Anderson along with a set of Warrant officer Bars General Layton shook his hand and wished him luck. When, now Warrant Officer Anderson stepped back McNeil spoke, "congratulation Chief Anderson. Now go get those bars pinned on a shirt and get back here."

"Are those the two men you spoke of?" asked General Layton when he saw PVT Mendez and PVT Hatfield enter the tent behind Tiny.

"Yes sir it is," answered McNeil as he motioned for the two men to come forward, "you two go and report to the general."

No one could understand what the two really said since one had an accent and the other had a southern drawl so thick it could be cut with a knife but apparently it satisfied General Layton. When PVT Hatfield said Sir, it came out sounding like SUR and he pronounced the word General as Genial. PVT Mendez's speech wasn't much better but at least he was understood. Sir and General came out as Saar and Generail. "As I understand it you two have been doing an outstanding job of patrolling the shore lines and let me add my thanks for taking care of that sniper today. Your work has earned each of you a promotion. Congratulations," said General Layton as he shook each man's hand then handed them a set of PFC strips and the order. Both men saluted, did a sharp about face and was about to leave when McNeil stopped them.

"Congratulations PFC Mendez and PFC Hatfield," said McNeil shaking each man's hand, "now you have about thirty minutes to get those stripes sewn on and ready to go back to the landing." They both saluted McNeil and when he returned the salute PFC Mendez and PFC Hatfield left the tent with big smiles. They went two happy men.

"Now," said General Layton looking at the officers gathered in the tent, "is there any more business to discuss, more promotions to be made, problems?"

McNeil looked at Captain Downs who was looking at the ground. Now is your time to speak up, it's now or never, thought McNeil. Captain Downs didn't speak and none of the others had anything to say. "There is one more bit of business to take care of then Captain McNeil and I have some things to discuss in private. Captain McNeil would you step forward?"

McNeil took his place in front of General Layton and saluted, wondering what this was all about.

"Stand at ease. An almost impossible task was placed on this young man's shoulders, to rebuild a battalion from on hand assets. I wasn't sure he could accomplish the task but as one can see he did it. Not a complete battalion but a working one. None of the other battalions have a complete staff either because they have taken a page from the book of a deceased commander and stripped the battalions to put men on the line. This man received an order, and without questioning it, did what he was told to do. All of you men, as far as that goes, all units in Korea, are laboring under a very difficult situation. We know how important this peninsula is to the North Koreans but you men have kept it out of their hands. Don't expect any help from R O K for a while because they are still reeling from the sudden attacks in the cities of South Korea. Knowing what I know now, when I leave here I'll go back to General Walker and ask for more men. If I could meet with General MacArthur I would beg for more men, if I thought it would do some good. The man power just isn't available right now. I do want you men to know that you haven't been forgotten out here on the peninsula. Mac, would you read an abbreviated version of the order please?"

"Attention to orders. Department of the Army special order 342 dated 20 Oct 1950. Captain Charley R. McNeil, serial number 0-637813 is promoted to the rank of Lieutenant Colonel with date of rank 20 Oct 1950. The same order assigns Lieutenant Colonel McNeil as Commander of the 1/5 Infantry Battalion."

McNeil was flabbergasted; surprised to the point he almost let his mouth drop open. He had hoped the orders would relieve him of his present position and allow him to go back to Baker Company Commander. Why not put Capt. Downs in this position, or possibly the new Captain, Capt. Donohue. How much time in grade does the new Captain have? I'll have to check on that. Why is this happening to me? I've just been promoted to Lieutenant Colonel and at such a young age and with little experience? I certainly hope General Layton's confidence in me isn't wasted.

"Here are a set of silver oak leafs and the order," said General Layton, "and congratulations."

"My congratulations also," added Col. MacMasters.

"I'm speechless," said McNeil, "but thank you both." He was reeling with the shock of what just happened. There was no chance of getting out of the almost impossible situation now because he had the rank for the job and he had the job, on orders.

"Time is moving fast so if you men have nothing further Colonel McNeil and I .have some business to discuss," said General Layton.

The first to congratulate McNeil was Lt Johnson. They were once corporals together now each of them were officers. Lt. Hampton congratulated McNeil and followed Johnson out the tent door. Captain Downs waited until last. "That should have been my promotion," he said in a low voice to McNeil.

"You had your chance to protest but it's now too late. I sincerely hope we can work together Captain Downs, if not please ask for a transfer. If you will excuse me the general is waiting."

"I believe you said you wanted to discuss something with me," said General Layton after the men left the tent, "but before we start I would like a quick tour of the M L R. Before we do that lets get those silver oak leaves pinned on. Mac, give me a hand here," General Layton said as he started to remove the captain rank from McNeil's collar.

After the new rank was pinned on he replied, "Yes sir. This way please," said McNeil as he walked out of the CP. The MP escorts rushed to their jeeps but General Layton spoke, "not this time gentlemen."

"But sir we are not supposed to let you out of our sight," protested the MP Lieutenant.

"I feel sure I will be safe with both Ltc. McNeil and Col. MacMasters with me plus all those men on the line. You wait here," said General Layton as he climbed in the Raider six jeep.

"Any particular place or thing you wish to see sir?" asked McNeil as he drove up to the M L R.

"Just drive the line and I'll tell you where to stop." said General Layton.

By now word had spread that a General Officer was in the area so when General Layton called stop and he got out of the jeep the man on the berm came to attention and waited for the general without saluting. General Layton walked up and spoke to the man and took a look over the berm. When he got back in the jeep he spoke, "that young man tells me he is not allowed to salute officers while on the line per your orders, why"

"That's something else snipers look for. If a man is saluted then the sniper knows he has an officer in his sight."

"I see. Stop here for a minute," said General Layton. He again got out of the jeep and walked up to the line and spoke to the man.

When General Layton was back in the jeep and McNeil drove on down the line he called out to stop near where the mortar tube was set up. "Is that the tube I read about in one of your reports? Is it functional?"

"That's the one sir and yes it does function. We have sent many rounds back to the enemy with it and stopped several fire fights."

"I believe I've seen enough Col. McNeil. Good men you have here. They obey orders very well. One thing I must ask though is why do the men have more than one weapon? If I know my rifles they have Russian Ak-47's. Where did they come by those weapons?"

"I'm a student of Sun Tzu sir. An Army must rely on native people for assistance. It also teaches that whenever possible enemy supplies and weapons and ammo should be used to ease the burden on one's own supply system."

"I'm aware of the teachings of Sun Tzu but that doesn't answer my question. I'm sure there are no weapons like that issued to men in the division."

"In my younger and ignorant days as a corporal I went out and took those weapons off dead North Koreans along with the ammo. I also brought back grenades and tins of food to supplement the men's rations. The mortar was being used by the North Koreans to harass my people so I took it and turned it on them."

"I see you are a Ranger," said Col. MacMasters, "but weren't you taking a big chance going out on the battle field alone?"

"One man can move quieter and faster than several. Speed and stealth gets the job done."

"I would hope that you have out grown such temptations by now," said General Layton.

"Yes sir I have."

"Let's head back to the CP."

When McNeil stopped in front of the CP General Layton spoke, "I believe you said you had something to discuss with me?"

"Yes sir I do. Would you come inside so I can show you on the map sir?"

"You don't mind if Mac joins us do you? I like to have him near to keep notes and remind me later what was said and any promises I may have made."

"Not at all sir."

"I have four items to discuss sir," said Col. McNeil when the three were gathered at the big map. "The first is the stench of the battle field. It's not so bad now with the weather cooling down but when it's hot the odor is almost unbearable. We have to sleep and eat with the odor. I don't have the assets to form a burial detail but I do have a solution which brings up my next item. I have no idea what assets are on hand in Korea but I'm sure that somewhere there is an idle light Engineer Company, either on hand or due in, that needs something to do. If I could have them for a while they could very quickly bury the dead using machinery and relieve us of the odor. The other use I would have for them, with your approval sir, is to clear a one hundred yard wide area across the peninsula this side of the 38th parallel. We are fighting a delayed action here by being so far from the 38th parallel. If we could move forward and have a clear field of fire we could stop any border crossing. Right now there are several abandoned villages between us and the 38th parallel that the North Koreans can reach and hold up in. In fact the weapons carrier took out a squad of North Koreans a week ago that were camped in one of the villages.

"With your permission sir I would like to move the battalions forward after the Engineers finish, if any are available, and establish a base camp at the 38th parallel."

"Hmm," said General Layton as he studied the map, "give me your thoughts Mac?"

"McNeil has made some good point's sir. It's not humane to leave bodies on the battle field. Though enemies they are still humans and need to be buried. What about marking the burial sites, have you given any thought to that?"

"I suppose we can mark each burial site with a marker as the Army Engineers did in Europe after WW2. Something like, 'several hundred North Koreans buried here'."

"That should work just in case the North Koreans decide they want to recover and identify the bodies once this police action is over. The idea of moving forward bears merit. I can see McNeil's point about better defending the border if the battalion was at it rather that far behind it."

"Let me look into the matter further McNeil and I'll get back to you on that. But, no matter if your request to move the battalion is approved or not, I want it understood that there will be no border crossing for any reason. Your orders are to only fire across the 38th parallel if and when you are fired on. Have I your word on that?"

"Yes sir. I understand sir."

"I believe you said four items. What's next? And speaking of items, are you up on the L O P mission?"

"Yes sir. We get daily reports and the current man, Lt. Calloway is due to be replaced this month."

"Ok, what else is on your mind?"

"Winter is almost upon us sir. I haven't spent one here but I understand they can be cold. The men do not have proper winter clothes to remain on the M L R day after day without getting frost bite, or something more serious. Can something be done about getting them heavy winter clothing?"

"That very same thing was brought up in a staff meeting sir," said Col. MacMasters.

"Has anything been done about it?" asked General Layton.

"Not to my knowledge sir."

"Make a note and let's see what can be done. Now let me recap. You would like to get a light engineer company over here for a two- fold job; First to bury the dead then to clear a strip along the 38th parallel. Is that about it?"

"That's it sir."

"I can't make you any promises but I'll check around and see what is available. Anything further Col. McNeil?"

"Nothing further sir I've taken up far too much of you time as it is."

"Then let's get moving Mac, I have a meeting in, what?"

"An hour and a half sir."

"That should give us enough time to get back."

The mike boat was waiting when the small convey reached the beach.

Again General Layton congratulated Col. McNeil and asked him to keep up the good work. As he was about to get on the mike boat he stopped and turned around, "Col. McNeil, you can expect a shipment of food for the Thanksgiving meal."

"Thank you very much sir. That will please the men."

"For what it's worth sir, I think you made the right decision in reference to McNeil," said Col. MacMasters after the mike boat left shore, "though young he seems to have a natural ability to command."

"What? Oh yeah," answered General Layton who was in deep thought, "He certainly came up with some good ideas didn't he?"

"Yes he did. I can't believe that Captain Downs didn't speak up. You gave him every opportunity to protest both the promotion and assignment of McNeil."

"It's sad to think that a man has reached this point in his Army career but won't speak up to defend himself. I don't believe he could stand the stress of taking over a battalion."

"I would say his career is about over."

"Mac, about that engineer company. I know one is due in tomorrow. Remind me to speak to General Walker about borrowing it. If this idea of McNeil's pans out maybe we should think about clearing a strip all along the 38th parallel on the main land, from coast to coast. I don't believe General MacArthur is correct in his assessment that we'll be home by Christmas. I think we are here for the long haul. Let's do what we can for the men. And don't let me forget to look into the winter clothes thing."

It had been overcast most all day and before the mike boat reached the mainland it started raining.

# McNeil

## Ongjin Peninsula

**Chapter 13**
**18 Dec 1950**

The rain that fell that day turned into sleet before night fall. The cold days of winter had set in and there was no sign that the men in Korea would be home by Christmas. Snow was on the ground the next day and seldom did the temperature get above freezing during the next several days.

Lt. Calloway had been replaced on the island by Lt. Hampton of Dog Company. Lt. Calloway was now Dog Company Commander.

McNeil had some good commanders and he didn't want to change them so he made the decision to keep Captain Donohue in the Battalion to assist him. He spoke with Captain Donohue because he was not one to assign a person where he could not be beneficial to the good of the battalion. If a man is not somewhat happy then he won't do a good job. Even though this was war time, happiness was not a factor to be considered, yet McNeil thought a man should know why he was being assigned to a position. "Do you have any command time Captain Donohue?" McNeil asked one day after the General's visit and he and Captain Donohue had time for coffee.

"Yes sir. I had a year before coming over here."

"I realize combat command time on your records would look good but I have a greater need for you here in battalion. Later I'll see about moving you to one of the companies."

"What would you have me doing sir?"

"The time will go on your records as staff time, but mostly you'll be taking some of the pressure off me. I don't have the luxury of an XO so you will be filling that position, among many more."

"Sir, if you think I am needed here then no complaints from me. I have to say though that I have no experience at staff work."

"We'll take care of that. I never leave a man in the cold. You will be working in all the staff sections."

General Layton came through with the heavy winter clothes so the men had some protection from the cold as they guarded the 38th parallel.

A sergeant, an E-7, with four new men arrived shortly after the general's visit so McNeil assigned the sergeant, Sfc Biddle, as 1st Sergeant of Baker Company to relieve Tiny of some of his duties so he could better perform his duties at battalion. Five men are not much but McNeil, as he had said before, welcomed any warm body.

There was a shipment of food for the Thanksgiving meal just as General Layton had promised. That in itself was a great moral booster for the men.

Three days after General Layton's visit to the peninsula the 1/5th Infantry battalion received a radio call that an engineer company with equipment was headed for the peninsula. When McNeil met the company commander, a Captain Bronsky, he welcomed him and asked what the 1/5th Infantry Battalion could do to assist him.

"Colonel, we were told there wasn't much on the peninsula so we brought all the assets we need with us," McNeil was told, "all we need is a place to set up camp and someone to show us what needs to be done and where to do it."

McNeil wasn't use to being called colonel so when someone used that title he had the urge to turn and see which colonel was present.

"Your people can set up anywhere at the rear of the battalion for now. The first order of business is to bury the bodies which you can see on the battle field. When you are ready I'll show you the next project. How long do you estimate the burial to take you?"

"From what I can see I estimate two or three day's work sir. Will we be putting up any markers?"

"Yes, dig a hole and push the bodies in and cover them, then place a marker at the site."

McNeil knew it was callous to bury bodies that way but no one knew who the North Koreans were and there wasn't time to try and identify them.

"Sir, I won't need all my men and equipment for this job so do you want to show me what else there is to do?"

"Get in the jeep and we'll go to the 38th parallel," said McNeil as he got in the jeep and picked up the mick, "raider six for wasp one. Come in wasp one."

"Wasp one."

"Meet me at the berm crossover between Baker and Charlie."

"Roger."

"Wasp one raider six coming up behind you," said McNeil a few minutes later, "run a recon ahead of me to the 38th."

"Roger raider six. Wasp moving."

"If I may ask sir what is this wasp?"

"A weapons carrier converted to carry a fifty. It's a mean machine and very effective. Once your men are working near the 38th I'll have one with you at all times because one never knows just what those North Koreans next move will be."

"I was wondering how my men would be able to work and guard themselves at the same time. And you did say the 38th Parallel?"

"I did. That's where we are headed now and where your next project will be. Have no fear captain it's all been taken care of. In fact the entire battalion and companies will be moving forward as soon as you start work up there. Once you finish burying the bodies I would suggest you think about moving up behind us. You do have a surveyor with you don't you?"

"One of the best."

"You'll need him to lay out the 38th parallel so we don't cross it. I don't want a border crossing incident."

When they reached what McNeil guessed to be the 38th Parallel he stopped the jeep well back from it. The wasp stopped further back with a commanding view of the 38th and the fifty was in constant motion sweeping the 38th. McNeil explained exactly what he wanted the engineers to do. "First, dig a hole, or holes, back a couple hundred yards and bury those bodies you see out there. There are South Korean Soldiers but there are so many of them and the bodies have deteriorated to a point that they can't be identified. Once you have removed the bodies clear an area across the peninsula from shore to shore from the 38th parallel back a hundred yards. Clear the strip of all vegetation and trees and push up a berm about five feet high at the south edge of the cleared strip." Nothing fancy McNeil told Captain Bronsky. "Just so there are no holes, mounds, trees or brush that the enemy can hide behind or in. Ever so many feet, that will have to be worked out; I want a guard tower built. Later there will be phone lines connecting each tower to a switch board. My plan is to man the towers twenty four hours a day then in case of an attack the other men will fill in between the towers in prepared fighting positions."

"I don't see any problem with what you want sir," said Captain Bronsky. "I'll get some of the equipment up here tomorrow and get started. As soon as the other project is completed I'll move the rest of the equipment and tents. I can't guess how long it will take here until we get started and see how fast the work goes."

The abandon villages scattered over the area worried McNeil. He had always thought they may be a place for any North Koreans to hold up or even store supplies, now that he had seen a couple on his way to and back from the 38th they bothered him even more. McNeil stopped the jeep and reached for the mick. "Wasp one join up with Raider six jeep." Shortly wasp one skidded to a stop beside the jeep. Wasp two what's your twenty?" "Wasp two is patrolling west shore line." Lt Johnson had asked permission to convert one of his weapons carrier's into a wasp and McNeil gave his permission.

"Wasp two pick up two men at Charlie Company. Wasp one go back and pick up two men at Baker Company. You wasps will do a search of all villages, every house. Copy?"

"Wasp two copies and is moving."

"Wasp one copies." The wasp one vehicle sped away heading back to the MLR.

"Raider six for raider five."

"Go raider six, Raider five here," came the voice of Captain Donohue.

"Notify Charlie and Baker Companies to supply two men each to the wasps for a patrol. Copy?"

"Copy Raider six," Replied Capt. Donohue.

"That man in the wasp does have a way with words doesn't he Colonel?" commented Captain Bronsky after the wasp left them. "How do you understand what he says?"

"We have gotten use to it. He's just a good old boy from the deep south."

Nothing was heard from the wasps until McNeil had dropped off Captain Bronsky and returned to the battalion CP.

"No activity at first village. Wasp two headed for next one."

"Signs of activity at center village. Wasp one checking."

"Wasp one taking fire. One man wounded. Two POW's down four surrendered."

McNeil had been listening to the reports. "Wasp one this is Raider six. Search, secure, and blind fold the POW's. How bad is your wounded?

"Through and through to the leg. First aid administered."

"Hold position for Wasp two. Break, Break, Wasp two join Wasp one and assist."

"Wasp two moving."

"POW's secured and searched."

"Has Wasp two joined you yet?"

"In sight."

"Have Wasp two continue search. Wasp one transport wounded and POW's to CP."

"Roger."

"Rodgers, tell SSgt. Hicks we have a wounded man inbound."

"Yes sir."

"Willis, contact Blue Stallion commo. Need mike boat to transport four POW's immediately."

"On it sir," replied Willis as he encoded the short message and turned to the big radio to make the call.

McNeil, Sergeant Hicks and one of his men were standing by when Wasp one arrived at the CP. "Sergeant Hicks," said McNeil, "the mike boat is on the way can you handle the wounded or should we evacuate him?"

"I'll check him over and let you know sir," he replied as he and his man started moving the man from the truck onto a stretcher.

"Colonel," said the man, Pfc Holden, "I would rather remain here. I trust Sergeant Hicks. The wound isn't all that bad, just stings."

"We'll wait and see what Sergeant Hick's diagnosis is. But I can't blame you," said McNeil, "I wouldn't want to be evacuated from this tropical paradise either." Pfc Holden was smiling at the comment as he was carried to the hospital tent.

"Good job you two," said McNeil to PFC Mendez and PFC Hatfield. Now get the POW's to the landing and on the mike boat. Report in when that's accomplished. Captain Donohue will ride with you so wait for him."

McNeil went back into the CP to tell Captain Donohue of his decision for him to accompany the POW's. He was just a bit afraid that Billy Joe might get a bit trigger happy and the POW's wouldn't reach the boat, alive that is.

Wasp two was on the radio when McNeil went into the CP. "What's their status Willis?" asked McNeil.

"They located a stash of supplies and weapons in one of the houses. They want to know what to do with it."

"Tell them to load it and transport it to battalion CP. Rodgers, I need Mr. Anderson. Would you locate him for me?"

"On the way sir."

"Yes sir?' asked Warrant Officer Anderson as he entered the CP behind Rodgers.

"Wasp two is inbound with a load of enemy supplies. Get one or more of your people and get the Wasp unloaded so it can return to patrol."

"Yes sir," replied Mr. Anderson as he turned and left the CP.

When Wasp two stopped in front of the CP it was quickly unloaded by Mr. Anderson, his two men and the two men from Charlie Company. McNeil spoke to the driver of Wasp two. "Good job men. First, get those two men back to Charlie Company. Next catch up with that engineer equipment you hear moving up to the 38th. Stay with them and provide security as long as they work. Under no circumstances are you to fire across the border unless you are fired on. Return fire only after receiving permission from me. You protect yourselves and the engineers from any border crossing North Koreans. Do you understand?"

"We understand sir."

"You are unloaded so move out."

"What have we here?" McNeil asked Mr. Anderson after Wasp two left.

"There are six AK-47's with several cases of ammo for them.. Several cases of grenades and ammo for a mortar, plus rations, but I have no idea what they are."

"Get the rations to SSgt. Leeks. He'll use what he can of them. Divide the ammo, both Ak-47 and mortar, and grenades between Baker and Charlie Companies. Use any vehicle."

The companies had been alerted for a move out so they, knowing what to expect this being their third move, were packed and ready for the signal the evening of 3 December 1950. This would be the last forward move of the 1/5th Infantry Battalion since they would be on the 38th parallel and camping at the border.

The men of the 1/5th Infantry Battalion spent a cold night but everyone was up and ready well before daylight with breakfast over. It was three weeks before Christmas when the men crossed the berm and as usual Ltc. McNeil moved with his men taking the lead as they spread out and moved on line. Captain Donohue brought up the rear with all vehicles. It was a coordinated move and all four companies were instructed to be on the alert and check all abandoned houses in each village they came to.

Because of the distance from the current location to the 38th Parallel it took them most all day to reach the new location and set up operations.

For more than two weeks now, after the move, there was little action from the North Koreans other than small probing attacks. That worried McNeil. What was even more worrisome was the fact that no encounter was made with any enemy during the move. McNeil had expected, and alerted the companies, to meet some resistance during the move. Possibly the only North Koreans this side of the 38th had been captured, or killed. Just what are they up to, he asked himself several times over the next few days.

The North Koreans have been far too quiet so maybe we can expect something during the Christmas holiday time, not that there would be much celebration going on. Division did come through with turkeys and all the extras for Christmas dinner and for that I, and I'm sure the men, are thankful. But here it's near Christmas time and no word about going home. I suppose General MacArthur's speech about being home for Christmas was just a wild guess with no facts.

The men and machines of the triple duce engineer company that Captain Bronsky had sent forward were working hard. All the bodies had been removed and buried by the time the entire battalion was settled in. The area in front of Dog Company was finished except for a couple of guard towers. Once the triple duce had made camp the entire company and all machinery went to work.

During the time the engineer people were working there had been only an occasional shot fired at them from across the border. No one was hit and no machinery was damaged. It was as if the North Koreans were trying to provoke a fire fight. Maybe cause a border incident.

It stayed cold enough that the frozen turkeys sent over for Christmas dinner stayed frozen. The weather would warm up to the high thirties then it would snow and the temperature would drop back down. The men were cold and the only consolidation was that the North Koreans were cold also. The triple duce Engineer Company with all their equipment and men available in one place was able to work much faster and complete the strip clearing and berm building much faster. By Christmas Eve they were working in front of Able Company.

The Engineer people pushed down enough trees to build the twenty four guard towers; that is four posts to support the tower and a five foot high log front to absorb bullets. Other materials were sent to the peninsula to complete the towers. The towers were not too high, the bottoms were just a bit higher than the top of the berm, but each required three additional sides to protect the guards from the elements plus roof, steps, and a door.

After General Layton's visit it seemed that whatever was requested, within reason, was granted. Each request sent in by Mr. Anderson was accompanied with a justification. Either warehouses were being emptied or the supply line was operational.

It seemed that the mike boat came every day with a load of supplies. Rolls of commo wire which had never been used on the peninsula. Field phones to connect each tower, six towers per company, plus five small switchboards, one for each company plus one for battalion; Binoculars for each tower plus one for each commander, thirty caliber machine guns, plus ammo, for the towers. Small space heaters were received for each tower so the guards could stay warm while on duty. There were larger heaters for all the tents. Tables and chairs for the mess tents so the men could eat inside and out of the harsh cold. McNeil altered some of his earlier orders and allowed cots for the men so they could sleep off the cold ground. His justification was that the only move from here would be off the peninsula. Where the battalion and companies were set up would be home for an unspecified length of time.

He changed his policy about men on the line now that the towers were complete. He required two men to a tower and each tower to be manned twenty four hours a day plus roving patrols. In case of need the other men would be called for to man the fighting positions. Since both Able and Dog companies had the responsibility of coast watch McNeil allowed them to modify their 3/4 ton weapon carrier to a wasp so they could better patrol their area of responsibility. That gave the battalion a total of four of the modified weapons carriers.

Two days before Christmas a small group of men came over on the mike boat. Though small in number, and it would take many more to bring the battalion up to strength, the twenty men were most welcome. McNeil had decided to only allow one promotion per month per company to keep up morale. Dog Company lost its clerk, due to an emergency leave so Pfc Rogers was sent to replace him, but not before McNeil promoted him to Corporal.

The lack of activity of the North Koreans still worried McNeil. They had to see and know what was happening along the 38th parallel, he reasoned, so why didn't they try and stop it? Some artillery and mortar rounds would have destroyed some equipment and slowed down the berm building. A concentration of small arms fire would have taken out some men and really slowed down the operation. What are they waiting for, a Holiday? Maybe that's it? Since it's been so long since we've had any action maybe the North Koreans think we have been lulled into a sense of relaxation, let our guard down. Maybe Christmas is the day they have chosen to hit us?

Even though McNeil had the men in a high state of alert Christmas came and went without a single incident. There was turkey and all the trimmings, and even two cans of beer for each man who wanted it.

The mail sack was extra heavy with letters and cards for the men plus several of the men received packages from home. There were several copies of the Stars and Stripes Newspaper in the mail sack which was received with great delight by the men because it would give them an idea of what was happening in other places in Korea. The item that the paper headlined didn't mean much to some but McNeil read it very carefully. Lieutenant General Walton H. Walker, the commander of the 8th Army in Korea, was killed, but not by bullets in battle. He was killed in a jeep accident the day before Christmas Eve, December 23 1950. For such a highly decorated general a jeep accident wasn't a very flattering way to die on the battlefield was McNeil's thought.

The day after Christmas orders arrived promoting the lieutenants to captains. Lieutenants, Johnson, Calloway, and Hampton were now captains. Lt. Hampton would have to wait until his return from the island to receive his promotion. Captain Allgood, a young captain, arrived with the promotion orders. He would take over Baker Company which would relieve McNeil of some of his responsibility.

Three days after Christmas Captain Bronsky drove up to battalion to report that he was finished with the project. "Would you care to inspect it?" he asked Ltc. McNeil.

"If it's all as good as what I see out there then I have no need to inspect your work. What happens to you now?"

"My boss will be flying over to inspect the work and take pictures. Then we wait and see."

"If I don't see you before you depart then let me say thanks for a job well done," said McNeil shaking Captain Bronsky's hand, "relay to your men my thanks also."

A day later a helicopter flew over, staying well back from the border, making several passes before it flew away. Two days later word came by radio from Wasp two that several large landing craft, Navy markings, had beached behind Able Company and the Engineers were loading their equipment on them. The 1/5st Infantry Battalion was once again alone on the peninsula.

Without the noise of the engineer equipment it was quiet and peaceful on the Ongjin Peninsula. No mortar, no artillery, and no small arms fire could be heard. Even though the peace and quiet was welcome it didn't help ease the worry of McNeil. Something had to happen, and soon.

# McNeil

## 38th Parallel
## Ongjin peninsula
## South Korea

**Chapter 14**
**30 Dec 1950**

The short cold days on the peninsula were made bearable by the heated tents even though some men had to brave the cold to perform their duties. It was a constant struggle to keep water from freezing but several submergible heaters helped with that problem so the men could have warm showers. Adapting to the harsh cold was a constant struggle.

As the final days of 1950 slowly passed still no attack occurred. Christmas came and went with no attack. McNeil constantly worried about the reason. Either he or Captain Donohue made a daily trip along the berm to speak with the commanders and the men on guard. It made the men feel better to know battalion wasn't camped around a heater while they were outside freezing.

The day before New Year's Eve 1/5st Infantry Battalion received a coded radio message. Willis decoded it and passed it to McNeil. It seemed that finally the intelligence service had some ears and eyes at work. **; be advised that North Korean elements are massing for an attack.** End of message. So, thought McNeil, my fear was not in-vane. They have picked the end of the year to launch an attack.

"Willis, can you set up a conference call to all commanders through the switch board?"

"Yes sir."

"Let me know when all four are on line." while he waited he sat down and wrote out what he wanted to say.

"All commanders are standing by sir," said Willis a few minutes later.

"This is Raider Six. Be advised that all battalion personnel are now in a state of high alert. Have all weapons checked and cleaned. Check all equipment. Since an attack is preceded by either an artillery or mortar barrage, or sometimes both, the safest place for people will be on the line. Tomorrow evening, immediately after dark, have all men on the line and ready. Keep the wasps back and ready to move to where the heaviest fighting occurs. The intelligence report indicates the attack should occur sometime during New Year's Eve. I suppose they believe thay will catch the men celebrating. But we know there is little to celebrate here."

"Is this going to be one of those false alerts like we had at Christmas?" broke in Captain Downs.

"It's better to be prepared with no attack than not be prepared and have an attack. We'll chalk up the Christmas alert to training. As I read the intelligence report it has a high degree of probability. That's all I have."

"Break it down for me Willis," said McNeil handing him the phone.

"Captain Donohue you heard so make sure battalion personal are ready and the wasps are serviced and have plenty of ammo."

McNeil took his M1 rifle to a table and broke it down, cleaned and oiled it, and reassembled it. He inserted a clip of ammo then filled every pocket on his ammo belt with clips of ammo. When the others saw what he was doing they decided it was time for them to do the same.

When McNeil finished cleaning his rifle he set it aside then stepped outside the tent and lit a cigar. Clouds had moved in and a few flakes of snow started falling.

"It's going to be one cold miserable night," stated Tiny who had stepped up beside McNeil.

"Think warm Tiny, think warm. It would be nice if they would plan their attacks on warm days, wouldn't it?"

"I suppose we'll do as we have always done Boss, we'll take what we can get and make do with what we have. We have come a long way haven't we Boss?"

"Yes we have Tiny," answered McNeil as he thought about it. In just over a year I've gone from a Private, learning to be a soldier, to a Lieutenant Colonel commanding a battalion in combat. If the North Koreans had waited a few months I would have been gone from here and out of the Army. But dwelling on what could have been doesn't help the situation now. I should have better than seven hundred men in the battalion but I have no headquarters company and a stripped down battalion and we are suppose to operate with less than eighty percent strength. Every one of those men is looking to me to keep them alive. I guess we'll find a way, somehow.

"Something on your mind Boss?" asked Tiny.

"Just doing some thinking Tiny. If you haven't done it yet notify SSgt. Leeks to plan for an early evening meal and let him know I expect him and his men on the line after dark. Are we missing anything Tiny?"

"I can't think of a thing Boss. I'll go see SSgt. Leeks now," said Tiny as he walked away turning up his coat collar to keep snowflakes off his neck.

Any and everything that could be done was done, now it was just waiting. The snow continued to fall during and after the evening meal and it was accumulating on the frozen ground. The temperature hovered around the freezing mark, everyone was thankful that the wind wasn't blowing to make it colder than it was. But then what are a few degrees one way or the other when one is cold.

The companies were set up a hundred yards back from the berm in the trees which provided some protection from the wind. Battalion was set up between and behind Baker and Charlie companies. The evening of New Year's Eve, 1950, after a hot meal, the men started moving from the units to take their place on the new MLR.

# MCNEIL

## 1/5 BATTALION M L R

### Chapter 15
### 31 Dec 1950

In many places around the world people were drinking and celebrating the end of 1950. On the Ongjin Peninsula and other places in South Korea it was a different story. There was nothing to celebrate and nothing to celebrate with. The only thing the men on the peninsula had to look forward to was hope, hope that they would be alive come daylight of the New Year.

McNeil was wondering if other units were in as bad a shape as the 1/5st Infantry Battalion. Most all of the trucks were jury rigged to keep them running. Those that were beyond repair were stripped of usable parts to keep others running. There were several abandoned truck hulks out behind what passed for the motor pool. Weapons were starting to wear out due to the excessive amount of rounds fired through them. Baker and Charley Company were luckier than most because of the AK-47's that McNeil had supplied them with. The men had been instructed to use the AK-47's first and save the M-1 ammo.

As soon as darkness fell, per instructions, men started to move to the M L R when their normal duties were finished. Everybody shouldered weapons, except for the medics who would have their hands full soon enough, and stood ready.

McNeil walked the line speaking to the men and giving encouragement to them. The mortar tube now had some experienced men so he spent a few minutes giving final instructions to them before he moved to a vacate position and looked over the berm. There was little to see but white. Before the Christmas alert McNeil had taken Tiny and a couple of men and instructed them on how to set up trip wires using grenades. He had advised the Company Commanders to do the same. They had set up twenty of them on the far side of the cleared strip in front of Baker Company. Using tin cans anchored in the ground the pin was pulled from a grenade and the grenade was eased into the can. A trip wire was tied to the grenade and stretched out on short stakes about six inches above ground. If and when someone caught their boot on the wire it would pull the grenade out of the can. The snow now hid all evidence that the booby traps existed. As McNeil looked out over the berm he couldn't see any of the stakes or the wires.

Just before midnight when most people would start counting down the seconds until the New Year mortar rounds started falling behind the M L R. The tubes were too far away for the men to hear the rounds leave the tubes but they could hear the rounds whistle as they passed overhead. Since there was nothing to shoot at yet all the men huddled down in their firing positions hoping the shrapnel would pass over their heads. The exploding rounds shook the ground and shrapnel bounced off vehicles and punched a few holes in the tents. There was a direct hit on one of the tents and a 6x6 truck. Few rounds fell directly on the M L R. The same thing that was happening at Baker and Charley companies was happening at the other two companies. The light from the exploding mortars could be seen plus the sound of the explosions echoed on the cold night air. So maybe, thought McNeil, they are dropping the rounds on the tents hoping to catch men sleeping, or celebrating?

Even though it was bitter cold in the fighting positions each and every man was glad that their commander had ordered them to the berm tonight. As the men huddled in the fighting positions they could see the mortar rounds dropping into the area where the tents were. It was on the minds of many that they would not have survived this night if they were still in the warm tents drinking and celebrating. Each man, new men and veterans', had the fear that a bullet or mortar round would have their name on it as they huddled in the firing positions and tried to make themselves as small as possible.

One mortar round fell on top of a guard tower but before anyone could get to it to check on the two men inside whistles and horns sounded and from across the border men could be heard shouting. The mortar barrage was being lifted and when McNeil looked over the berm he saw a sight he hoped he would never see again. It was unbelievable. So many times in the past the North Koreans had attacked in mass and it hadn't worked, yet they were doing it again. The difference now was the sheer number of men starting to cross the cleared area. It was a blunt nose wedge formation of about a hundred men leading and the rest were winged out on each side. The center of the wedge formation was directly between Baker and Charlie Companies.

The wasp moved into position and the fifties opened up and so did the thirty caliber machine guns in the towers. Soon the Ak-47's on the line opened up and bullets were flying outbound and inbound. The wasp gunner had to stop and change the hot gun barrel because they were burning through so many rounds. The mortar tube gunners did as McNeil had instructed them to do. First, they lowered the barrel and dropped several rounds behind the advancing hoard of North Koreans. McNeil had thought the rounds might catch some of the officers who were directing the charge. Then they raised the barrel and started dropping rounds in the middle of the formation of North Koreans. The mortar tube in Charlie Company was busy also. When the mass of North Koreans ran into the booby traps and the grenades started exploding they thought they were in a mine field and they froze. It was like shooting fish in a barrel for the men on the line. So many North Koreans were being killed that they were falling in heaps. Some of the braver North Koreans decided to use their fallen comrades as shields and they dropped down behind the bodies and started firing. The fifty caliber machine guns punched through dead bodies and killed the men hiding behind them. When the North Korean, the few left alive, decided it was time to retreat they were mowed down by a heavy barrage of fire as they ran for the safety of the trees on the North Korean side of the 38th parallel.

With the lull in the fighting McNeil decided to go check on the men in the tower that had its roof blown off. As he stepped up on the steps a round struck his helmet, punching through it and creasing his head knocking him out. As he started to fall three more rounds hit him. One in the left side of his chest, one just creased his left side, and one in his left leg. Those he did not feel since he was unconscious.

The bullet that hit McNeil's leg spun him around and he fell on his back in the snow. The snow was deep enough that the only part of McNeil that could be seen was his hands.

Tiny, never far from his Boss, saw McNeil fall and he jumped up and ran to him calling for a medic. Tiny wasn't sure if McNeil was alive or dead until he touched the side of his neck and felt a pulse. Sergeant Hicks heard Tiny yell that the Boss was down and he hurried to where Tiny was kneeling in the snow. First, Hicks pulled the helmet off McNeil's head and he could see a gash in the right side of his forehead. It was bleeding, which was good. Hicks surmised that that was why McNeil was unconscious. He washed away the blood and sprinkled some Sulphur powder on the gash before applying a small bandage. Next he brushed off the snow and pulled off McNeil's web gear and field jacket. He located the chest wound and a gash. Both wounds were bleeding and there was no exit wound that he could find for the bullet, the bullet was still in McNeil. Hicks again sprinkled Sulphur powder on both wounds and applied a bandage to stop the bleeding. Last was the leg. He ripped open McNeil's pants leg and he could see the bullet had passed through the lower thigh. He cleaned both holes and added the sulphur powder before wrapping the wounds with bandages.

Sergeant Hicks helper came by with a stretcher about the time Hicks was finished checking McNeil over. Working together, with the aide of Tiny they got McNeil onto the stretcher. "Tiny," said Sergeant Hicks, "looks like the Colonel is out of it for a long while. I suggest you locate Captain Donohue and tell him he is in Command. After you do that come by the medic tent so I can take a look at your arm."

"Why?" asked Tiny. "What's wrong with my arm?"

"There's blood on your coat sleeve so I must assume you have been wounded."

"I never felt a thing," replied Tiny as he raised his right arm so he could see what Hicks was talking about.

"Come by and we'll take a look at it. Right now I have to get the colonel to the hospital tent."

"Have you checked on those two men in tower B-12 Sergeant Hicks?" asked Tiny. McNeil had the towers numbered starting with number one at the shore line of Abel Company. Each tower had a letter and a number for quick reference.

"I have. They are more mad than hurt. A few splinters from the shattered wood and their machine gun is jammed."

Tiny located Captain Donohue further down the line toward Abel Company. He was staring out at the mass of dead bodies wondering why, and was thankful it didn't happen; the North Koreans didn't use artillery. If they had used it we may not be here now, or most of us wouldn't be. The noise of battle had died down now except for a few scattered shots. There were cries and moans out on the battle field from men who would never see a medic or receive help. When the men on the M L R saw movement they fired and put the man out of his misery. Captain Donohue jumped when he heard his name called. "Yeah, what? Oh, it's your Sergeant Brockman."

"Yes sir. As of now you have the battalion. The boss is down."

"Down! How bad is he?"

"Wounded four times and he was unconscious when he was taken to the medic's tent. I don't have further word on him yet."

"Thank you Sergeant Brockman." Now what would the colonel do, Captain Donohue asked himself. The first thing is to check on the men. But I don't have the time to go to each unit. The phone, use the phone. I'll get to the CP and check on them with the phone; that is if they are still working.

When he entered the CP he heard Corporal Willis on the phone getting information from the units. Good man, thought Captain Donohue as he loosened his coat to wait on the information.

When Willis hung up the phone Captain Donohue spoke, "do you have a complete status of personnel and equipment yet Corporal?"

"Not a full report sir. Two units are still checking. They will call me."

"Any status on the battalion yet?"

"I'm waiting for Colonel McNeil to bring me something."

"He won't be bringing anything, for a while that is. He was wounded and the medics are working on him. I'll go check on him and get a status from Sergeant Hicks. You man the phones until I get back."

The tent that served as the battalion hospital was a bee hive of activity when Captain Donohue entered it. Every medic plus some men who wasn't a medic was busy treating wounded men. None of them were of the battalion. "Sergeant Hicks," spoke Captain Donohue to get his attention, "how is the colonel?"

"We'll have to talk while I work sir," said Sergeant Hicks as he continued to treat a man's bullet wound, "at this time he's still unconscious. His vitals are strong except for his blood pressure which, understandably, is a bit low. He has a bullet lodged somewhere in the left chest. I feel he should be evacuated along with two more men come morning."

"I see. Can you give me a personnel status, Battalion only?"

"As it stands now, one K I A and four men W I A. You'll have to see Mr. Anderson about the equipment."

"Thank you Sergeant Hicks I'll get out of your way but keep the CP informed if there is a change in the condition of Colonel McNeil."

"Will do sir," replied Hicks as he finished one man and turned to another.

When Capt. Donohue returned to the CP Willis had all the information from the units and when Captain Donohue handed him the list of battalion casualties Willis added it to his list. Captain Donohue sat down to draft out a message to division so Willis could encode it. **Heavy mortar barrage, no artillery, on 1/5ˢᵗ Battalion. Repelled extreme large ground attack. Need mike boat at earliest convenience for K I A and W I A.**

After he finished drafting the message and checked it over he handed it to Willis. "Encode this and get it to division."

Tiny entered the CP with his right arm out of his coat sleeve sporting a bandage. "I see you are one of the walking wounded Sergeant Brockman. Bad?"

"Yes sir but its not bad sir."

"Will you be able to type?"

"I'll do what I can sir."

"Good because we have a lot of paper work to get done." He had all the information from Sergeant Hicks for the wounded and the purple hearts which he placed on the table near the typewriter so Tiny could get them typed up along with the casualty and equipment loss report. The units would be sending in their written reports shortly. What else needs to be done? Captain Donohue asked himself.

When the last man had been treated Sergeant Hicks stood up and stretched. He heard a low moan from one of the wounded men occupying a bed. He turned to see which one it was and saw McNeil move his leg. He walked over to him and started taking his vitals. "I see you are back among the living colonel."

"What happened and why am I in bed? What is this hooked up to my arm?"

"First you were wounded and you are in bed because I put you there," replied Sergeant Hicks as he recorded the vital information, "that's an IV in your arm; a saline solution. You need blood but I don't have any."

"I remember something hitting me in the head but that's no reason for me to be in bed."

"A bullet is the something that hit your head. Went through your helmet and cut a gash in the right side of your head. You have three more wounds also."

"I don't remember any more wounds."

"Apparently you were knocked unconscious so you wouldn't remember the other three wounds. One, a through and through, in your upper left thigh and one in your left chest plus another grazed your side. The bullet is still in your chest. I have no idea how much damage has been done so I've set you up for an evacuation to the 4088 MASH unit come morning."

McNeil began to feel a bit cramped so he moved his body and then he felt the pain, plus something else. "Would it be safe to say that there are no stones in my bed Sergeant Hicks?" asked McNeal moving his body around on the bed.

"Stones? Certainly not in one of my beds sir."

"Then what is it that I feel under me?"

"I have no idea but let's see," said Sergeant Hicks as he gently rolled McNeil over onto his right side. "It's the bullet sir. It's lodged under the skin just inside of the shoulder blade."

"Then a simple slit of the skin and the bullet can be popped out, correct?"

"Sounds simple but I don't have what I would need to do that. I have run out of sutures and there is no anesthetic. It's best we get you to the MASH unit where they have what is needed and qualified people to do the job."

"Sergeant Hicks, though I'm in a bit of pain I still have all my faculties. You treated a man last month, Holland I believe his name was---

"Pfc Holden," interrupted Sfc Hicks, "I remember him."

"--who did not want to be evacuated," continued McNeil, "and he said he trusted you to treat him. I feel the same way. I cannot leave my command at a time like this. I trust you to take care of me. This is a direct order Sergeant

Hicks. You will not evacuate me. You will radio a list of what you need to the 4088 MASH unit through division. The message should read: unable to evacuate, which will be true because I gave you a direct order, send supplies or a doctor. List what you need in the message. Do it now Sergeant Hicks."

"Under protest I'll do it sir. But I can't make any promises that I'll do you any good."

"Your protest is noted and you are much better than you give yourself credit for."

Sergeant Hicks went to the battalion CP to draft the message. He found Tiny and Captain Donohue were busy with reports. He decided to tell Captain Donohue about the direct order in hopes he might have a suggestion, "Could I speak with you a moment Sir."

"What is it Sergeant Hicks? How is the colonel? Has he regained conscious yet?"

"He has and he is the reason I am here and need a word with you. He should be evacuated to where there are qualified people to care for him."

"So let's add him to the list of evacuees."

"That's the problem sir. He refuses to be evacuated. He gave me a direct order to not evacuated him and get what supplies are needed to care for him here."

"Sergeant Hicks, I have heard the story about the colonel, when he was a captain, shooting up a coffee pot when one of his orders was violated. If he gave you a direct order then I suggest you carry it out."

"Yes sir," replied a reluctant Sergeant Hicks as he started drafting out the message. "Oh, by the way sir," added Sergeant Hicks, "draft up orders for Col. McNeil's fifth, sixth, seventh, and eighth award for the purple heart."

The 5th Infantry Division headquarters had followed the battalions in slimming down on man power. Non-essential men were sent to battalions, which sent them to the companies, where they were needed to fill vacancies. But with all the action going on the work load of division didn't decrease.

Blue Stallion commo was a busy place day and night. Men took messages, other men decoded them, and runners got the messages to the correct people. Such was the message that came in over the radio well before daylight New Year's morning. An unusual message from the 1/5th Infantry Battalion. Once it was decoded and handed to a runner he left to locate Col. MacMasters.

Col .MacMasters read the message, laughed, then went to see General Layton.

"Sorry to bother you sir but I think you should see this," he said passing over the message.

General Layton read the message and passed it back. "Mac, I'm not about to start countermanding my battalion commanders orders. Col. McNeil knows what he's doing and he does have good men with him that know their job."

"What's this part about not wanting to be the coffee pot?"

"I guess that happened before your time Mac. When the previous 1/5st Infantry Battalion Commander, Ltc. Winters, now deceased, made McNeil a Captain and gave him Baker company McNeil issued certain orders, good orders I might add. One was that there would be no open fires or light after dark. One evening he found a cook boiling coffee on an open flame. Captain McNeil pulled his forty five and blew a hole in the pot which put out the fire. After that incident he never had trouble with men disobeying his orders. What I suggest you do Mac is draft an order to the 4088 MASH over my signature. **Send requested supplies, or a doctor if one is available, on next medevac flight to the 1/5th Infantry Battalion on Ongjin peninsula."**

"It would be my guess that they will send the supplies because doctors don't wish to leave the security and warmth of their tents to go out in the cold, especially to the Ongjin Peninsula."

"Yes sir I'll take care of it," replied Col Masters as he turned to leave the commanders office.

# MCNEIL

## ONGJIN PENINSULA

### Chapter 16
### 14 Jan 1951

The weather seldom got above freezing and the cold wind kept the wind chill very low. Snow fell until it was a more than a foot deep, snow drifts was even deeper, all over the peninsula. The men fared well with their heavy winter clothes and the heaters kept the chill out of the tents and guard towers.

The New Year's battle would never be forgotten by the men of the 1/5th Infantry Battalion. The fact that the battle was a last ditch effort for the North Koreans to take the Ongjin Peninsula would not be known to the men who defended the peninsula for a while. Nor would they know that the fierce battle, not only on the peninsula but all along the 38th parallel, broke the back of the North Koreans. It wasn't that they didn't have the manpower just that their main forces were in the wrong place, roaming around in South Korea. The war wasn't over yet, just slowed down some.

Before a unit of the engineers were called back to rebuild two of the guard towers and bury the dead, the bodies were counted. Once the mass of bodies were counted by each company and totaled, close to two thousand, and checked, it didn't take a military genius to figure out that they were not regular military. Many of the dead wore only a cap to identify them as military. When the weapons were collected and counted there were five hundred less than the number of dead men. Because of this bit of information one could assume that the North Korean Army was not doing too well.

The Ongjin Peninsula was isolated and without news the men had no idea of what was happening in the war other than what happened to them. McNeil had often wondered why the North Koreans didn't use aircraft. He didn't know it but they tried and US Air Force quickly established air superiority. With their radar, which could reach out across the border, and the F-82, they shot down anything that left the ground, especially if it headed toward South Korea.

With permission from the President of the United States General

MacArthur pulled units from both Okinawi and Hawaii to assist the 8th Army in retaking ports and towns of South Korea. The push started well before the New Year's battle but word of that never reached the men on the peninsula.

US Navy Battle ships patrolled the waters of the Korean Bay and the Yellow Sea blowing up anything on the water that did not have US markings. This made the **L O P Mission** virtually useless but the men on the peninsula didn't know that.

With the now cleared strip of land at the 38thparallel spanning across the mainland from the Yellow Sea to the Sea of Japan the 5th Infantry Division was tasked with guarding the border. 2nd, 3rd, and 4th Battalions were beefed up with several artillery batteries and mortar crews plus extra men. This was not known to the men on the peninsula.

General MacArthur had issued a surrender demand to the North Koreans with no results. This wasn't known to the men on the peninsula.

The medicine and supplies Sergeant Hicks requested arrived on the first helicopter sent over to pick up the wounded. Air ambulances were something new to the Army and to the men. But it was a much quicker way to get the wounded to a MASH unit and would probably save many lives.

Sergeant Hicks took down the bottle of saline solution and hung a bottle of antibiotic and started a slow drip into McNeil's arm. "Sir, I have never done anything like this before," said Sergeant Hicks as he opened the roll of medical equipment.

"After you finish with me then you won't be able to say that will you? Stop stalling and let's get on with it," said McNeil.

"Yes sir," replied a reluctant Sergeant Hicks.

Sergeant Hicks filled a syringe with anesthesia then injected some in and around each of the areas he would soon be stitching up. After the anesthesia took effect he began stitching up, first the head wound then he moved down to the leg. He saved the chest wound and removing the bullet for last. He gently rolled McNeil over onto his right side, located the bullet, and pinched it up in the loose skin, then using a sterilized scalpel slit the skin. The bloody bullet popped out onto the cot. Hicks picked it up and wrapped it in a piece of gauze. He let the opening bleed a minute to help cleanse it. He then cleaned the opening with iodine and stitched it up. Then he moved to the front of McNeil and did the same with the bullet entrance hole. He cleaned each area with alcohol then dabbed on some iodine. He left the stitched up wounds uncovered for faster healing. After he cleaned up the tools he used he cleaned the bullet with alcohol and handed it to McNeil. "Here's a souvenir for you sir."

"Thanks Sergeant Hicks for a job well done," said McNeal reaching for the bullet.

"Let's hold the thanks until we make sure there is no infection," replied Sergeant Hicks.

"Oh ye of little faith. Why, may I ask aren't you in, or at least thinking about, going to medical school to be a doctor? You have skilled hands and a passion for healing."

"I've never given it much though sir."

"Think about it. Once this mess is over you qualify for the G I bill which will put you through school. Give it a lot of thought."

Once McNeil wounds showed signs of healing he asked to be moved from the medic tent into the battalion CP where he could do some good and lend a hand to Captain Donohue. He and his cot, four men helping, was moved into the CP tent and set up near the radios.

The harsh cold continued into the month of February. It was either cold and snow, or cold and mud when the temperature climbed high enough to melt some of the snow. The life on the peninsula became routine with very few probes on the 38th parallel. For the men it was guard duty in the towers and trying to keep warm. Frost bite was the main concern for McNeil and the medics. He had given orders to the officers and NCO's to be on the alert for any signs of frost bite in hopes of catching it before it got to far along.

McNeil slowly healed to the point that he could get around on a crutch after Sergeant Hicks removed the stitches. McNeal kept the bullet; Sergeant Hicks had removed from his back, in his pocket as a reminder of how close he had come to being dead. A few more inches to the left and his lights would have been out for good.

When it came time to replace the man on the island, the L O P Mission, McNeil decided to send Captain Calloway back since he was experienced. No need to train another man. Lt. Hampton was promoted upon his return and he again took command of Dog Company.

It seemed there was no letup in the paper work, mostly making daily entries in the staff journals, and with a pile of it to do the lull in the fighting gave the men at battalion time to catch up on it.

It had been months since the men had so much free time and they soon became bored with all the leisure time. It was sleep, eat, and play cards, plus trying to stay warm.

Other than daily reports to division and alerts when the mike boat was due the radio was mostly silent. On one of those cold evenings in late February when the temperature dropped and snow started to fall the men of the battalion were huddled around the heater when the radio sounded with a message. Corporal Willis quickly moved to it and started copying a message.

It was a longer than usual and after Willis decoded it he shook his head then passed it to McNeil. McNeil read it, and reread it.

Message number 5112 from Blue Stallion six to Raider Six.
Eyes only. Classified Secret. Confirm receipt.
Part one of three.
Alert. Alert.
1/5th is alerted to a move. Prepare but no action until part two
Has been received.
Blue Stallion Commo.

"Willis, report receipt of message. You better read this," said McNeil passing it to Captain Donohue.

"I'm not sure I understand sir, move to where?" asked Capt. Donohue, "We can't move any further forward."

"This is just an alert," answered McNeal, "We'll have to wait for part two."

"Should we do anything now?"

"Without knowing what it's all about there is little we can do but sit tight."

Two days later another message came in but it wasn't part two nor did it have anything to do with a move.

Message number 5114 from Blue Stallion six to Raider six.
Eyes only. Classified Secret. Confirm receipt.
Meet mike boat at zero seven hundred hours 15 February 51.
One passenger plus rations.
Blue Stallion Commo.

This certainly doesn't have anything to do with the alert message, thought McNeil after Willis decoded the message and handed it to him. He was deep in thought as he read the message. Why just one passenger and rations, no supplies? Why no ammo, and who is the lone passenger? There's no need for me to dwell on it now, I'll have to wait until tomorrow to find out what this is all about.

"Rodgers, I need Mr. Anderson. Would you locate him for me?" a clerk typist had arrived and Rogers was moved back to battalion.

"Yes sir."

"Is that part two sir?" asked Captain Donohue.

"No. This is something different."

"You sent for me sir," said Mr. Anderson entering the CP a few minutes later.

"Yes I did. The Mike boat will arrive at zero seven hundred tomorrow. You'll need a truck and some men to off load rations. I'll go along in my jeep plus we should have a wasp with us. Set it up please."

"Will do sir."

"You have any idea what this is about?" asked Captain Donohue after he read the message and after Mr. Anderson departed.

"You know as much as I do," replied McNeil as he went back to work on the ledgers.

Tiny looked at Captain Donohue with raised eyebrows and Captain Donohue nodded his head. No words were needed to express their thoughts. Tiny would be the jeep driver come morning.

# MCNEIL

## ONGJIN PENINSULA
## GENERAL LAYTON VISITS

**Chapter 17**
**20 Feb 1951**

When McNeil stepped out of the CP the next morning well before daylight he found a 6x6 with four men in it, the wasp from Charlie Company, Baker Company wasp was destroyed by a direct mortar round killing both Pfc Mendez and Billie Joe Hatfield, plus his jeep with Tiny standing by. "I'm perfectly capable of driving myself," McNeil said to Tiny.

"Sergeant Hicks and I decided to not allow you to take a chance Charley. Please get in."

"You and Sergeant Hicks are bordering on in subornation Tiny."

"Yes sir. We had a good teacher. Please get in the jeep sir."

McNeil, using a walking stick, had a smile on his face when he walked around and got in the jeep. He had not failed to notice that Tiny was never far from his side lately and the B A R was seldom out of his hand.

The wasp sat off to the side waiting and the 6x6 was backed up to the shore line when the Mike boat touched shore and lowered its ramp. A lone figure stepped off the mike boat but even though it wasn't full daylight yet it wasn't hard for McNeil to recognize the man. McNeil saluted him and spoke, "good morning sir and welcome to the peninsula general."

McNeil looked back at the mike boat but there was no other passengers getting off: no Chief of staff nor an MP escort. "Surprised Colonel McNeil?" asked General Layton, "even generals can do damn foolish stunts."

I suppose that's my reprimand for not allowing myself to be evacuated, thought McNeil, and it was done with great tack.

"I'll probably catch hell for sneaking off without my chief of staff and an MP escort when I return but sometimes it feels good to do something alone. Don't you agree Colonel McNeil?"

"Absolutely sir. Sir, your message didn't provide much information so may I ask the purpose of this visit?" McNeil did notice that his general stars were not visible this time.

"I see you still have an escort," commented General Layton without answering McNeil's question.

"Yes sir. I had to borrow one since Baker Company's was destroyed along with the two men you personally promoted."

"Sorry to hear that. Shall we get moving?"

"By all means sir," replied McNeil as he slid into the rear seat of the jeep, not without a bit of discomfort.

"Good morning to you Sergeant Brockman," greeted General Layton as he got in the right seat of the jeep.

"Good morning general," replied Tiny rendering a salute.

"Back to the CP," said McNeil.

"I should think we are in time for coffee and food?" spoke General Layton as the jeep started moving and the wasp led off.

"That would be a good assumption sir," answered McNeil still trying to figure out what General Layton was doing on the peninsula.

"How are the wounds Colonel? I see you still use a cane."

"Looks can be deceiving general. I'm doing real well sir."

Nothing more was said until Tiny stopped the jeep in front of the Battalion CP. "Sergeant," spoke General Layton, "would you mind letting the Colonel drive that is unless he has forgotten how?"

"I'm sure I can handle it sir," replied McNeil as he eased out of the rear of the jeep and slid into the driver's seat that Tiny had reluctantly vacated, "where to general?"

"Up toward the line or any place where we can have a quiet conversation in private."

"What shape is the battalion in?" asked General Layton as McNeil got the jeep moving.

"Sir, the battalion is in fine shape except for----"

"I know," interrupted General Layton, "except for manpower and equipment. There is a trickle of men coming in but the pipe line for personnel isn't fully operational yet. This will do fine." said General Layton. They were half way between Baker Company and the line.

"I could have sent a lengthy message but I knew there would be questions. I could have sent Colonel MacMasters but I felt I needed some time away from the division so here I am."

"It's always a pleasure to have you here General."

"What I have to say is for your ears only, for now. I'm sure it won't be long before every one hears about it. You have received the first part of three messages so you are aware that the 1/5st Infantry Battalion will be leaving the peninsula soon. What I wanted to alert you about is that the Korean people are steeped in tradition. Even though the 17th Infantry Regiment, which has a long list of victories and is sort of famous to the R O K Army, was lost here on the peninsula, the R O K Army is reviving the 17th. It'll be a modified 17th Infantry Regiment commanded by a Brigadier General Wang. I've met him and he's a good military man trained in the U S A. He'll try to regain the honor of the 17th. When he arrives here, and I don't have a date and time yet, you will afford him all honors short of a parade. He's assured me he will have enough English speaking men with him so the turnover will go smoothly. Under no circumstances are the 1/5st Infantry Battalion to depart the peninsula until so relieved by General Wang. Do you understand what I'm saying?"

"Yes sir, I understand."

"Any questions so far?"

"No questions so far sir."

"I wanted to tell you personally about the 17th so you could get the word out to the men. I don't want to hear of any derogatory remarks made by your people about, or to, the 17th. Do you understand?"

"I understand sir. I'll make sure of that."

"Good. Now, there is a package for you marked, Personal, which came on the mike boat. You'll find a copy of the new T O E (**T**able of **O**rganization and **E**quipment) for the battalion and companies. Just a little heads up for you so you have advanced information of what is to happen. You'll have time to study the new T O E and decide which men to keep and where to assign them, or which ones to get rid of.. Any questions so far?"

"Two comes to mind sir if you can answer them? When is the change of command to take place and where will the battalion go to from here?"

"The change of command here depends on the R O K. They will let the division know and you'll be informed. The 1/5th Battalion will move from here to Japan. It'll be a double R & R. **Retrofit** and **Resupply** for the battalion plus **Rest** and **Recuperation** for the men. The men will be paid full pay for the time, which is estimated to be two months, so you'll have your hands full with men with money in their pockets and no women and whisky in a long time."

"Where will the 1/5st Infantry Battalion be assigned after the retrofit, sir?"

"The 1/5st will replace the 2/5th so they can go through the same retrofit. The 2nd will replace the 3rd, and so forth. Now, knowing all that's to take place do you think you can handle it? Or should I replace you. I realize you are young but you have proven yourself to be a capable combat commander, so far. If you decide you want to be replaced now is the time to speak up. I can assure you that if you decide you want a replacement, and if I can find a replacement, I'll find a place for you in the division and there will be no black marks on your records."

McNeil was silent for several seconds before he made a decision. If he could handle a battalion in war time what reason could he give for not being able to manage a battalion in a peace time mode for a couple of months. "No replacement is necessary sir. I will handle the battalion."

"I felt that might be your decision and I'm glad because as you should know by now there is no one to replace you with. At least not here, but maybe where you are going. Now I have a question for you. How is Able Company faring under the command of Captain Downs?"

"About as well as could be expected sir. We have our moment's but--"

"He's not too happy with your promotion and assignment. He had his chance to speak up but just between you and I, I don't believe he has what it takes to command, that is anything higher than a company. You rate him so be truthful. If you decide to replace him I'll go along with your decision. Any more questions or comments?"

McNeil took a while before answering. "You have given me a lot to digest sir but at this time I have no questions, maybe later."

"That's all I have at this time so what say we go get some food?"

"That sounds good sir," replied McNeil as he started the jeep and headed back to the battalion and the cook tent.

# MCNEIL

## ONGJIN PENINSULA
## 1ST BATTALION RELIEVED

**Chapter 18**
**22 Feb 1951**

Two days after General Layton departed the peninsula part two of the alert message arrived.

> Message number 5118
> From Blue Stallion Six for Raider Six.
> Eyes only. Classified Secret. Confirm Receipt.
> Part two of three.
> 1/5th will be replaced on peninsula by new R O K 17th Infantry Regiment.
> All equipment will remain in place for use by 17th except personnel gear.
> Date of departure and destination to be announced in part three.
> Blue Stallion Commo.

"Well this explains thing a bit better," said McNeil passing the message to Captain Donohue after he finished reading it. McNeil knew what was going to happen but he couldn't let the others know that.

"Good God. We're actually going to leave this peninsula?" exclaimed Captain Donohue.

"Seems that we are. Let me write the information out so it will be better understood then I want you, Captain Donohue, to bundle up then go to each company and make sure each commander reads it. We'll have to wait for part three to know when the move will take place. I know there will be questions but as of now I have no answers. Another thing, make sure that you explain that it's my desire that no one make derogatory remarks about the R O K 17th Infantry Regiment. You were not here so let me explain. We had the original 17th on line at the 38th parallel. They were, let's just say they were a bit lax in their duty, rolled over and every man lost. This is a new reinforced R O K 17th Infantry Regiment."

"I understand sir," replied Captain Donohue as he prepared to battle the cold to get the information to the companies.

Three days later the final message came in.

Message number 5121 from Blue Stallion to Raider Six
Eyes only. Classified Secret. Confirm receipt.
Part three of three.
Raider Six will meet Commander of R O K 17th Infantry Regiment,
General Wang, at landing morning of 25 Feb 1951.
1/5th will be released only after General Wang has been
Briefed and has control of security.
1/5th will proceed to Camp Drake in Japan for R & R,
(Retrofit and Replacement of personnel). Transportation
Provided from peninsula and in Japan.
Blue Stallion Six.

McNeil decided to call the commanders to battalion to personally brief them on the latest.

It was decided that two of the 6x6 trucks were needed to carry the personal gear of the men of each company plus one for battalion. Those nine loaded trucks were the only vehicles that would be leaving the peninsula when the battalion left. All other vehicles, radios and tents, would remain on site to be used as needed by the incoming 17th R O K.

The morning of the twenty fifth, well before daylight, McNeil with a detail of men not needed at their units were waiting at the landing. He had dispatched a couple of trucks to the companies collecting forty men, ten from each unit plus a good NCO, to secure the area at the landing. Captain Donohue was left at battalion to handle any last minute details but McNeil brought Mr. Anderson with him.. It would be SSgt. Leeks responsibility to shuttle food to the men at the landing during the day.

McNeil selected a camp site among the trees well back from the landing yet near the road. Once the area was secure and guards posted he allowed the men to have small fires to ward of the early morning chill. McNeil selected a spot; near where his jeep was parked so he could hear the radio, and lay down to get some sleep. As he stretched out he ran his hand in his pocket and fingered the bullet, the bullet that almost cost him his life. He was still a bit sore and stiff but the cane helped him to get around.

Just before daylight a guard called out, "Lights on the water," which brought everyone to their feet. McNeil, like most of the other men, was instantly on his feet and alert. Without knowing if the lights were friendly or not each man took up a good position and waited. Now more lights could be seen out on the water. Not bright lights but more like black out lights.

McNeil reasoned that if General Wang was landing here this morning then the area should have been cleared so the lights must be from friendly ships. A few bumps and metal to metal sounds reached the men on shore then the lights went out and nothing could be seen or heard.

About daylight, just as Sergeant Leeks arrived and passed out hot food and coffee, sounds of motors running could be heard and a few lights could be seen again on the water.

"Mr. Anderson," called McNeil, quietly, "have the men ready and standing by, put out the fires, we are about to have visitors."

McNeil walked down to the water's edge and stood waiting, leaning on his cane. Soon he could hear what sounded like a motor start up and head his way. It had to be a boat. Soon other motors could be heard out on the water.

It was light enough now that McNeil could see several Mike Boats running around in a circle out on the water. One mike boat left the circling boats and came toward the landing. When the mike boat touched shore and dropped the ramp two jeeps drove off the boat. There was no mistaking who were in the two jeeps. Both jeeps had antennas and radios. When the lead jeep stopped beside McNeil he came to attention and saluted. "Welcome to the Ongjin Peninsula General Wang. I'm Lieutenant Colonel McNeil, commander of the 1/5th Infantry Battalion."

"Thank you for meeting me here Col McNeil," spoke the small wiry man in perfect English returning the salute. McNeil remembered from General Layton's briefing than General Wang had been schooled in America. It was obvious from his bearing he was a general and it was obvious from the way the men in the second jeep jumped out and stood behind General Wang at attention that he was respected.

"My pleasure sir".

"How are your wounds progressing Col McNeil?"

"Very well sir."

"Colonel McNeil let me say how much I appreciate you and your men's effort in protecting my home land. My children are the fourth generation to own and farm land on the Ongjin Peninsula."

"Thank you general and that's quite an accomplishment."

"Maybe one day they will be able to return here and farm the land once again."

"I'm sure they will sir. May I say you have a beautiful country. Maybe one day I can come back and see it when there is no war."

"You would be most welcome as my quest."

"Thank you very much sir. Have you been briefed on the L O P mission sir?"

"I have," said General Wang holding up one finger. One of his people ran to a jeep and spoke on the radio. "As you can see two of the mike boats are now headed for the islands. If you will contact your man he can be returned to you when the mike boat returns."

McNeil turned and pointed to Willis who was waiting with him. Corporal Wills ran back to the jeep and made the call to Lt. Callaway who was on the island. It was light enough now that McNeil could indeed see two mike boats leave the circling boats and head for the islands. He could also see two large L S T ships anchored plus two Navy destroyers circling the anchored ships, all with US Navy markings. General Wang made another motion with his fingers and a man ran to the other radio and spoke. The circling mike boats started peeling off and heading for the landing. As soon as the boats touched shore and the ramps were lowered 6x6 trucks drove off loaded with R O K troops. When a mike boat was unloaded it returned to the L S T for another load. Soon there were a dozen 6x6's parked on the road. "General Wang," spoke McNeil, "if you and your people will follow me I'll lead you to the 38th parallel."

McNeil briefed Mr. Anderson and left him in charge of the landing then he got in his jeep and moved to the head of the parked trucks. General Wang and his two jeeps followed. The wasp pulled ahead of McNeil's jeep. The convoy started out with the loaded trucks spaced out behind.

When they reached the battalion area McNeil gave instructions to Willis. "General Wang, my communications man is about to notify the units so if you have your communications people ready they can observe the operation."

General Wang turned and spoke to a man standing behind him, his aide assumed McNeil, the man ran off and returned with three R O K troops. In rapid fire Korean General Wang gave them instructions as they stood at attention. They saluted then followed Willis into the tent.

"Would you care for a cup of coffee while I brief you General Wang?" asked McNeil.

"Coffee would be fine, but first, where is your 1st company?"

"Able company is to the west at the coast. Then Baker Company in front of us, Charlie, and Dog Company is to the east on the coast."

Again the General gave rapid fire instructions to his aide who ran off to deliver the information. "While we have coffee the units will be moving to their designated areas of responsibility."

McNeil briefed the general on the set up and how he and his people had managed the security situation. While McNeil talked General Wang would turn and give instructions to his aide who was taking notes. "I don't have anything else General Wang unless you have questions for me?"

"What was that odd vehicle that escorted the convoy? Looked like a modified weapons carrier to me."

"That's what it was general. It was created out of necessity because we didn't have the man power to patrol the coast lines. It, I should say three of them, there were four but one was destroyed during the New Year's day battle, has a triple mission. Not only does it patrol the coast but it does escort duty and the Wasp's, as they have been named, can rapidly move to hot spots along the M L R."

"And you will be leaving them with me?"

"Absolutely sir. And sir may I ask a favor of you?"

"If it's with in my power?"

"My instructions were to leave all equipment and vehicles with you. We'll be taking only the nine 6x6 trucks loaded with our personal gear. Would it be possible for your men to transport my people to the landing after they are relieved?"

"That will be no trouble as I'm sure your people are anxious to depart this peninsula." he turned and gave more rapid fire instructions to his aide who ran from the CP .

A 6x6 from Charlie Company drove up and parked. This truck would load the ledgers, American flag and battalion guidon, after the battalion was relieved. Two hours later a man came from the CP and handed a message to General Wang. He read it then turned to McNeil. "Colonel it seems all my people have been briefed and responsibility of the M L R is in the hands of the R O K 17th Infantry Regiment. Under the circumstances there will be no formal change of command. I hereby relieve the 1/5th Infantry Battalion of the Ongjin Peninsula security responsibility." McNeil Saluted and it was returned by General Wang.

"I wish you luck general and it's a pleasure to meet you."

"We shall meet again one day Colonel," spoke General Wang offering his hand, "and may I say again, thank you and your men for defending my homeland. The family farm here on the peninsula has been in my family for four generations. My children are managing it now, or we hope to again in the near future."

"It has been an experience sir. Strike the colors and load the truck," McNeil said turning to the waiting men.

The road was a muddy mess with all the traffic on it. On the way to the landing there were vehicles moving in both directions. Trucks of the R O K 17th Infantry Regiment loaded with supplies and many of them pulling artillery pieces. The R O K 17th was a modified Infantry Division, self-supporting. McNeil was a bit envious of all the man power and equipment.

One of the wasps' led and McNeil's jeep followed with the last 6x6 bringing up the rear along the muddy road. A R O K troop rode in the jeep and one in the wasp so they could return the vehicles to General Wang. Once all individual and crew served weapons were cleared the ammo would be deposited in the wasp before they departed the landing. McNeil didn't want any live ammo on the ship to cause an incident.

There was a steady stream of 6x6's dropping off 1/5th Infantry Battalion men and returning empty. Well before dark all the 1/5th men and equipment were standing by at the landing. McNeil called a meeting of his officers to pass out last minute instructions.

# MCNEIL

## JAPAN
## CAMP DRAKE

**Chapter 19**
**25 Feb 1951**

It was two hours before official daylight time as the convoy of buses, escorted by an MP jeep, followed by the 6x6's and an MP jeep bringing up the rear, passed by stinking rice paddies. A smell the men thought they had smelled the last of for a while. The convoy passed through a couple of small towns but other than that there wasn't much to see even though the restless men kept turning their heads so as to not miss anything. A few lighted windows in homes where people had to get up early, very light traffic with a few bicycles mixed in was all there was to see out the dark windows of the buses. What was unusual was the peace and quiet, civilization, no guns firing and no mortars rounds falling. The buses were well heated but the outside temperature was cold with a fine mist falling.

Yesterday, which now seems a lifetime away, after the 1/5th Infantry Battalion was relieved on the Ongjin Peninsula and all the men were gathered at the landing the mike boats once again took to the water as if a signal had been passed to them, maybe general Wang had sent a signal, and headed for the landing.

It almost took a direct order for Tiny to accompany Captain Donohue, he thought his place was by McNeil's side to offer him protecting, on the first mike boat so they could direct the men to their quarters on the ships and make sure they were taken care of. Two companies, with vehicles, to a L S T. When the last mike touched shore and the last of the men boarded, McNeil stood and looked back at the peninsula that had been his and the 1/5th's home for better than eight months. So many men had been wounded, and many had lost their lives, on the peninsula. He came to attention and rendered a salute to the piece of land they had defended before he stepped onto the mike boat for the trip to the L S T.

The cruise was uneventful because there was no booze to give the men false courage and no women to stir up the juices of manhood. The men did have a bunk with clean sheets, plenty of hot food and coffee, and an abundance of hot water to bath and shave with, simple luxuries they had been without for a long time. They were out of the war for a while now and they could relax, play cards, or walk the deck and smoke.

For the officers and N C O's there was work still to be done and McNeil kept them busy during the voyage. Equipment lost to combat and transferred to the R O K 17th had to be accounted for plus all the other small items lost to combat. Letters had to be written plus there were orders to be cut for awards, many were for the Purple Heart.

The envelope that General Layton had told McNeil about earlier on the peninsula had been forgotten about until McNeil had a shower and lent a hand with most of the back log of paper work. He opened the manila envelope in the privacy of his cabin and pulled out the new, modified, battalion T O E plus a copy of one for the companies. All four companies, except for Headquarters Company, would be the same.

The new, modified T O E, would almost double the number of men assigned. Where, wondered McNeil as he studied the T O E, would the men come from? If there are not enough people now, how will all the new positions be filled? Those men who have been there, those who have been loyal, those who have been wounded, I'll make sure they are taken care of first. He decided as he opened a pad of paper and started making notes.

McNeil had a couple of hours of sleep before he heard the ship engines shut down and he could hear the bustle of activity on deck. He quickly got dressed to face whatever waited the 1/5th Infantry Battalion.

It was still dark when the L S T's were docked by the use of tug boats at some unknown port. It had to be Japan because lights could be seen lighting up the dock area plus buildings. No mike boats now. The ship doors were opened and the 6x6's were driven off onto the port docks. The men would walk off using the docks. MP's were everywhere directing the unloading process. A line of buses waited on the dock for the men and the MP's were directing the men to them.

Major Ellis, a man in his middle thirties and a bit on the short side and losing some of his hair was rushing around trying to locate the commander of the 1/5 Infantry Battalion. He expected to find a weather beaten older man but was surprised to find a rather young man wearing the silver oak leaves of a Lieutenant Colonel; a man who looked about old enough to be a First Lieutenant. And the Captains with the young colonel looked like they should have been back in school. But this was a unit that had survived in war. "Sir," spoke Major Ellis who was hoping he would get a command so he would be able to pin on the silver leaves of a lieutenant colonel, "I'm here as your liaison."

"I'm glad to meet you Major Ellis and I'm thankful someone was kind enough to think of providing assistance. Is adequate quarters ready for my men?"

"Yes sir they are. I'm to give this to you," said Major Ellis handing McNeil a manila envelope.

"What's the procedure here?" asked McNeil taking the envelope. He couldn't help but notice the clean and well starched uniform Major Ellis wore.

"Once everyone is off the ships and loaded on the buses we'll have an MP escort to Camp Drake where we'll get your people settled in. Food is being prepared as we speak."

"And how long will you be with us Major Ellis?"

"Until you release me sir."

"What's the schedule of activities after the men eat?"

"I believe that information is in that envelope I gave you sir."

"Major Ellis," spoke McNeil, as long as you are associated with this unit I want you to remember one thing. When I ask for information I expect to get it or hear you say you don't know but you'll get it for me. I ask again, what is the schedule of activities?"

"Sorry sir. I don't know the exact schedule but I do know your people will be paid; draw new uniforms, new equipment, and get replacement personal from the local holding company. There will be an awards ceremony plus you have a meeting, make that several meetings. One is with the post commander, General Dickerson, and you have a meeting with a Colonel Ashcraft. I have no idea what that's about. I'd have to see the itinerary to give you more information."

"We'll get into the itinerary later. Right now let's get loaded up and move out."

The convoy pulled through the gate of Camp Drake and turned right, stopping in the middle of many buildings. At the far end one could see a high fence with double barbed wire topping it. At the opposite end stood a two story building. Along each side of the open area were several buildings, all with lights burning on the outside. Only one building was lit up on the inside. As they exited the bus McNeil called out to Tiny. "Sergeant Brockman, have the first sergeants form and hold the companies. Mr. Anderson, round up all the officers. Major Ellis, is the buildings marked in any way?"

I don't believe, thought Major Ellis, I have ever seen or heard a commander who could issue rapid fire orders so fast and accurate. "Yes sir. I took the liberty of marking each building for your units."

"Very well. I thank you for that. There'll be less confusion that way. Will there be plenty of hot water?"

"I made sure the boilers were fired before I left to meet you at the docks sir."

Once the officers had gathered around McNeil he spoke. "Major Ellis tells me he has the buildings marked so locate your unit buildings and have the men move in. Once they have secured their weapons and dropped their field gear I believe we'll be eating. Is that correct Major Ellis?"

"Yes sir it is. That's the mess hall," he said pointing to the building all lite up, "where steak and eggs are being prepared as we speak. We can go eat any time sir."

"Major Ellis, please keep this in mind as long as you are associated with the 1/5th Infantry Battalion. No officer or N C O eats or takes comfort until the lowest private has done so. We take care of the men and they take care of us in combat. Without the men we wouldn't be needed."

"Sorry sir. I just meant you and your people could eat any time you are ready."

"Where are the BOQ and BEQ located?"

"The first building on the left is the BOQ and the next has been set up as the BEQ sir."

"Right now each of you know as much as I do," spoke McNeil turning to his officers, "get your men settled in then to the mess hall. I'll have more for you later. Shall we check out the BOQ and headquarters building Major Ellis?"

"By all means sir." Sir, spoke Major Ellis as they walked to the BOQ, "aren't you missing several officers? I only saw eight just now."

"The battalion is missing many officers but we have been operating with the number you just saw."

McNeil selected the first room inside the front door of the BOQ and secured his gear and weapon in a wall locker. He locked it then locked the room door as he left. He checked out the rest of the building. There were sixteen private rooms on the ground floor and the same number on the second floor. A community bath served each floors which was a step up from what they were used to. At least they wouldn't have to walk through the snow to take a bath. After a tour of the headquarters building McNeil spoke again to Major Ellis. "I want six jeeps delivered here this morning Major Ellis. Six jeeps with operational radios and the correct markings on the bumpers."

"I'm not sure that will be possible until later sir."

"Nothing is impossible Major Ellis. I have looked over the new T O E and I know I'm authorized twelve jeeps which should have been ready long before now. See about having six of them delivered tomorrow, and see about getting me an assigned driver. A man who knows his way around Camp Drake. See General Dickerson if there is a problem," said McNeil as they entered the mess hall.

The aroma of food was strong on the air as they entered the building. A long line of men were waiting for food. Several Japanese women were rushing around lending a hand. "Sir," spoke Major Ellis, the officers are served in the section reserved for officers. The camp mess halls use local labor to which you and your people will be asked to contribute, monetary, that is as soon as you get paid." Major Ellis had noticed that Col McNeil had a slight limp and he favored his left shoulder but he thought it best to not ask questions or comment on it.

McNeil had decided he could get around without the cane so he abandoned it on the ship.

"I understand Major Ellis."

"Shall we get seated sir?"

"Coffee only until all my men have been fed. Keep that in mind major. You, on the other hand may eat when you are ready."

"Yes sir, I will. I'll wait for you sir."

McNeil selected a table off to the side then went about moving chairs so he could push three of the four man tables together so his people could be seated together when they arrived. He knew this would turn into a working breakfast and he wanted everyone close. A pretty Japanese woman came to the table and spoke with just a trace of an accent. "May I bring you gentlemen some food?"

"Thank you but just coffee for now," answered McNeil. As he looked at the woman walking away he was reminded of just how long he had been without female companionship.

While waiting for the coffee McNeil opened the envelope Major Ellis had handed him earlier. He pulled out a typed sheet of paper and read it. It was a letter from the Camp Commander, Brigadier General Dickerson, welcoming the 1/5th Infantry Battalion to Camp Drake. It also stated that if there were any problems to not hesitate to get in touch with his office. After McNeil read it he passed it to Major Ellis. "Take this with you tomorrow, no make that today, Major Ellis. It should be your passport to getting what I want done much easier. Because when the jeeps are delivered I want enough drivers to take the eight 6x6's back with them. They will be unloaded in a couple of hours."

"I don't think the Camp motor pool will pick up and deliver vehicles sir. People are supposed to take vehicles to and pick up vehicles from the camp motor pool."

"Major Ellis you must start looking at things in a logical way. My people don't know their way around Camp Drake plus everyone will be busy with other things this morning. See what you can do and if there is a problem call me."

Coffee was served and the other officers started coming in and sat down pouring coffee for themselves. "This itinerary is all wrong," said McNeil after he looked it over.

"But sir, that itinerary was drafted by General Dickerson's adjutant and approved by the general, so I'm told," said Major Ellis.

"Regardless of who drafted it or who approved it, it's still wrong. I said earlier Major Ellis you would have to start thinking logically. Those men, my men, have been on the M L R in combat for eight months with no breaks, no booze, or women, and only an occasional beer. Their uniforms are not up to military standards. What do you think would happen if they were paid full pay and turned loose right now?"

"We would be up all night answering calls and retrieving our men from the MP's," spoke up Captain Downs when Major Ellis hesitated. That surprised McNeil because he seldom spoke up and almost never agreed with him.

"Is that what they want to do, pay everyone a full pay?" asked Captain Johnson.

"First thing this morning."

"There's far too much to do before we allow them to have money in their pockets," said Captain Hampton.

McNeil started rearranging the itinerary adding a couple of items then he passed it to Captain Downs. "Check this over and I'm open for comments. Pass it to the others when you have finished with it.

When the itinerary came back to McNeil he checked it over and saw only one change from his. He handed it to Major Ellis. "This will put a burden on the finance people to pay a partial pay today and the balance Wednesday after the awards ceremony," he commented, "but that's the way I want it. Better an inconvenience for a few people than a burden for the MP's and these few officers. Make that point when you see this Colonel Tidwell."

Finally the line of men ended and the officers ordered food. As they ate McNeil spoke about the new T O E. "I have a copy of the new modified T O E and I have studied it in detail. It will be in the battalion headquarters for you people to see any time you want. I think you will be quite surprised at the changes; that is if we get the people we have been promised. Some of you have been with this battalion for a while and some of you are new comers. My question to you is do you wish to remain in your current positions or do you wish a transfer? Give it some thought and let me know by tomorrow."

"I don't believe I need to wait until tomorrow," spoke Captain Downs, "I have given it some thought and I believe my talents can be better used in another unit."

"If that's your decision the so be it Captain Downs. As soon as we get a typewriter I'll see that you have orders transferring you to the unassigned officer pool. Anyone else?"

"I would like to discuss this with you later in private," spoke Captain Johnson.

"Whenever I have a free moment we'll get together. Anyone else? No. Then Captain Callaway will be taking over Able Company. Also be advised that we will have a full headquarters company, plus a full battalion staff, when we leave here. As soon as we finish eating have your people unload the trucks so they can be turned in, hopefully today. Anything else I should be aware of? No. One other item then; I'll need a roster of each company's personnel, rank and serial number, this morning. Now, let's get on with settling in."

When McNeil entered the battalion building he found Tiny hard at work getting things organized. Tiny had the battalion and American flags set up behind McNeil's desk in the office designated as the Battalion Commanders. The guidon was posted outside the building as required. He had a typewriter set up with Rodgers pecking away at it in another room. "Do you have a minute Sergeant Brockman?" asked McNeil.

"Yes sir," replied Tiny as he got up and followed McNeil into the designated Battalion Commanders Office, closing the door behind him. "What's going on Charley?"

"I have a copy of the new modified T O E and according to it the battalion will be getting a Sergeant Major. I can't promote you to a Sergeant Major so that leaves two options for you Tiny. You can turn in those stripes and revert back to a corporal, or you can keep the stripes and become First Sergeant of the new Headquarters Company. Your choice Tiny. Think it over."

"Not much of a choice to make Charley. I have gotten quite use to these stripes and I don't want to lose them. I'll become the First Sergeant of Headquarters Company."

"Good choice Tiny because I believe you will make a good first sergeant. As of now I have no idea who your commander will be. So until you are relieved here get orders cut transferring Captain Downs to the Camp Drake holding company, his choice. You'll have to get the correct address of the holding company. Also cut orders for Captain Callaway to take command of Able Company."

"Yes sir I'll get right on it."

"Are the phones working?"

"Yes sir they are."

"Make sure I have the number."

Major Ellis returned midmorning with the news that the requested Jeeps would be delivered before noon and the nine trucks would be picked up. "Sir, I'm to tell you that you have a thirteen hundred appointment with General Dickerson."

"I guess we ruffled his feathers some. No problem Major. If you will show me the way I'll keep the appointment," said McNeil.

After the noon meal McNeil returned to battalion and saw six jeeps lined up in front of the battalion building. All had radios with the whip antennas tied down. Each had the correct markings on the bumpers. "Sergeant Brockman," called out McNeil as he entered the building, "get in touch with the commanders and have them pick up their jeeps. Alert them to a meeting upon my return, I'll call and let you know when. Captain Johnson has an appointment with me so set that up first. Anything new I should be aware of?"

"Just that you have a driver sir, Pfc Gooding."

"Where is he?"

"Right here sir." spoke a man who stood up.

"Have you checked out my jeep? Is it full of fuel and ready?"

"Yes sir. It's ready."

"I suppose you know where Camp Drake Headquarters is?"

"Yes sir I do."

"Stand by. We'll be leaving shortly. Do we have the personnel rosters I asked for Sergeant Brockman; and the order for Captain Downs?"

"Right here sir."

"I'll be taking them with me. Is Major Ellis around?"

"I see him coming now," answered Tiny.

"Is he always like that?" asked Pfc Gooding after McNeil went into his office.

"Always. You have to learn to stay one step ahead of him to get along with him otherwise he's a good commander."

The building the jeep stopped in front of wasn't very impressive for a Generals office but then this isn't back in the states, this is Japan. McNeil walked into the building followed by Major Ells. "Sergeant Major Alcorn I'm Lieutenant Colonel McNeil. I have a thirteen hundred appointment with General Dickerson."

"Yes sir he's expecting you. The door at the end of the hallway."

McNeil knocked on the door with a gold glitter sign which said this was the office of the Commander, General Dickerson. He heard a voice utter 'come in.'

McNeil went in. Stopped two foot from the desk from which sat a short heavy set man with thinning hair and reading glasses down on his nose. McNeil noticed that the general wasn't Infantry but was of the signal Corp. The array of fruit salad on his uniform told McNeil that the man had never seen combat. Most all his ribbons were of the 'I was there' variety. "Sir," spoke McNeil in a loud voice and rendering a salute, "Lieutenant Colonel Charley R. McNeil, Commander of the 1/5th Infantry Battalion, reporting to the general as ordered."

"At ease," said General Dickerson after he looked McNeil over and returned the salute. "Colonel, are you aware that its proper protocol for a senior officer to report to the commander upon entering a Post, Camp, or Station?"

"Yes sir I'm aware of the protocol. I had planned to get in touch with your sergeant major and see when you had an opening in your busy schedule to see me."

"Well be that as it may, you are here now. Why have you decided to change a perfectly good itinerary? The changes you requested will put a burden on the people here."

"I apologize sir. I'm an example of my men sir. We have just come off of eight months on the M L R. My people need time to unwind, to get haircuts, and proper uniforms. If they were turned loose with a pocket full----"

"Yes, yes," interrupted General Dickerson, "Major Ellis explained your reasons for the changes but it will be a strain on the finance people to make two paydays."

"I'm sure it will be a strain sir. But my reason was that it would be better this way than putting a strain on the MP's and my seven officers."

"Explain that please, and why only seven officers?"

"Due to the high attrition in combat there were no officers to replace those lost. I have seven, besides myself sir. The reason I say a strain on my officers and the MP's is that if my men were given full pay they would hit the streets of the town, in most cases out of uniform or improperly dressed, spreading pollen and trying to drink the bars dry. The MP's would be kept busy rounding up the men and my officers would be up all night extracting men from the MP's. I felt a partial pay today, this afternoon if possible, would be better so the men could get haircuts and have a drink at the club until I am informed of the proper procedures for passes."

"Hmm, well, I can see your reasoning. Is there any reason the awards ceremony cannot be held Wednesday morning as planned?"

"Wednesday morning will be fine sir. Then full pay for the men right after. By Wednesday I should hope the quartermaster will have issued uniforms to all my people so they can be properly dressed for the ceremony."

"Sergeant Major," called out General Dickerson.

"Yes sir?" asked Sergeant Major Alcorn when he entered the office.

"Get this itinerary retyped and notify the people of the changes. Col McNeil is very convincing."

"Yes sir. Col McNeil sir, I'll need a roster of your people for the awards Wednesday."

"I have them right here, plus an order transferring an officer out of the battalion."

"When you are so short of officers why would one wish to leave?" asked General Dickerson.

"I didn't ask sir but I can assume he didn't care for my method of commanding."

"I see. Speaking of officers, what's your opinion of Major Ellis?"

"I have only been around him today sir but he seems to be a qualified Infantry Officer."

"Then you would have no objections if he was transferred to you?"

"None whatever sir, that is if he is agreeable. I could use an XO."

"Sergeant Major cut the order, effective today. Send in Major Ellis on your way out."

"Yes sir."

Major Ellis knocked, entered, rendered a salute, and reported."

"At ease Major Ellis. Col. McNeil tells me he has no objection to you being assigned to the 1/5th Infantry Battalion. What's your thinking on that?"

"I–I haven't given it much thought sir. But from what I've heard, and now seen, the 1/5th Infantry Battalion has a fine record. I would be honored to be part of it."

"I thought you may say that. Orders are being cut as we speak assigning you as the XO of the 1/5th Infantry Battalion. Sign out at the holding company and sign in at the 1/5st today."

"Welcome aboard Major Ellis," said McNeil extending his hand. Major Ellis took it and smiled.

"Thank you Col McNeil."

"You may not wish to thank me when you learn where we are headed once we are retrofitted."

"I'll take my chances sir."

"Do we have anything else to discuss Col McNeil?" asked General Dickerson.

"Nothing that I can think of at present sir. We've taken up enough of your time."

Both McNeil and Major Ellis saluted and left the office.

"Sir," spoke Major Ellis from the rear seat of the jeep on their way back to battalion, "you mentioned that I might not like where we are headed at the generals office, are you permitted to say where the battalion is going from here?"

"Where else but back to Korea and the 38th Parallel."

There was a bustle of activity in the battalion area when the jeep stopped at the battalion building. Several 6x6's with racks of weapons and MP's to guard them. Three Lieutenants were recording the serial numbers of issued weapons as new rifles were exchanged for old ones. Men were lined up before all three lieutenants. Things seemed to be going well so McNeil decided he wasn't needed there. He went inside where the officers of the battalion waited for him. He had used the Camp Drake sergeant majors phone to let Tiny know he was returning and to call the officers together. "Gentlemen," spoke McNeil after all the officers were gathered in the conference room, "we have a battalion XO. Please greet Major Ellis and introduce yourselves to him. Afterwards you can get a look at the new T O E you will be operating from. Captain Johnson I believe you asked to see me."

"I did sir."

"Go into my office and I'll join you."

"Tiny, have Captain Downs report to battalion with his bags, an hour ago. Give him his orders and have him sign out."

"On it sir," Tiny replied without asking questions because he was used to McNeil's way of getting things done without delay.

"Major Ellis, a Captain Downs will be here shortly. Take him with you to the holding company when you go to pick up your bags and sign out. Use my jeep."

"Yes sir."

"Now Bob what's on your mind," Asked McNeil entering his office and closing the door.

"I hope what I'm going to ask will not create a problem for you Charley."

"I won't know until you ask me, will I?"

"If I'm to keep this rank, and it seems so now, I have had command experience but I need to expand my administration experience."

"Good thinking Bob. Which staff position would you like?"

"Too much too soon Charley. I was thinking along the line of taking over Headquarters Company. I could gain much experience from setting up a company from scratch plus I'd be closer to the battalion. What do you think?"

"I think that if that's what you want then you got it. I'll have Tiny cut the orders now. And speaking of Tiny, he'll be your first sergeant."

"That's great Charley. I'm sure we'll do fine."

"Do you have anything else for me Bob?

"I'm sure I'll have questions later but for now, nothing."

"Stay where you are until I get another captain to take your place. Right now let's get back to the conference room"

"Ok Charley."

"Capt. Donohue," called out McNeil when he entered the conference room to find every one leaning over the table looking at the new T O E.

"Yes sir?" he asked when turning to McNeil.

"I told you once you would get a command when one was available. That has happened. Have you changed your mind?"

"Absolutely not sir. When and where sir?"

"You can have command of Charley Company and how about tomorrow?"

"That sounds good sir, and thank you."

The camp finance people arrived, before the armory people finished, and set up operations in three of the empty rooms in the battalion building. As McNeil had requested, every man, regardless of rank, was paid a fifty dollar partial pay.

Tuesday was just as hectic as Monday. While one company was sent to the quartermaster to draw new uniforms another released its people to get haircuts and purchase needed toilet articles. The local tailor/laundry shop, having been alerted, added extra people to handle the rush of getting new uniforms pressed and all the chevrons of rank and shoulder patches sewed on.

Since the 1/5th Infantry Battalion arrival at Camp Drake the skies were overcast and snow was threatened, sometimes a few flakes would fall. A cold north wind blew to keep the temperature down. Wednesday morning dawned and the wind died down. The clouds parted and the day started out to be warmer than usual.

Wearing class 'A' uniforms and marching was something the men of the 1/5th had not done for better than eight months so it took some doing to get all six hundred and forty men to the small parade field and in position. They were in place and checked over a half hour before a couple of weapon carriers arrived and backed up to the platform at the side of the parade field. Speakers were set up and microphones checked out.

Two minutes after the specified time three jeeps arrived loaded with people. General Dickerson took his place on the platform along with his adjutant Colonel Tidwell plus six unknown captains. Cardboard boxes were taken up on the platform. Attention was called and the awards ceremony began with a speech form General Dickers about the valor of the 1/5th Infantry Battalion and braving the cold and surviving plus surviving in combat.

Col. Tidwell took over when General Dickerson sat down. "It's always a pleasure to award medals to men who serve and distinguish themselves in combat. Due to the unusual large number of medals and ribbons to be awarded today you men would be standing here well past the noon hour if we did it the normal way. I'm sure, after eight months of combat and being cooped up here on Camp Drake for two days you men are ready for wine, women, and song. What we'll do is call out the award, then call out all the names of those who will be receiving the award. When your name is called please line up at the, my left your right, platform steps. The method chosen will in no way demean the award, simply speed up the process. Everyone will be receiving the Korean service medal, and most all of you men will receive the Combat Infantry Badge, which will be handed out along with other awards. Captain Black will you begin?"

The first award called for was the Army Good Conduct ribbon. Ninety seven names were called out. There were three more minor awards handed out then the Purple Heart award was announced. Three hundred and nine names were called out. Almost half the men in the battalion had received combat wounds. It took a while to get though the list and pass out the medal and ribbon. Some of the same men were called back for the additional Purple Heart award, Oak leaf cluster, since they were wounded more than once. Ten men, who had distinguished themselves were called forward, individually, to receive the Bronze Star.

Three hours later General Dickerson walked to the microphone. "That concludes the awards ceremony, except for one man. Since he is receiving so many awards I decided to wait until last to call him forward. Would Lieutenant Colonel McNeil come forward?"

McNeil left his place in front of his battalion and Major Ellis stepped forward to stand in his place. He marched to the platform. A low mummer started as he walked and it grew louder as he approached the platform. Soon the chant taken up by all the battalion men could be distinguished, 'raider, raider, raider.'

McNeil stepped upon the platform, went to the microphone, and raised his hands out palms down. He made the motion with his hands to quiet down by moving his hands up and down. When the men were quiet he spoke. "I thank you men for that rendition but keep in mind that this is an awards ceremony and not a pep rally. You are still in the Army and all rules and regulations apply. While I have the microphone and with the generals permission, let me say that the awards you men received here today does not do justice to the acts you performed in combat. Let's also keep in mind that many of our friends are not with us today. Let's not ever forget them. Another sobering thought, we are here at Camp Drake to retrofit and pick up additional personnel because we are going back into combat. The war, some wish to call it a Police action but those of us who have been there know better, is not over. War still rages across South Korea. We will be relieving another battalion so they can enjoy some R & R as we will be doing soon. Be advised that the established duty hours will remain in effect until Monday. After you are released here, eat, then you'll be paid. Go spread some pollen among the native women and have a drink to those who didn't make it. I'm proud of each and every man here today and each of you is a proven combat veteran, but, we'll have to prove that fact once again. Thank you."

"Let me add my appreciation to you combat veterans of the 1/5th Infantry Battalion," said General Dickerson when he stepped back to the microphone, "and as Col. McNeil said, we should never forget those fallen comrades. The medals they earned will be awarded posthumously, to their wives or parents. I asked that Col. McNeil be the last to receive his awards for two reasons, first because he will be receiving many, and secondly, because he is the commander I thought each of you would enjoy watching him receive his without any interruption. So without further ado."

# MCNEIL

## CAMP DRAKE

**Chapter 20**
**28 Feb 1951**

McNeil decided it was time for him to start enjoying this leisure time at Camp Drake. The major hurdles were over and now the administrative work would begin. He had a competent executive officer now to shoulder some of the burden of command so why shouldn't he have some leisure time?

Before he left the platform at the awards ceremony he saw his jeep arrive and park at the rear of the platform, or viewing stand. Has Major Ellis started anticipating my desires, he wondered, as he waited for the ceremony to end? There was a vast array of medals and ribbons awarded to him, even a very prestigious Korean medal which he thought General Wang may have had something to do with. The highest medal awarded to McNeil was the Distinguished Service Cross. Next was the Silver Star medal, followed by two Bronze Star medal. He was awarded the Purple Heart medal plus seven oak leaf clusters. There were so many other medals that Colonel Tidwell only hit the high lights of the citations to expedite the time. All the medals and ribbons were placed in a box along with the citations and handed to McNeil.

After turning the men over to the company commanders to get paid he released them from duty for the rest of the day, but restricted to Camp Drake, so they could enjoy some free time. He went to his jeep and dropped the box in the rear. "What are you doing here Pfc Gooding?" he asked his driver.

"Sir, Major Ellis thought you might want to take care of a few things before returning to battalion."

"Well he thought correctly. First, to finance; You do know where that is don't you?"

"Yes sir I do," replied Pfc Gooding as he started the jeep.

"Are you paid up to date?"

"Yes sir."

"Good. After finance I need to go to the PX, after a couple of other stops we'll head back to battalion."

McNeil knew that five sets of duty uniforms, which would be the number issued, would not be enough so he purchased five more sets plus two pair of jump boots. The issue boots were ok but the jump boots, Corcoran boots, fit better plus they shined up better that issue boots. With money in his pocket he decided he needed some casual clothes, something warm to wear while he was here at Camp Drake. He couldn't resist buying a new suit since they were so inexpensive, the whole nine yards, shirt, tie, and shoes. The PX stocked his favorite cigars so he stocked up on them also. The next stop was the Class six store where he purchased two bottles of good scotch.

While the men were released from duty he had scheduled a meeting with his officers to go over the new T O E and decide where the currently assigned men would be transferred to. McNeil wanted to take care of them first before the influx of new people started arriving. The days of free promotions were over but there were some men in the companies he felt deserved a good assignment.

When they finished going over the new T O E they had a long list of vacate positions which would be presented to the holding company to be filled. McNeil had Pfc Gooding deliver it that evening. Now it would be wait and see.

The hectic days that McNeil had grown use to were slowly winding down and he suddenly felt useless, he was restless, but he knew the slow time wouldn't last long. With all the work caught up with, Major Ellis had taken care of most of it, McNeil decided it was time for him to get away from the battalion for a few hours and enjoy himself. He showered, shaved, and dressed in his new clothes. First stop was the Camp Drake officers club which he had not visited yet.

A sharply dressed First Lieutenant was guarding the portals of the club today and he stopped McNeil. "Sir, are you a member of the club?"

"No I'm not. I'm in transit."

"May I see some identification sir?"

"Certainly," replied McNeil taking the new ID card from his wallet and passing it to the lieutenant. The man's eyes grew large when he saw the rank of Lieutenant Colonel on the ID card.

"I'm, I, I, —"

"No apology necessary Lieutenant, you had no way of knowing," said McNeil to the flustered lieutenant as he took the ID card back.

"Yes sir. The bar is to the left and the dining room to your right sir. Enjoy."

McNeil had never been inside an officer's club so he found it different from the enlisted club. It wasn't noisy and crowded and it was warm and comfortable. A few people were at the bar but not anyone McNeil knew.

"What will it be sir," asked the Japanese bartender when McNeil pulled up a stool and sat down.

"A good scotch on ice, no water."

When the drink was placed before him he slid a quarter across to the bartender, not a regular quarter but a paper quarter, M P C money, funny money as people called it. **M**ilitary **P**ay **C**urrency. At the finance office it was optional as to how much money a man drew. Some took all that was owed to them while others, as did McNeil, only drew enough money to last until next month. He had no need for so much money so he left the balance with the finance office.

He took a sip of the drink and approved. It felt good to just sit and enjoy a drink without the constant worry of combat and the lives of over six hundred men. In about seven weeks the battalion would be back on the line and back in combat. But hopefully this time he would have a staff and enough people to take some of the pressure off his shoulders.

He finished another drink then went into the dining room where he sat down at a four person table with a white table cloth on it. After looking over the menu he ordered the biggest steak on the menu with all the trimmings plus a glass of red wine. The only thing left on the plate forty minutes after it was delivered was a bone, some fat trimmings, and the skin off the baked potato. McNeil sat back and lit a cigar while he enjoyed a second glass of wine. Several other officers sat down to eat while he was in the O-club but no one he knew.

When he left the battalion he told no one where he was going except Maj. Ellis, he did leave a note on his desk that he would be at the O-club for a while. Now that he was sated he felt he needed to walk off the large amount of food he had consumed.

After walking what he figured was about a mile around Camp Drake he came across a rather large building with a sign on it that read; Service Club/ Library. He went inside to find this building also warm and comfortable. A few men sat at tables and played chess or checkers while others sat in comfortable looking chairs and read books or newspapers. He spied a table with a big pot of coffee and some cups on it. Just what I need decided McNeil as he shed his heavy coat and poured himself a cup. When he located the library he went browsing to find something to read. The book he purchased, which now seemed so long ago but was only eight months, was dog eared from reading it so much.

There were several women working here, some were playing checkers with the men and some just sat and talked. As McNeil was looking for a book to read one of the women approached him and spoke, "See anything you like Lieutenant?" she asked. He looked to see who had spoken and saw a very petite redhead with a name tag on her blouse that read, U SO, Mrs. Clare. What a leading question, thought McNeil, I certainly do see something I like, you. I have been celibate far too long "Mrs. Clare, is it? I was looking for something on political science."

"Wrong isle," she said looking at McNeil with green eyes that he wanted to crawl into, "next isle over. Come, I'll show you Lieutenant." she said and brushed by him to move to the next isle.

The smell of a woman, there is nothing like it, thought McNeil as he followed her. And that's the second time today someone mistook me for a lieutenant.

"Are you with that battalion that's here for R & R Lieutenant?" she asked as she started looking for the book he wanted.

"Yes I am."

"We've had several of the men in here."

"That's good. Better they come here rather than spend time in the club."

"Ah, here we are," she said pulling a book from the shelf and handing it to McNeil.

"Thank you for your help Mrs. Clare."

"No trouble, just part of the job. But, why may I ask, political science?"

"My major, if I ever get back to college."

"You think that police action in Korea will last long?"

"It's already lasted longer that I care for."

"Do you mind if we sit and talk, or would you rather read?"

"Coffee and talk would be fine." Especially with someone as cute as you he thought but didn't voice it.

"I understand you have a real mean commander," said Clare as she got herself a cup of coffee and sat down across a table from McNeil.

"Mean in what way?"

"Some of the men were saying he once shot up a coffee pot just to put out a fire, Anything to it?"

"I do believe something like that did happen."

"Why would a man shoot a coffee pot?"

"As you said, to put out a fire that might be seen by the enemy."

"I suppose that makes sense. I would guess you are anxious to get back home to your wife and family."

"No wife and no family, that is except for my mother."

No wife, well that's good to know. He's such a hunk of a man I can't imagine why some lucky lady hasn't grabbed onto him. Take a chance Clare. Not too many young good looking men around, especially officers. "Have you had a chance to see any of the sights in Tokyo yet?"

"I haven't even been off the base yet. We just arrived Monday."

"That's a shame."

"What about you Mrs. Clare? You are a long way from home and hearth. Or is your family here with you?"

"My family is somewhere on the other side of the world. Dad's a colonel in the Air Force and mom is with him. I tried the home and hearth bit but it didn't work out. I'm here to get away from too many memories."

"Memories have a habit of following. They are hard to leave behind."

"I found that out, but, at least the one who caused the bad memories isn't here."

"How long have you been here?"

"A bit over a year now. Another few months to go. How about you?"

"Ten months with an unknown time to go."

"Look, I really enjoy talking to you but I don't even know your name."

"Just call me Charley."

"As I said I really enjoy talking to you Charley but I need to mingle with the other people. I'm off Saturday so how does a guided tour around Tokyo sound, if that mean colonel will let you off?"

"Some time off base sounds great and yes, I believe I can get some time off. Where and when?"

"I have one of those little Japanese cars so how about we meet here at eight Saturday morning? Can do?"

"Can and will. Take care Mrs. Clare."

"You also Charley. Watch out for that mean colonel."

McNeil sat and watched her walk away and start talking to a young man who had just entered the building. They had spent so much time talking that it was now dark outside. McNeil checked out the book and walked back to the battalion.

There was a note on his desk for him: Col. McNeil, you have a zero eight hundred meeting with a Colonel Ashcroft at building 1021. Maj. Ellis.

# MCNEIL

## CAREER COUNSELING

**Chapter 21**
**3 Mar 1951**

After breakfast Thursday morning McNeil went to battalion to find Pfc Gooding standing ready. "Good morning Gooding. Is my jeep ready?"

"Good morning to you sir. The jeep is ready and I saw the note so I located building 1021. It's about ten minutes away."

"Very good. We'll leave here in fifteen minutes then. I have a few things to take care of first."

"Major Ellis, good morning. You're here early."

"Yes sir. I had some urgent things to take care of. We have four men to go on emergency leave, Red Cross approved. The paper work is about completed so all that is needed is your signature and we can get them on the way."

"Anything else I should be aware of?"

"There is some controversy about that list of needed people we sent over to the base adjutant."

"That list has been approved by me, it stands."

"I expressed that to the colonel sir."

"If I'm not here act in my name until I return. Is that the reason we haven't started receiving personnel yet?"

"That would be my guess sir."

"If the situation has not been resolved by the time I return I'll handle it. You know where I'll be for a while. By the way, have you any idea who this Colonel Ashcroft is?"

"Never heard of him sir, but if you like I can make some inquiries?"

"That won't be necessary. I'll find out for myself shortly. Let me sign those leave orders then I'll be on my way."

When Pfc Gooding stopped the jeep in front of a rather run down building, building 1021, McNeil wasn't too impressed with it. If this meeting is so important why is it being held in such a rundown building with no indication of what business goes on here? But then I haven't seen to many modern buildings on Camp Drake.

"I have no idea how long I'll be here PFC Gooding so come inside where it should be somewhat warmer while you wait."

A sergeant jumped up from behind a desk when he saw the silver oak leaves on McNeil's collar. "Good morning sir. May I help you?"

"I'm Lieutenant Colonel McNeil here to see Colonel Ashcroft."

"Yes sir. He's expecting you. Go right in sir. That door at the end of the hall."

McNeil knocked then entered when he heard someone call out, 'enter'. A full colonel sat on a couch with reading glasses down on his nose with papers in his hand. He had almost white hair and looked to be in his forties or even fifties. "Come in Colonel McNeil and have a seat," said the colonel motioning with his hand for McNeil to sit on the couch, "coffee?"

"Thank you very much sir for the offer but none for me," replied McNeil sitting down.

"How is the weather outside?"

"It's a bit nippy sir. A few flakes of snow fell on the way over here."

"Strange weather we are having this year. I'm Colonel Ashcroft and among my other duties I'm the OCC (Officer Career Counselor) for Camp Drake. Have you ever been counseled? No I guess not being that you are so young and with little time in grade," he said answering his own question.

"You moved up through the ranks very fast didn't you Colonel McNeil."

"Strange things happen when it's for the exigency of the service sir."

"Yes, I suppose so. You were on the M L R for eight months and went from Corporal to Colonel. That's quite a jump. I understand that letter for, field promotions, was canceled."

"Yes sir it was, just prior to the battalion leaving the Ongjin Peninsula."

"I suppose the letter was necessary under the circumstances but the normal promotion system is a bit fouled up right now."

"I'm sure it will work it's self out once we start getting the men and supplies we need to fight this war sir."

"Police action I believe it's being called."

"War, by another name is still war sir. Men are getting killed every day."

"Yes, I suppose so. What are your plans now Colonel McNeil?"

"I believe the President has made plans for me sir. I'll have to follow his orders."

"Yes, yes. For the duration plus six months. I mean are you considering making a career of the Army?"

"I haven't thought that far ahead sir. My original plans were to serve my time then get back to college. Obviously that plan was changed for me."

"If you decide to make the Army a career, or not, you will have the G I Bill to pay for your college. Most times men on active duty can go to college at the expense of the government. Choices you have."

"Sir, why am I really here, to see you I mean? Have I stepped on some ones toes? Am I in error somehow?"

"No, no. I suppose you did irk General Dickerson, and his people, some but that's not the reason you are here. Every officer, at some time in his career, needs counseling to set his goals and to make sure his desires and what the Army needs coincide. I was at your awards ceremony yesterday; you have distinguished yourself in the short time you have been commissioned. Colonel, I have to ask this, do you have friends in high places?"

McNeil gave the question some thought before answering. That's a strange question. Do I have friends in high places, none that I can think of. "I'd have to answer that in the negative sir. The highest ranking person I know and have met is General Layton, the 5th Infantry Division Commander, and now General Dickerson. Why do you ask sir?"

"There are four Lieutenant Colonels here at Camp Drake, which I'm aware of, who have much time in grade and are chomping at the bit, so to speak, to get command of the1/5th Infantry Battalion. I saw a letter, that came from for way up the command line, that stated you, Ltc. Charley R McNeil, were to retain command of the 1/5th Infantry Battalion for six more months from the time you arrived at Camp Drake. Unless you decided to relinquish command for some reason"

"I have not made any request sir and I have no knowledge of such a letter. May I ask who initiated such a letter?"

"You may but I can't divulge that information. I would assume that after eight months of being in the line of fire one would be ready and willing for a less stressful position."

"Command is a very special position Sir, command in combat is even more satisfying. It gets in the blood and it's hard to explain. The more one gets the more one wants."

"I see. Speaking of command brings us to another point. Since you are so young and have so little time in grade you will not be getting another command for a long time. At least until you catch up with your constitutes. If you do decide to remain on active duty it will be a while before you can expect a promotion. I do hope you understand because it's not a punishment, just a fact. Normally those who are promoted ahead of their years and experience are reduced back several grades once the situation, war that is, is resolved. You on the other hand will retain the rank of Lieutenant Colonel. So the same letter states. "

"I do understand sir and I'm grateful. If I do decide to remain on active duty what's in store for me?"

"First, you will have to attend the yearlong C & G S school (Command and general Staff) at Fort Leavenworth Kansas. That is when you depart Korea, whenever that might be. Let me also add that attending the school will gain you some college credits, just how many I don't know."

"Sir, to complete my masters I need a foreign language. I understand the Army has a fine language school in California. Is there a chance I can attend that school?"

"Yes, the Presidio, near San Francisco, a fine language school. You do realize that if you are accepted at the language school plus the C & G S several years will be tacked onto your time to serve in the military."

"Yes sir I understand that. I suppose it will be worth it to complete my masters. What about after the schools, what will I be doing?"

"My best guess will be a tour in the Pentagon. Every young officer should have knowledge of what goes on there. It's good military education for the future."

"What about now, after the six months of command is over?"

"I would say that's up to whomever is your commander. Possible some staff experience, until such time as this police action is over."

"So what happens to me now sir?"

"I'll draft up a letter expressing your desires, send it to through S-1 to G-1. Then we play the old Army game of waiting. Someone at Army level will check your desires against what the Army needs. Any more questions Colonel McNeil?"

"I can't think of anything at this time sir."

"Then I'm sure you have duties to get back to and I have letters to draft."

"Yes sir. Thank you sir for your very informative time," said McNeil standing up and reaching for the colonel's hand. He had thought about rendering a salute but Col Ashcroft was still sitting down.

On the ride back to battalion McNeil had time to do some thinking. It's funny how ones plans can be altered in such a short time. If I had not run out of money and had to drop out of college to work the draft would not have gotten me for a while yet. If this Korean uprising had not happened I would be heading back home and college in a couple of months. Now it looks as if I'm here to stay, in the Army that is. Maybe it's for the better since I'll begetting some free education. And speaking of home, I should write a letter to mother. It's been a while since I wrote to her. I wonder how she is getting along so far from town and living all by herself.

# MCNEIL

## RETROFIT

**Chapter 22**
**5 Mar 1951**

The influx of personnel for the battalion started shortly after the noon meal. A bus arrived with officers, Captains and First and Second Lieutenants and a couple of Warrant Officers. As the officers were signing in McNeil called Major Ellis aside, "Major Ellis, you are the Battalion Chief of Staff so you handle the assignments. You know what we need. Twenty lieutenant's to the companies and any extra send back. Select the most qualified four captains for staff duty.

"Yes sir I'll handle it."

Next a bus load of enlisted men arrived with three First Sergeants and a Sergeant Major. Since Major Ellis was busy with the officers McNeil called the Sergeant Major aside and spoke to him. "Welcome aboard Sergeant Major Lenear. I'm Colonel McNeil, the commander of the 1/5th Infantry Battalion. How long will it take you to get settled in here?"

"Glad to be with you sir and it normally takes a couple of days to get organized."

"We don't have the luxury of time. This battalion has been without a Sergeant Major for the past six or seven months."

"Who has been taking care of that position sir?"

"See that big man over there, Master Sergeant Brockman. He has been wearing two hats for a long time. He held the position of Baker Company first sergeant and the battalion sergeant major. I'm sure he'll be glad for your presence because as soon as you are ready he'll be taking over the headquarters company of which we never had."

"How did a battalion operate without a headquarters company sir?"

"In combat one learns quickly to operate with what is at hand. Every one wore more than one hat and helped where help was needed. Just drop your bags over there for now because your expertise is needed with this influx of personnel. Sergeant Brockman will show you to the B E Q later. Let me introduce you to him. "Sergeant Brockman," called out McNeil to get Tiny's attention where he was busy getting the men signed in.

"Yes sir?"

"Come meet your replacement. Sergeant Major Lenear, Master Sergeant Brockman."

"Very pleased to meet you Sergeant Major and may I say welcome, said Tiny shaking the Sergeant Major's hand."

"Sergeant Brockman, as soon as you get the Sergeant Major up to speed cut your orders, sign out here then sign in at the headquarters company."

"Colonel, do you have a moment?" asked Major Ellis of Colonel McNeil.

"Certainly, what's up?"

"Those four captains wish to speak to you about their assignments," said Major Ellis pointing to where four captains stood waiting.

McNeil looked at the four men then spoke to Major Ellis, "What is it that they don't understand and you can't help them with?"

"They were told they would become company commanders by someone."

"Gentleman," said McNeil walking to where the four stood together, "I'm Lieutenant Colonel McNeil, commander of the 1/5th. Welcome. You wished to speak with me?"

"Yes sir," spoke up a Captain Cobb, "we were informed that we would be taking over companies not staff positions."

"Who informed you of that, someone from this battalion?"

"No sir. Word was passed out at the holding company."

"Your displeasure is duly noted captain but you were misinformed by someone. All the command positions are filled. If you don't wish to become staff officers I suggest you get back on the bus and return to the pool of officers waiting assignments. As I'm sure Major Ellis has explained, we have an urgent need for staff officers. What will it be?"

"Sir," spoke Captain Murtagh, "I have never worked in a staff position before. I'm not sure I can handle it."

"We all climb the ladder of experience one rung at a time. If you ever need guidance speak with Major Ellis or, myself. You have six weeks to get read in on the job before we return to combat. My suggestion is for you to accept the position offered and get started by selecting, from the incoming personnel, your NCO and additional personnel required. The choice is yours."

Reluctantly the four captains accepted the offer because they had no desire to return to the holding company where they had been for a month now. Captain Johnson walked in just as they agreed. McNeil called him over. "Captain Johnson have you met your replacement yet?"

"Yes sir, I just left him."

"As soon as he is ready to take command you move to headquarters Company. Right now would you show these four staff officers to the BOQ?"

"My pleasure sir. This way gentlemen."

On the walk to the BOQ Captain Roshon spoke. "Captain Johnson have you been with the 1/5th very long?"

"From the very beginning."

"Is there any truth to the rumor that the colonel once shot up a coffee pot because he didn't like the cook's coffee?"

Bob had to smile at that. It's funny how the truth gets changed the more it's passed around. Bob didn't want to admit or deny the rumor and he didn't have time to give the correct version. "Let's just say, he did shoot a coffee pot when he was a captain. He can be a mean S O B if his orders are not followed."

"He looks so young to be a colonel," commented Captain Kirby.

"Young in age but not in experience," answered Bob, "He's an airborne ranger and he just received the Distinguished Service medal, the silver and bronze star and his eighth purple heart earned during eight months of combat. I'll follow him back into combat anytime."

Even though the influx of personnel continued through Friday several positions remained to be filled. McNeil decided to do something he had not done in a very long time, take a day off, Saturday to be exact. He had a tour date with Mrs. Clare. This would be the first time he would be out of touch with his battalion since he took over command of it. He notified Major Ellis of his plans. "Pass the word that there will be an officer's call at zero seven hundred Sunday morning. All officers and I'll accept no excuse."

"I'll get the word out sir."

Saturday morning McNeil, dressed in his new suit and was waiting at the U S O club when Mrs. Clare arrived in her small Japanese car. "Good morning to you Mrs. Clare," greeted McNeil as he finally wormed his way into the small vehicle and closed the door.

"Good morning Charley. Been waiting long?"

"Just a few minutes."

At the Japanese restaurant when McNeil helped her off with her coat he almost whistled. She certainly had a body that filled out the skirt and sweater she wore, even though she was petite. Her red hair was cut short and suited her almost childlike face. She was a very beautiful young woman. When they were seated McNeil asked, "Is Clare your first or last name?"

"Clare is my first name, Clare Marie O' Brien. I retook my family name after the divorce but as yet I'm not sure if I'm a Miss or a Mrs. What's your handle Charley?"

"Charley Michael McNeil, just call me Charley."

They had spent the morning sightseeing and talking, sometimes walking and sometimes driving around They ate at a very nice Japanese restaurant where the waiter spoke enough English, Clare spoke only a few words of Japanese, so they could order a meal and know what they were eating.

Clare told him she was an only child born in Virginia. She was a military brat and therefore had no roots. She told him about the many places she had been around the world before she left her family to attend college and start a life of her own. It was obvious that a failed marriage with no kids still weighed heavy on her mind.

McNeil told her he was from Kentucky and never left until he was drafted. He told her about his brother and sister whom he had not seen since the funeral of his father. He told her about his mother, not that she lived in a bottle just that she was in bad health. In a couple of more months he would be back there to care for her except for this Korean war.

"Is it really as bad over there as the papers say it is?" she asked.

"I have no criteria, nor the experience, to judge by, but I can say men are getting killed each day this war drags on."

"And soon you will be back in it."

"That's what men in uniform do. We train for war until a war happens; the we go to the war."

After eating they continued the tour. Clare drove by the Dai Ichi building where the very famous General Douglas MacArthur was headquartered. Clare proved to be a very capable tour guide and she regaled McNeil with little known facts about the Japanese baths and other places in Japan.

That evening she drove to a hotel, the Imperial, a very clean looking hotel that Clare explained was taken over by the State Department and was used to house State Department personnel which she and the other U S O workers were considered part of. It had a fine dining room and a bar. They sat at a booth and McNeil ordered a scotch, neat. Clare had a Manhattan.

They continued their conversation during the very excellent meal. And when coffee and brandy was ordered the talk continued. Even though they had only met and talked twice it was as if they had known each other a long time. "You know Charley, I have really enjoyed this day."

"It's been very enjoyable for me also Clare. It's been a while since I've talked with a woman."

"I think what made it so enjoyable for me is the fact that you are not the demanding type, no pressure, just a very relaxing day of sightseeing. I really hate for it to end."

"All good things must come to an end sometime. It is getting late, should we be getting back? Oh, that's right, you live right here. I'll just catch a taxi and save you the trip out to the camp."

"Charley," Clare said placing her hand on his arm, "my roommate is working until midnight and I really don't want to go to my room alone."

"Then after I pay the bill I'll escort you to your door then catch a taxi."

"Charley, there are no strings attached."

"I see. Well what are we waiting for?"

Once they were inside Clare's room, which was just large enough for two beds and a couple of dressers, and the door was locked they grabbed each other. It had been a year for Clare and about that long for McNeil. They couldn't get enough of each other and as they half stumbled and half walked toward the bedroom they left a trail of clothes in their wake. After they fell on the bed and coupled it was over far too soon. After they caught their breath they started working up more passion. This time it lasted longer and each time thereafter it was better and lasted longer.

It was a no hole barred sexual marathon until McNeil checked his watch. They were both exhausted but McNeil slowly got out of bed and located his clothes. Clare was barely awake when he told her he had to leave. She just grunted and went back to sleep. McNeil was able to catch a taxi outside the hotel and was driven back to Camp Drake arriving just after midnight.

The next morning McNeil felt alive and refreshed, not worn out and drowsy as he thought he would be. He had eaten and was in the conference room waiting for his officers. When they arrived and were all seated he started.

"Good morning. Some of you know who I am but for those who I haven't met, I'm Lieutenant Colonel McNeil, I'm the commander of the 1/5 Infantry Battalion. I'm sure there were some grumbling about a Sunday morning meeting so let me clear the air on that. As an officer we are never off duty until we die or retire. We are on duty twenty four hours a day. Keep that in mind for the future.

"Next subject is the men. We eat when they eat, we sleep when they sleep, but at no time will we eat before the enlisted men have eaten. Granted, officers have a privilege of rank, but in garrison only. From this day forward as long as you are assigned to this battalion, we will not buck a line, we will wait and make sure the lowest private has been fed before we take food. No one will sleep on a mattress unless you are assured the lowest private is sleeping on a mattress. We have been trained, and we are here to command men, so without those enlisted men we would not be needed. We would be without a job. When we depart here we will be going into combat. It's been my experience that if we take care of the men assigned to us they will, in turn, take care of us.

"I said we would be going into combat. What we will be doing is relieving the 2/5th Infantry Battalion, who is currently operating on the 38th Parallel, so they can come here and get updated plus enjoy some R &R. How long we'll be on the M L R is up to the North Koreans. How much longer we'll be in Korea is up to the North Koreans.

"If none of you have been in combat I suggest you learn from those who have been there. We tend to throw away the book because where we will be isn't in school, but the real thing. Paint over that rank emblem on your helmets which is a target for snipers. When you are on the line make sure your rank doesn't show, tuck in your collars. That shinny rank is a target for snipers. Never go on the line with a radio man dogging your heels. An antenna is letting a sniper know that an officer is present. Most of what I'm saying should be common sense, but some will tend to forget and those are the ones who will not be returning, alive that is.

"One last item before you're released. If I give you an order I expect it to be carried out. I will tolerate no excuses for disobeying an order no matter how inane you think the order may be.

"My main goal is first, to carry out the assigned mission. Second, to try and keep each of you alive so you can return to your wives, your families, your girlfriends, and your parents. Writing letters to the families of deceased is a very unpleasant undertaking.

"I desire that each of you use the proper chain of command. I believe you have met my executive officer and chief of staff, Major Ellis. He is in the chain of command right under me. I can't make that much plainer.

"Much has been done and much remains to be done while we are at Camp Drake. I have nothing further so you are released to get back to your units, and duty stations, and take care of what needs to be done."

Major Ellis jumped up and called the room to attention as McNeil walked out. Major Ellis noticed the smile on Captain Johnson's face. "Do you find something funny you would care to share with us Captain Johnson?"

"Sorry sir. I was just remembering when, then Captain McNeil, threw beds and mattresses out of a tent because the men on the line didn't have such comfort."

"You can reminisce some other time. Right now we have much work to get done. Several things I wish to speak to you about."

Major Ellis kept the officers another twenty minutes passing out information he felt they should have to better perform their duties. He answered many questions.

Personnel continued to arrive until the battalion strength swelled to almost full strength. More and more of the work load was taken from McNeil until he began to feel sort of left out. What the many were doing he once did with far less.

Time moved on and the time for departure from Camp Drake drew closer. New vehicles arrived, new equipment arrived, until there were rows of vehicles lined up near the rear fence. A new, up to date, commo van arrived filled with the newest communication equipment. No longer would truck batteries have to be kept charged to supply power for the radios. The van was a self-contained unit with its own power supply.

Corporal Willis, the most experienced man, took over the van and since communications came under control of the S-2 he did also.

One of the new Warrant officers, Mr. Waterman, took over as motor maintenance officer and worked from Headquarters Company through the S-4.

Even though new men arrived daily, the supply was becoming less and less, McNeil was under no illusion that all the new position would be filled in the new T O E. There would always be a vacant slot.

Camp Drake had a small firing range where everyone in the battalion went to, not to qualify, but to check out the new weapons and zero them. That took several days because not all the people could be released at once.

McNeil did get back to the U S O/ Library to have coffee and chat with Clare several times. When he found out she had an evening off he invited her to dine with him. When he arrived at the building at the designated time he found her a bit out of sorts as if she had a lot on her mind. Once they were in her car with the windows rolled up he found out why she was so withdrawn. "You lied to me," she almost shouted. At least she was lady enough to not blow off steam in the building and in front of others.

"I beg your pardon. How did I lie to you?"

"You allowed me to run off at the mouth about some big bad colonel and you're he."

"You assumed, as others have done, that I was a lieutenant and I didn't correct you. That's not a lie."

"You could have spoken up Colonel McNeil and corrected that misconception. How can this be? You are about half the age of my father and he's a full colonel." By the way, my name is O'Brien."

"It seems we both have bit of Irish in us. I'm McNeil and you're O'Brien. If you feel I have deceived you I do apologize."

"How can someone so young be a colonel?"

"Lieutenant Colonel. If you will get this car started I'll relate the details to you over a steak dinner."

"You have friends, or a relative, in high places and you have been fast tracked. Is that it?"

"A warm club, a glass of wine, and a big steak await us."

"Being a colonel I'm sure you can afford a steak."

"Lieutenant Colonel," he said correcting her again.

"Ok, Lieutenant Colonel," she replied as she started the car.

"Good afternoon Colonel," greeted the keeper of the portals at the club, "will it be the bar or the dining room sir?"

"Straight to the dining room today," answered McNeil as he guided Clare to a table off to the side near a window where they could talk in private.

"I should think coffee while we clear the air some, then wine with the steak, if you are still hungry?"

"Let's get on with this incredible story of yours then we'll see."

First he told Clare about his family. About how his snobbish brother and sister had left home and not returned except for his father's funeral after he was killed in a job related accident. He told about his mother, who wasn't really ill but just lived in a bottle. He told her about his college days and after the insurance money got low he dropped out for a semester to work and the draft caught him. He spoke of his plans to stay at Fort Benning as long as he could so he could get home more often. About how he received orders for Korea and hoping to be here only ten or eleven months before he could get back home to care for his mother and complete his college requirements.

He related the June 25th incident when the North Koreans crossed the 38th parallel and war broke out. He told Clare about the need for a classified mission requiring and officer when N C O's were commanding companies and no officer was available. How he was commissioned because of his R O T C experience, first as a lieutenant, then a captain. How the entire battalion was wiped out, leaving out the gory details, except for one man.

Clare sipped her coffee as she listened to his story. He skipped most of the gory details but related that with no qualified officers available he was appointed to rebuild the battalion. Later the silver leaves of Lieutenant Colonel were pinned on him. "And there you have my story in a nut shell. And you are the first person I have ever related that much information about me to."

"Should I feel flattered?"

"Feel anyway you like. You now know all the facts. Shall we order or would you like to leave?"

"I could eat a steak so let's order."

McNeil called the waiter over and placed both orders plus a good red wine to go with the meal.

"Sounds so incredible," spoke Clare after the waiter left to fill the order, "What we read in the paper is nothing compared to what you just related."

"If everything that happened, good and bad, was printed in the news then the North Koreans would know far too much about us."

"I suppose there is some truth there. You said only one man survived the lost battalion. What happened to him? Was he sent out of Korea?"

"He's still with me. I promoted him and he'll be going back with me.

"What about you Charley. In most cases those who receive battle field promotion are reduced in grade once the war is over. What will you be doing? Leaving the service or staying in?"

"So many questions. First, I have been promised that I will be allowed to keep the current rank but to not look for any kind of promotion for a long time. Yes. I'll be staying in the Army and continuing my education at the expense of the government. Once I leave Korea, whenever that might be, I'll go home to check up on mother."

"You could ask for a compassionate transfer. I'm sure you would be granted one."

"That's right you are a military brat and know all about such things. But what good would I serve at home other that being there. Don't get me wrong, I love my mother but she is an emotional cripple. She has no concept of time or events. When I got my draft notice I told her I would be going away. He response was; that's nice, be careful. She probably thinks I'm away for a few days at college."

"That's so sad. Why didn't you tell me this earlier?"

"My problems are mine and mine alone and I'll deal with them. What purpose would it serve relating my problems to, anyone, for that matter. As I said you are the only one who knows my life story. In my position I can't go around feeling sorry for myself. There are too many others I have to look out for."

The food arrived along with the wine so they started eating but Clare wasn't through with the questions. "So, you just came out of combat and you are headed right back. What happens now?"

"I'm told I'll have command of this new battalion for the next four months then I'll have to turn it over to someone else."

"I mean after Korea?"

"I'm scheduled to attend the Army Language school in California, the Command and General Staff College in Kansas, then a tour in the Pentagon. That should account for my next three or four years of service. When I leave here is unknown at this time."

They finished the meal, more wine, and ordered coffee and brandy. Clare seemed to be back to herself now. "I forgive you for your oversight Charley," she said placing her hand on his, "is it possible that you are free this evening?"

"I suppose the colonel could declare himself free from duty?" McNeil wondered if she was suggesting what he thought she was suggesting. He supposed women had the same want, needs, and desires as a man. They can't just go around expressing themselves as we can.

"I'm off duty in two hours," said Clare with a down cast look, "can you meet me at the USO building?"

"Sure, I'll be there. Let me pay the tab and we'll get out of here."

Their relationship was definitely not platonic. As Clare had said, no strings. They spent time together several more times before McNeil had to depart Camp Drake.

# MCNEIL

## DEPART CAMP DRAKE

## Chapter 23
## 7 Apr 1951

The cold days of winter passed into warmer days of spring and the snow changed to rain. All equipment that was authorized was not available but what was on hand was issued to the 1/5th Infantry Battalion with promises that the items not on hand would be shipped as soon as they arrived. All required personnel that were available were assigned to the 1/5th Infantry Battalion until the strength rose to over a thousand men. One of the most welcome additions to the battalion was a 105 Howitzer Battery, complete with men, an Artillery Captain, Capt. Follett. to command it, vehicles to move the guns, around plus the ammo.

After the loss of the original battalion and most all equipment the re-born battalion had never had a mess facility, they used Baker companies mess. Now the 1/5th Infantry Battalion Headquarters Company had its own mess facility with a mess sergeant, Sfc Merrill plus five cooks. SSgt. Leeks expressed his desire to be transferred shortly after arriving at Camp Drake and McNeil thought that was a good idea and approved his request.

By the end of the first week of April all preparations were made for the trip back to Korea and the 38thparallel. McNeil purchased several boxes of those Cuban cigars he had grown to like plus a couple of bottles of good scotch. He paid his respects to General Dickerson to thank him for his support. The last night before departing Camp Drake he went to the club to feast on a big steak with all the trimmings.

Since there wasn't anything between him and Clare, no strings she had said, and he figured he would never see her again, he wrote her a long letter rather than going by to say goodbye.

With a full staff to handle all plans and details there was little for McNeil to do except watch and wait. Since this would be a large movement of vehicles the MP's decided it would be best to make the move to the docks at night when there would be less traffic. Midnight was the time selected.

All the barracks were cleaned and all personal gear loaded on the trucks prior to the evening meal. Drivers were assigned to the trucks and all others would ride in the buses provided. McNeil had Willis transmit a last message to 5th Infantry Division Headquarters prior to midnight giving the time of departure from Camp Drake of the 1/5 Battalion.Everything that could be done was done well before midnight.

The weather had changed from cold and snow to warm and balmy. Rain fell often but didn't last long, just April showers.

At the stroke of midnight the signal was given to start engines, the convoy moved out led by an MP jeep with one bringing up the rear of the long convoy.

The normal procedure is that the last vehicle loaded on the L S T is the first vehicle off so McNeil made sure his and Major Ellis's jeeps were the last loaded plus a 6x6 with over three tons of rifle ammo and grenades. McNeil, having been in Korea, wanted his people prepared when they hit land. Each person would get a hundred round of ammo and two grenades upon leaving the ship.

As soon as McNeil's jeep was loaded on the L S T the mooring ropes were untied and the ship was pushed away from the dock. When both L S T's were out in the bay and moving, two destroyer escorts took up position alongside.

The plan was to make it to Korea and have most of the ships unloaded before full light of the next day. They would spend the rest of the night and the next day on the water. The captains of these medium size ships got nervous when they were too close to land. They wanted to be far out to sea and out of reach of any artillery as quickly as possible.

Per instructions, the men were drilled on safety, personal hygiene, what to expect in combat, and what had become to be known as Raiders rules. No lights outside a tent after dark, no comforts before the lowest ranking man was taken care of, etc., etc.

Classes were conducted by the Corporal squad leaders, by the Platoon sergeants, and by the company First Sergeants. Classes went on continuously except for time off to sleep and eat.

McNeil and Major Ellis had briefing sessions with the officers to remind them of the Raider rules plus what would be expected of the officers at the 38th Parallel. Plans were made as to where each unit and each part of each unit would set up in relation to each other. McNeil was not familiar with the area but he had a good working idea. He knew some of the plans may have to be altered once he saw the area.

Some changes had been made with the new T O E. No longer was there a Dog Company, now it was Delta Company. Headquarters Company was now designated Able Company and Echo Company was added.

Captain Kirby and his S-2 Sergeant spent some time coming up with a list of call signs. A commander is always Six and his second in command is Five, but the other officers and key NCO's needed a call sign, or number, for communication purposes.

It was an hour before dawn when the L S T's stopped engines and dropped anchors. This time it was not at the familiar Ongjin Peninsula landing but on the main land about two miles south of the where the 5th Division was set up. No sooner had the anchors been dropped than the big front door were opened and the mike boats went into the water. As planned, McNeil's jeep plus Major Ellis' were on the first mike boat and headed for shore along with as many men as could get on the boat. There was a light fog across the water making it hard to see more than a few feet but the mike boat operators knew where to go.

There were MP's and a line of 6x6 trucks waiting on the beach plus Blue Stallion six. When LTC. Albright, the commander of the 2/5th Infantry Battalion saw Col. McNeil got out of the jeep he made a commented to General Layton. "He looks even younger that I expected sir."

"He's young but one hell of a combat commander, and that's not saying my other commanders are not good, just that somehow McNeil has a way of earning the respect of his men and they are devoted to him. I wouldn't want what I just said to get back to him."

"Understood sir."

McNeil had Pfc Gooding pull his jeep off to the side and park. He left his jeep and went to General Layton to report in. "Sir, Lieutenant Colonel McNeil with the men of the 1/5 Infantry Battalion reporting for duty."

"Good to have you back Col. McNeil. Have you met Col. Albright, the 2/5th Infantry Battalion commander?"

"I haven't had the pleasure. Good to meet you colonel," said McNeil reaching for his hand.

"My pleasure Colonel. How was the trip?"

"Smooth but long and boring."

"General may I present my battalion XO Major Ellis. Major Ellis, General Layton, the 5th Infantry Division Commander."

"Glad to meet you sir," said Major Ellis.

"Major Ellis, welcome aboard."

"Thank you very much sir."

"Col McNeil, those 6x6's are to carry your men who don't have a ride. The MP's will lead your convoy to the 38th parallel. I want you to get with Col. Albright and brief him on what to expect at Camp Drake and he can brief you on the situation of your new area of responsibility. I expect to see you at the division staff meeting today at seventeen hundred."

"Yes sir, I'll be there. Sir, with your permission, I would like to get my staff officers and NCO's together with their division counterparts so they can get briefed on the current situation and what will be expected of them. I think now would be a good time."

"By all means. A good idea."

"Major Ellis you are in charge of the landing site. I'll be with Col. Albright."

"Yes sir."

After they were both in McNeil's jeep and moving up the road, which was now a muddy mess and soon to get worse with all the traffic, McNeil spoke, "those Mike boats are fast so make sure your people and vehicles are ready."

"They are lined up and waiting, that is except for those at the M L R waiting for your people." Unlike the 1/5th Infantry Battalion who had left all their vehicles and equipment on the Ongjin Peninsula the 2/5th Infantry Battalion would be taking everything with them so there was a long line of loaded trucks beside the road.

Before departing the L S T McNeil had instructed his officers that all men, to include officer, would stop by the 6x6 ammo truck and pick up a basic load of ammo for their weapons plus two grenades. He didn't want men on the line without ammo.

# MCNEIL

## South Korea main Land 38th Parallel

**Chapter 24**
**10 Apr 1951**

Very little changed for the 1/5th Infantry Battalion as they moved into the designated areas, took over security from the 2/5<sup>nd</sup> Infantry Battalion, and started setting up tents. The big difference was now they were on the mainland part of the 38<sup>th</sup> parallel and their rear would have to be protected from retreating North Koreans.

Where the Ongjin Peninsula was mostly open land with rice paddies the area the 1/5 was moving into was mostly wooded, especially to the rear of the designated area of responsibility.

Very quickly men were designated to take over the guard towers so the rest of the 2/5th Infantry Battalion people could depart. The plot maps, drawn up on the ship, had to be altered some to take advantage of cover and concealment, the use of trees and terrain. Camouflage nets had been issued at Camp Drake so they were used once the tents were set up and the vehicles were parked.

The 105 Battery Commander, Capt. Follett, decided it would be best to divide his battery in half since there was such a large area to cover. Six guns behind Baker and Charlie companies and six guns behind Delta and Echo Companies was his decision and McNeil agreed to it.

Each of the guard towers had a 30 caliber machine gun plus each of the company's platoons had a 30 caliber machine gun and a gun crew. Each company had a mortar tube and a mortar crew. It was an awesome display of fire power compared to what was available when they were on the Ongjin Peninsula.

When Pfc Gooding drove McNeil to the seventeen hundred meeting at Division that evening McNeil had him return to the 1/5th Infantry Battalion, and return. "You should memorize the road, ever crook and turn, since we'll be returning after dark and using only black out lights," he told Gooding that was his reason for having him make an extra trip.

It was dark with just a touch of hazy fog on the return trip from Division. Just before they reached the battalion area a man with a gun pointed at them stepped in front of the jeep. A man appeared at each side of the jeep with weapons ready. McNeil was hoping this would happen.

He knew there were supposed to be men guarding the access road plus a roving patrol in the woods. If his jeep had not been stopped he would have had to step on some toes about the lax security procedures.

Pfc Gooding, on the other hand, was not prepared for a man with a weapon to step in front of the jeep. His hands gripped the steering wheel and he locked the brakes causing the jeep wheels to slide on the dirt road.

The man in front called out 'ten' after the jeep stopped sliding.

McNeil replied with five. The pass word today was fifteen. "Sorry to stop you sir, "the man said when he saw who was in the jeep, "but we were instructed to stop all vehicles."

"No apology necessary soldier. You would have been sorrier if you had not stopped me. Keep up the good work soldier and keep alert. One never knows when the North Koreans may decide to sneak up on our rear."

"Yes sir. We'll be alert sir."

"What's your name soldier?" McNeil asked.

"I'm PFC Hartford sir, of Delta Company."

"Stay alert PFC Hartford."

"Yes sir I will. Good night sir."

"Drive on Gooding."

The cold of winter had masked the foul odor of Korea but with the weather warming up some the smell of Korea was returning, it was in the night air. Though not as strong as it was a year ago, the foul odor was still there. One reason the odor wasn't as strong was because of the unstable situation in Korea. Not too many farmers wanted to take a chance of planting and having their crop destroyed or confiscated by retreating North Korean troops so not too many were anxious to work the fields.

The spring rains wet the ground and mud was everywhere. It didn't take a certain odor to remind McNeil that he was still in Korea. His two years of military service would have been up this month, if the North Koreans had stayed home.

# MCNEIL

## 38TH PARALLEL

### Chapter 25
### 23 Jun 1951

Duty on the main land side of the 38th parallel wasn't near as hectic as on the Ongjin Peninsula. Other than a few probes to check defenses there had not been any major attacks since the 1/5th Infantry Battalion returned from Japan.

It was almost like garrison duty these days. A movie was shown at each company twice a week and even the two-beer –per- person limit was relaxed some.

On the night of June 25th, which just happened to be the day, a year ago, that the North Koreans crossed the 38th Parallel, McNeil retired after completing his routine of duty, paper work and checking with each unit commander to assure himself that everything was fine.

At zero three hundred hours he felt a hand shake him awake. "What is it?" he asked the dark figure. No light was on so he couldn't see who was shaking him.

"Major Ellis here sir. We have a situation on the line."

"I'll be right there," said McNeil feeling for his clothes. "Has the alert gone out?"

"Yes sir. Everyone has been alerted."

"I'll see you in operations then."

When McNeil walked into the operations side of the tent it was to find everyone gathered around the radios listening. Most all of the men were out of uniform. McNeil, not knowing just what to expect, had taken the time to get fully dressed, to include his carbine, which he had to trade his old trusty M-1 in for. "Gentlemen," he called out to get their attention, "this is not a drill or test, this is the real thing. Get yourselves and your people in the proper uniform, with weapons and have them stand by. Don't crowd Capt. Kirby and Willis, they have their hands full. Is the situation board updated Captain Kirby?"

"Yes sir. With all the information we have."

"What is the current situation?"

"An attack is going on along the M L R sir. It seems to be concentrated near the boundary of Charlie and Baker Companies. So far it's just small arms fire."

McNeil felt a nudge on his arm and Sergeant Major Lenear handed him a steaming cup of coffee. When McNeil took the cup he looked at Lenear with raised eyebrows.

"My contribution sir. A hot plate and a big coffee pot. I thought we could all use some hot coffee."

"My profound thanks Sergeant Major," said McNeil as he took a sip of the coffee then set it down and unwrapped and lit a cigar.

"Where would you like for me to assist sir?"

"Willis will soon need help with the radios and phones so lend him a hand, plus keep people from crowding him. He's a good man and he can handle the communications but not with people leaning over his shoulder."

"Understood sir."

"Captain Follett. You or one of your men grab a radio and get to the line. Stay in contact."

"Yes sir."

McNeil sipped his hot coffee as he stood studying the situation map. Something was tugging at his mind but he couldn't put his finger on it. The loud whump of an exploding mortar round finally jogged his memory. This was a draw. Something the North Koreans had used before. The probes were to analyze the response of the battalion then they could figure out where to best start their draw. Their plan was to draw the troops away from where the real action would take place. "Get Able Six on the radio now," McNeil called out without turning around, "and notify all units to stay in place. Do not move to the action area."

"Sir, Able six is on the line."

"Sir, what's going on?" asked Captain Murtagh, the S-3 officer, "I know an attack has happened on the M L R but I get the feeling you think it's a prelude to something bigger."

"Could be that you are right. Is the map up-to-date?"

"As of ten minutes ago Sir."

"Not good enough. Get the latest information and make sure the map is current."

The switch board was constantly ringing and calls could be heard coming in over the radio. More and more people gathering in operations to take their positions. Everyone was now in the proper uniform.

"Able Six, this is Raider six," spoke McNeil as he took the mike, "Get to your unit. Able company is reserve force. Get a 6x6 loaded with twenty men and a machine gun, full load of ammo. Move to a position three hundred yards to the rear of Echo Company, on the water. Deploy the men and watch. Copy?"

"Copy raider six. Moving as we speak."

"Willis, notify Echo Company that they have friendly's to their rear."

"Yes sir."

"Fox six for Raider commo. I see a mass of moving humanity on the north side of the cleared strip. Unable to determine number. Small arms fire used on the M L R plus a mortar round occasionally. Copy?"

"Copy Fox six. Stand by."

McNeil, even though his mind was busy analyzing the situation, had heard the report. He called out instructions. "Flare rounds over the area, now."

"Roving patrol to raider commo. Taking fire. Half mile east of dirt road. Copy?"

"Flare rounds on the way," came a report from Fox Six who had apparently heard the report and acted without instructions.

"Notify Able Company," called out McNeil, "A weapons carrier, six men plus a medic, to assist the roving patrol."

"Able Six in position. No movement on water."

"Flares over area. Maybe two or three hundred men moving on the M L R."

"Tell Fox Six to drop Canister rounds to their rear and walk them forward."

"Roving patrol has one wounded."

"Hold position. Assistance is headed your way."

"Movement on the water," came a call from Able six, "could be friendly's?"

"Negative on the friendly," called out McNeil, "blow them away as soon as they are close enough." his orders were repeated over the radio.

The ground shook as the 105 Canister rounds started exploding. A few mortar rounds continued to fall but they were starting to slack off some.

"Able six to raider commo. One boat nearing shore."

"Hold fire to make sure no one escapes."

"Shouldn't we be taking prisoners sir?" asked Captain Kirby who had walked up behind McNeil and was watching and listening to the fast paced orders.

"You want prisoners? Feel free to go get them. Right now we don't have the time to ask them to surrender."

"Able six to Raider commo. Boat destroyed. Looks to be about twenty bodies in the water. I have one wounded."

"Hold position Able six. Get a medic to Able six. Make sure no bodies are moving able six."

"The tide has turned," came a call from Fox Six, "the canister rounds are taking a toll on the North Koreans."

"What is the location of Raider five/" asked McNeil of Willis.

"I'll locate him sir."

"Sir. He's on the M L R. Do you wish to speak with him?"

"Roger that. I need a situation report from the line."

Two minutes later Sergeant Major Lenear handed McNeil a penciled message. Flare rounds worked. Attackers retreating. Canister rounds have taken a large toll. Two wounded on line. Men in high spirits.

"Able six for raider commo. Wounded treated. No movement on water."

"Stand by Able six."

"Roving patrol to Raider commo. Relief force arrived. Attackers broke off. Six of the seven attackers dead."

"Hold position roving patrol."

As Sergeant Major Lenear handed McNeil a fresh cup of coffee his respect for the young Lieutenant Colonel went up several notches. When he was first assigned to the battalion he had doubts that such a young officer could effective command a battalion. Now he had seen McNeil in action in combat and his mind was changed. In the past he thought age was the prime factor, because in age one should have experience. But here this young colonel, a man ten years younger than he was, had stood before the situation map and gave orders, precise orders, and never faltered nor lost his cool. He had anticipated the North Koreans and out-smarted them. Sergeant Major Lenear also noticed how the older staff officers, captains who were much older than this young man, carried out his rapid fire orders without questioning them.

"Raider five and Fox six to command center. Able six to keep detail on site until zero six hundred. Able six back to company. Roving patrol support to remain on site until zero six hundred also," spoke McNeil passing out orders which was instantly relayed over the radio and phones.

"Captain Cobb, gather the data and get the citations started for those wounded. Captain Kirby, work with Captain Murtagh and get the battle information on paper while it's still fresh in our minds. Captain Roshon, I'll need a report on ammo expended and any equipment damaged. You'll need that information in order to draw supplies. Major Ellis will assist where needed. The Sergeant Major and I will be taking breakfast at Charlie Company. Any questions?"

McNeil had a smile on his face as his jeep speed through the woods on the way to Baker Company. He had wanted so much to just drop everything and rush to the M L R and direct the battle as he had done in the past. But those days were over. Now he had a full staff to handle the details which only served to make him feel inadequate. Going to Baker Company, after eating at Charley Company, would serve a dual purpose. First, it would allow him to get out of the tent for a while, and second, he wanted to find out if anyone remained in Baker Company who had firsthand knowledge of the WASP because he saw a great need for one, no make that two, now.

It was two days later at an early morning staff meeting that McNeil revealed his plans for reactivating the WASP. "The WASP is not an authorized vehicle but a necessary one, he explained to his officers, but they were used extensively on the Ongjin Peninsula and saved many lives. I purpose to use two of them here."

"I don't believe I have ever heard of, what did you call it? A WASP," spoke Captain Roshon. "Where will we acquire one?"

"A WASP is nothing more than a modified weapons carrier and as the man who came up with the idea said, they carry a big sting. We do have some fifty caliber machine guns don't we Mr. Anderson?"

"Yes sir, four to be exact. I made sure we had them before we departed Camp Drake."

"And I checked and we have enough radios for two WASP's. There are some people in Baker Company who has firsthand experience with the WASP plus there are others scattered about. Use them Mr. Waterman and build me two WASP's. Use a weapons carrier from Baker Company and one from Echo Company. Here is the patrol route for them, plus, Captain Kirby look into setting up a listening post about here," said McNeil passing a penciled map to his S-2 officer.

Corporal Willis entered and handed McNeil a folded piece of paper. He unfolded it and read: see Col. MacMasters at ten hundred hours. McNeil refolded the paper and continued with his meeting.

"We were hit by a three pronged attack yesterday and we were lucky to survive it. They, the North Koreans, are fairly predictable. What they tried has been tried before, without success. With the WASP's patrolling, one on the water and the other the west boundary, we'll have advanced warning and a faster response time. If you have any doubt speak with those who have been there when the WASP's were used successfully. Now I'll hear from the staff officers. Please start Captain Cobb."

During the rest of the staff meeting and even on the ride to Division McNeil's mind was on the message. He had been told he could have the battalion for six more months, four after leaving Camp Drake, and the time to relinquish command was fast approaching. Could this be it? Am I to be told today? What will I do without a command? It seems as if I have always had command responsibility and I have grown to really enjoy it. I guess one can have his cake and eat only so much of it before he has to start sharing. But, it's been a great experience, one I'll never forget.

He found Col MacMasters leaving General Layton's office. "Right on time I see Col. McNeil. We, the general and I, were just discussing you. Come on in."

McNeil knew right away this was to be informal because he found General Layton sitting on his sofa reading a paper with his reading glasses down on his nose. "Morning McNeil, he said and motioned for McNeil to take a seat. "Coffee?"

"No thanks sir," replied McNeil as he took a seat.

"McNeil, began General Layton, there are several unpleasant tasks that a commander must perform and topping the list is writing letters to families of deceased men. The next unpleasant task is sending men on emergency leave. Mac, take it from here."

"Yes sir. Colonel McNeil, last night the division received a message from the Red Cross. "I'll let you read it," he said passing a message to McNeil.

The message simply read; To Col. McNeil, and the address of the 5th Infantry Division. Your mother, Mrs. Janice N. McNeil is gravely ill. Your presence is requested. There was a signature of the Red Cross representative.

The look of surprise on McNeil's face was mistaken for sorrow. "Please accept my sympathy," spoke General Layton.

"My sympathy also Col. McNeil," added Col. MacMasters.

"Thank you both but I hope you don't think me callus. This is way overdue. I have been expecting something like this for a while. What really surprises me is how did the Red Cross locate me?"

"Surly someone knew your address Col. McNeil," stated General Layton."

"No one sir. You see, when my father was killed, in a job related accident my mother took to the bottle. When I was drafted and had to leave I told her I would be away for a while. Her only response was; that's nice, be careful. Then she went back to her puzzle book. So no one knows where I am."

"Apparently someone knew because the message reached you."

"It would seem so sir."

"Be that as it may. Here are your emergency leave orders and Mac has your transportation laid on."

"The orders are for two weeks McNeil but if you need more time notify the closest military installation. You have just enough time to get back to the battalion and pack you bag. Have Major Ellis assume command in your absence. A helicopter will get you from here to K-1 in Pusan where you can catch a ride to Japan and Camp Drake. See the finance officer then get to Tachikown airport where you can catch a plane to the states. Any questions?"

"No sir. I suppose I better get a move on," said McNeil getting up from the sofa. He was almost out the door when he remembered something. "Sir, unless you have objections, the WASP program will be revived."

"Yes, I read you're after action report. They hit you from three sides did they?"

"Yes sir they did. The battalion is very vulnerable on the water side. A WASP would be able to cover more ground and give advanced warning to the battalion."

"Do you have the assets?"

"Yes sir, and the experienced people."

"Mac, follow up on the progress and it's possible the WASP may be a help to the 4th battalion."

"Yes sir. I'll make note of that.

As soon as McNeil was in the jeep he reached for the radio. "Raider six for Raider commo."

"Raider commo, go Raider six."

"Raider six in route. Have Raider five meet me. Copy/"

"Copy and will comply sir"

Major Ellis was standing in front of the command tent waiting for McNeil. "Keep the jeep ready," he said to Gooding as he got out, "I'll be returning to division shortly"

"Thank you for waiting for me Major Ellis. I don't have much time so follow me while I pack. I'm on emergency leave starting now, my mother."

"My sympathy sir."

"Thank you. Have orders cut for you to assume command of the battalion effective today, VOCG of the Division Commander. You are also in charge of the WASP program. Get it up and running because Col. MacMasters will be monitoring it. Use the expertise available. We need some kind of early warning along the coast so the battalion can react to an attack in time. I don't have time so would you pass on my profound thanks to the men?"

"Yes sir I'll do that. Any idea when you'll be returning?"

"Not at this time. Well, that's that," said McNeil picking up his small bag and reaching for Major Ellis' hand. It's been a pleasure major."

"More than a pleasure Sir, and experience. Have a safe trip."

# MCNEIL

## DUCKENS KENTUCKY

**Chapter 26**
**26 Jun 1951**


McNeil could tell that very little had changed since his last visit to the Duckens area. It was April, fourteen months ago, that he came home to visit his mother before shipping off to Korea. Now he was returning, for what he wasn't sure.

Sometimes, because of the short time McNeil was an officer on active duty, he tended to forget that field grade officers were not forgotten in the rush of things. On the flight from Korea he was wondering just how he was going to get from the airfield to Camp Drake and get through the procedures in time to catch his flight to the states. That problem was solved when a Major Jefferson met him with a jeep at the airport. Camp Drake had been notified, probably by General Layton, and Major Jefferson told McNeil that everything had been expedited for his benefit. Finance was waiting and McNeil withdrew the funds which he calculated he would need for the trip. He located his footlocker in the big warehouse and changed into a class 'A' uniform. His suit and essentials were packed in the suit bag and he was ready to go.

An Air Force C-54 for the long over the water flight to San Francisco. There he was able to book a flight, with a couple of stops, to the Capital City Airport in Frankfort Kentucky. After changing out of his uniform, using the airport bathroom, into the dark grey suit he rented a car for the five mile trip to the family home place. The familiar road wasn't straight nor flat but curved and hilly. Forests and mountainsides boarded the road of each side. He turned off the paved road onto a graded road which curved through thick forests of pine, maple, oak, and poplar trees all waving their green foliage. He finally arrived at the driveway to the McNeil residence, marked by only a mailbox.

The old wood frame, three bed room, house where he, and his brother and sister, were born and raised was dark and deserted and looked so cold and uninviting. When he stopped the car and got out he stood and looked around wondering why there were no cars in sight. Where is everyone? He often wondered why his father had decided to build the house so far from the city and a major road. The house was built in the center of the five acres of land so maybe Dad wanted his privacy.

When he tried the door he found it locked then he noticed a note tacked to it. When he unfolded the note he saw it was addressed to Charley McNeil and signed by the Reverend Jasper who was the preacher at the small church where the McNeil family attended services when his father was alive. The note read; Service and viewing for Mrs. McNeil today at ten. Interment at eleven.

She deteriorated fast, thought McNeil, reading the note, from gravely ill to deceased in two or three days. He hung his head feeling the sorrow of losing his mother. He had hoped to make the long trip and see his mother before she passed away but that wasn't to be. He checked his watch. It's ten thirty. I'm too late for the church service but if I hurry I can make the grave side service. There isn't time to retrieve the hidden key and look inside the house, maybe later.

The small country church was a twenty minute ride from the McNeil house and McNeil arrived just as Preacher Jasper finished his speech. There were no more than twenty people gathered around the open grave when McNeil walked up and stood with head bowed. Only a few of the people did he recognize. He surmised some of them were his mother's coworkers.

He saw his brother and his wife Janice but his sister Katherine wasn't there. Preacher Jasper was shaking hands and speaking to those gathered and finally he stood in front of McNeil. "Charley, please accept my condolences for your loss," he said reaching to shake hands.

"Thank you very much Preacher Jasper. I'm just sorry that I couldn't be here before mother passed. Do we owe anything here?" asked McNeil looking at the double headstone with both his mother and fathers name on it.

"Your mother took care of everything, preplanned and prepaid. I was with her before she passed and she asked me to give you this," said Preacher Jasper taking a small bundle of letters from his jacket pocket that was tied together with a blue ribbon, "the letters is how I knew where to contact you."

"So you are the one who called the Red Cross."

"I did."

"Could we keep this between us preacher."

"If you wish. Your mother also asked me to give you this," he said handing McNeil a small box. When McNeil opened it he recognized his mother's wedding ring.

"She said for me to tell you to give it to the lucky woman you will one day marry. I got the feeling she didn't want the rings to fall into the wrong hands."

"I thank you for everything Preacher." McNeil felt a hand clamp down on his shoulder as he put the ring box in his pocket along with the letters. He turned to see his brother Ken with his wife Janice.

"I'm so sorry Charley," said Janice leaning closer and bussing his cheek.

"Thank you Janice. You're looking great." Janice wasn't a tall woman but the high heels she wore made her look tall. Her dark hair was cut short and he could see the sadness in her dark eyes. She wore a very form fitted, dark blue skirt and jacket which did nothing to hide her feminine body.

"Where have you been Charley my boy?" spoke Ken in his arrogant voice without giving Janice a chance to reply, "Maybe if you had been here this wouldn't have happened." Ken showed no remorse at the loss of his mother and he wasn't even wearing a suit and tie but rather jeans and a jacket.

Ken had a way of getting under the skin of people, especially McNeil. McNeil wanted to say 'why wasn't you here to take care of mother' but he knew Ken loved to argue and McNeil didn't want to give in to him. "I don't think now is the time and place for this," spoke Janice.

"Yeah, Ok. Well, tomorrow we'll settle this. Be at the house tomorrow brother because the Lawyer will be there at ten to probate the will."

McNeil could feel his temper rising and he knew he would never show up at the house to listen to Ken ramble about who did what and who should have done what. McNeil took a note book from his pocket and wrote;

To Whom it may Concern;
I Charley R. McNeil, being of sound mind do hereby relinquish all rights and claims to any and all assets of the McNeil estate this twenty six day of June, 1951.

Charley R. McNeil
Witness----Reverend Jasper P. Story

He turned to Preacher Jasper who was still standing and watching the two brothers. "I have written a statement Preacher, would you be so kind and witness my signature?"

After Preacher Jasper read what McNeil wrote he looked at McNeil and asked, "are you sure about this?"

"What is going on here?" asked Ken when he realized he was being ignored.

"Absolutely," replied McNeil to Preacher Jasper's question.

After Preacher Jasper signed the note as a witness McNeil tore out the page and handed it to Ken. "I won't be there tomorrow Ken but this paper should make you very happy."

McNeil turned and looked at the grave where his father was already in the ground and the casket holding his mother was ready to enter the grave. Now both his parents were gone and he had not seen his sister since the day of his father's funeral and he had just handed his arrogant brother what was left of the family estate. The slate was clean and he probably would not see either his brother or sister again.

McNeil, with a heavy heart, nodded to Preacher Jasper then turned and walked away without saying another word to his brother and sister in law.

After driving back to the airport McNeil turned in the rental car and booked himself on a flight to San Francisco. With an hour to kill he went into the airport restaurant and ordered a big steak with all the trimmings. While he ate he remembered the stack of letters and he removed them from his pocket. When he untied the ribbon he found that only one of the letters had been opened, the one he sent to his mother after he arrived in Korea.

He knew what the other letter said and he didn't want to open them just now. Why his mother never opened and read his letters was a mystery to him. Maybe she had her reason but it escaped him. He put the letters and the box of rings in his bag before he boarded the plane.

He had thought about getting something from the house as a memento but it was too late now. He had signed away his rights, besides; there was no room for such things now that his home was the Army. Maybe mother was smarter than I gave her credit for. She made sure I had the letters and the rings. What more memories could I ask for?

# MCNEIL

## SOUTH KOREA

**Chapter 27**
**30 June 1951**

It took far longer to get back to the 5th Infantry Division than it did to leave it since he was ahead of schedule there was no one expecting him and no one to plan transportation for him.

Once he arrived back at Camp Drake, after catching a ride in an MP jeep, he went to the warehouse and retrieved his foot locker. He stored his class 'A' uniform and suit plus the letters and rings. With no schedule to keep, he still had several days of emergency leave left, he went to the Camp Drake U S O/ Library hoping to find Clare and inviting her out to eat. She no longer worked there said one of the ladies. Her time was up and she went back to the states.

With nothing more to keep him away from Korea he went out to the airfield and using his emergency leave orders caught a flight to Korea. He spent a day catching rides across Korea to get back to the division. All total he had been gone from the division four days.

He finally reached the 5th Infantry Division late in the evening of the fifth day since his departure. He had just signed in and started to step back from the desk and bumped into General Layton. "Excuse me sir. I wasn't paying attention and didn't see you"

General Layton, who had been reading a paper, looked up to see who had spoken. "Colonel McNeil what are you doing back here so soon? I certainly didn't expect to see you for a while." My God, thought General Layton, he looks like forty miles of bad road. It must have been rough on him.

"Let's just say, I came home early sir."

"I see. I think. Well since the hour is late come on in the office. You look like you could use a drink."

"With profound thanks sir and could you make that a double sir?"

"That bad huh," asked General Layton as he poured Scotch into two glasses and handed one to McNeil. "Sit down."

"Mother passed away before I arrived and I just made it in time for the funeral."

"Then please accept my condolences Colonel McNeil. Shall we drink to your mother, and to all mothers, where ever they may be."

"Thank you very much sir," said McNeil as he raised his glass and took a healthy slug of the good Scotch. "I suppose the reason I came back so soon is that I had no place to go. Between losing my mother and my brother making an ass of himself I had to get away from there. Since I signed away my rights to the estate I had no home to go to. I suppose now I can call the Army my home."

General Layton realized that McNeil needed someone to talk to so he placed the papers on his desk and sat down. "Why did you sign away your rights to the estate?"

"To prevent a confrontation with an arrogant brother who has answers for everything, right or wrong. I couldn't see myself standing in the house arguing over trifle things with my mother recently committed to the grave."

"You have just the one brother?"

"One brother sir but I have a sister who didn't hang around for the grave side service so I didn't get to see her."

"Sibling rivalry, I suppose it happens in the best of families," commented General Layton.

"The thing between me and my brother goes far beyond competition sir. He thinks the world owes him something and when a thing doesn't go his way it's never his fault."

"I wish things could have been different for you McNeil. It's bad enough when one loses a parent then to have such a confrontation with your kin doesn't allow much room for grieving."

"No sir it doesn't. But, that's my problem and it's in the past. I'm ready for duty sir."

"Let me replenish the drinks," said General Layton taking both glasses and going to his desk to add more Scotch to them. He sat back down and handed one glass to McNeil. "If only you had stayed a few more days we would have gotten your orders to you and you wouldn't have had to return here."

"Orders sir?"

"Orders McNeil. We all get orders. A Colonel Gallenger, your replacement, arrived here two days ago bringing your orders with him. I had hoped to send then on to you so you would not have to return to Korea."

"I realize I was due for assignment orders Sir but I was also informed that I had another month of command time."

"It seems someone jumped the gun."

"So what happens to me now sir?"

"I have read the orders but let's get a copy in here so you can read them," said General Layton as he punched his intercom and made the request.

A sergeant arrived ten minutes later and handed General Layton a manila envelope, which he passed to McNeil. While they waited for the orders General Layton had refreshed their drinks again and McNeil had unwrapped a cigar and lit it. McNeil looked at the orders and shook his head. "Something bothering you?" asked General Layton.

"It seems rather foolish for me to go to D C, then back to California, to Kansas, then back to D C. That's a lot of unnecessary traveling sir."

"Not for us to reason why, but to obey."

"Is it possibly to amend the orders and cancel this three week leave sir?"

"You have so much leave built up that you will have to take it eventually. Why cancel it?"

"No place to go sir. I would rather spend the time here, in familiar surroundings."

"I suppose we could handle that. I'll talk to Mac and see if he can use you for three weeks."

"Sir do you have any idea who this Colonel Minion is and why I'm to see him in D C?"

General Layton did indeed know but he wasn't to tell McNeil what it was all about. "McNeil, you have questioned legitimate orders. I suggest you comply with them and stop trying to guess why such things are done. I'll see about canceling the leave and you can spend that time here at division if you desire."

"Sorry sir. I suppose I'm feeling sorry for myself."

"That's understandable. Are you sure you don't want to take some more time off?"

"No sir, I'm fine. Work is what I need."

The orders were changed and McNeil spent the three weeks learning about staff duty at division level. He also had time to retrieve his gear from the battalion and speak to the friends he had made during the past year and a half, especially Bob, Tiny, and Willis.

Willis did get his stripes, a promotion to buck sergeant. Once General Layton realized who the man was he personally went to the battalion and shook Willis' hand after the orders were read.

When the day of McNeil's departure arrived he said goodbye to Bob, Tiny, and Willis. Four people who were united by war. Four men who came to Korea as young inexperienced men and now would depart as officers and NCO's, battle hardened veterans.

After saying goodbye to his friends McNeil signed out and didn't look back. He had put a lot of his life into the 5th Infantry Division in a short time. The 1/5th Infantry Battalion was his first command and, as he was told, it would be a long time before he could expect another command.

He was too young for the rank he held but who but the president of the United States would argue about the orders personally signed by General Douglas MacArthur. McNeil had been told it would be a long time before he could expect to have a command again. He would have a long wait until his counterparts caught up to him.

# McNeil

## Washington D C

**Chapter 28**
**23 July 1951**

It was hot and muggy that day in late July when McNeil arrived in the Washington D C area. The place of mystic, the place of power, the place most people only heard of or read about and few ever visited. It was the place where McNeil had high hopes of finding work if he ever got around to completing his degree in Political Science. Now here he was, a country boy from the hills of Kentucky, at the seat of power.

It seemed he had been traveling for ages. First the trip from Korea to his mother's funeral in Kentucky and back to Korea, then this trip from Korea to Washington D C. According to his orders his traveling wasn't over with.

From Korea to Japan where he recovered his footlocker and packed his clothes, then an Air Force C-54 flight to San Francisco. When he stepped off the plane in California he was thinking about booking a flight to DC then having a leisure steak dinner but that was not to be. He was approached by an Air Force Major who informed McNeil that he was there to make sure he was taken care of.

"Major Gill, said McNeil, "I thank you for your concern but I'm perfectly capable of taking care of myself."

"I'm sure you are sir but I have orders to get you to the other side of the airfield where an air force plane is waiting to get you to D C. Would you follow me please."

Without further word McNeil allowed his bags to be loaded in an Air Force staff car, with the help of the driver. Apparently his itinerary was known and his travels were being expedited, by someone. Five minutes later the staff car pulled up beside a gleaming Super Constellation with Air Force markings.

"What is going on here Major Gill?" asked McNeil as he stepped out of the staff car and looked up at the newest and biggest plane he had ever seen.

"I have no idea Sir, I'm simply following orders, which were to see that you were on this plane which is headed for Andrews Air Force Base. Have a safe flight sir."

After McNeil's bags were stowed, by an Air force Sergeant, he boarded and knew right away this was no ordinary Air Force plane, it was for VIP's. The interior was plush with wide comfortable looking seats. A stewardess, this time a good looking woman in an Air Force uniform, directed McNeil to a seat and made sure he was strapped in. The engines were running by the time he was seated and the plane moved out to the runway. There were more than one of the lovely Air Force ladies to cater to the wants and needs of the passengers, and there were several. McNeil had time to look around before he was seated and he saw several Generals, both Air Force and Army, and a couple of Navy Admirals, all looked very unhappy that they had to wait in the heat for a mere Lieutenant Colonel to board. Toward the rear of the plane were seated several enlisted men.

Once the plane was in the air and headed east a stewardess stopped by McNeil's seat and spoke to him. "Welcome aboard sir. Would you care for a drink?"

"As in?"

"Your choice sir,." the very pretty blond relied with a smile.

"Would I be wrong in presuming that this is no ordinary flight and something other than soft drinks are available?"

"That would be correct sir."

"Then I'll have a Scotch, ice."

"I'll be right back with it sir."

The clean smell of the lovely blond lingered as McNeil waited for his drink. He was reminded of just how long he had been without a woman.

When the lovely stewardess returned with the drink she handed McNeil a current San Francisco newspaper and a menu. "Enjoy the drink sir and ring if you need a refill. Make your selection of food and I'll be by to pick up the menu later." A man could easily get use to such service, thought McNeil as he tasted his drink then set it down. He removed a cigar from his pocket, removed the paper from it and lit it. When he had the cigar lit he opened to paper to get the latest news.

Even though the new Super Constellation airplane was faster than the C-54 it took several hours for it to reach its destination. McNeil had plenty of time to think. I have been in combat and survived and I have both the physical and mental scars to prove it. I have seen men die, I have killed men. How will that affect me later in life? The good book say's killing is a sin, is there a provision somewhere that excludes soldiers from that rule? If so I don't remember ever reading it. How will we soldiers be appraised when, and if, we see St Peter?

When the big Super Connie landed and taxied to the terminal at Andrews Air force base there were several staff cars and a bus waiting. McNeil assumed the staff cars were for all the brass aboard, the Generals and Admirals. The bus had to be for the enlisted men. He waited until all the brass had deplaned before he picked up his carryon bag and left the plane. When he reached the ground he saw an Air Force sergeant separating his bags from the few remaining. "I'll take those and thank you sergeant."

"Sir, I was told to put your bags in the staff car."

"You don't like the shiny staff car I came to pick you up in Col. McNeil?" asked an Army Lieutenant Colonel who had walked up behind McNeil.

"I assumed those staff cars were for all the brass Col. Scott. I was going to call for transportation as soon as I contacted a Col. Minor."

"Col. Minor is the one who arranged this flight for you and the staff car, he is aware of your arrival. How was your flight?"

"Good, but a bit chilly on board."

"I'm sure the brass wasn't too happy having to wait in California for a Lieutenant Colonel to board. This way please and we'll get you to your hotel."

"Colonel, just what is going on here?"

"I'm not sure. I'm just following----"

"I know, just following orders. I'm beginning to feel like a dog on a leash. I'm being led somewhere but I have no idea where and for what."

"I'm sure once we have you settled in Col. Minor will explain everything to you."

The weather was hot and humid and the staff car air condition was working on high to cool the vehicle and the men inside as the driver made his way from the Air Force base to down town D.C. Since LTC Scott had said he didn't have any idea what was going on McNeil refrained from asking any more questions. However, it seemed the staff car driver knew where to go. The early morning traffic was heavy but the driver seemed to know his way around as if he had driven here many times.

McNeil assumed they were headed for one of the several military bases around the DC area where he would be given quarters until this business with COL Minor was completed, whatever that business was.

When the Air Force staff car turned into the entrance of the D C Hilton and stopped under the portico two porters came out pushing a cart.

"Why are we stopping here?" McNeil asked of LTC Scott.

"This is where COL Minor has put you up during your stay in D C."

"For a man who doesn't know much you seem to have information I'm not getting."

"I'm sorry colonel but I was given specific orders but without a reason. If you will follow me sir we'll get you settled in."

With the help of the driver McNeil's bags were removed from the staff car and loaded on the cart. McNeil got out of the car and looked around at the majestic hotel. The building was six stories tall and made of some kind of stone. Flowers were in bloom everywhere he looked. This is certainly several steps up from what I just left, tent city in Korea, not a place I would go unless I was taking a good looking woman for one night to impress her. If the inside is as impressive as the outside it must cost a small fortune to stay here. McNeil turned to LTC Scott who was waiting for him. "I'm just a poor boy from Kentucky colonel, certainly not rich; I could have made do with a BOQ room somewhere. I'm sure the cost of lodging here for one night is more than the quarters allowance for a colonel for a month."

McNeil did have money, more than he had ever had or seen in his life. He couldn't believe how much money was being held in finance for him until he watched the finance officer start counting out twenty dollar bills, real money, not that military funny money. The money was in a thick envelope inside the attach case he had purchased at Camp Drake to keep his files and other papers he had accumulated. There was far too much money to fit in his wallet or leave lying around. Maybe the hotel had a safe he could put the money in for safe keeping?

"This is where COL Minor said to bring you sir, and I'm just following---

"I know, just following orders."

"I failed to tell you. There is a fine restaurant and bar inside and your bill for each is to be charged to the room; all courtesy of the U S Army. Shall we get you signed in?"

Apparently McNeil was expected because the manager, Mr. Paine, met him and greeted him by name. "Welcome to the Hilton Col. McNeil. Your room is ready if you will just sign the card. If you need anything please call me."

Once all the bags were dropped off in room 305 and the porters left Col. Scott made a call from the room phone. "He made it ok." It was a one sided conversation for McNeil who had started to remove his jacket.

"Is he checked in ok?

"Yes, no problem there."

"How does he look?

"A bit travel worn."

"Uniform and hair cut?"

"Not so good."

"Get him to Fort McNair Quartermaster now. I'll call ahead so they will be expecting you."

"Yes sir I'll take care of that."

"With a new uniform and a haircut will he look presentable tomorrow?"

"Yes sir."

"After your return from Ft. McNair tell Col. McNeil I'll see him for breakfast in the hotel dining room at six AM then you can get on with your other duties. I don't think a colonel needs a sitter overnight."

"Yes sir."

"I'm supposed to call a Col. Minor upon my arrival," spoke McNeil after Col. Scott put down the phone

"No need to. I just spoke with him. Right now he is calling the Fort McNair Quartermaster. Your uniform is a bit mussed and you could stand a haircut. Put your jacket back on and we'll take a ride. You'll be issued a new uniform and while it's being pressed we'll get that hair cut for you."

Reluctantly McNeil, who was still feeling like a dog on a leash, buttoned his jacket and followed Col. Scott out of the room. He had been traveling for the past twenty hours now and he was beginning to feel it. What he really needed was food, a drink, a bath, then bed, and in that order if possible.

Three hours later Col. Scott dropped McNeil back at the hotel with a new pressed class 'A' uniform with all the ribbons and badges in place. There really wasn't anything wrong with the pink and green uniform he wore except that it needed cleaning and pressing but, he now had an extra uniform, at no cost to him.

"Col. Minor will meet you in the dining room at zero six hundred hours. Class 'A' uniform, "said Col. Scott just before he got back in the staff car.

McNeil went to his room to hang up the uniform and he altered his wants and needs a bit. First he took a long hot bath then dressed in casual clothes before going down to the hotel dining room. It was noon and since nothing was apparently on schedule he ordered a tall Scotch over ice while he went over the very long and impressive menu. With all the fancy food he could have ordered he stuck with the basic, a salad and a big steak with the trimmings. With the food he ordered a good red wine. Afterwards he switched to coffee with a small desert.

While he sat eating he noticed two well dressed women enter the bar and order drinks. He guessed by their manner of dress and the way they eyed the customers that they were hookers. He thought about inviting one to his table but with all the unknown happening plus the early morning meeting he thought it best to not get involved.

Before he signed his bill he ordered a bottle of Scotch to take back to his room. Why not, he decided, since all this is being catered by the Army for some unknown reason.

His plans were to go back to his room and have a drink while reading a newspaper to see just what was happening in the world. He got undressed ,mixed a drink, and lit a cigar. He sat down in the easy chair to smoke and read the newspaper. He found the local D C paper to be as uninformative about Korea as the other papers he had read since his return to the states. Nothing was mentioned of the hard ships the men suffered due to the lack of equipment, supplies, and man power shortage. When he felt his eyes get heavy he stubbed out his cigar, laid the paper on the coffee table, and crawled into the bed. His body had traveled many miles and went through several time zones and the effects were now being felt.

A year ago, no, make that two years ago, someone would have had to wake McNeil so he wouldn't be late for class. Now, after better than a year in combat and being awaken at all hours of the night and learning to get by on less sleep, he awoke feeling refreshed at four AM the next morning. He had slept for better than twelve hours. After a bath and shave he dressed in the new uniform and checked himself over in the mirror. When he was satisfied he left his room at exactly ten minutes till six AM and headed down stairs for the dining room.

He was surprised to see there were a few other early risers seated in the dining room. It wasn't hard to spot Col. Minor because he was the only man there in a military uniform and he was seated in a booth away from the other patrons. Col. Minor saw McNeil approach the booth and stood up.

What McNeil saw was an officer who looked like a recruiting poster of what an Army officer should look like. Col. Minor was a tall, very distinguished looking, well-built and wore a pencil thin mustache. He looked like one of those movie stars. His uniform did not come off the rack at the quartermaster. It was made of very fine cloth and tailored to fit him perfectly.

"Good morning Col. McNeil," spoke Col. Minor extending his hand, "we finally meet."

"Good morning Col. Minor. I would have called according to my orders but Col. Scott said he had taken care of notifying you of my arrival."

"He did indeed. Please, have a seat."

"May I assume sir, that you are the man with some answers?"

"You may. But right now have some coffee and they make the best Eggs Benedict here which is what I'm having."

"I bow to your judgment sir."

"Then I'll order the same for the both of us."

After the order was placed and McNeil had a cup of coffee in front of him he spoke, "Colonel, just why am I here, in D C?"

"You do cut right to the point don't you Col McNeil?"

"I find that it saves time sir."

"Well, first, let's talk about Korea so you'll have a better idea of why you are here. According to the papers I received on you, you were there, in Korea, from the first. Is that correct?"

"Even before the border crossing incident which is being called a police action but just another name for a war."

"You sound a bit bitter."

"One would have had to be there sir. Because of inadequate planning, lack of properly trained men, and a shortage of supplies and equipment, thousands of men are being killed or wounded needlessly."

"You said are, rather than was. I was under the impression that men and material was available over there now."

"It's arriving slowly, but a bit too late and nowhere near enough."

"You were wounded eight times I believe."

"I never could learn to keep my head down sir."

"Would you say the same thing to the Army Chief of Staff if you met him?"

"I would if he asked me sir. I don't believe in sugar coating information. The truth is always better. Will I be meeting him sir?"

"Anything is possibly but meeting the Army Chief of Staff isn't on the schedule. Because of the situation in Korea, of which you have firsthand knowledge of, not only the Army but all branches of the military are having a hard time recruiting personnel. What would you suggest to correct this problem?"

The food arrived and they continued to talk as they ate. "First, I can well understand why men are not anxious to rush over there and get killed because of the lack of training and proper equipment. I would venture to say that those responsible for the lack of proper planning will never come forward and admit their mistakes. Identifying and eliminating those at fault would be the way to start correcting this inadequacy."

"Would you believe the President has been slapping, those responsible, on the wrist. Plus some have been relieved of duty. Take it from me that the problem has been recognized and action taken to make sure it never happens again."

"I have not read or heard anything along those lines sir but I'll take your word on that."

"If that got out to the press it would be like throwing fuel on a fire, bad publicity."

"What part of the military establishment do you represent sir? I don't recognize that insignia you are wearing."

"I'm with the office of Military Public Affairs, better known as the Public Information office, or P I O."

"Is the P I O tasked with covering up this inadequacy of military planning? If so just what part am I to play in it?"

"As I said before Colonel, you do cut right to the point, don't you. But to answer your question, no, the P I O has not been tasked with any cover up. As to why you are here and I'm surprised that you have no clue. Maybe the Army can keep a secret. Lieutenant Colonel Charley R. McNeil you are here to receive the highest award that can be bestowed on a military man, the Congressional Medal of Honor."

"I sincerely hope this is a joke sir," said a very surprised McNeil. "Are you sure you have the right man?"

"I assure you this isn't a joke and if you are Charley R. McNeil, serial number 0-637815 Lieutenant Colonel, U S Army Infantry, then I have the correct man."

"Colonel, there are many men, both dead and alive, who did as much or more than I did who deserve recognition. Do I have the option of declining the medal?"

"Since you like to get right to the point, allow me to also. I'm sure there are other men who are as deserving as you, but they were not recommended, you were. No, you don't have the option of declining the medal. Why would you? It's a very distinguished award and several things go with the Medal. First, there is extra pay. I don't know the exact amount right off. Secondly, even generals must salute the wearer of the Medal. Third, your children, when and if you have any, are automatically accepted at West Point, or any other Military Academy."

"That's the up side sir. I'm a student of military history so I know for a fact that the holder of the Medal cannot serve in a war. It seems ironic that once a man proves himself in battle to the point that he earns the Medal he can never again lead men into battle. I had high hopes of going back to Korea; that is if the war over there is still going on when I finish my schools."

"I wasn't aware of that fact Colonel, and I agree it's ironic. But the fact is, orders have been cut and approved for you to receive the Medal. In less than an hour you will be standing before the President of the United States to receive the Medal. I'm sure you believe in obeying orders. We all receive them, from Generals on down the line. After you have the Medal you will spend some time with the P I O making a short recruiting film. If you have any more questions now is the time to ask them because in about ten minutes a staff car will arrive to take you and I to the white house where the President will give us five minutes of his most valuable time."

McNeil pushed his plate away and took a last sip of coffee. He knew about orders and it seemed he had no choice in this matter. "No questions sir."

The staff car was stopped at the white house gate and checked; names were checked off a list before it was allowed to proceed. Inside the White House door a man in civilian clothes, Secret Service McNeil realized, patted them down and had Col. Minor open his brief case. McNeil was glad he had put his attache case in the hotel safe. He might have had to explain all the money in it.

They were escorted down a hall and stopped outside a door where another man in civilian clothes took over. "The President has allocated only five minutes for the ceremony. Please don't ask questions and cause the time to be extended. That would really mess up the schedule. I have allowed only two reporters to accompany you inside, one from a local paper plus your own Army reporter. We'll go in if you are ready?"

"We're as ready as we'll ever be," said Col. Minor.

When they entered the oval office the man who escorted them in went to the President and whispered something to him. President Harry S. Truman walked from behind his desk and stood there while the citation was being read.

McNeil stood at attention beside Col. Minor as the bull shit citation was read. McNeil was much calmer than he thought he would be as he listened to the reading of the citation but he did have a sour look on his face that the President must have seen. When the president moved forward to drape the blue ribbon with white stars over McNeil's head he spoke softly to him, "every war must have a hero son, and you have been chosen. Congratulations Colonel," he said shaking McNeil's hand.

"Thank you very much Mr. President."

"Now gentleman if you will follow me outside we'll let the President get on with business of state," said the man in civilian clothes. He never introduced himself and McNeil never found out who he was.

Outside the white house door several reporters cornered them with questions but Col. Minor held up his hands to quiet them. "Gentlemen, please. The reporters who were allowed inside have been instructed to pass to you what they have plus here are press releases," he said opening his attache case and passing out a stack of papers, "we have a schedule to keep so there is no time to answer questions. Sorry."

There may not have been time for questions but that didn't stop the reporters from taking pictures as several flash bulbs went off as the two officers made their way to the staff car. Once in the car and out the gate Col. Minor spoke, "Congratulations Col. McNeil. I thought that went very well. Here is the other part of the award," Col. Minor said passing a black box to McNeil which contained the small blue back ground with white stars on a ribbon he was to wear with his other decorations. "Also here are your amended orders reinstating your three week leave that you declined in Korea. That should give you enough time, after we are finished here, to get to California and the Language School. Right now, since we are in dress uniform, we'll go to George Town University for the first part of the film I spoke of. We'll have you sit in a class room to emphasize the education available to the military."

For the balance of that day and the next McNeil was filmed at various locations. He was dressed as a corporal standing in the ranks then as an officer with troops around him. That was titled from commanded to commander. To emphasize entertainment and relaxation McNeil was filmed on a golf course, at a bowling alley, in front of a movie theater, in the officer's club where a very attractive W A C was recruited to dance with him while it was being filmed.

At the end of the two days and after Col. Minor was satisfied they had everything on film that was needed he released McNeil to start his leave. Col. Minor sent McNeil back to the Hilton with a Captain to settle the bill. McNeil, before he checked out, went to the bar and picked up another bottle of Scotch then stopped at the hotel tobacco store for a couple of boxes of those good cigars he liked. He felt he had been used so let the Army pay for that use. Once he was cleared out of the Hilton he had the staff car take him to Fort McNair where he shipped all his military clothes, except one dress uniform, to Fort Leavenworth Kansas. His reason was that he wouldn't need any military uniforms until he reported in there so why lug them around for the next six or seven months. They would be there when he arrived to start the school.

Once he was free of all commitments to the P I O he packed the balance of his clothes, dressed in the suit, and caught a taxi to a motel close to the pentagon.

He believed in the five P's, Prior Planning Prevents Poor Performance. He had heard so much about the Pentagon, and since he would eventually be assigned here, he wanted a firsthand look at the monolith structure, the largest building in the world. He was able to sign onto a tour and he learned much about the Pentagon. Over twenty four thousand people from all branches of the service plus civilians worked here daily. That was as many people as was in an Army Division. The building was completed on land that was filled, swamp land, and was first occupied in the early forties. It was five sided, hence its name, and five stories tall. It was called the puzzle palace and McNeil had to wonder how many people got lost before they got use to the many miles of hallways.

The tour ended back where it started three hours later and McNeil was impressed with what he saw but he certainly wasn't looking forward to working here.

Back at the motel several things was on his mind as he sat in the dining room enjoying a good meal and washing it down with excellent wine. What about the friends I left behind? How are they doing? They are eating army food while I'm enjoying good food. Are they still alive? Are they wounded? How much longer will they be in Korea? The other thing he thought about, and again it was about prior planning, was that with the Korean War heating up the D C area would be flooded with both military and civilians who would need a place to stay. There are just so many VIP quarters and BOQ rooms near the pentagon and they would be filled according to rank. R H I P (Rank Has It's Privilege). It's best for me to plan ahead now rather than wait.

The next morning McNeil called for a taxi. When the cab arrived and he got in and closed the door the driver asked, "Where to sir?"

"Being a taxi driver I'm sure you have extensive knowledge of the area. Do you know where a fellow might find a house to buy? I'm looking for something not too far from the pentagon but near enough that public transportation won't be a problem; nothing elaborate nor expensive."

"A real estate office is where you should go for that information sir."

"I will eventually."

"I do happen to know of a fairly new housing development just started," answered the cab driver, "It's not too far from here."

"Would you please take me to it?"

Without further word the taxi driver left the motel and headed west. About five miles past Falls Church Virginia the taxi turned off the main road onto a secondary road, then onto a freshly paved street lined with trees. He stopped in front of a building with a sign in front; Corner Development, Sales Office. McNeil paid the cab driver then got out and looked around.

Besides the sales office, which also served as a model house, there were only four other houses, three completed and one under construction. Several of the available lots were cleared and ready for construction. He was impressed with what he saw. When the lots were cleared many of the trees were left for shade. He could see many Maple, Oak, and Poplar trees up and down the street.

A smiling middle aged woman opened the door for McNeil, welcomed him to the Corner Development and offered him coffee. He accepted the coffee and a seat. "May I assume you are here about a house sir?"

"That's very possible," McNeal replied as he started asking questions and listening to her sales speech. As McNeil looked over several available floor plans he listened to what she wasn't saying rather that to what she said. He knew that the Korean War happened so soon after WW11 and people were afraid to spend money. Money was far more valuable than assets when families needed to be provided for. It was a buyers-market and he intended to take advantage of it.

"Not too many houses have been started have they?" he asked the lady, a Mrs. Adel.

"No sir. The developer is waiting for some of the completed houses to sell before he starts more."

"Then I would guess that if one of those For Sale signs had SOLD painted on them it would be good for business?"

"That goes without saying sir. Anytime people see other people buying it generates interest."

"Then if I bought a house here it would help generate sales. What kind of a deal are you prepared to offer me?"

"Deal sir?"

"Yes, a deal. If a house sale would help the company why not a deal for me? A reduced price or maybe help with financing?"

"Well sir, you said your name was McNeil?"

"Yes ma'am, McNeil."

"I was told to offer a thousand dollars off if a party seemed real interested."

McNeil figured he could get at least two or three thousand dollars off since the houses were not selling. "How about three thousand dollars off the asking price?"

"I would have to get approval for that much."

"While you are getting approval, make that two houses at three thousand off, per house."

His offer was approved as he thought it would be and just looking at the floor plans he selected the two houses he wanted. Mrs. Adel drove him to a local bank where the Corner Development had made prior arrangements for financing and McNeil signed all the papers for two houses after opening an account and deposing enough money to cover six months of house payments.

He thanked Mrs. Adel then caught a taxi from the bank to the nearest real estate office where he made a deal for them to keep the two houses rented for him. One he would need in eighteen months when he returned here he explained.

## 29 Jul 51

With the housing problem for the D C area taken care of he checked out of the motel and caught a plane to Columbus Georgia. He reasoned that somewhere in the future, since he was Infantry, he would be stationed at Fort Benning and it would be nice to have a house waiting for him there. After the plane landed at Columbus Metro airport and he collected his bags he rented a car and went looking.

He found several houses but they were far out of his price range. He did find one just off route 27 near the Chattahoochee River. It wasn't water front property but the river was near enough that a person could walk to it. It was an older house but well built. The trees and shrubbery needed trimming and the yard needed mowing and the grass fertilized. The inside of the house needed no work but the paint was peeling on the outside and some boards needed replacing. The yard was fenced with a paved drive way leading to the one car garage. Because of the state of repair and the fact that it had been on the market a while McNeil was able to get a good deal on it.

Once he signed all the papers and made the same deal as before in Virginia, he went looking for the needed repairmen. During his traveling to and from the motel, where he rented a room, he noticed a piece of land beside the highway. It was eroded clay land with a few stunted pines trees on it. It had once been fenced but now neglected but nailed to a post was a faded sign, FOR SALE, and a phone number. Land was a valuable commodity and someday, being so near Fort Benning, there might be a need for the piece of land to build houses on. The price of land and houses were climbing each month he had found out by looking at the want ads and reading the finance section of the papers. If he could purchase the land his investment would earn more than money in a bank. Nothing ventured, nothing gained, so McNeil copied down the phone number and stopped at the very next public phone and dialed the number.

On the fourth ring an elderly woman answered. "Yes?"

"Ma'am. I saw this phone number on a For Sale sign and thought I would call and see if the property is still available."

"You must be talking about that worthless piece of property by Forest Road."

"I believe that's the one Ma'am. Is it still for sale?"

"I told my husband Harrel, now deceased, we needed to get rid of that ten acres long ago. With my husband gone it's hard for me to keep up the taxes on it. Why are you interested in such a worthless piece of property young man? I don't believe I caught your name."

"No ma'am. I'm Charley McNeil. I have some money I would like to invest. What are you asking for the property?"

"We were asking a hundred an acre but I suppose the market has gone up so how about two hundred an acre?"

"I could possible go one fifty per acre."

"Young man, that's ten acres and it'll have to be cash money."

"I wouldn't have it any other way. How soon can we close the deal?"

"I'll call my lawyer and have him get started on the papers."

"Ma'am, I'm running short of time. I have to leave for California within the next two days."

"I'll tell him to speed it up then. Where can he reach you, Mr. McNeil?"

"I'll give you the number at the motel where I'm staying."

Within three days the house repair was completed and it was turned over to a real estate company to keep rented for him. Mrs. Gladis Holster's lawyer called and after McNeil signed the papers and paid the money he now owned ten acres of worthless, property as Mrs. Gladis called it.

## 2 Jun 51

The next morning McNeil was on a plane headed for Kansas City Kansas.

He knew he would be at Fort Leavenworth Kansas in six months so he wanted to have a place to stay while he was there for the yearlong C&GS School, the Command and General Staff School. Since only field grade officers, Major's and above, attended the school there had to be plenty of B O Q rooms but McNeil wanted his privacy and he knew he wouldn't get it in a building where many other officers resided. Besides, he still carried quite a bit of money in his attach case plus he would draw more at the Presidio when he reported in.

He rented a car at the Kansas City airport and drove the twenty miles to Fort Leavenworth which is right on the Missouri river and just north of the town of Leavenworth Kansas. It was a small town and owed its existence to the military men who were stationed at Fort Leavenworth. Not only was the C&GS School hosted there but the big Military prison was there.

He stopped in at the Beattie Real Estate office where he met Mrs. Beattie. Lil, she said to call her. She was a very animated and talkative woman. She had greenish eyes and short brown hair. Probably because of her job she carried a few extra pounds but it was spread around in all the right places. It was obvious she was married because of the ring on her finger and the picture of her and, he guessed, her husband displayed on her desk. Apparently she assumed McNeal was married also when he told her he was house hunting.

She drove him a ways out of town to a housing development where a house was for sale. It was fairly new and one of those modern ones with the upper floor cantilevered out over the lower floor. It was now occupied she said but would be available soon. During her conversation she did mention that it had been on the market for a while, owned by a major who wouldn't be returning here and wished to sell it.

McNeil filed away that bit of information but told Lil that the house was too far out and too big for his needs. Something closer to town and a bit smaller was what he was looking for. "I may have misled you Ma'am," said McNeil on the ride back to town.

"Lil. Call me Lil."

"Ok Lil. I'm not married so I need a small house."

"Let me show you one you might like in town then," she said as she moved her skirt a bit higher up her legs, and fine legs they were, McNeal observed

The house she stopped at was a wood frame house on a tree lined back street, 124 Kildare Street, with a fenced yard. The house just felt right when he walked inside. It was cool and well kept. The location, the price, and the size were just what he was looking for.

During their conversations the two had gotten on a first name basis and when McNeil told her he was in the army and would be assigned here, that was the reason for the house, she offered to take him out to the base and the officers club, which I'm a member of she said very proudly.

"I wouldn't care to get on the wrong side of your husband Lil, but thanks for the offer."

"My husband is a lush and probable on cloud nine right now. He has his own business but for the life of me I don't know how he manages it."

"I'm sorry to hear that Lil. But I'll wait until I'm officially here to visit the club."

McNeil made an offer on both houses and when the deal was made and all the papers signed, and money was deposited, both houses were turned over to Lil to keep rented until he returned, they shook hands and she held his hand longer than was necessary and before releasing it she gave it a squeeze. "Charley," she said, "if you need anything, and I mean anything, please call me or come see me." the message was obvious and even though she was a desirable woman she was married and McNeil did not want to go there.

## 4 Jun 51

After everything was settled in Leavenworth McNeil drove back to Kansas City and the Lawrence Municipal Airport where he turned in the rental car and booked a flight to San Francisco California.

He had made a round trip across the states and now he was back in sunny California. It was the second week of July and hot but there was a cool breeze coming off the ocean to make the heat bearable.

With enough money left and seven days of leave remaining McNeil intended to relax and enjoy himself. With all the military and personal business out of the way it was time to enjoy some free time before he had to report in to the Presidio and the Language school.

Not wanting to waste money on a long taxi ride, and it was a long way from the airport to the town of San Francisco; McNeil took a bus and got off in the town of Daly City. From there he took a taxi to the coast road, the Great Highway it was called for some reason. There were many motels along the road but the prices were much too high for what he wanted. Just south of San Francisco he found a moderately priced motel that offered efficiency apartments that rented by the day, week, or month. He took an apartment and paid for a week. Just up the road a ways was a small shopping center which he walked to for his needed purchases. He bought food, beer and a cooler, magazines and newspapers, and visited a clothing store where he bought a bathing suit and more casual clothes.

When he returned to his home away from home he was soaked with sweat. He put away his purchases; the place came with a small refrigerator and stove. He could now cook his own meals and have ice for drinks. He opened a can of cold beer and downed most of it then he took a cool shower to wash away the sweat. He dressed in his bathing suit, finished the beer, packed the cooler, put on the new sun glasses, draped a towel around his neck and headed for the beach.

He had never been to a beach even though he had read about them and seen them in pictures. He was glad he had thought to purchase shower shoes because the beach sand was hot as he stepped off the trail onto the sand. With the new cooler full of iced beer and a couple of sandwiches he went looking for a place to spread out his towel.

There was a mass of people on the beach with hardly enough room to walk between the sun bathers. Ball games were in progress, kids running around and shouting, dogs chasing balls and barking. McNeil shook his head and almost changed his mind about the beach when he noticed that the crowd seemed to thin out to his left. There was a large rock formation that seemed to be the end of the beach. He started walking toward the rocks in hopes of finding a quiet place away from the crowd.

As he neared the large rock formation he realized it wasn't the end of the beach because he could see beyond it and there wasn't near as many people west of the rock formation. When he was even with the formation of rocks he noticed foot prints that seemed to lead right up to the rocks but he couldn't see any openings. Curiosity got the best of him and he decided to see just where the tracks led to. The opening between the rocks was well hidden and the trail zigzagged between rocks that were as high as his head. Several feet into the formation he came to an opening; about a ten by ten foot opening with pure white sand. From the open area to the west one could see the ocean washing up on the beach. The rocks afforded privacy and blocked the traffic and any other noise. The only sound was the wave hitting shore. McNeil spread his towel, then took off his shirt, and dropped everything as he went through the rocks and stood at the edge of the Pacific Ocean.

He waded into the mildly warm water until it was up to his waste. He found the salt water very refreshing. He started swimming back and forth until he realized he was panting for air and his muscles were burning. He left the water and went back into the rocks where he toweled off and applied sun tan lotion. He opened a can of beer and downed most of it before he lay down on the towel. The warm sand felt good to his back and the sun warmed the rest of his body. He finished the first beer and opened another one. Before he finished the second one he felt himself dozing off.

Sometime later he felt, rather than heard, the faint vibrations of footsteps. He opened his eyes and turned his head to look over his shoulder in the direction of the sound.

A most striking woman appeared between the rocks. In her late thirties McNeil guessed. Long tanned legs extended from a white two piece bathing suit that was stretched to its limit by the very rounded body it incased. She had on a white beach shirt, sunglasses, and a straw hat hid her features. Long blond hair, which it seemed most California women liked, fell down her back. She carried the normal beach paraphernalia on her arm.

After she removed the sunglasses and looked around she realized she wasn't alone. She gasped. "I'm so sorry to intrude sir. I had no idea this place was known to anyone but myself. I'll leave it to you."

"It seems I'm the intruder Ma'am," replied McNeil as he raised up and rested on his elbow, "I should be the one to leave."

"No, no. this is a private beach and I wouldn't have any right to ask you to leave. I am rather surprised to find someone who values privacy though."

"There are too many people and too much noise out there for me. I just lucked upon this spot but as I said, I do apologize for my intruding into your private spot."

"No apology necessary sir. I do hope you don't mind me joining you though?"

"By all means; there is plenty of room. By the way, I'm Charley."

"Liz here," she replied as she spread her towel, took off her shirt, hat, and sunglasses. McNeil couldn't help looking as he lay back down on his towel. There was a battle going on within that two piece bathing suit as she raised her arms to tuck her hair into a bathing cap; a battle of female body parts that almost defied the strength of the cloth. McNeil was so aroused that he had to turn over to hide the bulge in his bathing suit. He still had not stopped long enough to get his ashes hauled and he had to do something about that before he started school.

"I prefer a dip before I settle down to enjoy the sun," said Liz as she headed for the water.

"Yes ma'am I agree. I've already been in the water and it feels fine." he said as he watched Liz walk away.

He sure is such a good looking young man, thought Liz when she returned to the hidden area, and he seems so polite. I wonder what those spots are on his back, side, and chest. Looks like small buttons. That's none of my business though. No ring on his finger and no white place which would be there if he removed it. He doesn't stare at me as some men would. "Ah, that feels so good," she said as she dried off and sat down to rub sun tan lotion on her body.

She did see McNeil watching her through half closed eyes. He wanted so much to get up and offer to rub the lotion on her but the bulge in his pants would be far too embarrassing. "The water is very invigorating indeed. This is my first time on a beach," he offered.

"No kidding; your first time. Where are you from if you don't mind me asking?"

"I don't mind. I'm from Kentucky."

"That's beautiful country. I've passed through it several times but never stopped. Is your family here with you?" God I hope he says no. she though as she finished with the sun tan lotion and settled down on the towel.

"No family. I'm traveling alone."

"I'm from New England, Vermont to be exact. After my husband passed away I decided to come out here and buy a place. Now I divide my time between here and there."

"Sorry to hear about your husband Ma'am."

"Thank you but that was a while ago and I've gotten over it. I did tell you my name was Liz which I prefer more so than Ma'am."

"Sorry about that ma--Liz. Old habits die hard. Liz, I'm going to have another cold beer, would you care to join me?"

"A cold beer sounds good if you have an extra one."

"I have and extra one plus a sandwich if you would care to eat with me?"

They sat up and ate and drank and continued to talk. McNeil found her not only attractive but easy to talk to. After they finished the beer and food McNeil stood up now that the bulge had gone done. He started gathering up his gear. "I believe I have had enough sun for now."

"I believe I have also," replied Liz as she got up and started gathering her things.

"Please allow me to help you," said McNeil reaching for her bag.

"That's very kind of you. My car is just across the road in the parking lot."

And a fine car it was, a white Jaguar four door. Liz unlocked the car door, got inside and started the engine, turned the air on full blast, then touched a hidden button to unlock the trunk. "Just put my things in the trunk will you Charley?" she asked as she got back out of the car.

McNeil put her gear in the car trunk and closed the lid then offered his hand to her. "It's been a good day on the beach with good conversation."

Liz took his hand and looked at him with sad eyes, "the day doesn't have to end yet Charley. Unless you have other plans get in and go with me. Please. "

He could tell she was lonely so he just nodded his head. Liz reopened the car trunk so he could stow his gear. She left the parking lot and turned left on the beach road. No words were spoken as she turned off the beach road after a mile and onto another road. She pulled up to an iron gate then reached over the sun visor and touched a button and the gates swung open, then closed behind the car. Up a winding driveway which was lined with what looked like stunted pine trees she stopped in front of a rather large house sitting on a bluff with a breath taking view of the Pacific Ocean.

They spent five days together in the big house. She never offered her last name nor did he. It was five days and nights of unbridled marathon sex with short periods of rest when they were hungry. Each night they fell into exhausted sleep in the early morning hours. They never dressed. Liz wore a short robe and she offered McNeil the same. They made love where ever they were when the mood hit them, on the couch, on the floor, in the kitchen up against the cabinets, but most often in bed. It was something they both needed and no promises were made and no strings were attached. They gave to each other what was needed and wanted.

McNeil woke early on Friday morning and went to the kitchen and made coffee. He took two cups back to the bedroom where he found Liz still sleeping. He set the cups down and shook her awake. "What is it Charley?" she asked in a sleepy voice.

"It's that time Liz."

"What time? Come back to bed Charley."

"It's time for me to leave Liz. Here, I've made you some coffee."

"Must you go Charley?" asked Liz as she pushed the covers off and swung her legs off the bed to sit unashamed with nothing on. She took the cup of coffee and took a sip.

"I can't remember when I was ever offered coffee in bed. You really have to go Charley?" she asked again.

"I really have to Liz. It's been great meeting you and I've had a wonderful time here but all good things must end.

There was no pleading from Liz, just resignation that it was over. "Then I'll drive you to where you have to go. Let me get some clothes on."

"That's very thoughtful Liz but unnecessary."

"I want to do it Charley, for you."

At the motel they kissed and said goodbye with no mention of the future.

McNeil packed his clothes, checked out of the motel that he had used very little, and caught a bus headed in the right direction. After two bus changes he finally arrived at the Presidio of California. A very old yet beautiful military post where the Army language school was located.

He first located the school and signed in. Then he looked over the bulletin board where apartments were listed for rent. After he located what he thought was suitable he caught a taxi and went to find it. He left his bags in the apartment after agreeing to the deal and signing a six month lease; then headed back to the Presidio and the finance office. There he turned in all his travel vouchers and leave papers and he was paid up to date. His next stop was the PX (Post Exchange) where he purchased several more sets of casual clothes plus other items he would need at the apartment.

He spent the weekend putting away his clothes and doing some studying that he had neglected over the past several weeks. When he was in Washington he purchased a German language book which he found very useful now. He read the book to refresh his memory of the German language. The other thing he had neglected was the study material he picked up at Fort Benning. He knew he didn't have to worry about the Infantry officers basic and advanced course of instruction but he felt he may learn something plus when completed it would be on his records.

# McNeil

## Army Language School
## Class 51-03

**Chapter 29**
**21 Aug 1951**

McNeil was glad the he could wear civilian clothes at the school. If he had to wear a uniform someone would notice that blue ribbon with the white stars and questions would be asked. If the school commandant or even the post commander knew they had a recipient of the medal on base there would be all kinds of formal events he would be asked to attend. All he wanted to do was get through the school with as little notice as possible.

When he located the correct room on Monday he saw a name on a placard on the door and again the name was printed on the black board when he entered the room, Frau Ursula Heinz. McNeil knew right away that his teacher was a married woman. Frau was the same as Mrs. He had studied over the weekend and much of what his friend in college had taught him came back to him.

Frau Heinz was a big lady and she spoke perfect English when she greeted her students. As she explained that today would be get acquainted day but starting tomorrow all conversation would be in the German language. She made sure everyone had the correct books then she passed out a small test of twenty questions, written in German. "So I will know just how much of the language each of you has knowledge of," was her explanation for the test.

The next morning as she had said, she greeted everyone in her native language and she asked each student to reply in the language. When it came to McNeil's turn he spoke as if he was a native which surprised Frau Heinz. She started asking him questions in German which he answered in German. "Have you spent time in Germany Herr McNeil?"

"No, but I would like to visit your country someday."

"Where did you learn the language?"

"From a German, exchange student at college. We studied in the language."

"You learned it very well."

"Thank you very much Frau Heinz."

The other students were looking at each other wondering what was going on. It was obvious some spoke the language but others did not.

After lunch Frau Heinz called McNeil outside of the room and told him to go to another room where some tests would be administered.

He was tested in the language, both reading and writing. He was asked to wait while the tests were graded. After an hour of waiting he was escorted to the administrative office where he met a Professor Bennet. "Mr. McNeil, or should I call you Colonel?"

"Either will do but neither is necessary sir."

"The reason you are here is that sometimes we get a person, like you, who has extensive knowledge of the language you were sent here to study. All your tests graded out with a score high enough for you to pass. Here are the certificates and you may sign out and get back to your unit."

"That's good news sir but I don't really have a unit to get back to. If I leave here now I'll have six months to wait for my next school to begin."

"What is your next school Col. McNeil?"

"The C&GS school (Command and General Staff School) at Fort Leavenworth Kansas."

"Is it possible you have knowledge of another language which you could study?"

"The only other language I have ever studied is Spanish. I took two years of it in high school."

"Would you care to try it?"

He was sent to the proper room and started class 51-04, his second language study. It had been so long since he had taken Spanish in school that he had forgotten much of it. He found that he would have to really bear down and do some hard studying to pass it. He checked out some spoken Spanish tapes and books from the school library and each night after school he studied. He did find time to complete the course exams for the infantry school but that left him little time to socialize. All work and no play was bad. He started going to the officers club one night a week just to break up the studying.

He was able to team up with another Spanish language student and they were able to get together a couple nights a week which really helped. Even though there were several women studying the Spanish language he wasn't lucky enough to team up with one, he had to settle for a young man. The more he learned about the language the more he realized he did have a flare for languages. With the help of team study plus the books and tapes from the school library McNeil was able to complete the class and received his certificate for the Spanish language.

Because of all the time devoted to class and studying the six months seemed to fly by. Before McNeil realized it he had to sign out and start the trip to Kansas.

During his time at the school he thought many times about Liz on the beach. Her long blond hair and long tanned legs. He thought about calling her but he had failed to get her phone number. He though several times about just showing up on the beach and surprising her but he gave that up as a bad idea. She may have a man friend or possibly even be married by now. She may not want to renew an old friendship. What he finally decided was to move on and forget the past. What has been will be memories to carry forward in life; memories to warm the heart on cold winter nights.

Constantly he thought about the friends he had left in Korea. Were they still there, or did they finally get out? Were they dead or wounded? Will I ever see them again? There was always something in the local newspaper about the Korean situation but most of it was just a reporter's opinion. He knew much of what was written was what the Army passed out as press releases.

A month before he was to depart the school McNeil mailed a letter to Liz Beattie of the Beattie Real Estate to let her know of his arrival date so the house would be available upon his arrival.

Before he departed the Presidio he went by finance to be paid up to date, not that he needed money but he thought it better to keep his pay records updated. He signed out at the school, packed his bags, checked out of the apartment, and decided that since he had never rode a train it would be a good way to return to Kansas and going by train he would have a chance to see some of the Western lands.

# MCNEIL

## FORT LEAVENWORTH KANSAS
## C & G S CLASS 52- 01

### Chapter 30
### 28 Feb 1952

It was midevening before the train left the station for the long ride across the Rocky Mountains and deserts of the west. McNeil took his attache case and located the club car which had an observation deck where he could sit, order drinks, and have a good view of the country side. It would also afford him time to work on some of the military lessons he was behind on.

He ordered a Scotch over ice then spread out the material he had to study. Every now and again he would glance up at the passing view. What he saw out the window reminded him of scenes from a western movie. There were mountains, plateaus, weird rock formations, and plenty of desert land. Very little greenery could he see, mostly cactus and dried weeds. It was picturesque but not a place he would care to be in. He preferred green trees and grass. Even though it was February and probably a bit cold in the desert he could imagine just how hot it would be during the summer months.

People came and went in the observation deck but he noticed a woman with dark shoulder length hair who sat on the opposite side of the car from him. She was nursing a drink and staring out the window. She seemed to be alone with lots on her mind.

When McNeil ordered his next drink he also ordered one for the woman. When the porter, or whatever the people who work on a train is called, set the drink in front of the lady McNeil saw her speak. The porter pointed to him. He raised his drink in a toast then went back to his studying. He figured that such a young and good looking woman had to have a husband or be traveling with someone. He soon put her from his mind as he buried himself in the tests.

Several minutes later a half dozen men, well into their drink, came up the stairs bringing much noise with them. Up until now the observation deck was quite with few people in the seats.

That's such a good looking man and I don't see a ring on his finger, thought the petit woman. He did buy me a drink but made no move on me. If I don't move from here or do something those drunken men, one or more, will try to buy me drinks and pick me up. I think I'll take my chances with that nice gentleman because I don't really want to be alone just now.

McNeil was in deep thought about a question on tactics when he realized that someone was standing at his table. He looked up to see the willowy woman standing there holding her glass. She wore skin tight dark tan colored slacks and a white sweater, of which she filled out very well. McNeil stood up, "I'm so sorry Ma'am I didn't see you."

"I apologize for disturbing you sir but I wanted to say thanks for the drink."

"No thanks are necessary ma'am but would you care to sit?"

"That's very kind of you sir. Maybe if I sit here with you those men won't bother me."

"Please do ma'am. By the way," said McNeil as he gathered up the material he had spread out and put it in the attache case, "I'm Charley McNeil."

"I've caused you to stop your work, I apologize."

"No apology necessary ma'am. I have missed far too much of the scenery while working. It's time I stopped anyway."

"I'm Carol Bender from Missouri and you have just a hint of a twang in your voice so you must be from that area also."

"I'm from Kentucky."

"Then we're practically neighbors. Is your family here? On the train I mean?"

"My parents have passed on, my sister has disassociated herself from the family name and my brother, well, it's probably better if we stay apart."

"That's so sad Charley. No wife?"

"No wife. I assume since you are headed east you are headed home?"

"Reluctantly."

"Divorce is a sad situation."

"How did you know that? I mean that I'm divorced?"

"Your finger says you once wore a ring but no more."

Carol looked at her ring finger and saw what he was speaking of. There was a white ring where the gold band once was. She started to take a sip of her drink then realized she had emptied the glass. McNeil caught the waiter's eye and held up two fingers.

"Did you have children?" he asked Carol while they waited for the drinks.

"Thankfully, No."

"I gather you aren't too thrilled about going home."

"You are very observant Charley. I would rather go anywhere but home and have my parents say, I told you so." She was finding it so easy to just sit and talk to this man. He wasn't pushy and he was a good listener. There had not been anyone she could confide in for a long time.

She found herself telling everything to a stranger. How she had married her highschool sweetheart and following him out to California with promises of the good life. The promises and the good life both went away once they were settled in California and the bum, Carl Bender, starting noticing all the skimpy dressed blonds on and around the beach. It wasn't long before he was late coming home in the evenings. Then he was spending nights at work, his excuse was he had to work late. It didn't take her long to find out his work was on top of a blonde. She related more incidents that finally convinced her that the life she had dreamed of with Carl was over. "And I don't believe I have sat here and poured out all my troubles to a stranger. I apologize for burning your ear Charley."

She had such a sweet voice and such a gorgeous body that McNeil had to wonder how any man could find a woman who could top this one.

"That's what neighbors are for Carol. You don't have to apologize."

"Have you ever been married Charley?"

"I'm still waiting for Miss Right to come along and sweep me off my feet."

Carol laughed at that. "I believe you have that backwards Charley. You are supposed to sweep the right woman off her feet."

"Maybe that's why I'm still waiting around then."

They had talked through two more drinks and darkness was falling. "Carol, I have my limit of drink and it's time for me to find some food to absorb some of that alcohol. Would you care to join me in the dining car?"

"Haven't I bored you enough and taken up far too much of your time Charley?"

"We do have to eat and I don't find you boring at all."

"You are so very kind Charley."

They ate and savored a glass of wine with the food. Their conversation was as if they had known each other a long time. When the meal was finished Carol asked a question." Have you booked sleeping quarters for the night Charley?"

"Those seats in the pull-man car lean back and seem very comfortable. I'll spend the night there, maybe do some more work. How about you Carol?"

"I have a compartment thanks to a generous settlement of my ex-husband. If I'm not imposing too much would you walk me to my room? We could order a night cap," said Carol as she looked at the table rather than at McNeil.

"It would be my pleasure to escort you and I have some very good Scotch in my attache. But if you prefer something else?"

"No. Scotch is fine."

One thing led to another; a bump here and a touch there. After two drinks and more conversation they found themselves in each other's arms.

Carol had all the attributes required of a woman and everything was in the right places. She turned out to be a wildcat and she wasn't shy once in bed. It was a wild night and sometime well after midnight they fell into an exhausted sleep.

The porter woke them by tapping on the door and announcing that they were pulling into the Kansas station. "Are you getting off here also Charley, Carol asked as they scurried around trying to locate clothes that were scattered last night.

"Yes I am. You also?"

"I have to switch trains. Are you on a schedule Charley?"

"No I'm not. Why do you ask?"

"As you noticed I'm not too anxious to get home and I really enjoy your company."

It was cold with a few flakes of snow falling to add to what was already on the ground as they stepped from the train. They located their bags and caught a taxi to the nearest hotel. After securing a room and eating breakfast they went to the room. Carol had stated she wasn't too anxious to get home so they spent the next several days and the nights enjoying more of each other. Carol couldn't seem to get enough sex and McNeil didn't hold back.

Early one morning, a Friday, he told Carol that he really had to go. No tears were shed, no phone numbers were exchanged, No promises were made. They parted as friends, Carol to her parents and he back to the Army.

He found the house in Leavenworth empty and cold with no power. There was a note on the table with numbers for him to call to get the power turned on and the phone connected. No phone meant he would have to get to a pay phone somewhere to make the calls.

Apparently the utility companies were used to the quick comings and goings of the military, plus maybe because of the cold, because the power was on in a couple of hours. The phone was on an hour later. Even though the house had central heat and air it also had a fire place and there was a supply of wood. McNeil built a fire to aid in warming up the house. No food in the pantry so he would have to venture out in the cold once again. With everything out here some distance away, including the Army base, he knew he would have to have a car.

He called a taxi and had himself delivered to Fort Leavenworth. There he located the PX and the base bulletin board where, as he knew, there would be someone who was leaving and needing to sell a car.

After looking at a couple of cars he settled on a nineteen fifty ford that was in fair shape. After signing all the necessary papers he registered it on base then went to the commissary to purchase food. He also stopped by the class six store for some scotch and the PX for the needed supplies for the house. When he finally got back to the house it was warm and comfortable inside. There was about an inch of snow on the ground and more falling. The temperature was down in the thirties. Quite a contrast to what the weather was when he left California. McNeil made coffee and sandwiches and settled down in front of the fireplace to eat.

He had less than a week before he had to report in so he made good use of the time. He completed more of the school tests then went to the local post office and handed in a change of address plus sent a change of address card with one of his lessons to Fort Benning. He went out to the base and picked up a booklet which offered him information on what to expect while attending the school. He also joined the officers club which is required of an officer.

Liz Beattie came by the house a couple of times to welcome McNeil back and to see if he needed anything. She still gave off strong vibrations and made hints of what could be. McNeil had no desire to get involved with a married woman so he pretended he didn't get the hints.

The day finally came when he had to report in to start the school. He had to dress in his class 'A' uniform to do that. He hoped to get through that day without anyone noticing the blue starred ribbon he wore. The normal uniform for the school was the duty uniform.

The first day he met a Major Astern who was looking for a place off post. McNeil offered to share his house with him provided there would be no wild parties and he had to share the cost of everything.

A month into the course and a Major Tindal had the class on unusual military tactics and command decisions on the battle field. When he got to speaking about the use of what was called the WASP McNeil sat up and paid attention. Just how did the school learn about the wasps he wondered? His question was answered. "From lessons learned and battle field reports we learned about a strange vehicle that proved its worth during the battles in Korea. Just what is a wasp and why is it called such? How did they come into existence? Why don't we let the man who was there and used them most effectively tell us? Would you care to elaborate on the wasp Col. McNeil? Why did they come into existence?"

McNeil stood up. "First I'm surprised that the information you spoke of reached the school. But the reason for the wasp was born out of necessity. The idea came from an Alabama man who I suppose got the idea from running shine."

"What was the necessity Col. McNeil? Wasn't tanks available over there?"

"Tanks were not available to the 1/5th Infantry Battalion which was un-mechanized. The necessity came about upon receipt of a message that stated no personnel or equipment would be forth coming. Make do with what's available."

"And exactly what was a Wasp and how did you use them? Before you answer let me explain something to rest of the class," said Maj. Tindal. "Col. McNeil was there and commanded a Battalion on the Ongjin Peninsula, a very vital piece of real estate. Go ahead please."

"A Wasp was nothing but a 3/4 ton weapons carrier with a radio and a fifty caliber machine mounted on it. I had better than twenty miles of coast line to patrol and no men to do it. The wasp proved to be fast and maneuverable. Two wasps could patrol the coast line several times a day plus with a radio one of the Wasps could be called to aid when a battle was taking place. The 3/4 ton trucks were just sitting idle so we put them to good use. I had four of them."

"Did you lose any?"

"I lost one. A well placed mortar round got it."

"So, as you can see," continued Maj. Tindal to the class, "battle field decisions are made in a time of need and far outside the scope of regulations but necessary. If you gentlemen will follow me we'll go to the sandbox and discuss this further."

When McNeil looked over the sand box which was supposed to be a replicate of the Ongjin Peninsula and the placements of his battalion, companies, and men, he just shook his head.

"You don't approve of my sand box display Col. McNeil?"

McNeil explained that the peninsula was flat land with a few high places and plenty of rice paddies, not hills like what was depicted. The Peninsula had gentle rises of ground in some places and some ridges probably made by rainwater runoff. "And we were not on the 38th parallel, at first," he explained.

"Please show us just where the 1/5th Infantry Battalion was first located."

"We were operating back here. The ROK 17thInfantry Regiment was defending the 38th Parallel until they got rolled over in the first border crossing. We were there as advisors only."

"And where did you move to after the border crossing?"

"At the time I was commander of Baker Company of the 1/5th Infantry Battalion and we finally got permission to move forward to about here."

"What happened then," coached Maj. Tindal.

"The entire Battalion, because the commander refused to relocate, got wiped out. 80% equipment loss and only one man survived."

"Please continue Col. McNeil."

"I was ordered to rebuild the battalion using on hand assets. At the time we had some sergeants as company commanders due to the lack of officers."

"May I ask a question here?" spoke up a portly, nearly bald headed Lieutenant Colonel who looked to be in his late forties.

"Certainly sir," replied Maj. Tindal.

"Col. McNeil, I wasn't there and I have no reason to doubt you, but aren't you a bit young to be a Lieutenant colonel?"

"I suppose so colonel but I had captains who looked like they should be back in high school and teenagers for first sergeants. As I said before we had to make do with what we had on hand."

"Let me add something here," said Maj. Tindal, "Since I called on Col. McNeil. What he has said is true, all of it. He was wounded eight times and he did such a good job of rebuilding the lost battalion and protecting the 38th Parallel and the Ongjin Peninsula that he was promoted to colonel far ahead of his time. He was so outstanding in his duties that he was awarded the big medal, the Congressional Medal of Honor. Let me say congratulations Col. McNeil; Not only for the medal but for an outstanding job under the most trying situation. I salute you sir."

"Thank you very much Major Tindal but I was hoping to get through the school without any publicity. I suppose that's impossible now."

There were twenty lieutenant colonels and three majors in the class and during the break each one stopped by to offer congratulations and shake McNeil's hand.

Later on McNeil received letters asking him to join the Purple Hearts Club and the order of Congressional Medal of Honor recipients. He answered the letters and joined.

Once the ice was broken the notoriety of the medal wasn't as bad as McNeil feared it would be.

When McNeil settled down and started to work on the Fort Benning officers infantry correspondence course he found that most of the material fell into the category of; been there and done that.

A lot of the instructions at the C & G S also fell into the category of already done that. McNeil also noticed that some of the tactics of past battles played out on the sand table were WW2 or older. Some of them so outdated that if the tactics were used in modern combat the troops would get rolled over very quickly.

From experience, he knew that a commander in combat must have the flexibility to employ tactics based on weather, terrain, available supplies, troop strength and capability, plus status of the enemy. If a combat commander, be it a platoon leader a company or battalion commander, is restricted to or forced to use predetermined tactics the battle will be lost before it really begins. But he was here to get through the school, not to make waves and try to change what was being taught.

When the notice went out for the spring ball at the officers club it stated that mess whites or dress blues would be worn. McNeil had to put out some money for a dress blue uniform since he didn't own one. He knew that it would come in handy later on. Later he would purchase the expensive mess white uniform. The one drawback was that only medals, no ribbons, were worn on the dress blue or mess dress uniforms.

The evening of the ball he showed up with the Blue starred ribbon hung around his neck and an array of medals hanging from his jacket. As he stood in the doorway looking around a full colonel approached him. "Col. McNeil, I'm Colonel McAlister, the adjutant to General Miller, the post commander. It's the desire of the general that you sit at his table. Will you follow me please."

Major General Miller was a big man going to fat. When he saw his adjutant and Col. McNeil headed his way he stood up, came to attention, and saluted. "I'm so very glad to finally meet you Col .McNeil and it's a pleasure to have you here in the school."

"Thank you general and it's my pleasure to be here in such a fine institute of higher military learning."

"May I present my wife Adel? Adel, meet Col McNeil."

"I'm pleased to meet you colonel."

"It's my pleasure to meet you ma'am."

"Please sit colonel. What would you like to drink?"

"I prefer a good Scotch over ice."

"Splendid. We'll all have the same."

It was military custom that the guest of honor dance with the wife of the host, at least once. McNeil danced with both the Generals wife and the chief of staff's wife. He had just sat back down and took a sip of his drink when he felt a hand on his shoulder. He looked up to see Mrs. Liz Beattie standing there in an evening gown smiling down at him. He stood up. "Good evening Mrs. Beattie. I'm so very surprised to see you here." She looked rather chic in the aqua colored dress she wore that left plenty of cleavage and a bare back. The high heels she wore made her seem much taller than she was.

"Have you met General Miller?"

"Oh. The general and I are on a first name basis. I help incoming and outgoing officers find housing and make sure they have what they need. I had you pegged as a lieutenant being assigned here and here you are a lieutenant colonel. You kept that fact from me."

"I don't remember the question of my rank coming up in conversation."

"Well, anyway. You owe me a dance," she said tugging on his hand.

When Liz danced she danced close. She had her body plastered to McNeal's. It was hard for him to not feel something when a woman, any woman, danced that close to a man. "I hear that you have taken in a border Charley."

"You heard correctly."

"You don't know what you will be missing." she was very out spoken and suggestive. McNeil had to get his mind off the warm body next to his.

"Are you here alone Mrs. Beattie?"

"My husband wouldn't miss one of these affairs where the booze flows freely. He's over there somewhere in an alcohol daze," she said waving her hand in no specific direction. Remember, my name is Liz, not ma'am. "As usual I'll have to get someone to help me pour Carl into the car then help me get him to bed." hint, hint.

McNeil decided it wouldn't be him to help her get her husband home. Let some other horny officer have the pleasure. A few minutes of pleasure wasn't worth a lifetime of regret. "Sorry Liz but I'll be tied up here for a while. I'm sure you will find willing help among all these men."

There were three other occasions when McNeil had to appear in dress blues. The next time was the Christmas party at the O-club. The second time was the annual New Year's Eve party and the last was at the class graduation. Mrs. Beattie was there at each of the gatherings and each time McNeil had a ready excuse as to why he couldn't help her with her drunken husband.

McNeil did finish both the basic and advanced infantry school Officers correspondence courses while at Fort Leavenworth and received his diplomas. He finished twentieth in his class at the C and G S.

After the graduation ceremony McNeil sold his car to an incoming officer, packed his bags, closed down the house and turned it over to Beattie Real Estate to be rented out once again. Liz offered to drive him to Kansas City to the airport but he declined. Best to make a clean break he decided. To Liz he would forever be the one that got away.

When he left Kansas he stopped off at Kentucky State College, the college he had attended in Kentucky, to pick up extracts of his records and credits so he could turn them in when he registered at Georgetown University in Washington D C to complete his degree in Political Science. The language school and the C & G S would earn him some credits, how many he had no idea and would have to wait and see.

With three weeks of leave McNeil had plenty of time to get to Virginia and the house he owned there.

# MCNEIL

## WASHINGTON D C

### Chapter 31
### 10 Mar 1953

After taking care of business at the C & G S, such as clearing himself and signing out, he was able to catch a late bus to Kansas City Airport where he was able to book himself on an early morning flight to the capital City Airport at Frankfort Kentucky. He rented a car and drove to Kentucky State College to pick up the paper he needed. He gave some thought about possibly driving out to the old home place but gave it up. Knowing his brother it was probably sold by now. Since he didn't know his sister's or Ken's address McNeil decided it wasn't a good idea to try and located either. A visit by him would only stir up old trouble.

He turned in the rental car and booked a flight to Washington D C, vie Atlanta Georgia. He had just enough time to check his bags, buy a newspaper, and have a bite to eat, before his flight was called at one in the morning. Once he was seated and the plane was in the air McNeil relaxed and opened the newspaper. There was a brief mention about the ongoing Korean War, Police Action. He scanned it but saved it for later reading. What he came across inside the paper surprised him. An article released by the military about a Korean War Hero, a Medal of Honor holder, had just completed the Army Command and Staff College at Fort Leavenworth Kansas. Lieutenant Colonel Charley R. McNeil had completed the school in the top ten percent of the class. His next assignment was not released for security reasons. It went on to mention his accomplishments, which wasn't many since he had very little time on active duty.

There was even a picture in the paper that he could not remember anyone taking of him. It had to be at one of the club functions because there he was in dress blues with all those medals on his uniform. "A very good likeness," spoke a soft voice over his shoulder.

McNeil quickly folded the paper and looked to see who had spoken. One of the stewardesses stood there smiling at him. "Would you care for something to drink sir," she asked with a big smile.

"Coffee please and would you be so kind and not mention what you just saw?"

"Sure. My lips are sealed she replied with a smile. I'll be right back with the coffee."

It was the wee hours of morning when the plane landed at Dulles airport. McNeil decided that with all the bags he had and it being so far out to the Country Corner Estates a rental car was called for. He could turn it in later. He had notified the sales/rental office of his arrival date by letter in hopes that at least one of the houses he owned would be empty. A reply said the house nearest the sales office would be ready for him upon his arrival.

A cold March wind was blowing when McNeil finally located the Country Corner Estate just about daylight. Little had changed since he was last here except that now there were several more completed houses and it looked as if most of them were sold. At least there were signs of activity at them, such as lights on in the houses. His house on the other hand was dark and looked cold. Snow was on the ground and the trees were barren.

It was cold when he opened the door and stepped inside the house. He felt for a light switch hoping that the power might be on. It was, and he went to the thermostat and turned it up to warm the place up. Since he had never lived here the house was bare of furniture. Another problem he would have to solve since he would be here for at least a year and a half, or maybe longer. There was a refrigerator and stove in the kitchen but the refrigerator was shut off and empty. He turned it on so it could cool down. He brought his bags in from the rental car and stacked them in one of the empty bedrooms. First thing he had to do was get to the shopping center and pick up food before turning in the car.

He spent much more time shopping than he expected to but since there was nothing in the house he had to purchase everything. He wanting a good barbequed steak but he thought it might be a bit too cold to cook out just yet. Even so he added a small grill plus charcoal to his already long shopping list plus several large steaks. The shopping center furniture store was running a special and since McNeil would need a bed he went inside. If one purchased a complete bedroom suit, dresser, bed, and night stands, the store would throw in lamps, comforter, and sheets, plus free delivery. When he explained his situation, no bed, they agreed to deliver it that evening since it was a cash deal.

He drove back out to the Country Corner Estate and unloaded the car and after putting away his purchases he drove back to the small town and turned in the car. He caught a taxi back out to the house. He now had a warm house, a bed, or would have later today, and food.

The bedroom furniture was delivered, as promised, and set up. Being up most of last night plus all the traveling McNeil slept well the first night in his house. He was up early and had coffee perking by day break. The wind had died down some but there was still plenty of snow on the ground and it was cold. He dressed warmly then he took his cup of coffee and his, still boxed grill, to the small patio at the rear of the house and unpacked the parts. The patio and picnic table was clear of snow so he spread parts out all over the picnic table and sipped his coffee while trying to interpret the confusing assembly instructions. A very pleasant voice called out, "Hello."

McNeil looked up to see who was invading his privacy. Being a gentleman he stood up quickly when he saw who had called to him. A very shapely well-dressed woman stood at the edge of the patio. Even though the woman wore a coat he could tell she had a fine body. She had light brown eyes with just a sprinkle of freckles on her cheeks and nose. Short light brown coiffured hair, some would call blond. She wore a dark wool skirt, a white blouse with a sweater under her coat.

"Good morning. May I help you?" asked McNeil.

"I'm Barbara Morehouse the resident sales agent for the Country Corner Estates. I make it a point to visit each family after they are settled in. I know this unit was sold a while ago but I don't remember seeing you here."

"I'm Charley McNeil. I own two of the houses; this one and the one across the street. I wrote and asked for one of them to be empty when I arrived."

"I do remember the letter and I helped the family that rented it to find another house. Will your family be joining you soon Mr. McNeil?"

"I'm the only family that will be living here Miss Morehouse. I'm not married."

"Oh. I see. Please make that Mrs. I was once married but not anymore. I'm a widower." I wonder why some woman hasn't latched on to this handsome, rugged but handsome, man? Could be that he has latent idiosyncrasies that no woman can put up with. Stop being so judgmental Barbs, she scolded herself.

She said she was a widower so there wouldn't be a ring on her finger, thought McNeil. The ring on a finger was the first thing he looked for.

"I glanced out the window earlier and you looked lost with whatever you are trying to do here, in the cold." she said waving her hand at the mass of black pieces of metal on the table.

"I suppose I was, and still am a bit lost."

"What is it that you are trying to assemble, if you don't mind me asking? And isn't it far too cold to be out here this early in the morning?"

"It is a bit chilly but no, I don't mind you asking. The writing on the box says it's a barbeque grill. I'm not so sure now. The assembly instructions must have been drafted by an inmate of some insane asylum just to drive unsuspecting people like me up a wall. If I can figure out how to insert 'X' piece into slot 'H' before 'A' goes into hole 'C' I have high hopes of building a fire and turning red meat into mouth watering steaks this afternoon."

"Isn't it a bit early in the year for cooking out?"

"Depends on how much one desires a good grilled steak. This is, cook outside and eat inside weather."

"I can't remember how long it's been since I smelled food cooking on a grill or tasted anything barbequed outdoors. Would you allow me to help, with the assembly, I mean?"

"I can't accept free labor Mrs. Morehouse. If you wish to assist, and we are successful in this endeavor, and if you don't have a prior engagement, I insist you join me for steaks and potatoes later this evening. Of course, as I said, cook out and eat in."

"I really wasn't fishing for an invitation Mr. McNeil."

"I didn't think you were. Please call me Charley."

"Call me Babs, Let me check the office and get my coffee and I'll be back to lend a hand."

"Cups and coffee I have."

"Then I'll be back shortly."

With Babs, as she asked to be called, reading the instructions and pointing out the parts McNeil was able to finally get the grill together. He had watched her walk away earlier and then watched her return. She had poise in her walk, she had manners, and she was a very good looking woman. The question on McNeil's mind was why was she working when she could be married to anyone she chose? Why was she way out here in the country in real estate sales? Her clothes spoke money so why was she working?

With the grill together and the coffee finished Babs excused herself saying that she had work to do. They agreed on a time to fire up the grill. "I sometimes have to work late so I have everything for a salad in the model home. If you don't mind Charley I'll prepare the salad for us while the steaks cook; my contribution. That is if you are sure you don't mind my intruding?"

"I accept Mrs. Morehouse --- "

"No, no. Babs," she said interrupting him

"Sorry, Force of habit. Babs, you will not be intruding and a salad would go well with the steaks."

After watching Babs walk away he went inside to unpack his bags and spent the balance of the day putting away his clothes and putting the house in order which didn't take long since the house was barren of furniture.

McNeil had purchased paper plates and plastic ware and knowing he liked a drink in the evening he bought a set of real glasses. That evening when it was about time to light the grill he made a fresh pot of coffee and opened a bottle of red wine so it could breathe. After lighting the charcoal he took the marinating steaks from the refrigerator. While waiting for the charcoal to burn down he set the table with the paper ware. When the charcoal had burned down he placed the marinated steaks on the grill.

Babs had timed it perfectly. While the steaks were cooking she came over with a bowl of salad and set it on the dining room table. "That sure smells good, she said coming back outside."

"I have high hopes that they will taste as good as they smell," replied McNeil as he turned the steaks for the last time.

With the table set and the food ready they went back inside to enjoy the meal and talk.

"Charley, you can relax," said Babs as she chewed on a small piece of steak while spreading butter on her baked potato, "the steak taste even better than they smelled."

"Then my first attempt at burning steaks in such a long time is a success," replied McNeil as he poured the wine.

"You said no family Charley. You have never been married?"

"I never had the time Babs. I was drafted from college and sent to Korea. As yet I haven't met the woman I would care to spend my life with. What about you Babs? You did say you were widowed. I should offer my condolences."

"Thank you Charlie but it happened three years ago."

"Do you have any children?"

"One, a son."

"Must be rough having to work and raise a son."

"In a way I was fortunate. Joe, that was my husband, was a lawyer and worked for a big firm and carried a big insurance policy. Even though I was left alone there was a big house and enough money so I didn't have to worry. Before his accident I was a legal secretary for a rather large advertising agency. I suppose you are wondering why I'm working now. Well, I didn't want to be a secretary for the rest of my life and I'd go out of my mind if I had to sit at home all the time so I got my real estate license and this job. Now I'm working to get my Brokers license so I can open my own real estate office someday. That's the story of my life."

"Is your son old enough to care for himself?"

"He's a junior in high school, a boarding school. He's also taking ROTC and has plans to go to V M I (Virginia Military Institute) after high school. So, yes, he's old enough that I don't have to worry about him."

"That's good that he knows what he wants at an early age. The Virginia Military Institute is a good college. It has turned out some very fine officers."

"I know. I read all the material when he decided he wanted to go there. I wanted to make sure it was what it was advertised to be. You seem to know a lot about the military Charley. Oh yes, you did say you were drafted."

"Yes, I was drafted and I should know about the military because I'm an officer on active duty. I'm here for a tour of duty at the pentagon."

"Oh. I had no idea. Doesn't the army furnish quarters for their officers?"

"They do. But there are so many officers around the D C area and not enough quarters for them. That's why I bought the house here."

"You did say you owned two houses. Why two?"

"I bought one to live in and one as an investment."

"That's good planning. House shortages are causing the cost to rise monthly. You should make a good profit when and if you do sell."

"If I do decide to sell I'll contact you."

"Wait until I get my license."

"I'm sure I won't be selling in the near future."

"What about your family Charley? Where are you from?"

"I was born and raised in Kentucky. Went to school and college there, that is, until the draft caught me. Both my parents are dead. I have a sister who has disinherited the family and a brother who can't get alone with anyone, especially me. I don't have an address or phone number for either so I have no idea where they are and they have no idea where I am. That's the story of Charley McNeil."

"It's sad when families drift apart like that," commented Babs as she finished off her steak.

It is but I guess it happens more than we know," added McNeil as he poured the last bit of wine in their glasses.

"That was a great steak Charley. I really enjoyed it."

"And the salad was outstanding Babs. Now you just sit while I clean up and I'll bring us some coffee."

"I can't do that. I'll help," she said as she got up and started gathering up the throw away plates and utensils.

"I have a favor to ask Babs," spoke McNeil after they sat back down with coffee, "but not if it interferes with your schedule."

"We won't know until you ask will we?"

"No we won't. I need a woman's feel for decorating the house and purchasing furniture. I'll understand if you decline."

"What are you looking for exactly?"

"I want the house to feel warm and lived in without being cluttered and cold; something other than early Salvation Army. Something that is easy to maintain. Other than the small bedroom I'll need the whole nine yards, from curtains to dishes."

"Sounds like fun. I suppose I can get away for a few hours sometime. Where is your car Charley? I didn't see one out front."

"With the traffic so heavy and parking at a premium at the pentagon I decided not to buy one. I'll use a taxi service and the bus to get around and to work."

"I suppose we can use my car then, when we go shopping I mean."

"I'll spring for the gas then."

Babs went back to the sales office and picked up a note book, pencil, and a small tape measure. When she came back she went from room to room taking measurements and making notes. "I know just the place to go to get most of what you need here Charley. How much longer do you have before you must go to work?"

"About three weeks."

"We should be able to get the job done in less than a week," said Babs as she made some final notes.

When Babs needed time off to visit her son, or he was coming home for a weekend, she had someone stand in for her at the sales office. She had the lady stand in for her the next day so she was able to take off to help McNeil select the furniture and other items she decided was necessary to decorate the house. They shopped and ate out several times over the next few days. They were good together and the conversation was easy between them. One day, a week later, after the house was finished to her liking McNeil asked her a question. "Babs, just how much do you know about the military? I mean soon you'll have a son doing military things so shouldn't you have some knowledge of what he will be going through so you two can talk."

"I suppose what you say is true and I have very little military knowledge."

"Would you care to accompanying me to the Officers club one evening for food, drinks, and dancing?"

"I think I would like that."

They used Babs car, a Cadillac, which she insisted McNeil drive since she had no idea of where they were headed. A maître-d' met them at the Fort McNair Officers club door and since McNeil was not in uniform he had to show his ID card. "Good evening Colonel and welcome." Babs just looked at McNeil with raised eye brows. "Will you be using the club at a later date?"

"I'm sure I will."

"If you will complete this form sir, I'll have a club card ready before you depart."

With that taken care of the Maître-d' said, "again welcome and the bar is to the left and the dining room is to your right. Please enjoy."

"Thank you very much," said McNeil as he escorted Babs into the club.

They decided to take a seat in the dining room and order a drink while looking over the menu.

"What was that all about at the door Charley? I heard the Maître-d' call you a colonel. I would have guessed you were a lieutenant, or at the most a captain."

"I do get that a lot. I mean not looking old enough to be a colonel."

Before he could continue and explain to her, the club manager, a retired Major named Mainer, came to their table. "I had no way of knowing Colonel McNeil or I would have met you at the door. I'm sorry."

"No need to be. As you said, you had no way of knowing."

"Then allow me to say that your, and of course the lady's, meals will be on the club tonight. I also took the liberty of having Champagne brought to your table, Ah, here it is now," he said as a waiter entered with an ice bucket and a bottle of champagne. "Enjoy the club services and if there is anything I can do for you please don't hesitate to call me."

"I'm sure we will be ok Maj. Mainer and I'm sure you have more to care for than us. Thank you very much for the service."

"It's my pleasure sir."

"Why do I get the impression that something was left out of the story of Charley McNeil as you told it the other day?" asked Babs as soon as the club manager left them alone.

"I suppose I did leave one small item out and I apologize. Just how much do you know about the ongoing Korean war?"

"Nothing more than what I read in the papers----Oh my God, you were there?"

"I was there before the beginning and until about eighteen months ago."

"I see. So you are a war hero. Is that why all this bowing and scraping?"

"There's a bit more to the story Babs."

"Oh. Please, continue Charley."

A waiter came and took their orders for food. "You said there was more to the story Charley," Babs repeated after the waiter left.

"Yes I did. The reason I'm a colonel at a young age is that I commanded a Battalion when there was no one else to do it. I was promoted on the battlefield."

"And that makes you unique?"

"There's more to the story Babs. I'm having a hard time here since I have never had to tell it to anyone before."

"I'm sorry Charley if I have pushed you into a corner? If it makes you uneasy please forget it?"

"No, it's not that. You see what just happened here and the same thing happens when word gets out. And I have no idea how the club manager found out."

"I don't understand Charley. When word gets out about what?"

"I've thought about this a lot Babs and I did nothing more than many other men did over there. Like the President said to me----"

"You have met and spoke to the President, our President?" interrupted Babs.

"I did. He's the one who pinned the medal on me and he----"

"What medal Charley, interrupted Babs again.

"The Congressional Medal of Honor Babs."

"Oh my God; Here I'm sitting with a military celebrity."

"Not so loud Babs or we'll never have any privacy," said McNeil putting his finger to his lips.

"Sorry. What did the President say to you?" asked Babs in a low voice.

"He said that every war must have a hero and I was chosen for this one."

"You must have done something outstanding to get noticed Charley. Were you wounded?"

"More than once but so were many other men. The big medal isn't awarded for wounds, a purple heart is."

They talked through the meal and McNeil told Babs everything that happened to him in Korea and why. He relayed much about the military that Babs was unaware of. After eating McNeil ordered coffee. Since he was driving he didn't want anything else to drink. They did have a chance to dance several times before it was time to depart. Before they left the Club manager came by and handed McNeil his club card and said he hoped to see them back soon.

They both realized they were very comfortable together and McNeil talked more about himself than he ever did with anyone else. He told her all about his family and the things that happened in the past.

Babs took a couple of days off from work and they went shopping for other item that were needed for the house to complete the decorating process. It took McNeil, and Babs when she could get away from the office, another two days to hang all the curtains and arrange the furniture that was delivered. The house now had the warm lived in feel.

During the remainder of McNeil's leave time they visited some of the historical sites in the D C area and McNeil took Babs to another military post during the day so she could see more of the military in action. She was beginning to see just what her son would be involved in later on when he pinned on the bars of a second lieutenant.

All too soon the three weeks of leave came to an end and it was time for McNeil to get back to work, whatever that would be.

## 24 Jan 52

When McNeil signed in at the pentagon he found a note waiting for him. He was to report to a Colonel Hopper, room 103, the office of R T P. It took McNeil a while to find out that the office of R T P, (Research, Test, and Procurement) was a branch of the R & D, (Research and Development) department. It took him even longer to locate room 103 in the vast warrens of the pentagon. He expected at any time to come across a skeleton of a man looking for an exit out of here.

A full Colonel, one grade below a general, does not sit out front in a room. When McNeil opened the door to room 103 he found two civilian women busy typing and a young Lieutenant looking at some papers. Lt. Black looked up when the door opened and asked, "May I help you sir?" both the ladies looked up and smiled at McNeil then went back to typing.

"I certainly hope so. I'm Lieutenant Colonel McNeil here to see Col. Hopper."

"We have been expecting you sir and may I say welcome. One moment while I see if the colonel is free," he said opening a door behind him without knocking and closing the door after himself. He came back and spoke, "Col. Hopper will see you now sir."

"Thank you very much Lt. Black.

McNeil put his hat under his left arm and switched the attache case to his left hand as he entered the office. He stopped in front of a desk littered with file folders and a pudgy balding colonel sat behind it. "Sir, Lieutenant Colonel McNeil reporting for duty."

Col. Hopper slowly looked up from the papers in front of him and gave McNeil the once over. Young, but rugged looking, and the medal will go a long ways when he goes to the hill. He finally returned McNeil's salute then said, "Stand at ease colonel."

"Are you another Audie Murphy Col. McNeil?" he asked after a short wait.

"Absolutely not sir," replied McNeil wondering just where the colonel was going with that question.

"Good. Don't you ever let the medal get in the way of your duties during your tour here at the Pentagon."

That's a hell of a way to greet someone, thought McNeil, I have never hid behind the medal and I see no reason to start now. "I resent the fact that you would even think that of me sir."

"Resent, the hell you say? You just keep in mind that the mission come's first Colonel McNeil."

"The mission is always first in my mind Sir. But I'm in the dark as to what my duties are sir."

"Your duty is whatever I tell you to do."

"I understand sir." I think. I wonder just why this man has a burr under his saddle. If he's an example of the other officers in the pentagon then this will be a long miserable tour of duty.

"Do you know what our mission is Col. McNeil?"

"I'm sorry to say I don't sir."

"Here," he said passing over a hard back booklet, "this will explain everything and consider this your incoming briefing. Along with that," he said handing McNeil one of the folders full of papers from his desk, "read and study the material and I expect you to know what's in there as well or better than I do because in two weeks you will accompany me to the hill where we'll beg for funds for the purpose of purchase and test. Any questions colonel?"

"Just one question sir. Where would you have me work?"

"Black," yelled Col. Hopper into his intercom. The door opened and Lt. Black entered.

"Yes sir?"

"Is that office ready for Col. McNeil?"

"Yes sir it is."

"Show him to it. Dismissed." and Col. Hopper went back to his work.

"If you'll follow me sir," said Lt. Black. "We have been allocated a group of offices on the lower level." explained Lt. Black as he led McNeil down a hall and some stairs to a lower level of the pentagon. "This is yours sir, 100B," said Lt. Black stopping in front of a closed door. There was a name plate attached to the door, Ltc. McNeil. R. T. P. Dept.

It was a small room McNeil saw as he opened door and went inside. A grey metal desk with a cushioned chair behind it and two hard seated chairs in front of the desk for visitors; a grey metal file cabinet in a corner and a coat tree behind the door. There was just enough room between the desk and the wall for a man to get through. On the desk were a reading lamp and a phone. McNeil opened one of the desk drawers and saw a supply of pencils and paper and other paraphernalia that would be needed to perform his tasks. "I though a diagram of the pentagon might be useful sir," spoke Lt. Black, "at least until you get used to where everything is. I marked this room and the main office on the diagram."

"That's very thoughtful lieutenant. What if I need something typed? I don't see a typewriter."

"Down the hall on the left is a typing pool for you and all the other assistants assigned to R T P department. They also maintain the coffee machine of which you will be asked to contribute to."

"And the latrine?"

"Down the hall on the left also."

"Lieutenant I have to turn in my records so where do I go?"

"I'll mark the proper room on the diagram sir," he said as he took a pen from his pocket and proceeded to do so. "Will there be anything else sir?"

"The phone, how do I get in touch with your office if I have questions?"

"In the top right desk drawer is a pentagon phone directory."

"You're very efficient lieutenant, I thank you. Right now I can't think of anything else."

"Then I best get back to my duties sir, have a good day."

McNeil walked down the hall and located the latrine. Well at least there is more than one urinal. No waiting in line. He went to the room that was marked as typing pool. "Good morning ladies. I'm Lieutenant Colonel McNeil in room 100B," he said to the five women seated at desks pecking away on typewriters.

"Good morning Col. McNeil," spoke the elder of the women who sat at the front desk, "I'm Mrs. Lancaster. I'm in charge of this room. Nothing comes in or goes out without coming across my desk. What can I do for you this morning?"

"I had hoped to pay my dues to the coffee fund."

Mrs. Lancaster pulled a small ledger from her desk drawer and started writing. "Ltc. McNeil, Room 100B," she said out loud as she wrote then looked up at McNeil. "Colonel, the fee is ten dollars a month. For twelve dollars you will be caught up for the rest of this month through next month. You furnish your own cup."

"Sounds fair to me," he said as he counted out the money. The other four women kept glancing up at McNeil but quickly looked down and kept on typing. Mrs. Lancaster must be hell on wheels to work for, he though after he paid his dues and left the room.

McNeil decided that he wanted nothing to disturb him once he took off his jacket and got to work. He folded the pentagon diagram and put it in his pocket, picked up his attache case and went to locate the pentagon officer's record section.

It was near noon by the time he finished turning in all his records and got paid so he located the rear door that led out to the court yard and the snack bar. There were shade trees and benches for those who ate here so he purchased a hamburger and coffee and sat down to eat. Even though it was cold with snow on the ground the high walls of the pentagon blocked the wind and directed what little sun there was into the center of the Pentagon open area.

After lunch McNeil found his way back to his small office, which was no small feat, pulled off his jacket and sat down at his desk to start work. After he read through the briefing booklet he sat it aside and opened the file folder

Col. Hopper had given him. As he read he made notes. Taking his notes with him he located the Pentagon library to do some research. By the end of the first week he had a stack of papers that needed to be typed up.

Seldom did the phone on his desk ring and that suited McNeil just fine. But a courier did drop off envelopes from time to time. Other than that he was left alone in the small office on the lower level of the pentagon. He found keys, to the file cabinet, in the desk so he could lock up his papers each night. There was no way to lock the room door but since the file folders were marked 'Classified' he thought it best to secure them each night.

Three days before Col. Hopper was scheduled to appear before a Congressional committee he had McNeil bring all his research papers to his office so he could go over them. "Very good colonel," he said after he glanced through the material, "is this my copy."

"Yes sir."

"Lt. Black will keep you informed but I expect you to accompany me to the committee meeting. Will that be a problem for you?"

"No sir. I'll be ready."

McNeil was already at work on the next project when he received the call from Lt. Black with the schedule.

On the ride from the pentagon to the congressional building Col. Hopper was busy reading some papers which didn't seem to be related to what this briefing was about. But he is the briefer and I'm just along for the ride.

McNeil had everything memorized so he sat back and watched the scenery as the driver made his way through the maze of streets and traffic.

When they were seated at a long table in front of the Congressional Committee and Col. Hopper had the material spread out the Committee chairman called the meeting to order. "As I understand it Col. Hopper you are here today to ask for funds to purchase a new weapon for test and evaluation. Is that correct?"

"Yes sir it is. The weapons currently in inventory, though proven in combat, are getting old. We would like to start testing something to replace them with."

"And what will that weapon be colonel? What I see here in the picture looks to be a toy."

"A toy it may look like sir but the factory results have proven it to be a very effective weapon."

"But you want to test it further, hence the requested funds."

"Correct sir. We need to get the weapon into the hands of military men who will test it in the field rather than in a closed environment. If it please the committee I'll let my assistant, Lieutenant Colonel McNeil explain the reason for needing the weapon for tests."

"Then let's hear from Col. McNeil. Colonel you look young for the rank you hold," spoke the chairman."

"I suppose I am sir and I hear that a lot." McNeil stood up thinking, I have been sandbagged here. What is Col. Hopper trying to do, make me look bad?

"Just what are your Credentials Colonel?"

"If I may," spoke Col. Hopper, before McNeil could form and answer. "I failed to mention that Col. McNeil is both a paratrooper and a ranger. During that training he had extensive training on all weapons. Also he has eighteen months of combat experience where he either used or observed weapons being used under actual combat situations."

"Thank you Col. Hopper. Now back to Col. McNeil. I've read your briefing paper but its most confusion and much of it I don't understand."

"I have high hopes of explaining it sir. First; and I'm only speaking for the Army today, we have a total of six weapons in the inventory—"

"Why six different weapons Colonel?" interrupted one of the committee members.

"I have no idea sir but I would guess that somewhere in the past new weapons were bought, tested, and issued to the troops and the old weapons were not dropped from inventory. If it's important I can do research and give you a better answer?"

"No. That won't be necessary but it does sound like a waste of time and money to have so many different weapons which require maintenance and so many different types of ammo must be kept on hand."

"I agree with you sir. We have hopes of reducing the number of weapons to simplify the situation. First, let's take the pistol, a forty five caliber automatic used by officers and some noncombatants. It's called the 1911 for a reason sir. It was manufactured by the Colt Arms Company in the early nineteen hundreds and has been in contentious use since. It's a great pistol, very reliable, and has good knock down power for close work. But those pistols in current inventory are getting a bit old and require extensive maintenance."

"What is on the books to replace the pistol?"

"Nothing at this time Sir, maybe later. The Navy is currently using a colt revolver but we would like to keep the Colt forty five automatic for a while longer. Next is shoulder fired weapons; we won't get into crew served machine guns of which there are several. The oldest of these is the 45 caliber sub Thompson which I'm sure most everyone is familiar with. It was also developed in the early nineteen hundreds and has been in contentions use since. The army used it in WW2 and gave many away to the French underground. It's a heavy, over 9 pounds, weapon using either 20 round clips or 50 round drums. A man has to be well trained in its use and maintenance because it takes a special tool to disassemble it. Lack of or too much oil will cause misfires. Clips must be handled carefully because the slightest dent will cause the weapon to misfire. It's a good weapon for close work but not for long range firing.

"The next weapon is also of 45 caliber. The M3 submachine gun or grease gun as its commonly called by those who use it. It is a low cost gun with easy maintenance. Since it was made for drivers, tankers, and paratroopers, it has a metal folding stock. It's also for close work since it has no range to it. Because of the short barrel, only eight inches, it tends to quickly overheat when a full twenty round clip is fired rapidly. Having to wait for a barrel to cool down while the enemy is headed your way is not a very good position to be in.

"The next and last weapons to be discussed are all 30 caliber. The first one is the B A R, (Browning Automatic Rifle) also manufactured in the early nineteen hundreds. It has excellent fire power for long ranges and it's easy to maintain. It's a shoulder fired weapon or comes with a bi-pod for more accurate fire power. It's a heavy weapon, over 15 pounds, and because of the rapid fire capability, 500 rounds per minute, an ammo bearer must accompany the weapon. It requires over forty pounds of ammo for one minute of firing.

"Next is the M1 Carbine. It weighs only five pounds and is a short weapon using a fifteen round clip. It's a very effective weapon and very accurate for close or long range work. One design had a folding stock for use by tankers, drivers, and paratroopers. This weapon entered service during WW2.

"The last weapon we'll discuss is the most used weapon in the inventory today, the M1 Garand rifle. It's a heavy weapon, over nine pounds but easy to maintain. It's very effective at any range. The weapon has been known to continue firing even after being in the rain and mud. It was designed and issued to replace the 30-06 Springfield rifle which was a bolt action rifle. It's a clip fired weapon and the clips hold eight rounds. The one drawback to the weapon is the clip. They are hard to load, especially with frozen fingers, and if the rounds are not seated just right it'll cause the weapon to misfire. If clips must be loaded in the muddy trenches and mud gets in the clips a misfire will occur.

"What we would like to have is a light weight weapon that can be used for close work or long range. One that's easy to maintain and can be used by all troops. We need to have only one weapon, one rifle, in the inventory. In a case study performed by NATO they found that most member nations, and we are a member nation, have so many different caliber weapons that it would be next to impossible to store enough ammo for all the different weapons. They found out that most nations are switching to the 7.62 caliber round so I feel sure that sometime in the near future all member nations will switch over to the more common caliber bullets.

"We, as a leading nation, should have a leg up and stay ahead by starting early to come up with a suitable weapon that will fire the 7.62 caliber bullet.

"Sir, that concludes my briefing unless the committee has questions for me?"

"Do you believe the weapon in the pamphlet is the answer to your, the Army's, needs?" asked a panel member.

"We won't know until we have a chance to test them sir."

"Why a hundred weapon?" asked another panel member, "why not ten or twenty?"

"To properly test and evaluate a weapon sir it must be tested in all environments; Cold, heat, sand, and high humidity. It would take a couple of years with only ten or twenty weapons to test them in so many different environments."

"You are asking to purchase a hundred of the weapons at a cost of three hundred dollars each which comes to thirty thousand dollars, so why are you asking for funds totaling four hundred thousand dollars?"

"There will be the expenses of food and lodging plus transportation for the men testing the weapons sir. Since the weapon fires three different types of ammo that will have to be purchases for testing plus extra clips."

"Whoa, back up a minute here. I thought the whole idea was to reduce the ammo requirement to one type but I just heard you say tree types of ammo didn't I?"

"You did sir but let me explain. These weapons all fire the same caliber of ammo but three different types. We have ball ammo which is the common ammo. There is also a tracer round used to mark targets plus a blank used for training. We need to test all three rounds for effectiveness."

"Does anyone have more questions for the colonel?" asked the committee chairman as he looked at each member.

"One final question," asked an elderly man who looked as if he had slept through the entire meeting, "if the funds were made available how soon could testing begin and how soon would the results be known to us?"

"Since I'm new at this I'll have to defer that question to Col. Hopper," said McNeil as he sat down.

After all questions had been asked and answered Col. Hopper and McNeil were released from the committee meeting. Col. Hopper spoke as they left the building headed for the waiting staff car, "for your first time out that was a good briefing Col. McNeil but, just how much of what you said is factual?"

McNeil knew right then that the briefing paper he had given to Col. Hopper well before the scheduled meeting had not been read. "I can't believe a fellow officer would accuse me of passing out false information to a Congressional committee sir."

"Don't go there Col. McNeil, you are treading very close to insubordination."

"Then I apologize colonel."

"My question still stands colonel."

"All the information in my briefing paper came from data on file in the pentagon library. I believe it to be factual sir."

The pentagon library, thought Col. Hopper. The library was a place he had always wanted to visit but never seemed to have time. Instead he sent his assistants to do research for him.

After they were in the car and on the way back to the pentagon Col. Hopper spoke, "In addition to your other work Col. McNeil you will be the case officer for testing the new weapon. You'll have to coordinate with the various posts to set up training and firing schedule. I expect full reports of the results."

"Then you believe our request for funds will be approved?"

"One never knows with such a committee, but it looks favorable."

Tonight was school night for McNeil, his first class at Georgetown University. He had decided he would wear a suit to work then change into his uniform which he kept in the office. That worked out well and since this was school night he changed into the suit since he didn't want to show up at the university in a military uniform. Not that he was ashamed of the uniform but because there were some antiwar protesters on campus and seeing a man in a military uniform might be fuel for their fire.

He was spending about six dollars a day for bus and taxi fares, and since pentagon duty was six days a week, McNeil figured it was costing him about a hundred and forty four dollars a month, a bit more on school nights, for transportation. To own a car would cost him much more when the cost of insurance, fuel, and maintenance was added in, plus the lost time and frustration of traffic delays. He found it much less expensive, and faster, to travel by public transportation than with a car.

It was well after dark, close to ten Pm, when he reached the house this night. When he opened the door he saw Babs sleeping on the sofa. She was fully dressed, less her shoes which were lying on the floor along with a book. He thought about waking her but she looked so peaceful sleeping there that he decided to leave her alone. He took a blanket and spread it over her then went to change and take a shower. Not knowing how long it would take him to get home after school he had grabbed a bit to eat before leaving the pentagon. So after his shower he went to bed.

The smell of coffee woke him the next morning. It took him a few minutes to realize he wasn't dreaming, the smell was real. He got up and belted on a robe and went to the bathroom to splash cold water on his face. He dried off, ran his fingers through his short hair, and went to the kitchen which was well lit up. He found Babs pouring herself a cup of coffee. "Did I wake you Charley? I tried to be quite."

"Good morning Babs. You didn't wake me but the smell of coffee did, besides, it was time for me to get up anyway. He looked at Babs, as she poured another cup of coffee and handed it to McNeil, whose hair was a bit tousled and her clothes were wrinkle from sleeping in them, but she looked great, even in that state of disrepair.

"You're staring at me," she commented, "I must look awful."

"Not so. You look like just what you are, a woman who got up early from a night's sleep."

"I did sleep well. I didn't know when you would be home but I had intended to wait up for you and prepare some food for you but I fell asleep reading. Did you cover me up?"

"I did. You looked so peaceful sleeping I didn't have the heart to wake you. Hey, this is good coffee," he said after tasting it, "thanks."

Apparently it had been a long time since she was in a kitchen with a man so she was a bit nervous. As soon as she finished her cup of coffee she looked at her watch, "look at the time. I know you have to get ready for work and I need to shower and change. I'll see you later Charley," she said as she gathered up her coat and went out the rear door.

She had told McNeil that she sometimes stayed over at the model home which also served as her office; She kept extra clothes and toilet articles there.

Now that he had a better idea of what his schedule would be, and he relayed it to Babs, he often came home to find a hot meal waiting for him. Babs seemed to enjoy taking care of a man which McNeil was grateful for. The one thing he did notice was that Babs was not ready for any kind of an affair. The only time they had touched each other was when he took her hand to guide her across a street or when she linked her arm with his when they were walking, plus when they danced. He wanted so bad to taker her in his arms and smother her with kisses and tell her how much he appreciated having her around but he knew it wasn't the right time yet. He was afraid he might scare her off if he rushed her. Maybe in time she would get over her fears and inhibitions. He could wait. If it was a fling he wanted there was Helen, a wholesome blond who worked in the typing pool. Her body language and words said she was ready to go out with him.

He didn't have the time nor did he want to gain a reputation as a swinging bachelor. Besides, ten hour work days in the pentagon plus two to three nights a week at Georgetown University didn't leave much time for partying.

Old man winter finally released his grip on the area in April and spring took over. There were small green leaves showing on the trees and brown grass showed a touch of green in it. It was still cool but not the cold that had gripped the area for so long.

At least once a week McNeil and Babs cooked on the grill and ate out on the patio. With a regular schedule now he would come home to find a hot meal and Babs waiting for him. They fell into a routine. Unless it was school night for him they ate and had a glass of wine. While Babs cleared away the dishes he would shower and get into comfortable clothes. They would settle down on the couch with coffee and while McNeil did his homework Babs brought her business records up to date. On the weekends they spent time in DC visiting the famous landmarks and museums and eating out. On some weekends Babs went to visit her son or met him at the family home when he could get away from school. Those times that she was away McNeil realized he really missed having her around. She never talked about McNeil meeting her son and he never brought it up. Apparently she wanted to keep her personal life separated from business and her social life. He decided that was her privilege.

As time moved on McNeil began to notices little changes in the house. First there was the extra toothbrush in the bathroom that he knew belonged to Babs. A hair brush on the counter and her robe hung behind the bathroom door beside his. Since she spent time in his house he noticed she had moved some of her clothes into a bedroom closet. She never asked if she could and he never mentioned it. It wasn't long before Babs started using the spare bedroom. That started one night after they had eaten and finished their paper work. When she was ready to leave it was pouring down rain so she asked if she could use a bedroom tonight. McNeil agreed that was the best thing to do in this kind of weather.

Babs started spending more and more nights in the spare bedroom rather than go to her home or spent the night in the big empty model home. A week later after they had eaten, finished their paper work, bathed, and turned in, McNeil had just dozed off to sleep when he heard a light tap on his door. "What is it Babs?"

The door opened just as he reached to turn on the bedside lamp. "No, please don't turn on the light," said Babs as she entered and sat on the side of the bed.

"Something wrong Babs?" McNeil asked.

"Sorry to wake you Charley but I had a crazy nightmare. It seemed so real."

McNeil turned back the covers and without thinking Babs lay down and pulled the cover over her and snuggled close with her back to him. "Want to talk about it?" he asked as he felt the heat from her body through the thin cloth of her nightgown.

"I shouldn't trouble you with such nonsense, besides, without knowing all the details you wouldn't understand anyway."

"Anytime you need an ear I have an extra one Babs."

"So sweet of you Charley," she said as she stifled a yawn.

Babs fell asleep shortly after but it took McNeil a lot longer. Having such a beautiful, vibrate, woman sleeping in his house caused him to lose sleep but now that she was in his bed, laying so close to him, he found it extra hard to drift off to sleep.

He spent a restless night and when it was time for him to get up the next morning Babs was still sleeping soundly. He eased out of bed, put coffee on, showered and dressed. When he came back to the kitchen for his first cup of coffee he found Babs in her bathrobe pouring coffee for the both of them. "You should have waked me Charley," she said with a shy smile.

"You were sleeping so well that I didn't have the heart to disturb you."

"Thank you Charley," she said with a shy smile.

"For what Babs?"

"For being such a gentleman last night and not taking advantage of me."

"I have found that one person cannot force another to do what they don't want to do."

Two nights later after each completed the nightly ritual, bathed and went to separate bedrooms, McNeil heard the light tap on his door again and knew it was Babs. "Come on in Babs," he called out.

There was enough moon light coming through the bedroom window for him to see her as she entered the room and closed the door behind her. "Don't turn on the light Charley," she said when she saw him reaching for the switch.

He watched her drop her robe and this time there was no night gown. Instead she wore a short flimsy, almost sheer, thing. He turned back the covers and she got into bed but this time she didn't turn her back to him. She put her arms around him and placed her lips to his and gave him a kiss that was anything but casual.

"Are you sure about this Babs?" he asked rising up on his arm to better see her.

"It's been such a long time for me Charley, but yes, I'm sure."

As he put his hand on her he could feel her body heat through the flimsy material. "For me also," he managed to say as she reached down under his pajama bottoms and grasped him. He let out a sigh then started running his hands over her body. The few clothes they wore were soon on the floor and he moved on top of her. They were both so caught up in passion that it was over far too soon. They clung to each other and a few minutes later the fires of passion flared up again. There was no need to hurry so they took time to fan the flames even higher. An hour later they fell back exhausted and went to asleep cuddled in each other's arms.

When McNeil's mental alarm clock woke him the next morning he looked at Babs. She was sleeping so well that he decided to not wake her. He bathed, and shaved, dressed and put the coffee on. While he sat and drank the coffee he wrote a note to Babs.

> Babs
> Such a wonderful surprise you gave me last night.
> Thank you. I would have woke you this morning
> but you were sleeping so well, again, I didn't have the
> heart to disturb you. Have a great day and I'll see
> you this evening. I have classes tonight.
> Charley

When he finished his second cup of coffee he propped the note up on the counter. Just as he finished washing his coffee cup he heard a car horn blow. His taxi had arrived. He had an agreement with the Taxi Company to have a taxi pick him up every week day morning at five AM unless he called and canceled.

That night when he entered the house there was no Babs asleep on the couch as she would normally be. He went into the kitchen to find a note from her.

> Charlie
> Thanks for the note. I had a great time also.
> I made you a sandwich. I had so much energy
> today I cleaned both your house and the office.
> I must have overdone it because I couldn't keep
> my eyes open long enough to wait for you.
> Babs

McNeil found the sandwich and poured himself a glass of wine to go with it. As he sat down to eat he thought Babs had decided to sleep in the spare bedroom, or possibly at the model home, since she wasn't on the couch.

After finishing the sandwich and cleaning up the kitchen he went to the bedroom to get undressed before taking a shower. He was very surprised to find Babs in his bed.

Two weeks later McNeil found a note on his desk one morning attached to a manila envelope. STUDY CONTENTS AND BE PREPARED TO ACCOMPANY AND ASSIST GENERAL STEADMAN AT A CONGRESSIONAL HEARING.

He was rather surprised that he would be accompanying a general since they normally went to the hill with a full colonel, or sometimes two. When he opened the envelope he found that the material was about requesting funds for a major modification to an existing tank. He studied it over the next three days then he received a call to tell him where and what time to meet with the general.

General Steadman proved to be a good orator and McNeil really couldn't see where he was needed. All he did during the hearing was make sure the general had the right papers and when needed he passed certain specific data to the general. What he was, he decided, was a glorified clerk. Any young lieutenant could have done what he did for two hours.

Other than saying good morning when they met at the staff car General Steadman had not spoken until they were out of the meeting and in the hall. "I think that went rather well, don't you colonel?"

Before McNeil could answer a man in suit and tie hailed them. "Good morning general." then he turned to McNeil. "Colonel McNeil, Congressman Waldon wishes a moment of your time at your convenience."

General Steadman looked at McNeil with raised eye brows in question. McNeil had no idea who Congressman Waldon was and he couldn't think of any reason why a Congressman would want to speak with him. He just shrugged his shoulder.

"Unless you have something pressing how about now?" asked General Steadman.

"Nothing I can think of sir."

"Then make us proud colonel." with that the general turned and walked away.

When McNeil was escorted into the office of Congressman Waldon, by the man who had approached him in the hall, he saw a very slender gray haired man behind the massive desk. "Congressman Waldon, Lieutenant Colonel McNeil, said the man introducing the two.

"Yes, I know Fred, and thank you." with that the man left the office closing the door behind him.

He said, 'I know.' just how does he know me, wondered McNeil. I certainly don't remember every meeting a Congressman Waldon.

"Please, sit," said the Congressman after the man named Fred left the room. Would you care for a cup of coffee Colonel McNeil?"

McNeil saw a service of coffee complete with cups and condiments on a side table. "My mouth is a bit dry after two hours in the meeting. A cup of coffee would be nice sir."

The Congressman got up from his desk and poured the coffee for both of them. He handed McNeil a cup then sat back down behind his desk.

"From the look on your face when you entered the room I would guess you have no idea who I am, by that I mean which state I represent?"

"I must apologize sir but you are correct."

"Don't you think it's a bit odd that I know you?"

"I do sir."

"I'm the Congressman from the great state of Kentucky. Many years ago your father and I spent time together fishing. He had no political axe to grind and he knew where all the best fishing hole were. We got alone very well. Nothing yet?"

McNeil did remember when he was a small child, a distinguished looking man coming to the house. The man would pat him on the head. Could this be that man?"

"Sorry sir."

"You were very young then so I guess you wouldn't remember me."

"I suppose that's it sir. You did know dad was killed in a job related accident."

"I did. I wanted so much to attend his funeral but unfortunately I was out of the country at the time. How is your mother? I remember she set a fine table."

"She passed away about three years ago sir."

"Sorry to hear that son. I've heard your name mentioned several times here in Congress and I did some checking to see if you were the son of Robert Jon McNeil. I wanted to meet you."

"That's very nice of you sir."

"That's a lot of rank you are wearing but after doing some research and finding out you were awarded the medal I suppose both, the medal and rank, were well earned."

"Someone thought so sir."

"Are you being modest son?"

"Just truthful sir."

"I suppose you are anxious to get out of service and back to school now?"

"That was my original plans sir but with the Korean thing plus the President holding everyone on active duty I'll be around a while."

"What were your original plans?"

"To get a degree in Political Science and come to D C to work for the government."

"You haven't abandoned that plan have you?"

"Not entirely sir. At present I'm attending George Washington University."

"So everything is on hold with this Korean uprising. I'll tell you what. When you do make up your mind, and when this Korean thing is settled, come see me. I'm sure I can find a position for you on my staff.

"That's very kind of you sir and I'll certainly keep your offer in mind, but, as I said, there's no telling just how long this Korean thing will last."

"Unless I'm voted out of office I'll be around a long time. Colonel McNeil, I would like to sit and chat with you longer but I only have a few minutes before I have to attend a committee —"

There was a knock on the door and it opened. "I know Fred," Congressman Waldon said holding up his hand like a traffic cop, "we were just finishing up here."

McNeil set his cup down and stood up, "thank you for your time Congressman Waldon."

"It was my pleasure Colonel McNeil. Come see me anytime," said Congressman Waldon as he started gathering up his papers.

"I'll certainly keep that in mind sir, along with your offer," said McNeil reaching for the Congressman's hand.

When he got back to the pentagon and his desk he found a note. He was to call General Steadman. When he finally got through a secretary and the generals aide he spoke with General Steadman. "Colonel McNeil here sir. I have a note to call you."

"Ah, yes. Colonel McNeil. Colonel, curiosity overwhelms me. Why would a busy Congressman take time to speak with a lowly soldier?"

"Congressman Waldon is the congressman from my home state sir. He's also an old friend of my fathers. He just wanted to say hello."

"That's it? Nothing to do with anything military?"

"That's it sir."

"My curiosity is now satisfied. Back to work Colonel." The phone went dead. McNeil set it back in the cradle. He wasn't about to mention the job offer, not yet anyway.

Summer moved into fall and then old man winter took hold once again. This time he wasn't as harsh as last time. Winter passed and spring took over and soon the long warm days of summer were upon the land. Putting in long hours at the pentagon plus the night school made the time seem to past fast. He and Babs were good together and there had been no mentions of the future, no strings, just enjoy life. With Babs to keep him company he forgot about how much he grew to hate his job. Seventeen months he had spent in the cubby hole of a lower level office doing research and playing at being a glorified clerk. Months of going to the hill to plead for money to better equip the soldiers who do battle to preserve the freedom of the U S A.

The Korean armistice was signed on July 27th 1953. The letter from the president extending all military men on active duty plus six months was rescinded in January 1954. When McNeil heard the good news he thought about submitting his request for release from the service but since he hadn't completed his masters yet, plus he wasn't too thrilled about leaving Babs, he put it off.

Some of the better times were when he could get out of the pentagon and travel to various locations to observe and evaluate weapons testing. The down side of that was he was away from Babs.

The only good thing about being in a lower level office was that he didn't have to fetch coffee and pastry for generals as full colonels did on the upper levels. The down side was that he seemed to be forgotten down there. That is until someone needed some research done; research that any competent sergeant could do.

Officers normally knew what their next assignment was four to six months ahead of time. Here McNeil had been stationed at the pentagon for seventeen months, one month shy of the eighteen month tour, with no idea what was in store for him.

He though many times about the job offered by Congressman Waldon. But then, from what I've seen during my time in the Congressional building, I have to wonder if it's such a good idea. Everyone has to start somewhere and there are plenty of goffers running around in the halls of Congress. Would I be one of them? Was it a legitimate job offer or was it a political thing to gain votes? No, he said he was a friend of my fathers and he sounded sincere. If I left the Army and took the job I would be making double, or three times, as much money as I'm making now. Plus I would know each day where I would be, and each day I would be near Babs. I wonder how she would react if I told her I may leave the Army and become a Congressional staffer. Would she be pleased or would she think I'm nuts? On the other hand a staffer isn't doing much more that what I'm doing in the pentagon, a glorified gofer.

An evening, a month later, when he came home he found Babs had prepared a great meal and the wine was open and waiting. After he bathed and changed he asked, "What's the occasion Babs?"

"What makes you think there is a special occasion? I just felt like making a good meal for us."

"Come on Babs. You are walking on air and that smile hasn't left your face once. What's up?" Oh God, I hope she isn't going to tell me she is pregnant. But so what? We'll get married. No problem there.

"Ok. I can't keep it to myself any longer. Sit down and I'll tell you."

She kept smiling as she passed around the food and refrained from speaking until we had food on our plates. "You know I have been working toward getting my Real Estate Broker's License?"

"Sure. You have put in many nights of classes and studying."

"It finally happened. I got my license and I leased a building to set up my business."

"Well, that is good news Babs. Congratulations. I'm glad for you, but what about here? I mean your current job?"

"Oh, I have someone interested in taking it over. I should have her up to speed in a week."

"And then?"

"I'll open my own office and be in business. That is if I can come up with some customers. That brings up something else Charley. I need a favor."

"Just name it and if I can do it I will."

"Would you consider allowing me to handle your two houses and keep them rented, at least the other one?"

"They are yours. Set it up."

"Just one more small item; there is a house here, in the development that will be coming on the market soon. It's a smaller house that this one but the selling price is right. A young couple, the man works in some capacity for the government, got transferred and must sell the house."

"And you are going to handle it?"

"I was thinking along another line Charley. The two houses you bought have appreciated at a rate of around one hundred and fifty dollars a month. If you decided to sell one or both, and I hope you don't, you could make a nice profit. So why not have three houses? It would be a good investment for you."

"Babs, what you don't know is that I own a total of five house scattered around the states plus some vacate land in Georgia. I'm beginning to feel as if I'm in the real estate business myself."

"You failed to mention the other houses Charley. I had no idea. But, what is one more. It's a good investment. There will always be a need for housing here in the area."

Babs was so convincing McNeil finally conceded and allowed her to handle the purchasing of the other house and keep it rented for him. Money wasn't a problem; he just transferred some from other accounts.

Why am I still in the Army, McNeil asked himself one day? I never wanted a military career but I was caught in the draft, then the Korean thing, and here I am, still in the army. My dissertation is complete, approved, and accepted, after long hours of laboring over it. I only need five more credit hours to complete my degree which I can complete anytime and anywhere, in or out of the service.

Thoughts of resigning his commission were on his mind as the months passed by. He constantly went over the pros and cons. His original goal was not a military career but a political career. And now he had a chance to make that come true with the job offer from Congressman Waldon. Why not? He finally decided. He had been assigned to the pentagon for about twenty months now and still no orders for a new assignment. Had he been forgotten? He finally made up his mind as to what he wanted to do. He drafted up a letter to resign his commission and handed it to Mrs. Lancaster for typing. After McNeil picked up the four typed copies of the resignation letter he signed and dated them then placed a copy in his desk.

If he was in a line company he would know what the chain of command was but here in the pentagon the chain of command was a bit vague. Instead of going to the trouble to find out just what his chain of command was he put three copies of the typed letter of resignation in a manila envelope and addressed it to **Pentagon Senior Officer Records** then dropped it in the mail box. When the request reached the officer in charge of senior officer records they would know what to do with it. Either approve it or send it to whoever had the authority to approve or disapprove such a request.

Days went by and McNeil had not heard anything from his request to resign his commission. He had decided to wait until he had firm word to tell Babs of his plans.

# MCNEIL

## PENTAGON

## Chapter 32
## 8 Aug 1955

General Black, his four stars gleaming, sat at his desk where a mound of paper work waited for him. He had just taken two days off in conjunction with a week end to recharge his batteries. The result was a stack of papers that needed his attention and or decisions made. He was deep in thought when his door opened and one of his aides, Brigadier General Edwards, entered with a paper in his hand. He stood and waited until General Black raised his head to see who had invaded his inner sanctum. General Black knew he would have a lot of work to catch up on so he had left word he was not to be disturbed, unless the President called or war broke out, at least until after lunch.

"What is it Jerry," he asked as he kept his finger on the place he had been reading, "a fire that needs some water on it?"

"Not a fire yet sir. Let's just say it's smoldering."

"Let's have it," he said waving his hand at General Edwards to come forward.

He took the paper, flipped up the attached routing slip, and scanned the contents. After reading the short letter, of which there were three copies, he looked up at General Edwards. "You are aware that because we are top heavy with senior officers that a message went out a week ago requesting that any senior officer who wished to resign his commission could do so?"

"Yes sir, I'm aware of the message."

"Don't you suppose this is just one of hundreds of requests we'll be receiving?"

"Look at the date sir. This request is dated two weeks before the message went out."

"So what makes this request so special that you thought I should see it?"

"The name doesn't jog your memory sir?"

After looking at the name again he shook his head. "I don't recall the name Jerry."

"The young Lieutenant Colonel who was featured in that excellent Army recruiting film that did so much to get our recruiting program back on track."

"Apparently I didn't see the film."

"The young Lieutenant Colonel who was wounded eight times and awarded the Congressional Medal of Honor for protecting the South Korean Ongjin Peninsula from being taken over by the North Koreans."

"Jerry, the chief of personnel has the authority to approve or disapprove any request to resign a commission. I still don't see why you think this request is important enough to bring it to my attention."

"Picture the headlines sir; **DECORATED WAR HERO RESIGNS COMMISSION.** In smaller print; The Officer who believes so much in the Army that he made a valiant effort, on film, to say that the Army was not as bad as the public wishes to believe. The Army does not desert its men in a time of need. The film I'm speaking of sir that did so much for our recruiting program, and the man featured in it, has asked to resign his commission. How will that set with the young men of America when they read that the man who believes in the system has decided to leave the Army."

"I see where you are going with this Jerry. Where do we have this man working?"

"When the request was handed to me I took the time to do some checking. He's assigned to a lesser branch of the R & D department. He has a cubby hole of an office on the lower level. He's a proven Infantry Combat Commander based on his wounds, and the big medal, and many lesser medals. His duties have been nothing more than a glorified clerk."

"How long has he been assigned in this position Jerry?"

"Better than twenty months Sir. The system has really crapped on him. He's lost in the very system he really believes in. He has received no orders and has no idea of how much longer he will be here. At this time I have no idea who is responsible for the error but if you wish I'll look into it. If we have asked for senior offers to resign their commissions how can we disapprove his request? On the other hand how can we approve it with all the publicity his resignation will generate?"

General Black gave a lot of thought to what General Edwards had just said and he decided he was right. Too much negative publicity would hamper future recruiting needs. Something had to be done. "I'm open to suggestions Jerry."

"Sir, this Colonel's mentor was his commanding general, now Major General Layton. Maybe he will have some influence on the colonel."

"The location of this General Layton?" He knew General Edwards was a good officer and he knew he would have researched and would have all the answers before he brought a problem to him.

"He's currently on orders to take command of the 8th Infantry Division in Europe. Under the new regulation he must attend a special Protocol seminar at William and Mary in Williamsburg. He's about half way through that class now sir."

After giving it some thought General Black spoke. "Here's what you do Jerry. You know that we maintain a house in Georgetown for special VIP's."

"Yes sir, I'm aware of the house."

"Check and make sure the house is staffed and supplied. Then get General Layton on the phone and tell him it's my desire, and the reason, to be at the house this weekend. If he can't talk Colonel McNeil out of resigning his commission then we'll just have to live with it. If you run into any problems get back to me."

"I'll handle it sir," said General Edwards as he turned to leave the room.

"Oh, one more thing," said General Black holding up the letter of resignation, "put this in an envelope, marked for General Layton, and see that it's at the house waiting for him."

"Yes sir."

## 8 Aug 55

After General Edwards located the phone number for the William and Mary College located in Williamsburg Virginia and placed the call he had to ask for the correct number for the Protocol school. It was a new class and as yet the phone number was not listed. When he finally got the correct number and dialed it a lady with a very cultured voice answered; "William and Mary, Mrs. Horn of the office of the Protocol school. How may I help you?"

"Ma'am, Mrs. Horn, I'm General Edwards, aide to General Black at the pentagon. Is it possible to get General Layton, who is attending the Protocol seminar, to the phone?"

"Sir, the seminar class is about to take a break. Will you wait or should I ask the general to call you?"

"If it's not too much of a bother I'll wait."

"Then I'll put you on hold for a short time sir."

General Edwards could have had one of the many secretaries, or even a Lieutenant, make the call but he thought it important enough for him to make the call personally. He held the phone between his neck and shoulder and started to take care of some of the paper work that had accumulated on his desk. He had just finished the third paper when he heard the phone being picked up. "General Layton here. To whom am I speaking?"

"Sir, I'm General Edwards, aide to General Black the chief of staff. I'm calling on his behalf."

"I'm aware of who General Black is but why are you calling me?"

"We have a small problem here that General Black thought you could handle better than anyone else sir."

"I can't imagine any problem that a few hundred generals in the pentagon can't solve. What do you need of me?"

"You have knowledge of a Lieutenant Colonel McNeil general?"

"I do."

"The problem is with him sir. He has submitted a letter to resign his commission."

"Well, with that letter from the Department of the Army asking for volunteers to resign their commissions I don't see your problem."

General Edwards went on to explain the problem as he and General Black saw it and spoke of where Col. McNeil was currently assigned. "So you see general, it would be quite embarrassing to the Army if a man such as this was allowed to give it all up."

"General, that man, though young for his rank, is an excellent planner and one hell of a combat commander. He survived some vicious battles in Korea and won the medal for his exploits. Just who is the horse's ass who put him in the dungeon of the pentagon? If I was treated that way I would resign also. And I don't know why I'm jumping on you General Edwards, I'm sure you didn't have anything to do with his assignment. Just what is it that General Black wished me to do?"

Mrs. Horn had left the room when General Layton picked up the phone so she wouldn't be privy to any military discussions. He face would have been red had she stayed and heard the conversation.

"Speak with Colonel McNeil; reason with him, whatever it takes to convince him to remain on active duty."

"After such an assignment and after being treated the way he has been I'm not too sure I will have enough influence to cause him to change his decision."

"It's General Black's desire that you try sir."

"Then I'll do what I can but no promises."

"A valid effort is all we ask sir. An Air Force special mission's jet will pick you, and your wife, up at the local airport this afternoon at sixteen hundred. A staff car will meet you at Dulles and take you to 124 Georgetown. The house has been stocked and staffed for your arrival. You and your wife will be flown back to Williamsburg Sunday evening. How you contact Colonel McNeil and get him to the house is left up to you sir."

After giving it some thought General Layton spoke, "General Edwards, I'll need a copy of Colonel McNeil's request to resign his commission—"

"At the house waiting for you sir."

"I'll also need orders, all separate orders, when I call for them. One set of orders for Colonel McNeil to attend the Protocol seminar, one set of orders assigning him to the 8th Infantry Division, and another set of orders making him my aide. If this situation is as important as you say it is I'm sure there will be no problem in cutting the orders when I call for them. I'll need a copy of an order assigning Col. McNeil to the 8th Infantry Division at the house when I arrive. I may need that to convince him everything is on the up and up."

"I'm sure there will be no problem sir," replied General Edwards as he copied down all the requests.

"I have one other item General; a note, a hand written note, for Colonel McNeil. Get it to him today, with the address and date it for today.

COCKTAILS AT NINETEEN HUNDRED. DINER AT TWENTY HUNDRED. CASUAL DRESS 124 George Town."

"I'll handle that sir. Shall I say who? And shall I schedule a staff car for him?"

"No name and no staff car. As I said, he's a great planner; he'll get there on his own."

"Is there anything else sir?"

"That should do it."

"Of course you will keep me or General Black informed of the outcome."

"Of course." with that General Layton hung up the phone then he had a thought and picked it up again and dialed a number. When his wife answered the phone he said, "I, you and I, have been called to Washington for the weekend. Pack for two days and nights. I'll explain it on the way. I have this one last class then I'll be home. Love you."

Marie, his wife, a long time military wife, was use to these sudden, unannounced, trips. She didn't ask questions and started packing as soon as she got off the phone.

McNeil had spent the last two hours in the Pentagon Library, and the lower level archives where classified material was stored, doing research that any just commissioned second lieutenant, or any competent sergeant for that matter, could have done. A secretary, military or civilian, would have been nice to have but he was told it wasn't authorized for his office when he inquired about it.

He had found out that somewhere in the past Colonel Hopper, his immediate boss, had stepped on the wrong toes or made a wrong military decision which had cost him any chance of wearing the star of a general. Col. Hopper was assigned to his current position and told to accept it and like it or retire. He had over twenty four years of service so he had his time in for retirement. He was being an ass about everything when it came to McNeil so McNeil thought maybe Col. Hopper resented his fast rise in rank and the glory he had achieved on the battle field, plus the medal.

McNeil was assigned to his current position and was unlucky enough to be assigned under Col. Hopper. What was he supposed to do? Cry foul to someone? Who? The one consolation that always came to his mind was the fact that he wasn't upstairs fetching coffee and pastry for generals as many of the other Lieutenant Colonels, and some full colonels, were doing; out of sight, out of mind. But then maybe he was too far out of mind and sight or he would have had his assignment orders by now. That thought was constantly on his mind these days.

When he reached his office he started to place the stack of research papers on his desk while he washed his hands but then he remembered that some of the papers were classified so he took them with him to the latrine rather than take the time to open the file cabinet and secure them. It would take time to open the cabinet and store the papers only to have to reopen it and retrieve them five minutes later.

When he reentered the office and dropped the stack of papers on his desk he noticed an unsealed envelope on his desk with his name on it. He picked it up and removed the single piece of paper.

9 Aug 1955
124 GEORGETOWN
CASUAL DRESS
COCKTAILS AT NINETEEN HUNDRED
DINNER AT TWENTY HUNDRED

He reread the note, which was neatly typed, then turned it over but there was no signature. Who sent the note and why am I supposed to attend a cocktail party? Who will be there that's so unimportant that a lowly Lieutenant Colonel has been asked to attend? If this is some more of Col. Hopper's crap then I will be forced to make a formal complaint.

He took a few deep breaths to calm himself down then opened the city map and located Georgetown. He knew where Georgetown was because he attended Georgetown College but he wanted to locate the exact address. He figured he could catch the train that ran under the pentagon into DC, and a bus would get him close to Georgetown, then a taxi to the listed address. He checked his watch and realized he had just enough time to change out of his uniform into a suit, he had just brought in a freshly cleaned one, and get to the underground station in time to catch the train.

The reason for the note and who sent it was still on his mind as he secured the classified papers and changed clothes. He had decided when he was first assigned to the pentagon to travel in civilian clothes rather than in uniform so he always had a suit on hand at his office.

The taxi dropped McNeil off in front of 124 Georgetown with just five minutes to spare. He had wondered about the address since there was no street mentioned but the taxi knew exactly where to go. 124 Georgetown was a big red brick house, just off Wisconsin Avenue, very old, and looked much like the others on the tree lined street.

There are two theories about how Georgetown got its name. One; it was named after King George the second who was in power about the time the settlement was started. Two; it was named after the town's founders, George Gordon and George Beall. No one really knows for sure but regardless of how the town got its name Georgetown is an old settlement dating back to 1745. Since stones were plentiful in the area most all houses were built of field stone, or brownstone. Later some houses were built of sun baked brick. Georgetown was also where Georgetown University was located; a very old university and the one that McNeil attended.

When he got out of the cab and paid the taxi driver he looked up and down the street but no cars lined the street as there should be when a cocktail part was in progress. There wasn't too many people in Washington who would pass up a cocktail party where there was free booze and a chance to socialize. It was a party town and many decisions were reached over a drink in a relaxed atmosphere.

He checked his appearance and straightened his tie as he approached the house door. As any good military man will do he stopped and brushed each shoe on the rear of his pants leg to remove any dust that may have accumulated on the toe of his shoes.

It took a minute for the door to be opened after he rang the doorbell and it was opened by a well-dressed butler. "Good evening sir. May I help you?"

"I'm Colonel McNeil," was all he could say since he really didn't have an invitation to present. He really expected to hear loud conversation blast him when the door was opened but it was deathly quiet and he couldn't see anyone behind the butler as he should have been able to if a party was in progress.

"Yes sir. Please step inside and wait in the foyer and wait while I announce you."

McNeil stepped inside and the butler closed the door, turned and walked away. McNeil waited where indicated and watched the butler walk through the living room headed for a closed door at the rear of the room. Before he reached it the door opened and a very good looking woman stepped through. She had long black hair and Spanish facial features. Her, and the butler conversed then the butler continued through the door and the lady came toward where McNeil waited. "Good evening Colonel McNeil," she said in a very pleasant voice, "I have heard so much about you and it's a pleasure to finally meet you. I'm Marie Layton," she said holding out her hand.

Layton, Layton, he thought, the only Layton I know is General Layton. Could this be his home?

"Good evening Mrs. Layton. It's my pleasure to meet you," he replied taking her hand which was soft and warm.

"He's waiting for you in the den," she said without releasing is hand and leading him into the living room and to another door which was open now. She stopped just inside the door and called out, "Walter, our guest has arrived."

"So I see," replied General Layton rising from a high backed chair where he had been sitting in front of a small fire. "Please come on in Charley."

"Walter dear," said Mrs. Layton, "dinner in an hour," she said as she backed out of the room and closed the door.

"Come on over by the fire and have a seat. Since this is very informal what do I call you Charley, Charles, or Chuck?" It's August and he has a fire going? It's certainly not needed so he must just enjoy looking at a fire.

"My mother named me Charley so that's all I have ever been called sir."

"Then Charley it is. If memory serves I believe you are a Scotch drinker."

"Your memory is good sir."

General Layton, dressed in a suit and tie, went to a small table and built two glasses of Scotch on ice then handed one to McNeil before he sat back down.

"The cocktail hour is upon us so what shall we drink to Charley?"

"Let's drink to absent friends' sir."

"Yes. I agree. We both lost some good friends in Korea. To absent companions," he said touching his glass to McNeil's.

"How about a cigar? If I remember correctly you once smoked good cigars."

"Yes sir. A good cigar would go nice with the Scotch." After they both lit up General Layton spoke.

"How long has it been Charley?"

"Over three years since Korea Sir, almost four." McNeil wanted to ask about the friends he left behind but decided now wasn't he time.

"Time does seem to get away from a body these days. How did you find the C & G S School?"

"It's a very good and informative school sir but I found it hard to critique what I thought I did correct the first time."

"So the school is already teaching about the Korean war, is it?"

"Yes sir."

"What about your current assignment? What is it and what do they have you doing?"

"I'm with an obscure branch of the R & D department."

"Interesting work?"

"Sir, I'm in a cubby hole of an office on the lower level of the pentagon. What they having me doing could be done by any, just promoted second Lieutenant. I seem to have slipped through the cracks as far as the Army is concerned. And I apologize if it seems I am a bit bitter."

"I asked and I expected the truth from you. Besides, we are behind a closed door in a private home. Nothing said will ever be repeated."

"Yes sir. Speaking of home Sir; is this your home?

"As you once said Charley, the Army is my home. To answer your question though, this house is leased by the military for V I P's; a place to house visiting military dignitaries."

"Very interesting Sir. How about you general; what have you been up to?"

"Oh, a couple of routine assignments, the War College, and now I'm attending a protocol seminar at William and Mary. It's something new. Since we are not at war with anyone we are not conquers but considered guests of any country we are in. The seminar is mandatory for anyone selected for command in an overseas assignment."

"I can see the merits of such a school sir. What country will you be assigned sir? Certainly not back to Korea?"

"No. Not Korea. I have been tapped to command the 8th Infantry Division in EUROPE. The 9th Infantry Division is being deactivated and the 8th Infantry Division is being activated to replace it. With that said let me refill our glasses."

"Sir, going from commanding one division to commanding another doesn't seem to be progressing. I mean you are a combat commander and may I say a good one."

"Thank you Charley," said General Layton as he sat back down and handed McNeil a full glass of Scotch, "but I don't look at the assignment that way. We soldiers go where we are told and do what we are told to do. The 8th Infantry Division has a very long history. It's about two or three times the size of the 5th Infantry Division and it's mechanized. It even has two battalions of airborne plus its own aviation compliment."

"Yes sir. I stand rebuked sir. Allow me to apologize for sounding bitter with my assignment."

"No rebuke was intended Charley. From what I hear you have done a

322 | R. W. POWERS

good job. And having said that, I ask, why this?" said General Layton taking three pages of stapled together paper from a side table and handing them to McNeil. It was his request to resign his commission, he saw, and he wondered how General Layton got it.

The fire crackled and a sparks hit the guard screen. McNeil took a pull on his cigar then reached for his drink to delay what he was going to say in answer to General Layton's question. "Sir," he finally said, "anything I say in answer to your question will sound as if I'm complaining."

"Regardless of how it sounds the truth is always the best way to go."

"Yes sir, you're correct. To coin an old saying sir, with a slight change, never have I seen so many trying to lead so few with no results. The gentleman part of being an officer seems to be lost to those assigned to the pentagon. I have witnessed back stabbing, back biting, and officers walking over their friends to obtain that bit of recognition they so crave. Senior officers have been relegated to positions of coffee makers and gophers. Don't do as I do but as I told you to do because I outrank you is a common phrase around the pentagon. I felt I was in a dead end job here at the pentagon and nothing has happened to change my mind today. There are over four hundred light colonels assigned there at any one time and they all seem to be going around in little circles lost to the original mission.

"There are people, officers, company grade and up, who by their display of ribbons, have never heard a shot fired in anger. I feel sorry for the men who will have to serve under them in combat, if we ever have to go to combat again.

"I realize that I'm still far too young for the rank I hold and a command assignment is out of the question, at least for a long while. But hope springs eternal and it's very dishearten to see so many others leaving for command positions. I met and was offered a position on the staff of my Congressman from Kentucky. I'm enrolled at Georgetown University and I need only five more credits to complete my masters. I thought I would resign my commission and accept the congressman's offer and I could complete the last five credit hours at the university. That's about it sir"

"You failed to mention that as a congressional staffer your pay would be two or three times what you make now."

"That too sir, plus, the job would be in line with my goal of obtaining a degree in Political Science. I would gain a lot of experience."

"Well," said General Layton as he reached for his drink and took a sip, "I certainly can't fault a man for trying to better himself, money wise ,and it seems you have thought ahead."

"I'm glad you see it my way sir."

"Let me throw this in the equation and hopefully something for you to think about. For every desirable position in the Army there are three or four undesirable positions that must be filled to support the men in the field. When you and I were in combat there were many who desired to be there but couldn't because they were working to get supplies and equipment to us. Granted, they didn't do such a good job. We need all kinds of men in the Army, combat types and support types.

"The late Colonel Winters saw something in you that it took me a bit longer to see. You are that rare breed of commander, a natural born leader; A commander who commands by example rather than by fear as most commanders do; a man who leads from the front rather than from the rear; a man who has the loyalty of his men because they respect their leader rather than fear him; a man who, when given a seemly impossible assignment, gets the job done to the best of his ability with no complaints. How old are you now Charlie?"

"Twenty eight sir."

"Men who hold the rank you have are starting to get grey hair and are in their late thirties. Through no fault of your own, but out of desperation and necessity, you were promoted far ahead of your age but not of your abilities and experience. If I had the authority I would give you a command today, but I don't have the authority. What I can guarantee you is an assignment which will get you out of the pentagon. The only thing preventing you from getting that assignment are those papers in your left hand. It's decision time Charley and only you can make the correct decision."

McNeil looked at the request to resign his commission and thought about where he would be if he let it stand and weighed the pros and cons. Accepting the position Congressman Waldon offered me would be right in line with what I have always wanted; to work in the government someplace. I could remain at the Georgetown University and complete my masters with no further delay. I would be making much more money than I am now. I have a home here and a good woman to come home to even though she doesn't seem interested in marriage, just companionship. Everything isn't always a bed of roses though. How long can I stand the bickering and back stabbing that goes on in politics, especially for junior people? And I would be a junior staffer. What will I do if my dream turns out to be a nightmare? Surely the Army won't take me back at my current rank. I'll have to accept a lower rank in keeping with my age and start all over again. I know, as the general said, I'm a good commander, but when will I ever get another command? How many more shitty little assignments will I have to put up with before the Army decides I can have another command? The general did say he could guarantee me an assignment. I wonder just what he has in mind and why can he guarantee me something the Army has failed to do so far?

"Sir, am I permitted to ask what kind of assignment you have in mind?"

Without speaking General Layton handed McNeil another paper. McNeil saw it was a set of orders assigning him to the 8th Infantry Division but no position was indicated. "I believe you said you were to take command of the 8th Infantry Division sir?"

"Correct."

"What will I be doing there sir? Nothing is specified on the order and no date for the assignment is specified."

"Let this be a lesson for you Charley. Nothing is free. There is always a catch when someone offers you something."

"What is the catch here sir?"

"When playing poker a player never reveals his hand, not that we are playing a game here Charley. But the orders you hold are valid, as soon as they are dated and signed, and they will get you out of the pentagon and back into the field which is where you indicated you wished to be. But, I haven't heard a decision from you yet. Let me refresh our drinks, a weak one this time because it's near time for dinner."

General Layton got up and went to refresh both drinks and McNeil made his decision. He didn't want to leave something he really liked and get into something he may be sorry for later. Even though his plan was to acquire a government position in politics. He had to ask himself now if those plans were still valid. Is that what I really want? Command is such an awesome responsibility and yet so full filling but as the general said, its decision time. I can always resign later. Slowly he got up and dropped his request to resign his commission into the fire and watched it burn. The only other copy of the request was in his desk drawer. He sat back down and accepted the drink from General Layton.

"You did say the 8th Infantry Division had Airborne Battalions sir."

"I did."

"Jump status?"

"As I understand it those who are qualified are drawing jump pay."

"Then I would like to get back to the airborne school for a refresher course so I can get on jump status. But as yet you haven't mentioned what I would be doing if I accept this assignment sir. What's the catch?"

"Word is going out from the Department of Defense in a few days in the form of orders. We are no longer at war but are guests of the people of the country we are assigned to, in this case Germany. Each commander is, or will be, tasked with establishing classes for German American relations. I had a chance to scan your records and saw where you completed the language school and speak German. What I have in mind for you Charley is to make you my senior aide which will further your military education plus you will be tasked with establishing the German American Relations program for the 8th Infantry Division. It's a two-fold job but I feel you can handle it."

"No command sir."

"Maybe at a later date Charley. Sorry."

"Sir, I was just a lowly enlisted man until you pinned this rank on me. I have no idea what a general's aide is supposed to do. I would be working from a point of ignorance."

"I have faith in you Charley."

McNeil took a sip of the weak drink and took a drag on the very good cigar. Is this what I really want? To get out of the military and start over in a job I really don't know much about may be wrong for me? Where I'm at I know what I'm doing. Granted the pay isn't all that much. If I accept this offer it will get me out of the pentagon and back in the field. If I accept this offer I will be leaving behind a good woman, Babs. How will she react to this transfer when I spring it on her? She has her own money and now a career so she won't be left out in the cold. Why am I debating this with myself? I know I'm going to accept the assignment.

"Any more catches or surprises sir? And how soon will I have orders?"

"You will be required to attend the Protocol seminar of which I'm attending. That's just in case you do get a command later on. You will have orders next week with two weeks, one to clear yourself and one week leave, to get to William and Mary College. Is that quick enough for you? General Black is behind this so I feel certain there will be no delay in orders."

"General Black sir? The Chief of Staff? I had no idea I had ruffled feathers so far up the chain of command. Allow me to apologize for getting you involved sir."

"No apology is necessary Charley. Glad I was able to help when you needed it. Have you made a final decision yet?"

"The Protocol seminar at William and Mary followed by the airborne school, then on to the 8th Infantry Division where I will become your senior aide and the division German American Relations officer, plus I'll be on jump status. Is that about it Sir?"

"I believe that about covers it Charlie."

"Then I accept sir."

Without saying a word General Layton reached for the phone and dialed a number. When it was answered he spoke. "He has decided to withdraw his request General so get the orders, which I spoke to you about, cut and made official. This is how it will be. Orders for one week of leave before attending the protocol seminar at William and Mary. Another week leave before he attends the airborne school at Fort Benning Georgia. Add another week of leave time before Col. McNeil departs for Europe and the 8th Infantry Division. If for some reason there is a glitch and he doesn't receive the orders as I just called them out my advice to him is to resubmit his request to resign his commission. My God General, we can't go around treating a Medal of Honor winner as this man has been treated. Yes. I believe in three weeks but you better confirm that and get a class number. That's correct." General Layton hung up the phone and picked up more papers and handed them to McNeil.

"Might I infer sir that word of my decision to resign my commission has someone upset?"

"You may Charley. The Chief of Staff of the Army was very concerned when he heard of your decision. I just relayed word that his concern wasn't valid any longer."

"I apologize again sir if my decision has caused you any trouble."

"As I stated Charley, no apology is necessary. We all make mistakes. We tend to think of 'Me' rather than 'us' when making decisions. Your mistake, and General Blacks concern, was how your decision would affect the Army recruitment program especially if the man who won the medal and made such a good recruitment film suddenly decided to resign."

"Yes sir. You are correct. I was thinking of me rather than how my decision would affect others. What I would really like to do is resign this medal and get on with a normal military life."

"You know that can't be done Charley. It's a burden you'll have to bear."

"Yes sir."

"I'm sure my wife will be thrilled to hear you will be going with us. She has been worried that she may not be able to handle the social side of her duties since she doesn't speak the language and has no idea of the customs of the country. I haven't been in Germany since WW2 and we were then fighting for our lives rather than worrying about relations and good will. I'm sure much has changed since then. I'll need lots of help also."

There was a knock on the door and it opened, "dinner is served sir," spoke the butler.

"Shall we dine Charley?" said General Layton getting up from the easy chair.

"I'm so relieved to hear that you'll be joining us in Germany Charley," said Marie after they sat down to eat and General Layton told his wife about Charley deciding to accept the assignment, "maybe you can prevent me from making a fool of myself over there."

"I don't believe you are capable of that Mrs. Layton," replied McNeil, but I'll certainly help in any way I can."

Many questions were asked and McNeil answered them as best he could since he had never visited the country of whose language he spoke. Coffee and brandy was served along with another good cigar after the meal and Marie was reluctant to let McNeil go. It was near midnight when a cab was called far and he thanked the Layton's and left 124 George Town.

The decision was made and McNeil felt as if a burden was lifted from his shoulders. I'll be doing something I'm good at, something I enjoy, and something I understand, rather than getting into something I may not like. It's possible that later on I can rethink my goals and again think about resigning from the military.

# McNeil

## Rhine Main Airfield
## Frankfurt am Main Germany

**Chapter 33**
**10 Oct 55**

As soon as the buildings of New York City passed under the wings of the Super Constellation and the blue water of the Atlantic appeared the 'Unfasten seat belts and smoking' lights flashed on. A very lovely stewardess came down the aisle offering drinks. McNeil, even though it was a long flight, didn't think it proper to arrive at a new assignment with traces of alcohol on his breath, ordered coffee.

His orders had stated he could travel military air or commercial. McNeil envisioned a military plane with hard seats and limited facilities and service for a ten to twelve hour trip across the Atlantic ocean verses a commercial airliner with plush seats, full service and facilities. He elected to go commercial then get reimbursed later. As he sat in the plush seat and sipped coffee his thoughts turned to the time before his departure.

He knew he would have to tell Babs he was leaving the area but he put it off until he had the orders in his hand. He had no idea what to expect from her when he told her but she surprised him. "When we went into this relationship we knew this day would come," she said, "and as stated in the beginning, no strings attached. You have your career, which is God knows where, and I have mind here. We have a good relationship Charley but not good enough to sustain a marriage so don't even mention that.

"My home is here where I have a son to see after. Even though he is almost grown he is still my son and I'm his mother. I have no regrets Charley. I'll certainly miss having you around and I have enjoyed the time we spent together. Now that I have my license and a place of business I'll have something to occupy my time. The Country Corner Estates is closing down the sales office here, rather than hire someone else, and I have first choice of their business."

"I have really enjoyed our time together and I'll miss you also Babs. You are a very lovely and capable lady Babs and I believe you will go far in the profession you have chosen."

Until the day he actually packed his bags to leave nothing more was mentioned about him leaving. They continued as usual with cookouts, weather permitting, and going to the theater, dining out and dancing. Babs made herself scarce on the day of his departure so there were no sad goodbyes.

McNeil found the school, or seminar, at William and Mary very educational and enlightening. Some of the material discussed was a refresher for him but most was something he would need in his new position as German American Relations Officer at the 8th Infantry Division.

McNeil thought he was in great shape, physically, until the cadre started giving him and a hundred others physical training for the airborne school. McNeil had thought he would only have to go to an abbreviated refresher course at the airborne school but he soon found out there was no such thing as an abbreviated course. He had to go through the entire training phase all over again. For the first few days McNeil was sore and short winded which served to remind him that he was out of shape from riding a desk too long.

McNeil wasn't the youngest man in the class but he was the ranking man. It would have been embarrassing to fail the school after completing it years ago. He had to work harder than some of the other men and he suffered many aches and pains during the three week school. He didn't make the top ten or even the top twenty, but he made it, finally.

With leave time between the schools McNeil thought about going back to D C and seeing Babs again but he decided against it. They had made a clean break so it's best to leave it at that he decided. Instead he spent the leave time relaxing, working out the soreness, and studying.

Before boarding the small plane in Columbus Georgia he picked up some reading material to occupy his time. He changed planes in Atlanta then again in New York at La Guardia for the long over water flight. With little to do and see he drank coffee, read, and napped. The plane droned along across the Atlantic and made one stop at Gander Newfoundland and another in Prestwick Scotland before reaching its final destination at Rhine main, near Frankfurt Germany.

It was October and the weather was a bit colder in Germany than it was in New York. A cool North wind was blowing when he deplaned at the Frankfurt Germany Rhine Main terminal. As soon as the plane stopped there was a rush of passengers to retrieve luggage and the isle was crowded. McNeil couldn't see a reason to get in a hurry so he remained seated until some of the passengers deplaned. When there was room he stood in the isle and pulled on his coat and settled his hat on his head before removing his carry-on bag and attache case from the overhead rack. By the time he finished most all of the passengers had left the plane.

Once inside the terminal he located the sign directing him to the baggage pick-up and as he moved through the crowd in the terminal he heard many languages being spoken. Of those languages he understood three of them, English, Spanish, and German. It felt a bit strange to hear the language he had studied being spoken and even stranger to be able to understand what was said but here he was in the land where German was the native language. As he stood waiting with many others for the baggage to appear he listened and looked at the many Countries represented by both language and people.

What surprised him even more was to hear his name called. He had traveled commercial and he had not seen anyone whom he recognized so who would know him and use his name. Thinking he had heard wrong he waited and heard his name called once again. He turned to see just who might know him and saw a U S Army Captain wearing all the regalia of an aide to a two star general standing at attention and rendering a salute. Captain Waters was a young man, short cut dark hair and dark eyes. "Welcome to Germany Colonel McNeil sir."

McNeil returned the salute. "Thank you very much Captain Waters," he replied. He had seen the captains name tag and according to the regalia he wore McNeil knew he was an aide to a two star general. McNeil had to assume he was an aide to General Layton but the man wasn't familiar to him.

"General Layton sends his regards sir."

"That's very kind of the general. Is he in the area?"

"No sir. He sent me with a helicopter to escort you to Bad Kreuznach. I have an Air Force bus outside so let me help you with your bags and we can be on the way."

McNeil had been wondering just how he would travel to his destination, Bad Kreuznach. He decided the train, the most common means of local travel in Germany, was the best way to go. But then he had four pieces of luggage to manhandle which would be a problem, both in a taxi and getting on and off a train. That problem was now solved for him.

Once all his bags were retrieved McNeil followed Captain Waters out of the rear door of the terminal where a blue Air force Volkswagen bus waited. The airman saluted then stowed the bags in the rear of the bus. He then drove around the east end of the airfield, pass the Air Force terminal, and stopped at an H-19 helicopter which bore the symbol of the 8th Infantry Division, a blue shield with a white number eight and a gold arrow throw it; the Golden arrow Division. As soon as the bags and two men were aboard the pilot, who was in the cockpit waiting, started the big noisy engine and took off. There would be no conversation during the hour flight due to the noise.

McNeil wondered why he was on orders as an aide to General Layton when the general already had an aide. But then a general can have as many aides as he wishes, McNeil decided.

When the helicopter landed at the Rose Barracks airfield a staff car was waiting for them. As soon as the bags were loaded and the passengers seated the staff sergeant driver got behind the wheel and drove away. No questions were asked so it would seem everything had been preplanned. "Welcome to the 8th Infantry Division, Rose Barracks, and Bad Kreuznach," said Captain Waters when the staff car started moving.

"Thank you very much Captain Waters," replied McNeil. He looked out of the staff car window at the grey stucco buildings. Most were single story but occasionally one could see a two story building. The buildings were built during, or before, WW2 to house German troops. Now the casern was leased to the American Military to house American troops. It was a bleak day and most of the trees had shed their leaves in anticipation of the coming winter. McNeil felt just a tingle of excitement at being back in the field but he didn't let it show. He was back with the troops, not working with them directly but at least he was where he wanted to be.

The staff car stopped in front of a small building which Captain Waters explained was to be his home. It was one of several used for VIP's and since he was a Lieutenant Colonel, had the medal, and was to be an aide to a general, it had been decided to house him in a VIP building rather than regular transit quarters or BOQ. The building had its own bath, a small kitchen less a stove but with a counter and sink with a small refrigerator. There was a separate bed room and the living room, dining room, and kitchen was all one room in an L-shape.

"These quarters will be cleaned and cared for by local labor," explained Captain Waters after the bags were deposited in the bed room which had closets rather than grey metal lockers, "but you will be required to donate to the cleaning fund. First we have to get you dressed properly. General Layton sent over a small package which he said had everything you would need today," said Captain Waters as he opened the package and dumped out everything on the bed. There were all the regalia needed to represent a man who was an aide to a General. A federal shield with two stars at the top to indicate the rank of the General, a golden rope, an aiguillette it's called. What was unexpected was the box of Cuban cigars, a bottle of twelve year old Scotch, and an iron. McNeil laughed, and spoke, "how long have you been with the general Captain Waters?"

"Ten months sir, I'm to get a company the first of the year."

"If you don't know already I'd advise you to not play poker with General Layton. He holds all the aces."

"I assume you know the general well sir?"

"It's been my privilege to know the general since I was a Corporal."

"Sir?" said Captain Waters.

"Not important. I suppose you'll show me how all this goes together," said McNeil waving his hand at the items spread out on the bed, "I'm familiar with the cigars and Scotch but not the rest."

"Yes sir, if you'll let me have your jacket and pants."

"Jacket I understand but why the pants?"

"If you care to freshen up sir I'll run the iron over the pants."

"Yes, that would be good. Thank you." I did tell General Layton I would be working from a point of ignorance so I guess he sent his aide to set me on the right path. He certainly seems to know what he's doing.

McNeil decided a bath was called for after such a long time riding the plane. He took underwear and a towel plus his shaving kit with him to the bath room. He shaved while showering then after drying off he splashed on some after shave lotion. He felt somewhat refreshed when he went back to the bedroom and got dressed in the uniform of an aide to a general. While he did that Captain Waters gave instructions on what was expected of an aide-d-camp.

# MCNEIL

## 8TH INFANTRY DIVISION HEADQUARTERS BAD KREUZNACH GERMANY ROSE BARRACKS

**Chapter 34**
**12 Oct 55**

The staff car was waiting for them when they left the VIP quarters and Captain Waters continued his instructions as the staff car pulled away. A minute later the staff car stopped in front of a two story building with a large sign in front declaring that this was the Headquarters of the 8th Infantry Division, the Golden Arrow Division.

"If you'll follow me sir," said Captain Waters getting out and holding the car door for McNeil.

"The S-2 and commo are in the basement where they have a vault to store classified documents," explained Captain Waters as he pushed open the door and motioned for McNeil to enter the building, "the S-3 section is to our left at the end of the building and the S-4 at the other end. The balance of Headquarters is on the second floor."

The first room with the door open at the head of the stairs was the division Sergeant Majors office. As soon as he looked up and saw who was coming up the stairs he stood up, came from behind his desk, and stood at attention and rendered a salute. "Welcome to the 8th Infantry Division Colonel McNeil. I'm Sergeant Major Graves."

Sergeant Major Graves looked as if he had been around a while. He was bald and big and looked as if he could take care of himself in a fight or anything else. McNeil returned the salute. "Thank you Sergeant Major Graves it's a pleasure to be here."

"If I can help in any way just ask sir."

"I'll certainly keep that in mind Sergeant Major Graves."

"The Division S-1 section occupies the offices to our left," continued

Captain Waters, "And over here is the office of the division XO Colonel Campbell," said Captain Waters knocking at the closed door. A gruff voice called out, "come in."

Captain Waters pushed open the door and announced, "Sir, may I present Lieutenant Colonel McNeil?"

Colonel Campbell, a full colonel, stood up and rendered a salute. He wasn't saluting the man but the white ribbon with blue stars, the Congressional Medal of Honor that adorned McNeil's uniform. It was required of everyone, from generals on down, to salute the medal.

Colonel Campbell wore his hair longer than most men but it was neatly cut. He was tall and well-built, no fat on his body.

"Welcome to the 8th Infantry Division Colonel McNeil," he said after McNeil returned the salute. "Are you being taken care of?"

"Captain Waters is a very efficient man sir."

"After he signs in here we'll get him to finance sir," said Capt. Waters.

"Next stop is the Generals office I suppose?"

"Yes sir."

"I'll accompany you then."

They passed by a closed door with a name plate in place; Lt .Col McNeil. German American Relations Officer, it read. He had been expected and no time was wasted.

At another closed door with a sign that read; **General Layton, Commanding general, 8th Infantry Division**, they stopped and Colonel Campbell knocked and entered without waiting for an invitation. It was a big plush office with several soft chairs arranged around a coffee table. A big desk stood at the rear of the room and a very familiar man stood up and rendered a salute before Colonel Campbell could announce the new comer. "I see you found us ok Charley," said General Layton as McNeil returned the salute.

"Yes sir. You have a very efficient aide sir."

"I see Tom has introduced you to the division XO, and I suppose you have met our Sergeant Major?"

"Yes sir he has, and yes I've met the sergeant major."

"How was your trip?"

"It was much nicer than the trip to and from Korea Sir."

"Have you finished processing in yet?"

"As soon as he signs in I'll get him processed sir," answered Captain Waters.

"Have you had a chance to visit your office Charlie?"

"No Sir, not yet."

"There is an itinerary on your desk but I'll give you the gist of it now. We will take lunch at the O-Club today so you can meet the staff. Tomorrow we go to Seventh Army for lunch with General Clark where the press will be present. One of your first duties here is to meet and extend an invitation, in my name, to all local German dignitaries, from the mayor down, to attend a luncheon at the O-Club. You will of course set it up with the club manager and let me know the date and time. My purpose for this is so we can meet each other, formally, and hopefully they will get over the idea that we are barbarians. Sorry to throw all this at you on your first day here Charley but the pressure is on us to get the program up and running so that fact can be reported to Seventh Army."

"Yes sir. I understand sir. I'll set it up. You are aware that they, the Germans, will feel obligated to reciprocate in kind."

"I trust you will handle the details and keep me notified."

"Yes sir."

"It's good to see you again and have you here with us Charley, but I'll have to cut this short because I'm pressed for time. I'll also need my staff car. Bill," he said turning to Col. Campbell who had not said a word as yet, has the other staff car arrived?"

"I'll check sir," he replied picking up the phone.

"Sometime later, when you are settled in Charley, Marie and I will have you to my quarters for lunch."

"The car has just arrived sir," said Col. Campbell replacing the phone.

"Good. I have added a second staff car Charley but not for your personal use. It will have to be shared with the staff. Schedule the use of it through the Sergeant Major. Why don't you accompany me to the meeting Bill so Tom will be free to escort Charley around."

"As you wish sir."

"Feel free to come to me anytime if there is a problem Charley. And, again, welcome to the 8th Infantry Division."

"Yes sir and thank you for your time sir. I'll get out of your way now," said Col. McNeil as he saluted and left the generals office, followed by Capt. Waters.

"You didn't say much Bill," spoke General Layton after his office door was closed, "what's on your mind?"

"He's so young, both in age and time in service, to wear the rank he wears. Can he handle it? Most men who were fast promoted as a necessity in Korea were reduced in rank appropriate to their age."

"For your information, and I sincerely hope you spread the word, Lieutenant Colonel Charley R. McNeal, though young, is one hell of a combat commander. As a captain he was given the near impossible task of rebuilding a battalion headquarters, which was lost to combat operations. Only one man survived and less than twenty percent of the equipment was usable. He rebuilt a functional battalion from on hand assets while defending an important piece of real estate. He, because of lack of man power, commanded a company and the battalion. If my memory serves me correctly, that battalion functioned with only eight men in it. He was wounded eight times commanding the battalion and holding the important piece of land with only seventy percent of the authorized strength.

"He fully believes in the Infantry motto, Follow Me, but he leads from the front rather than from the rear. He commands by example rather than 'do it because I say so'. In fact, and he doesn't know that I know this, before he took command he would venture out on the battle field at night to scrounge for food, ammo, and weapons for his men. He never voiced a complaint nor cried impossible in what would seem impossible situations.

"Yes, he is young, but very experienced. He has several distinctions. One, he has never worn gold rank. Two, he is the youngest man to ever command a company or battalion in combat. Three, he went to Korea as a Corporal and left as a Lieutenant Colonel. He was allowed to keep the rank by order of General MacArthur. One other thing you will find out about Lieutenant Colonel McNeil Bill, he has no fear of rank, he respects rank but has no fear of it. He will do what's necessary to get the assigned job done and if he has men assigned under him he will protect them to the fullest.

"Granted, he is young. He is an officer with over four years in grade. He has the medal, which he has tried to return because he believes the medal interferes with his duties. He has attended C & G S and speaks both German and Spanish. He has also served his time in the Pentagon. And if you noticed he is an Airborne Ranger. I could say more but you get the idea."

"Yes sir. I understand. If there is any doubt among the staff I'll correct it."

"I know you will Bill. One other item you should look into. Once Charley is settled in he will need help. Should we hire a local who will know the language or should we use military? Do we have anyone qualified that speaks German? Check that out for me Bill"

"Yes sir. I'll work on it."

"Sergeant Major," spoke Capt. Waters as he entered the office, "the general will be using his car this afternoon and I understand we now have a second one available."

"Yes we do sir."

"Unless it's spoken for Col. McNeil and will I need it."

"Specialist Milligan, front and center," yelled out the sergeant major.

A Spec five came into the office from somewhere in the rear and answered, "yes sergeant major." Spec Five Milligan was a young man dressed in a stiffly starched uniform with shiny boots. He wore an airborne patch.

"Take the captain and colonel where they need to go."

"Yes Sergeant Major."

McNeil had cleared finance and turned in all his green money for the old familiar Military Script. He was paid up-to-date. After the medics checked his records to assure themselves he didn't need any shots he headed for the education center which was on the back side of the post. "Capt. Waters," spoke McNeil when they were back in the car and on the way to the education center, "until I get my feet on the ground, so to speak, I won't be much help to you but if you run into a problem or need any help contact me any time."

"Yes sir, I'll keep that in mind but I don't foresee any problems right now."

There was a healthy young lady behind the desk at the education center, Miss Caldwell, her name tag read. She had long blonde hair and deep blue eyes which seemed to be always smiling. "Good morning gentlemen. May I help you?" she asked in a Midwest accent

"Good morning Miss Caldwell, I'm Col. McNeil, checking in. I have some records to turn in."

"Col. McNeil, we have been expecting you. Professor Hurbert, the center director, received advance notice you would be arriving here but not when. I know both Professor Hurbert and Professor Edge, in charge of higher learning, would like to meet you but unfortunately they are both tied up right now. Could we schedule a meeting at a later date?"

"Since I'm pressed for time myself I think that would be best. But, I have no idea what my phone number is. Give me the number here and I'll call later with my number. Will that be ok?"

"That'll be fine sir. Here's the center number and we'll be waiting for your call. Have a nice day now."

"You also Miss Caldwell."

"How are we for time?" McNeil asked of Capt. Waters when they were back in the car and moving.

"We have fifteen minutes but that's not enough time to accomplish anything."

"Then let's head for the club where I'm sure there will be coffee."

"What is your first name Spec Five Milligan?" asked McNeil when the car stopped at the officers club. Normally the place is called the OOM, Officers Open Mess, or O-club.

"Timothy or Tim sir."

"Ok, Tim it is. We'll probably be here for an hour or more so you go eat and be back here at a quarter till."

"Yes sir."

"Sir," said Capt. Waters after the staff car left, it is not post policy to release the drivers that way."

"Though they are enlisted men and human beings they are part of the military. Hasn't anyone though they might have personal business to take care of? How do they eat? Maybe they need a latrine break. If I have violated a policy I'll take responsibility for it but as long as I have a driver I'll see to his wellbeing."

"Yes sir," replied Capt.. Waters as they entered the club. "Sir, there should be coffee right over there. If it's ok with you I'll check in with the club manager to make sure everything is set for the noon meal."

"I can manage from here Capt. Waters you take care of business."

He found the large coffee pot and poured himself a cup of coffee then lit a cigar as he walked back out into the main part of the club. As usual, an OOM is rather large to accommodate officer social functions. There was a dance floor and a band stage; also a dining room large enough to handle the assigned officers and their wives. There is also a stag bar where officers can stop by on their way home after work and drink a beer without having to get dressed up. At this hour there were only a few men at the bar and none in the dining room.

"I see you found the place ok Charley," said General Layton as he entered the club followed by Col. Campbell, "where is Tom?"

"He's checking with the club manager sir."

"How is the in-processing coming along?"

"We should be through in a couple more hours' sir."

General Layton spoke as he went and poured himself a cup of coffee. "We'll do this as an informal receiving line Charley."

During the next ten minutes officers started entered the club, checked their hats, then approached General Layton and saluted him. When they were introduced to McNeil each one saluted him then shook his hand and welcomed him to the 8th Infantry Division. Several of the officers outranked him but they were not saluting him but the ribbon he wore on his uniform. There were four more full colonels beside Col. Campbell, half a dozen Lieutenant Colonels, and about the same number of majors. Capt. Waters was the lowest ranking man present. Once everyone was seated General Layton gave a short speech before the food was served. "Gentlemen," he said after tapping his water glass to get attention, "everyone is here today to meet Lieutenant Colonel McNeil the newest member of the division. In addition to being my senior aide he is the division German American relations officer. You will be hearing more on that later. Also, and there's a DF on your desk about this Charley, he will be the post labor relations officer. Lieutenant Colonel McNeil comes to us from a pentagon assignment. Charley, I'm sure the men would like to hear something from you."

McNeil had been thinking he would be asked to speak so he had given it some thought. "Gentlemen, it's a great honor for me to be assigned to the 8th Infantry Division, A division with a long and proud history. I arrived this morning so I'm still processing in and learning my way around Rose Barracks, the home of the 8th Infantry Division. As you may or may not know General Layton is privileged to----"

"Privileged!" interrupted General Layton.

"I'm sorry sir. Honored, to know me since I was a corporal." that got some laughs from men who were in awe of a general officer.

"We met in Korea and I see form some of the ribbons around the table others of you were there also. Enough said about Korea. In accomplishing the task handed me I will probably step on some toes getting the job done. I sincerely hope we can work together to accomplish the mission set forth. It will take me some time to put names and positions with the faces of men I met today, please bear with me.

"As for the medal; as you know a large percent of the Congressional Medals of Honor are awarded posthumously so those people have little to say about it. For those of us who are still around, and I would say that most would agree with me, we tend to ask why? Why me? Others did just as much so why were they not awarded the medal. We are soldiers and we do what is asked of us. I never felt that I did more than the next man and I certainly never felt that I really earned the medal. But, once the medal is presented, it is with you for life. It can't be returned. I know because I tried.

"I see our food is starting to arrive so I'll cut this short. One item I have for Col. Griffin." Lieutenant Colonel Griffin is the Post Provost Marshal, "It's a heads up sir. Shortly there will be a formal reception at Rose Barracks and the OOM for some German dignitaries. I don't have a number or a date as yet but we'll need MP help to get them through the gate and to the club. As soon as I have the information I'll get it to you. Thank you for your attention gentlemen."

The balance of the day, after the in-processing was completed, was spent getting McNeil's uniforms to the cleaners and getting the correct shoulder patches sewn on. He had a list of what he needed in the quarters so he went shopping. He realized that three Class 'A' uniforms might make it but didn't want to take a chance and be caught short, he needed a fourth one. A trip to the clothing store solved that. It was after sixteen hundred when he finally completed everything, dropped his purchases at his quarters, and went to his office.

There were two DF's on his desk, as General Layton had said there would be, one designating him as German labor officer for Rose Barracks. A message also gave him the uniform and departure time for the trip to Seventh Army tomorrow. After getting a cup of coffee he settled down to read the literature on what was expected of him as the division German American Relations officer. He was so engrossed in reading and making notes he was unaware that General Layton stood in his office doorway, until he spoke. "How is it coming Charley?"

"Sorry sir. I didn't hear you enter. I have bits and pieces of the puzzle sir. Right now I'm trying to put them together as a plan of action."

"You have had a busy day Charley. Why don't you knock off early and get some rest. Tomorrow is another day. That was not a suggestion Charley."

"Yes sir. I understand sir. Maybe with a clear head all this will make sense tomorrow. Sir, I'm designated as your senior aide and I have told Tom if he needs any help to call me. How are we to work this out?"

"Priorities Charley. I'll let you know if I need something from you. Right now this German Relations program needs to get up and running. I'll see you tomorrow Charley."

"Yes sir. Good evening sir."

After he stopped by the snack bar for his evening meal he went to his quarters and took a shower. With a drink and a cigar he settled down in the easy chair and his thoughts turned to Babs. He wondered what she was doing right now. And he wondered why he was here. One never realizes how good they have it until they leave an assignment. Thinking back he realized that the Pentagon assignment really wasn't such a bad assignment. At least he was there with several hundred other lieutenant colonels and not here singled out as one. And there was Babs, who he could come home to each evening, have a drink, a meal, and good conversation. Maybe I should have kept my mouth shut and drifted along with the pentagon assignment. I'm still a long way from getting a command and I could just as well complete the waiting time there as here. I'm one here and every move I make, everything I do or don't do, is noticed. I feel like a fish in a bowl where everyone can watch me.

After finishing the drink and cigar he prepared a uniform for tomorrow, brushed his teeth, bathed, and went to bed. Because of the time difference, the long flight, plus the hectic activities of today, McNeil had no trouble falling asleep.

Even though he was up early and had a good breakfast he made very little progress in his reading during the few hours before he and General Layton had to depart for the trip to Seventh Army; a helicopter ride from Rose Barracks to Seventh Army Airfield outside of Stuttgart where a staff car waited to take them to Seventh Army Headquarters.

It was about what McNeil expected. He was introduced to so many officers that he would never remember their names. Lieutenant General Clark gave a short speech after the meal and then invited McNeil to say something. McNeil expounded on his earlier speech about those who received the medal never believed they really earned it. After the meal and speech a few selected reporters were allowed to take photographs and ask questions.

When they arrived back at Rose Barracks McNeil was relieved that the show was finally over and he could get down to some serious work. He was able to get out of the dress uniform and into fatigues which he was much more comfortable with. Especially since no medals were worn on fatigues.

McNeil, having spent better than four years riding a desk felt he was very much out of shape. That was proven when he went through the airborne training at Fort Benning Georgia. He checked the training schedule and attached himself with the first unit that was doing physical training. He continued to do that each morning until he began to feel he could again hold his own with the younger and more physically able troops.

Three days after the trip to Seventh Army he completed his early morning run, stopped by his quarters to shower and change, then after a meal at the O-club he went to his office to start the day.

When he entered his office he found a woman sitting at his desk. She was middle aged and wore a ring on her finger. Her hair was done up in a bun at the back of her head with was common for most German women. She wore a very conservative dress and was busy reading a paper and did not know McNeil was present until he spoke to her in German. "Good morning. May I help you?"

She dropped the paper on the desk and stood up all flustered. "Good morning sir. I'm Frau Olga Snelling. I was hired to work for a Colonel McNeil. I was told to come here and wait for him," she said as she started to move from behind the desk.

"I'm Colonel McNeil and please, stay where you are. It's my pleasure to meet you Frau Olga and I'm very glad to have your help. The desk is yours. You do type and speak English don't you?" He asked her in English.

"Yes sir," she replied in English.

"I'll move to the table since you'll need the desk more than I will. One thing we have to get straight if we are to work together. You can call me Colonel, or Charley. May I call you Olga?"

"Yes sir."

"What I'm tasked with is coming up with a training program," said McNeil as he hung his hat up and moved his things from the desk to the table in the corner of the room, "for German American relations. I could certainly use your help."

"I'll be glad to lend a hand sir. You have a message sir from the post education center," she said handing McNeil a slip of paper, "Miss Caldwell."

"Frau Ogle I completely forgot about the education center. I was supposed to call them with my phone number. Would you get Miss Caldwell on the phone while I get some coffee? Would you like a cup also?"

"I can get the coffee sir."

"That would be kind of hard to do while on the phone. You make the call and I'll get the coffee."

When he returned with two cups of coffee and set one on the desk for Frau Ogle she handed him the phone. "Miss Caldwell please accept my apology for not getting in touch with you as promised."

"No apology needed sir. I made a few calls and got your number. Would it be convenient for you to meet with Professor Hurbert today at thirteen hundred hours?"

"I can and will."

"We'll be looking forward to your visit then. Would you please call me Jesse? Miss Caldwell sounds so formal." He could call me anything and I'd be happy thought Jesse as she sat twirling a sprig of her hair while she talked.

"Only if you will consent and call me Charley."

"Ok Charley."

With the assistance of Frau Olga everything went into high gear at the office of German American Relations. Contact was made with the Mayor, that position in Germany is called **Burgermeister,** Herr Carl Shultz, of Bad Kreuznach.

When Frau Ogle made the call to the office of the Burgermeister and after she explained who she was and what the call was about the person to whom she was speaking allowed her to speak with Herr Shultz. She had to again explain who she was and to whom she worked for and what the call was about. Herr Shultz was thrilled that something was about to be done about the high incidence rate of American soldiers and he agreed to meet with McNeil and have all his key people present. He had some free time at nine the next morning if that would be convenient?

Frau Ogle covered the mouth piece and spoke to McNeil. "Sir, the Herr Burgermeister asks if nine tomorrow morning will be ok with you."

"With us Frau Ogle and yes that will be fine."

Frau Ogle accepted the invitation then hung up the phone and spoke to McNeil. "Sir, am I to accompany you to this meeting?"

"You are part of this team Frau Ogle and you need to be there to observe and lend a hand where needed. We'll go in a staff car."

McNeil and Frau Ogle worked to gather any and all notes they would need at tomorrow's meeting. McNeil did remember to make it to the education center and meet with Professor Hurbert. Together they lay out a schedule for him to attend classes to complete the necessary credits for his masters. For McNeil it would be back to night classes since there would be little free time during the day.

"Tim," spoke McNeil when the staff car parked in a visitors slot at the big old German Government building in downtown Bad Kreuznach, "I have no idea how long we'll be so stay with the car." As he and Frau Ogle got out of the staff car a German Policeman walked up and saluted. He spoke in German. "If you will follow me sir and Ma'am I'll escort you to the office of the Burgermeister."

The building which looked old and weather worn on the outside was clean and spotless inside. The floors were waxed and shiny. They followed the German Policeman up two flights of stairs then he stopped at a door and opened it. The room was rather large with a big long table in the center and twenty chairs around it. On the table were ashtrays, bottles of water at each place plus pencils and a tablet were laid out at each place. The German Policeman closed the door and stood with his back against it. Frau Ogle and I were left standing. It crossed my mind of just how ironic the situation was. He I am just a young man from the hills of Kentucky about to have a meeting with the Mayor of a German town. My thought was interrupted when another door opened and I could hear voices.

A man entered the room talking to someone behind him. The policeman came to attention so I knew this must be the mayor. Herr Shultz had dark hair splashed with grey; he was short and pudgy with fat jowls. Several more men followed him into the room. When the group realized their visitors were already in the room they stopped talking and Mayor Shultz put on his political smile and walked over to where Frau Ogle Snelling and I stood.

"Herr Oberstleutnant McNeil so good to meet you," he spoke in German and the man who accompanied him started translating. When he finished I answered in German which seemed to surprise everyone. We shook hands. Apparently they didn't expect anyone who spoke the language.

"I'm pleased you could find time in your busy schedule to receive us Herr Burgermeister. May I present my assistant Frau Ogle Shelling?"

Herr Shultz moved in front of Frau Ogle, did a brief bow, and reached for her hand. Welcome and I'm pleased to meet you Frau Snelling. Snelling that name rings a bell, a Helmut Snelling and I attended school together."

"Helmut is my husband sir," said a very surprised Frau Ogle.

"Small world isn't? What is Himmy doing these days?"

"He owns a small café and bakery sir."

"We'll have to get together sometime. Shall we be seated?" he said taking Frau Ogle to a chair and holding it for her.

The other two men were introduced as Herr Carl Hildebrand the Mayor's interpreter and Herr Kurt Wagner the secretary. There were only five people seated at the big table when Herr Shultz spoke. "Herr Oberstleutnant McNeil you asked for this meeting so please begin."

"Yes sir." McNeil started at the beginning and explained how concerned the Department of Defense was about the high incident rate of American

Soldiers and how a program was to be put into effect in hopes of curtailing it. He explained that he was tasked with setting up classes to make soldiers more aware of the customs of the German people. He spoke about what the American military would do in cooperation with the German Police. While he spoke Herr Shultz's secretary was busy taking notes as was Frau Ogle. Many questions were asked and answered as best as McNeil could at this time. Herr Shultz decided he would have to have meetings with his law enforcement people then get back with McNeil at a later date.

"Have you met our Commanding General, General Layton, sir," McNeil asked of Herr Shultz.

"Once, very briefly."

"We hope to remediate that soon Sir. General Layton extends an invitation to you and your wife plus as many of your law enforcement people, and their wives, as you deem necessary to meet their military counterparts. It will be a formal reception held at the Rose Barracks Officer's club."

"When will this take place Herr Oberstleutnant McNeil?" asked Herr Shultz.

"It's in the planning stage now sir. What we need from you is a list of people who will attend so we can make arrangements for passes and escorts."

"How do I get the list to you?"

"Frau Snelling will give you a phone number so Herr Wagner can call her with the list."

"Do we have anything else to discuss here today Herr McNeil?"

"Nothing from me sir but I feel sure we should have more meetings after you speak with your people."

"I'll keep you up-to-date on that. Thank you very much for the information and I hope to see your actions bear fruit Herr McNeil. We have work to do as I'm sure you do so until the next time Herr Oberstleutnant McNeil."

Hands were shook all around then Herr Shultz spoke to Frau Snelling.

"Frau Snelling," spoke Herr Shultz, "if you ever get tired of working for the Oberstleutnant McNeil come see me. I could use someone with your talents on my staff."

McNeil and Frau Snelling left the building with the ever ready police escort.

When they were back in the car and on the way to Rose Barracks Frau Ogle spoke. "I had no idea Herr Shultz and my husband knew each other. I wonder why Helmut never said anything to me."

"As you well know Frau Ogle, the German people are very class and social conscious. Maybe he didn't want to brag about knowing the Burgermeister."

"It's possible but I'll speak to him about it."

I'm sure she will do a bit more than just speak with her man, thought McNeil. Keeping secrets from a woman, regardless of how innocent they might be, is asking for trouble.

Three days after the meeting Herr Wagner called with a list of men and their wives who would be attending the formal reception. Once McNeil had the list of the attendees, and their ladies, he made up formal invitations. Then he notified Col. Griffin of the number of dignitaries who would be visiting Rose Barracks and the date and time. A week before Thanksgiving at seventeen hundred was the date and time.

Working with Frau Ogle he came up with a list of military personnel who would be attending which would have to be approved by General Layton.

Now that McNeil had most everything approved he had to come up with a list of wine and food to be served. He was leaning towards typical German food but Frau Ogle had a better suggestion. "Herr Oberstleutnant," she called McNeil that when she was serious about something. That was his rank in German, "this is a reception hosted by Americans so why not serve typical American food rather that German food?"

McNeil gave her suggestion some thought. When in Rome do as the Romans do and eat the local food. Why shouldn't that apply in this case? I'm sure when the Germans reciprocate they will serve typical German food. He made a quick decision and picked up the phone and dialed a number from memory. "Officers open mess, Sgt Haskell speaking."

"Sgt Haskell, this is Col. McNeil. Is the club manager, Major Steel available?"

"He's out in the club sir. If you'll hold I'll get him."

A few minutes later a new voice was on the phone. "Major Steel sir, what can the club do for you Col. McNeil?"

"I assume you are aware of my position and the task that has been handed to me?"

"Yes sir. I remember you sir."

"There will be a formal reception held at your club, date and time to be announced but sometime just before Thanksgiving.. Right now this office needs to get with you and bring you up to date so you can start preparing, that is hiring extra help, making sure there is sufficient food and drink on hand. What is a convenient time for you today?"

"I'll be freed up by fourteen hundred Sir. We can get together any time after that."

"I won't be there but my assistant will be there at fourteen hundred today. Please accord her, Frau Olga Snelling, every courtesy because she will be operating in my name."

"Yes sir. I'll be waiting for her."

"Thank you very much Major Steel."

When he hung up the phone Frau Olga was looking at him with a worried look on her face. "Sir, do you trust me to do this for you?"

"A better question is, why shouldn't I trust you? Until you give me reason to not trust you I have complete faith in you and your abilities. I'll send you to the club in the staff car so make sure you have all the papers and information you will need."

"Yes sir."

McNeil realized he had just given Frau Olga a promotion, now he would have to see about making it legal. The lady is over qualified for a secretary position and I can't help but wonder why her abilities and education wasn't noticed before.

That evening after he returned from the education center and sent Frau Olga to the club in the staff car he looked up the correct phone number for the office of local hiring. When he dialed it he got a sergeant who sounded as if didn't have the ability to handle such a job. "Sergeant Lawson, is Capt. Dellwood available"

"Yes sir. He's right here."

"This is Capt. Dellwood. To whom am I speaking?"

"Capt. Dellwood, you are speaking with Col. McNeil. I have been designated as the Camp Labor Relations officer. What I have for you is a request to promote a person whom I believe has been hired well below her education and ability. I have already promoted her to assistant to the 8th Infantry Division German Relations officer. I need to make that official."

"Who are you speaking of Col McNeil?"

"Frau Olga Snelling."

"One moment please while I pull her file Sir." McNeil heard a chair scrape and some papers rustling then Capt. Dellwood was back on the phone. "Sir I have her file here and what you want can't be done at this time."

"And why is that?"

"By the regulation a person hired is on one year probation. Nothing can be done until a person completes the probation period and is evaluated. Frau Olga has only been with us for two months now, she has ten months to go on her probation."

"Are you familiar with General Black Capt. Dellwood?"

"I've heard the name sir but never met the man. I believe he is Chief of staff at the pentagon."

"A Colonel once told General Black he couldn't do what he wanted done because regulations forbid it. That Colonel had trouble sitting down after he left General Black's office. That is not a threat captain but a statement of fact.

You, or your office, is in error. I'm simply pointing out the error to you and asking that it be corrected."

"I understand sir but my hands are tied."

"Who do you work for captain?"

"This office is directly under the Camp Commander, General Layton, so I assume he is next in my chain of command sir."

"You assume but you don't know. Let me assure you he is the man in charge and as I have just told you he appointed me to oversee the office of labor hiring. So in essence I am your boss now. General Layton is twenty feet from me right now but this error should not have to be presented to him. We, you and I, will correct this error Captain Dellwood. This is a direct order. You will correct this mistake and have the papers on my desk no later than quitting time tomorrow showing that Frau Olga Snelling has been hired as the assistant German Relations officer to Rose Barracks with appropriate pay and allowances. Is that clear Captain?"

"Yes sir. I'll see what can be done sir."

"You will see and do and comply with that direct order Captain. At ten hundred hours on the thirteenth I will be in your office to have a look at your files. I hope that I won't fine any more miss-hiring. I will also look at your grievance files. You do have such a file don't you Capt. Dellwood?"

"Yes sir we do."

"Have a nice day Capt.. Dellwood."

When Frau Olga returned with the information about the formal affair the two sat down and went over it making sure everything was correct. The only unknown was the list of military attendees. He would have to get the information to General Layton and see who he wanted to add to the list since he was hosting the affair.

When McNeil gathered up the package of information for the formal affair and went to present it to General Layton he found that the general had taken off early. He called the generals quarters and found out the general was home and relaxing so he decided it was important enough to get the information in his hands now since time was a factor.

"Sorry to do this to you Tim," McNeil apologized to the driver as they headed for General Layton's quarters.

"Not a problem sir."

"I shouldn't be here long so wait."

"Yes sir."

After he rang the doorbell and was admitted by the butler he was escorted to the den by the butler where he found General Layton relaxing by the fire with a cup of coffee and a stack of papers he was reading. "Good evening sir. Sorry to bother you at this late hour by I felt you should have the information as quickly as I could get it to you."

"No bother Charley and what information do you speak of?"

"I have a rough draft of the formal party sir, with a list of German dignitaries that will be attending. I have met with the Mayor and his top people and he is looking forward to the gathering. What I'm not sure of is the military side of this. I thought you should go over the package and make any additions you wish."

"There's coffee Charley if you have time?" said General Layton as he reached for the package.

"I don't want to intrude sir and I do have some last minute work to accomplish."

"As I said before Charlie, my door is always open to you, and so is my home. But before you rush off I have another favor to ask."

"Anything sir."

"I realize I have placed a heavy load on you in a short time but I have to ask this of you. Marie is still worried that she will make a mistake at the formal gathering, with the German dignitaries. Could I impose on you to sit down with her and explain what is expected of her?"

"I could sir but I have a better idea."

"Let me have it."

"We are hosting a formal affair for the elite of the local Germans, but what about some of the lesser individuals; those who come in contact with the ever day problems of German American relations. I realize we are unable to meet all of them but I believe if you met with a few of them it would send a message that you are serious about German American relations."

"And of course you have someone in mind?"

"I do sir. I believe a lady could better explain the correct protocol to your wife than I could; a lady who is fluent in English and well educated. Her husband owns a bakery and café in town so he sees the everyday problems, not as much as say a bar owner but enough of the problems. Maybe if you could see your way clear to have them both to a dinner, at your quarters, one evening, informal, it would send the correct message."

"Maybe you have something Charley. Let me discuss it with Marie and I'll get back to you. When do you need an answer on this package?"

"Yesterday sir."

"I'll go over it tonight and have it back tomorrow morning then. Sure you want have some coffee Charley?"

"The staff car is waiting sir and I really do have work that can't wait."

"Then I'll see you tomorrow Charley. But remember, all work and no play, etc. etc."

"Yes sir. I can see a good example of that statement right here sir."

"I sometimes fine that I can think better with a good cigar and a cup of coffee laced with good brandy."

"I understand sir. I'll be going now. Good evening sir."

Early the next morning, after McNeil finished his run, General Layton summed him to his office. "Good job on the preparations Charley. I have added three names of military people. Though they are subordinate to the division I feel they should be invited. Also make the dress, not mandatory, but preferred, Mess dress. You do have your mess dress uniform don't your Charley?"

"Yes sir, for a while now." McNeil had purchased a Mess Dress uniform shortly after he bought his Dress Blues..

"Also notify this Frau Olga Snelling that the General and Mrs. Layton extends an invitation to her and her husband for an evening meal on the fourteenth at nineteen hundred hours, Informal dress. Now, just who is this Frau Snelling?"

"She was sent to me as a secretary sir but due to her education and expertise I have upgraded her to assistant German American relations officer."

"Did you run into a problem doing that?"

"Nothing that I can't handle sir."

"Ok. I have something else for you Charley, not for publication, Col. Campbell's name has been submitted to Congress for his star. I have requested that he remain here as my division XO. That means, if the request is approved, he will need a staff car so we'll see about getting another one for you. No date as yet on that." That will be good for the colonel, thought McNeil, he wouldn't have to move and he would stay in the same office.

"I have one final item for you Charley, before I let you get on with your duties. In the near future two of the division battalions will be going on training maneuvers. Date and time plus the two battalions have not been decided yet. When this happens I want you to be with them. You will be my eyes and ears out there. I realize you have commanded a battalion in combat but these battalions are twice the size in personnel, equipment, and missions, as what we had in Korea. You need to observe their training as part of your military education."

"Yes sir. I'll be ready."

"Then that's all I have for you Charley, except that Marie and I expect to see you at the dinner next Thursday evening."

"Yes sir. I'll be there."

# McNeil

## 8th Infantry Division
## Bad Kreuznach Germany
## Rose barracks

**Chapter 35**
**28 Oct 55**

Capt. Dellwood found a way to accomplish what McNeil wanted just as McNeil knew he would. The paper up grading Frau Snelling's status from secretary to assistant German American Relations officer was delivered before quitting time as he had requested. Not by Capt. Dellwood but by Sgt Lawson.

McNeil placed the promotion order, along with the invitation to dine with the general, and a gate pass to get her and her husband on the base, on her desk so she would see it the first thing in the morning.

McNeil did his usual run then showered before coming to the office the next morning. Frau Snelling had a very pleasant surprised look on her face when he entered the office.

"Sir, I don't understand how this could happen. I was told I would have a year probation before I could be promoted."

"And you are talking about what Frau Snelling?" asked McNeil trying to pretend he didn't know anything about what she was talking about.

"This," she said holding up the promotion paper, "paper that promotes me from secretary to your assistant with more pay."

"I suppose your talents were recognized Frau Snelling. Congratulations."

"Thank you very much sir. What about this invitation to a dinner with the general? My husband is invited and it's casual wear. Do you know what it's about?"

"It'll be sort of a working dinner. The general's wife, Marie, needs some tutoring on protocol before the big party. I hope you don't mind that I volunteered you for the project?"

"Not, at all sir. I'll be glad to help any way I can. Not that I'm not pleased, but why my husband?"

"He's a business man so we are trying to make sure we don't leave any one out of this German American Relations bit. Besides, I didn't feel it would be right to invite you without inviting your husband. Rumors can be harmful."

"I think I understand sir. I just hope I can do the right thing and don't make a fool of myself."

"You'll do fine Frau Snelling. Don't worry. I've known the general a long time and he isn't the fire breathing dragon most people think him to be."

As McNeil was afraid of, Herr Snelling, after they arrived at the Generals quarters the following evening and the introductions were out of the way, spoke to McNeil in German. "So you are the young man who is stealing the heart of my wife."

"No sir," answered McNeil in German, "Your wife is very talented and useful in our work. You have her heart and I don't believe anyone can take it away from you."

Herr Snelling smiled and offered his hand to McNeil. "My wife said basically the same thing."

Herr Snelling was dressed in a grey suit and tie and Frau Snelling had her hair down and pulled back which was unusual since she always had it in a bun at the back of her head. She wore a very nice dark dress which wasn't flashy but dressy.

"The general and his wife are in the den," said McNeil after taking their coats, "come and I'll introduce you."

Herr Snelling spoke some English, probably taught to him by his wife, but was reluctant to use it in mixed company. McNeil helped him as they were offered drinks before going in to dinner. After the meal Marie and Frau Snelling remained at the dining room table to drink coffee so they could discuss protocol. The three men returned to the den for coffee, brandy, and cigars, and talk. Herr Snelling was a bit more relaxed now so he opened up and talked about some of the problems with the language barrier.

Shortly after arriving at Rose Barracks McNeil found out which one of the Airborne Battalions would be jumping and he attached himself to it. There were six H-19 helicopters assigned to the division which were used to jump from. Weather permitting more helicopters and sometimes airplanes were brought in to make the jumps out at the airfield. McNeil was able to make the required four jumps a month. It wasn't that he really liked to jump but he was qualified and there was extra pay when one made the required jumps.

Tom, Captain Waters, General Layton's junior aide departed for a command assignment and the general selected another aide; another Infantry

Captain; an unmarried man which was more suitable for the duties of a general's aide. Captain Henry Davenport was a hard charging man apparently trying to make a name for himself and impress the general.

When Tom introduced Capt. Davenport to McNeil, McNeil told him that he was the senior aide and if he ever ran into a problem come to him. His reply was, "I think I can handle everything sir. I won't be bothering you."

Several days after Capt. Davenport assumed the duty of Junior Aide to General Layton, General Layton stopped by McNeil's office to ask a question one day. "How is the pup sir?" McNeil asked. He had noticed that Capt. Davenport never let the general out of his sight.

"What." asked General Layton as he noticed the smile on McNeil's face? "Oh, you mean my bird dog. I'll have to have a talk with the man one day."

During one of the many meetings with Herr Shultz it came out that McNeil didn't own a car but was looking for one. One day when the phone rang and Frau Snelling answered it. She handed it to McNeil. "The front gate is calling for you sir."

"Col. McNeil, what can I do for you today?"

"Sir, I'm Corporal Davies at the front gate. I have a man here, a German who doesn't speak much English but he did ask for you."

"What does he want?"

"He won't say sir. Just keeps asking for you by name."

"I'll be right there corporal."

Since the main gate was quite a distance from the headquarters building McNeil had Tim drive him in the staff car to save time. They parked in the small parking lot beside a small building at the main gate used by the MP's to check in and out local hire people. When McNeil walked into the building a tall lanky MP walked up to him and saluted. "Sir I'm Corporal Davie. I called you. That's the man who is asking for you," he said pointing to where a bald German sat on one of the chairs in the waiting room. He was a big man dressed in a suit and tie of which no self-respecting German would be in public without. "Thank you very much Corporal Davies. I'll take it from here," said McNeil walking to where the man sat. The man saw him approaching and stood up.

"Good morning sir," greeted McNeil in German which surprised the man, "I'm Oberstleutnant McNeil. I understand you are looking for me."

"Good morning sir," he said offering his hand, "I'm Herr Ernest Montag."

"I'm very pleased to meet you Herr Montag. What can I do for you today?"

"Not what you can do for me Oberstleutnant McNeil but what I can do for you sir. Word reached me that you were in need of a car."

"I am, and the only person to who I related that fact to was Herr Shultz."

"Yes sir. He contacted me and told me of your needs. I have the BMW dealership in Bad Kreuznach and I have a very nice BMW outside for your approval. Would you care to look at the car sir?"

"I think I can save both of us some time Herr Montag. As I stated, I have need of a car, but not a new one which I can't afford. What I need is a small one, used but in good shape, just to get around in while I'm here."

"That's what I brought here for you to look at sir. It's a four year old BMW but in excellent shape. It's small and red in color. It has a few kilometers on it but will give you many more and with the small four cylinder engine it uses very little gas. Herr Shultz explained to me of your needs and I wouldn't want to bring the wrath of the Burgomaster down on me nor insult you sir. The price is right also. I took it in on trade so I do know something about the car."

"I'll look sir but I make no promises. Where is the car?"

"Right this way sir," he said going to the door of the building that led outside the gate.

The car had been cleaned, inside and out, and it gleamed in the dim light of a cold day. McNeil opened the car door and sat in it. He raised the hood and looked at the small engine. He kicked the tires and did everything that an amateur car buyer would do. Then he stood back and gave it a hard look. It was a very nice car, one that would be a pleasure to drive. But, as he had stated before, the price was way out of his range.

"Very nice Herr Montag but I can't afford such a car."

"How about three thousand sir?"

My God, he's talking German Marks, not dollars. That comes to about seven hundred and fifty dollars. That car would be worth more than three thousand dollars in the states. I have the money in the bank and I don't believe I can find a better car for the money. But, will this be misconstrued as something other than what it is? If I do take the car will it be seen as a bribe; but a bribe for what? It could turn into a favor for a favor in the future. If I turn it down this man will have to answer to the Burgomaster as to why. It is a nice car and the price is right.

"Herr Montag. It is a nice car and the price seems right. But, I don't have that kind of money on me right now, it's in the bank."

"No problem sir. If you want the car I'll take it back with me and get all the correct papers to transfer the car from German ownership to American ownership. Would it be possible for you to come to the dealership sometime tomorrow and pick it up?"

"Tomorrow would be much better for me than today Herr Montag. Three thousand Marks even you say?"

"Yes sir. Three even."

"Then I'll see you tomorrow about noon. Thank you very much for all your troubles Herr Montag."

"No trouble sir. Here's the information you will need to get the car insured and registered," said Herr Montag handing McNeil a paper and reaching for his hand.

McNeil had Tim drive him to the BMW dealership the next day after he went by the bank and withdrew the money. The little red car was sitting out front of the dealership office and it looked even better today than yesterday. Possibly Herr Montag had it polished again. McNeil was met and greeted by Herr Montag and led to an officer where McNeil signed all the necessary papers. "This was sent over by Herr Shultz," said Herr Montag handing McNeil a cardboard with writing on it, all in German. It was a special pass which allowed the car to be parked in any reserve parking space at any German government facility.

With all the paper work completed, and money paid, the two men shook hands and McNeil accepted the keys to the car. He drove back to Rose Barracks and marveled at how comfortable the small car was, and how well it handled.

After a lot of hard work and many hours McNeil presented his draft of the German American Relations program and class schedule to General Layton for his approval. The one thing McNeil wanted, and it was a requirement by regulation, was for the commander of a unit, of the man involved in an incident, to be the one to pick up his man from the German police or from the MP's. "I'm not so sure this is a good idea Charley," said General Layton, "a commander has a lot on his plate as it is. He's not going to be too pleased to have to get up in the early morning hours to sign for a man from jail."

"That was a requirement in the original letter and that's my point exactly sir. Granted a commander has a plate full but he is still the commander and he is responsible for what his men do or don't do. If just any company officer is allowed to pick up an arrested man the incident may not get the full attention as it would if the commander had to go pick up his man, or men. It was brought to my attention at one of the meetings with Herr Shultz that when arrested men were released to just anyone they were seen back in town the next day which indicated to the German police that no punishment was handed out."

"I see your point here Charley, but. Let me discuss this with Col. Campbell and this needs to be staffed since we are talking about new policy. I'll get back with you Charley."

The Draft of the German American Relations Program was presented at the very next Division Staff meeting. It was more for information purposes and to let all staff and commanders know what was expected of them. The one item they all balked at, as General Layton had expected, was the commander of a unit was required to sign for and pick up any of his men arrested by the American military MP's or German Police.

McNeil sat and listened to the bickering and the many reasons given as to why the idea was not good. An Idea came to him and he spoke. "Gentlemen, what you have in front of you is what came down as an order. But maybe we can, with the approval of General Layton, alter it somewhat. What if a commander designated an officer, on orders, and the orders would have to be in German also, to be his representative to sign for men from the arresting authority. This officer would then be responsible for that man until such time as the commander could see the man and decide what punishment was warranted, if any. What D O D is trying to do here is make sure a commander is aware of any German American incidents and that the incident doesn't fall through the crack. I can rewrite the SOP if that idea appeals to you commanders and is approved by General Layton."

After a bit of discussion by the staff General Layton spoke, "Col. McNeil is correct, I have read the original letter and it does require commanders to pick up their men when incarcerated. I'll approve the idea Col. McNeil proposed but, if I hear of any commander failing to take action and not reporting action taken, we'll revert back to the original letter of instructions. Gentlemen, time is moving on and we have more work to take care of so let's close out this staff meeting. Col. McNeil, redo the SOP with the new concept for my signature. That's all gentlemen."

McNeil rewrote the SOP then after getting it approved by General Layton he went to the S-3 section, (Plans, Operation, and training) to get the German American classes on the training schedule. He would give the first class to each of the major units and then an officer would be designated to give the class on a monthly schedule to all units, from detachments to companies, and up.

The office of Indigenous hiring was located in an older building on Rose Barracks. When McNeil entered the office, after leaving the S-3, he found it untidy with ratty furniture. Sgt Lawson was at a desk when McNeil entered and he did not get up but simply looked up and asked, "Good morning sir. May I help you?"

"You may Sgt Lawson by following proper protocol. You do know what to do when an officer enters don't you?"

"Yes sir but we have officers here all the time," he replied slowly standing up.

"All the more reason you should start showing a bit of courtesy. Where is Capt. Dellwood?"

"He just stepped out sir. He said he would be right back."

"Did he not tell you that an inspection would be made today?"

"No sir," replied Sgt Lawson.

"Do you know who I am sergeant?"

"No sir. But you must be a Generals aide."

"I'm 'the' Generals aide. Three things I want while we wait for Capt. Dellwood to return; first dust down that table and chair. Get me a cup of coffee. Then I wish to see the files on local hire. Start with the 'A's'. Can you handle that sergeant?"

"Yes sir," he replied as he pulled a rag from one of his desk drawers and started wiping the dust off the table and chair. After putting the rag back in his desk drawer he opened a file cabinet and pulled out a thin stack of files and placed them on the table in front of McNeil. "How do you take your coffee sir?"

"Black will do fine," replied McNeil as he opened the first file. The 'A' file was thin because not too many Germans had last names beginning with the letter 'A'.

As soon as McNeil finished the 'A file the now alert Sgt Lawson placed another pile of files before him and picked up the first file and returned it to the file cabinet. McNeil made notes on a legal pad as he looked over the files, mainly interested in the education and skill level and where the people worked. He found a couple that did not even have the hire date on them.

He was half way through the 'J' file when Capt. Dellwood opened the door and entered. "Good morning sir, sorry I'm late but I had an errand to run." McNeil didn't return his greeting but simply looked up at the captain then looked at his watch and continued to work. Captain Dellwood looked at Sgt Lawson who just shrugged his shoulders. Capt. Dellwood went on back to his office.

When McNeil completed the last file he looked up to see Sgt Lawson watching him. "The grievance file, Sergeant, if you please."

"That's in Capt. Dellwood's office sir."

"Am I supposed to go get it?"

"No sir, I'll get it."

Sergeant Lawson rushed into the rear office and returned with a file that was a bit thicker than the others and placed it before McNeil. McNeil flipped through the file but nowhere could he find any follow-up on the grievances. He did find a grievance filed by one of the two names he found that were miss-hired but nothing was done. At least no follow up was posted.

After making more notes on his legal pad he stood up, picked up the legal pad and the grievance file and went into Capt. Dellwood's office, closing the door. Capt. Dellwood stood up behind his desk. "At least you have the courtesy to stand up when a superior officer enters your office Capt. Dellwood.

You should so instruct your sergeant. You also failed to let your sergeant know there would be an inspection today so this office wasn't prepared."

"Sorry about that sir but I'll make sure it doesn't happen again."

"You also assured me that you would go over the files and make sure there were no more miss-hires. You failed to do that."

"I beg your pardon sir but I did go over the files."

"You found nothing wrong?"

"Everything looked good to me sir."

"I see. Have you or your sergeant attended any of the classes on German American relations that are being conducted almost every day somewhere on the base?"

"This is the first I have heard of this sir."

"How long have you had this duty assignment Capt. Dellwood?"

"Seven months next week sir. I was supposed to be here six months."

"Where do you go from here?"

"I had hoped to get a command sir."

"Captain, if you command a company the way you run this office you will never pin on the gold leaf of a major. This German American Relations isn't something dreamed up at Rose Barracks. It came from the Department of Defense, through the Department of Army, down to USUAR, and through Seventh Army. We, the American military, are no longer an occupation force; we are here at the request of the German Government as a deterrent force. We are guests in this country. The German people are no longer POW's or slaves. They are free people and human beings. We will treat them as such. Do you have pen and paper captain?"

"Yes sir," he replied placing a sheet of paper on his desk and reaching for a pen.

"Take notes captain because I don't want there to be any more misunderstandings. You will find out where and when a class on German American relations is being given and you and your sergeant will attend once a month to get your names on the roster. It's mandatory that each man, from the general down, attend a class once a month.

"You will clean up this office, dust, mop, and paint as needed to present a better first impression to the people coming here seeking work. Some of the furniture out there looks as if it will collapse anytime."

"Sir, I have tried to get better furniture from the quartermaster but with no results."

"Captain, I represent the commanding general, I am his senior aide. Use my name, or the general's if necessary, but get this place cleaned up and presentable as an office should look that the public sees. Get a detail if needed, but get it cleaned up.

"I found two more miss-hires in the files and one of those filed a grievance but no action was taken. In fact there are no action reports on any grievances in the files. Why? Don't answer that. I don't need any more excuses. In addition to you and your sergeant getting this office cleaned up and presentable plus attending monthly classes on German American relations, you will get the two miss-hires taken care of plus you will take the grievance file and go see each person listed, that is go see them personally rather than have them come here and miss work. Find out just what their problem is and make sure there is a report attached to the file. I will be back here in two weeks for another inspection and I expect to see a 100 hundred present improvement. Do you have any questions Capt. Dellwood?"

"That's a lot to get done in such a short time sir. I'm not sure I can get everything you asked for done in time."

"First, the problems and errors I have brought to your attention should have been corrected a long time ago. They should not even exist. Secondly, and you may have forgotten this so I'll remind you, an officer is on duty twenty four hours a day until he dies or retires. You have nights and weekends to work. Get help if needed, but get it done. I'll see you in two weeks Captain Dellwood."

Without another word McNeil started to leave but stopped at the door, "Capt. Dellwood, you and Sgt Lawson deal with German speaking people every day, do either of you speak the language?"

"No sir we don't."

"I would strongly suggest that both of you get to the education center and sign up for a Spoken German class." McNeil left the office, picked up his hat and walked out.

At the end of the two weeks McNeil returned to the office of Indigenous hire and found a remarkable change. Sgt Lawson jumped up when McNeil entered the office and called out, "attention," "As you were Sgt Lawson," said McNeil as he looked the office over. The floors were clean and waxed. Gone was the rickety worn out furniture and good used couches and chairs were in their place. The walls had been painted and curtains hung. When Capt. Dellwood heard Sgt Lawson call attention he came from his office to see who had entered the building. "Good morning sir.

"Good Morning Capt. Dellwood."

McNeil made no comments until he looked over the files using his previous notes. The two miss-hires had been up graded to a position in keeping with their education and training. There were follow up's attached to each of the grievances on file.

"Everything looks fine here," said McNeil. "You have done a remarkable job. My question is, have each of you attended a German American Relations class?"

"Yes sir we both have and I have the schedule for the next month's class."

"Did you take my advice and go to the education center."

"Yes sir we both did. We signed up for the spoken German class for two nights a week."

"If you can learn a few words of German it will not only benefit you in this job but anywhere you go in Germany. You have done a great job here, keep up the good work Capt. Dellwood."

Even though McNeil worked hard at what he had to do it wasn't always gravy, sometimes there were lumps that had to be smoothed out. One day as he worked on a report his intercom buzzed. It was Col. Campbell requesting his presence in his office.

"Good morning sir," said McNeil after he knocked and entered the 8th Infantry Division Executive Officer/Chief of Staff's office.

"Good morning Col. McNeil," replied Col. Campbell looking up from a paper he was reading. You are a hard man to keep up with. It's rather embarrassing when I'm asked where Col. McNeil is and I have no answer. I do realize you are the senior aide to General Layton but you are also involved in other things that I should be aware of."

I could just tell him to check with the general, was the first though McNeil had, but one does not piss of a man who will soon pin on his first star. Back pedal and use a bit of diplomacy here Charley. If he really needed to know where I was or what I was doing all he had to do was ask the general or my assistant, Frau Snelling.

"Please accept my apology sir and I'm sorry if my lack of military courtesy and procedures has caused you embarrassment sir. In the future I will check out with you."

"That would be very nice colonel and thank you for your time." said Col. Campbell as he went back to his reading. McNeil left the office and closed the door. I think I have just had my ass chewed, in a nice way.

Two days later when his intercom buzzed it was the general calling. "Yes sir," answered McNeil.

"My office with files and any papers dealing with the base indigenous hire."

"On the way sir," replied McNeil as he started pulling the file and wondering just what was going on. The general had seen and read everything he had done.

When he knocked and entered the general's office he saw a bald head major sitting in a chair in front of the general's desk. Capt. Davenport, the general's junior aide stood behind the general. McNeil said, "Good morning," then handed the general the file. "Have you met Maj. Hochstetler?" asked General Layton as he open the file and started reading it.

"I haven't had the pleasure. Good morning major. I'm Lieutenant Colonel McNeil; I'm the senior aide to General Layton.

"Good Morning sir, I'm Major Hochstetler; I'm in charge of base facilities and until lately I thought I was in charge of the indigenous hire office."

"When I talked with Capt. Dellwood he was under the impression that his office came under the control of division," said McNeil. "He never mentioned you major. When were you put in charge of the indigenous office?"

"A year ago, by the previous Division Commander."

"Apparently Capt. Dellwood wasn't made aware of that fact, or he failed to inform me of that fact."

"Major Hochstetler read this inspection report," said General Layton passing the file to him..

"Could we have coffee Henry?" asked General Layton.

"Yes sir. How does the major take his coffee?" asked Henry.

"Oh, black will do fine."

Major Hochstetler finished reading the file about the time Henry returned with the coffee. "Have you a comment Major Hochstetler?" asked General Layton.

"When I asked Capt. Dellwood how everything was he always said, going well. I had no idea these problems existed sir. I just assumed Capt. Dellwood had everything under control and was doing an excellent job."

"Assumption by a commander, or any officer for that matter, is the mother of all evil. In this division we rely on facts and knowledge major, not assumptions," said General Layton.

"May I ask a question here sir?"

"Go ahead Charley."

"Major Hochstetler, have you heard of or attended any of the German American relations Classes?"

"I have heard of them but I though the classes were for the enlisted men."

"Sounds like another assumption major. Get the facts. Even General Layton attends a monthly class. The German American Relations classes are for everyone in EUROPE. The Indigenous hire office is the first place a local sees and forms a first impression. That office falls under the German American relations program and it must be run according to regulations."

"Major Hochstetler," broke in General Layton, "since the Indigenous Hire office has been under you for such a long time I'm going to leave it that way. If Charley, Col. McNeil, decides to visit the office for another inspection he will go through you. What I don't want to find is another report such as this one. Do we understand each other Major?"

"Yes sir. I'll make sure the office is properly run sir."

"You do that. Now, unless you have something further I have work to do?"

"No sir. That's all Sir," said Major Hochstetler standing up and saluting. He picked up his hat and left the office.

"I'm sorry this came to your attention sir. I could have handled it if only the major had spoken to me about it."

"What's done is done Charley. Do you have anything for me?"

"One item sir, if you have the time?"

"Let's have it."

"The weather sir; with all the snow on the ground and the frozen streets I was thinking it might be a good idea to put out a notice for all off post residents to curtail POV (Private Owned Vehicles) movement. Maybe have a military truck pick up off post personnel to prevent any accidents and incidents during the inclement weather."

"I'll look into it. Make a note Henry."

"That's all I have sir."

"Then let's get some work done."

Just before the Thanksgiving holiday, the Germans did not celebrate the holiday, it's strictly an American holiday, the German American party was held at the 0-club. To say it went off without a hitch would not be true. Many small things went wrong but nothing major that would cause a strain on the relations the party was trying to generate. Most, but not all, officers appeared dressed in their mess dress uniforms. The German dignitaries were dressed in tuxedos and their wives wore evening gowns.

Because of the language barrier McNeil was designated to translate what was spoken by both General Layton and Burgermeister Herr Shultz when they gave their little speech.

The club Manager and his team did an outstanding job with the club decorating. It was decorated in the scheme of freedom and friendship and the band was able to play both American and German music.

McNeil had thought about the seating arrangements and came up with a plan to seat those who had corresponding jobs together so they would have something to discuss. The General and Marie were paired with the Burgermeister and his wife Inga. Of course, Frau Ogle and her husband were in attendance and Frau Ogle took Marie in tow and introduced her to all the German ladies. The post Provost Marshal, Ltc. Griffin was paired up with the chief of the German police.

The club went all out in the food and drink department. There were the typical American hamburgers and hotdogs plus several big roasts and hams. There was both Rhine wine and American wine served but the main attraction was the hard stuff. The Germans liked the American Scotch and bourbon.

Other than a few minor hitches the party went quite well. McNeil, having put in so much time before the party to set everything up and was constantly on the move during the party, was wore out by the time the party was over and the German guests were leaving. All in all it was declared a success by General Layton.

November and December were busy months for McNeil. He had very little time for himself with all that was going on. The holidays came and went and as usual McNeil got through them by keeping busy with his job plus night school. It was cold and miserable and it seemed the snow wouldn't stop falling. The cold north wind blew and the temperature stayed in the teens most of the time. It was a lonely time for McNeil but the aide duties and other work kept him too busy to really think much about it.

Weather permitting, which wasn't too often, he did get out and see some of the local sites and eat out just to keep current on the language. He could sit in a café and hear the language spoken and like any language, nuances and idioms were constantly changing. He needed to keep up on any language changes.

Thoughts of Babs surfaced often but he had made his decision and there was no turning back, but it did give him a warm feeling to think back on the good times they shared. Sometimes he wished he was back at the pentagon, or for that matter back in Korea. But at least here he wasn't getting shot at while he was cold and miserable.

There were two more functions that also kept McNeil busy, Henry tried but was unable to complete the tasks, which were the annual Commanders Christmas and New Year's party at the O-club. Once the parties were set up McNeil had little to do with them other than be there.

Before the end of the year McNeil was finally able to complete all the education requirements for his masters in Political Science but as yet he had heard nothing from the education center. He continued to attend classes to add credit hours to his minor in Military History.

Col. Campbell's promotion didn't come through until after the end of the year and assignment orders followed. He would remain in the division as the executive officer and another full Colonel would be added as the Chief of Staff. Colonel Steel, no relations to Major Steel, a starchy, gun-ho colonel reported to the division to assume the duties of Chief of staff. After receiving permission from General Layton, General Campbell who had not as yet selected an aide, asked McNeil to organize a small party for the staff and his personal friends to celebrate the promotion.

Two more staff cars were added to the division staff car fleet and SGM Graves was put in charge of the drivers and dispatching the cars. All the cars were equipped with snow chains now which helped them get around better in the foot of snow on the streets.

# MCNEIL

## 8TH INFANTRY DIVISION
## ROSE BARRACKS

### Chapter 36
### 7 Jan 1956

In the first week of January it was announced that the two Battalions, one Infantry battalion (505th) and one of the Airborne Battalions, (504th) would be going on field training exercises the later part of January. Since the general had told McNeil he would be going on the training exercise he made a call to the commander, Ltc. Davie, of the 504th Airborne Battalion to let him know that he would be attached to his battalion while on the training exercise.

"May I ask why you are being attached to my battalion Ltc. McNeil?"

"Without sounding like a smart ass colonel, the general told me I would be with one of the battalions. Since yours is airborne I thought it would be the best one, and I always try to go with the best."

"I see. What will your function be during this training exercise Col. McNeil?"

"To observe and further my military education, to quote the general. But I'll lend a hand where needed Col. Davie."

"I suppose I should say welcome aboard colonel. I'll get the itinerary to you."

"Thank you very much colonel."

On one of those days when nothing seemed to go right General Layton took off early and went to his quarters. He showered and went to the den, his favorite room in the house. A fire was going so he added some brandy to his coffee and settled down in the big easy chair with a cigar. As usual he brought home papers that he was unable to read at work. He was half way through the cigar and on his second cup of brandy laced coffee when his wife Marie entered the room and sat down. She seldom came in to the room when he was relaxing so he knew something was up. When he laid the paper he was reading down and looked at her he saw a very worried face. "What is it dear?"

"I received another letter from Connie."

"From the look on your face it's not good news."

"No it isn't Walter. Her divorce was final four months ago and she retook her maiden name and dropped Carl's. What she is asking is can she come stay with us for a spell."

"I see no reason she shouldn't dear. I'm sorry her marriage didn't work out but from her previous letters we knew things were not going well. Tell her she can come home anytime."

"I have already dear. But, I'm still not comfortable with a divorce. Marriage is supposed to be for life."

"We'll, there are always two sides to a story but in this case I tend to believe my daughter. When I first met Carl he had a shifty look like he was always trying to hide something. You are correct though dear, a marriage is supposed to be for life. But can you see anyone living a life of hell when they don't have to. When trust and love is lost in a marriage it's time to get out of it and move on. I'm not condoning divorce but it's the only way out of a bad marriage. When will she arrive?"

It was the first of January when this conversation took place. "When we spoke on the phone she said she was packed and ready but would wait until after the holidays to come. She should be here in a couple of days."

"It'll be good to have her back home."

"Yes it will."

A week before McNeil was to depart for Bamberg for the training exercise a letter arrived marked personally for him. It was from Herr Shultz, the Burgomaster of Bad Kreuznach,

Now that the holidays were over he was ready to reciprocate and have his reception, his own version of a German American relations party. His question was: when would be the best time for the American military?

McNeil went to the general's office but found that he had taken off early, again. He noticed two papers on his desk marked URGENT so he picked them up to take with him. He would drop them off with the general when he saw him at his quarters. He had intended to go into Bad Kreuznach to eat this evening so he stopped by his quarters to shower and dress in a suit and tie before seeing the general.

He had been to the generals quarters so often that now the butler just pointed to the den door after greeting him. As McNeil started walking toward the den he noticed a body through the open kitchen door. At first he thought it was Marie, Mrs. Layton. But this person, who looked so much like Mrs. Layton, was much younger and very well built with the same long black hair. When she sensed someone was looking at her she glanced his way and he could distinguish the same Spanish facial features as Mrs. Layton. The woman quickly looked away and hurried from the kitchen. McNeil decided that maybe the woman was a guest of the Layton's and possibly a relative of Mrs. Layton since she favored her so much. McNeil put the woman from his mind and went into the den where he found the general in his favorite chair with a cigar reading some regulation. "Good evening sir. Sorry to disturb you." spoke McNeil as he entered the room.

"Hello Charley. Come on in and stop that apologizing. What have you got for me? Would you care for a coffee and brandy?"

"Thanks for the offer sir but I'll pass. I'm headed off post from here. Two papers were on your desk marked URGENT plus the Mayor of Bad Kreuznach has been heard from. It's his desire to reciprocate with his own reception. He asked when it would be a good time for the American Military.?"

"Well, the holidays are over and we should be finished with the training exercises this month. Tell him the first week in February would be suitable for us."

"Yes sir I'll take care of it. Here are the two papers and I'll leave you to your work sir. Good evening."

"Thank you Charley."

When the intercom buzzed in McNeil's office the next morning he looked up from the paper he was working on to see who was calling. It was the general. "Yes sir?"

"Charley, come to the office."

"I'm on the way sir."

McNeil knocked and entered, closing the door behind him. Capt. Davenport stood in his usual place behind the general. "Good morning sir."

"Charley, are you all set for this training exercise."

"Yes sir. I've attached myself to the 504th. I've spoken with Col. Davie about it sir."

"General Campbell, and his aide, 1Lt. Jeffery, will be flying out to Bamberg in one of the choppers. I'm sure he won't mind if you catch a ride with him. That would be much better than a long cold ride in a vehicle."

"Yes sir. I'll speak with General Campbell and if it's ok with him I'll notify Col. Davie of the change in plans."

That was certainly a subtle way of giving an order, thought McNeil as he left the General's office on his way to see General Campbell, and it was nice of him to think of my health and welfare.

McNeil and Frau Snelling went to see Herr Shultz and pass on the information of when it would be the best time for the military for his reception plus give him the roster of military personal who would be attending. .

There were many things McNeil had to take care of before he departed from Rose Barracks. Many loose ends he had to tie up and turn over the information to Frau Ogle. She would be in charge of the German American relations program during his absence. He knew Frau Ogle could handle everything while he was away and she would keep General Layton updated.

# MCNEIL

## 504TH AIRBORNE INFANTRY BATTALION BAMBERG GERMANY

**Chapter 37**
**15 Jan 1956**

The convoy that had departed Rose Barracks at 04;00 this morning was now on site. The helicopter circled over the training area so General Campbell could get a bird's eye view. It was a bee hive of activity and many of the tents were already erected. McNeil had seen, had supervised, such a move in the cold of Korea and he knew what would happen. With all the traffic, both foot and vehicle, the ground would turn into a muddy mess. Once the tents were erected and the stoves lit the heat would start the snow melting inside the tents and the ground would become a muddy mess also. Nothing could be done about it; the troops would have to live with it.

When the helicopter set down by the other four helicopters and shut down there were two jeeps waiting. One had a one star general's flag waving. After LTC Davie saluted General Campbell and welcomed him to the training site he quickly got General Campbell and his aide in the jeep and on the way. A Lt Taylor approached McNeil and rendered a salute. "Sir, Col. Davie said to tell you the sleeping quarters are not ready yet and for me to take you to the mess tent where we can get some hot coffee while we wait."

"That sounds like a good plan to me. Lead on Lieutenant," said McNeil as he started loading his bags in the jeep with the assist of the driver and Lt. Taylor.

It was warm inside the cook tent and the odor of fresh brewed coffee wafted on the air. It was as McNeil thought it would be with the heat of the cook stoves warming the tent. Very little traffic had moved through the tent as yet but the ground was already starting to get muddy. He was thankful that he had put on his galoshes to keep his shiny jump boots clean, and help keep his feet warm.

As he stood drinking his coffee and staring at the flame under the coffee pot memories came flooding back of a time which seemed so long ago. A time when he had his own battalion and he never allowed any of his N C O's or officers to eat until all the lower ranks had been fed. His thoughts were interrupted by someone calling his name. He turned to see Major Steadman pouring himself a cup of coffee and looking his way. "I'm sorry major," McNeil apologized, "my mind was wandering. What did you say?"

"Just good morning sir."

"Good morning to you major." Major Steadman was the XO of the 504th under Col. Davie.

"I came to tell you the tent will be up and ready shortly. I smelled the coffee and decided a cup would be nice."

"It's very good coffee."

"You were in Korea sir?" asked Major Steadman as he joined McNeil keeping warm at the stove.

"Yes I was."

"I heard a story that came out of Korea so I was wondering if maybe, since you were there, you could tell me if it's fact or fiction. The story is that a captain emptied his pistol into a coffee pot because he didn't like the coffee, anything to that?"

My God, thought McNeil, that incident must be known around the world by now. And as I just heard it gets bigger and better the more it's told.

"The incident is a fact major but the reason is fiction. A young cook had a stove lit up in violation of no fire or light conditions. One pistol round allowed the coffee to pour out and extinguish the fire. That's all there is to the story major."

"Would I be safe in assuming you were the captain?"

"No comment major." McNeil knew he had said too much and by the no comment he might as well acknowledged that he was the captain. Now the story would make its rounds and he would be known as the man who shot up a coffee pot.

"The tent should be ready by now sir so let's get you settled in," said Major Steadman setting his coffee cup down.

Men who were designated as umpires and recognized by the strip of white cloth on their left sleeve started arriving by the truck loads. Some had come out with the convoy to watch and grade the move and set up. The others were here to grade and evaluate the training exercise. Their word would mean this was a success or that the two battalions would have to return for another exercise.

Once McNeil stored his bags it the tent that had been set up as sleeping quarters for senior officers he wandered around to observe what was going on. That's what General Layton had said for him to do, observe.

With four helicopters on site, the one that brought General Campbell out had departed to take him back to Rose Barracks, there were jump exercises that evening and McNeil was invited to participate. He was able to make three jumps with the 504th troops while at Bamberg. He only needed one more jump for his jump pay this month.

Defense positions were established, guard posts set up, roving patrols went out, and classes were being held out in the open. Everywhere there was activity there were several umpires with their clipboards making notes. McNeil saw several things he would change if he was in charge but that wasn't the case. He was here to observe. He did make notes in the small notebook he kept in his jacket pocket; notes as a reminder to him just in case General Layton had questions when he returned.

Early in the morning of the third day McNeil had finished breakfast and stepped outside the mess tent with a cup of coffee and a cigar to watch the dawning of the day. A jeep drove up and a young PFC stepped out and saluted, "Good morning sir. A message for you," he said handing over a piece of paper.

"McNeil returned the salute and read the message. He stepped inside the mess tent and set his cup down then he got in the right seat of the jeep. "Take me to the CP (Command Post)."

He found Col. Davie looking at maps and sketches inside the CP. "Good morning Colonel," said McNeil holding out the slip of paper with the message on it.

"Good morning. I've read the message and alerted the aviation people to have a helicopter ready."

"Then all I have to do is collect my gear. I do wish to say thank you for allowing me to tag along with the 504th. It's been a pleasure."

"Nice to have you colonel but I have no idea why you were ordered out here."

"We just do the bidding of our Commanders colonel."

When the helicopter set down at Rose Barracks airfield there was a staff car waiting with Capt. Davenport standing beside it. He and the driver helped to get McNeil's bags off the helicopter and into the staff car. When it started moving McNeil spoke, "do you have any idea what this is all about Henry?"

"Not a clue sir. I'm just following orders. I'm to get you to your quarters where you will get into a class 'A' uniform then we will go to the education center."

"I'll need a bath before I get dressed." There is something about Army field gear, a certain odor that is unique and seems to cling to the body. Those who have been there know the odor.

General Layton was already at the education center. He arrived at the post school earlier to speak with his daughter, Connie Layton, who he and Marie had finally convinced to get out of the house. She still refused to socialize but she did agree to take a teaching position. She had her teaching credentials and with some influence from General Layton she was hired as a teacher for dependent children. The post school was near the education center.

General Layton tried to talk Connie into attending the party at the education center but she refused. Even though she had met some of the women at the center she didn't feel ready to socialize yet. She certainly didn't feel up to a party, she told her dad.

When McNeil arrived at the education center he was met and escorted, by one of the lesser staff members, to one of the conference rooms where a party was ready to get started. He knew this because there was a punch bowl full of punch plus a coffee pot full of coffee but he was the only one there. He wondered just what was going on as he picked up a paper cup and filled it with coffee.

He heard a noise and the door opened and Jesse, Miss Caldwell, entered with a cake which she tried to keep McNeil from seeing. "Hello Charley," she greeted as she placed the cake on a table.

"Miss Caldwell, Jesse, it would seem I'm in the wrong place."

"No, no, Charley. You're in the correct place," she replied allowing her body to hide the cake.

The room door opened and in came General Layton followed by Professor Edger and Professor Hurbert. Bringing up the rear was the German lady, Frauline Ursula Mueller, who taught Spoken German at the education center, and several others who McNeil had seen around but didn't know them. Frauline Ursula closed the door behind her. "Welcome back Charley," said General Layton.

"It's good to be back sir. Sir just what is going on here?"

"All in good time Charley," replied General Layton as he helped himself to a cup of coffee.

The door opened and Capt. Davenport entered and apologized to General Layton. "Sorry I'm late sir."

"You're not late Henry. You're right on time."

Professor Hurbert spoke. "Ladies and gentlemen, without further delay let's get this celebration started. Colonel McNeil has been working for this day for the past eight years. He has been steadfast to complete the goal he set for himself. I admire a man who doesn't lose sight of his dream. Professor Edger will present the Diploma. Professor Edger."

"Thank you professor Hurbert. Ladies and gentlemen. We here in this small school of higher learning don't get to see something such as this everyday so we are just as pleased as I suspect Colonel McNeil will be. Colonel McNeil, it's with great pleasure that I present to you your certificate and diploma for your Master's Degree in Political Science. It's been a long hard road for you but

I'm sure the reward is well worth the wait. Congratulations Colonel McNeil," he said as he handed over the diploma and shook McNeil's hand.

"Thank you very much sir and it is with great pleasure that I accept this diploma. And to all of you here at the education center who made this possible, I thank you." McNeil felt like waving the diploma in the air and jumping up and down and shouting but he didn't think that would be proper behavior for a colonel.

Each one stepped up and congratulated him then Jesse started cutting the cake and passing it out but not before McNeil had a chance to see what was written on top of it, CONGRATULATIONS CHARLEY.

General Layton waited until last to offer his congratulations. "You finally made it Charley, congratulations."

"Thank you very much sir."

"Now you can go get that job offered to you in D C."

"I believe I'll stick around sir. I still have high hopes of getting a command in the near future."

"Hang in there Charley. It could happen."

"May I offer my profound congratulations sir," spoke Capt. Davenport, "and may I say I envy you."

"Thank you Henry but please don't envy me, imitate me. How much longer do you have to go in Germany?"

"I have about two more years' sir."

"Don't you think it would be nice to know some of the language, the customs and traditions, of our host country?"

"Yes sir it would."

"See that young woman pouring punch?"

"Yes sir."

"She teaches spoken German and I'm sure she would be grateful to have you in her class. Go speak to her Henry."

"You're not doing some match making are you Charlie," asked General Layton after Henry walked away.

"Absolutely not sir. The start of a trip is the first step."

"You feel he needs a push."

"I think he needs something to give him direction and hopefully to calm him down some."

"If going to night school will help I'm all for it then."

"Colonel McNeil," spoke Professor Hurbert, "may I have a word with you before you depart?"

McNeil turned to General Layton. "Nothing is on the calendar Charley. I have to get back to the office but I'll make sure there is a staff car for you. Take your time."

"Yes sir. I'm at your disposal Professor Hurbert."

"Right this way please."

"What I wanted to see you about," Professor Hurbert said as he closed the door to his office, "is all the credits you accumulated over the years. Credits you earned but not related to your masters. Also we can transfer some of the credits from your Political Science over to your minor, Military History, studies. No sense in retaking classes which is already on your records. By doing this you will be closer to accomplishing your second masters. That is if you plan to continue with your studies?"

"Professor Hurbert, I have been at this so long that it's like a habit that would be hard to break. Of course I'll continue with my studies."

"Good. Then I'll get on these credit transfers and get back with you. Again, congratulations Colonel McNeil."

"Thank you very much sir."

McNeil decided to go to the office now and change his uniform at lunch time. He expected to find a stack of paper work waiting for him but the ever efficient Frau Ogla Snelling had taken care of most of it and there was only a small stack that needed his attention.

Colonel Steel entered McNeil's office while he was busy bringing himself up-to-date on the latest material. Frau Olga had stepped out to get coffee. "Col. McNeil, where have you been for the past three days? I had some work for you but you weren't around."

"Sorry sir but I was complying with orders from General Layton. I was at Bamberg with the two battalions going through training."

"No one seemed to know where you were or what you were doing."

"Again, sorry sir, but both generals were aware of where I was."

"In the future check with me when you depart the area. I might have something that needs done."

"Sir, you are aware that I'm the senior aide to General Layton plus he has me doing other duties?"

"Such as?"

"I have been designated as the division German American relations officer plus the Rose Barracks labor relations officer."

"I wasn't made aware of that colonel."

"Sir may I make it easy for you? Frau Snelling, my assistant, knows where I'm at and how to reach me when I'm out of the office."

"Who is this Frau Snelling?"

"You haven't met her sir? Here she comes now. Frau Snelling, may I present the Division Chief of Staff, Colonel Steel? Colonel Steel, Frau Snelling."

"I'm very pleased to meet you sir. I've seen you around."

"My pleasure to meet you Ma'am." Not a trace of an accent as one would expect from a German broad, thought Col. Steel, I wonder if Colonel McNeal is balling her in his spare time. Not bad looking for an older woman. "I'll be checking in with you from time to time Frau Snelling."

"Sir, before you go," said Frau Olga opening a file and removing a card from it, "this is your invitation to a formal reception the first week of next month."

"A formal reception, for what?" asked Col. Steel looking the card over.

"Sir," spoke up McNeil, "the Germans, the Burgermeister, the Mayor of Bad Kreuznach, is hosting a formal gathering in reciprocal of one General Layton had for the top men of Bad Kreuznach. It falls under the German American Relations program."

Colonel Steel looked again at the card, shrugged his shoulders and walked away.

He certainly doesn't seem to be too well read in on his job here, or maybe it's that he doesn't care, thought McNeil.

When the day of the German reception arrived General Layton made the decision that if the military went to down town Bad Kreuznach with a convoy of military vehicles the Germans might think they were being invaded by the American military. He decided to go in his staff car and all others would travel in their own private vehicles.

The place, where the reception was to be held, wasn't all that hard to find with the directions provided. It was a rather large building well lit with plenty of parking places. The German Police were out in force, some with those big German Shepard dog's, patrolling the area and directing traffic. The sign over the door of the building, translated, read CLUB SOCIAL. The inside was well lit and it was obvious that a party was in progress.

When the staff car stopped in front of the building a military man opened the car door. A Bundeswehr Oberstleutnant, a Lieutenant Colonel of the German Army. Why a German army officer wondered McNeil? Maybe he was available or maybe he was the only local officer who spoke English. Whatever the reason he greeted everyone in English and checked the names off the list he had before escorting everyone up the steps to the door and announcing them.

The Burgermeister, Herr Shultz, was at the head of the receiving line, with his wife, to greet everyone as they entered. General Layton and party had timed it so as to be the last of the American Military to arrive. As soon as they went through the receiving line and were greeted by everyone Frau Snelling came over and spoke to Marie; Frau Snelling, Marie, and Frau Shultz walked away talking. The men were left to themselves and were quickly led to where a bar was set up with enough booze to get an army drunk.

The Germans really know how to throw a party and they know how to drink. A band was on hand to supply music for dancing and a large buffet was set up with what looked to be enough food, German cuisine, to also feed an army.

Most everyone attending had already met and while some stood around drinking others had their wives, or somebodies wife, out on the dance floor. When it comes to partying there is little shyness on the part of the American Military.

It was a great evening with plenty of food, booze, and dancing. Herr Shultz brought his interpreter tonight, Herr Hildebrand, who did the translating when Herr Shultz gave his speech. McNeil took over when General Layton gave his speech. Now that the speeches were over and everyone had eaten McNeil and General Layton were talking with a glass of brandy in their hands. Herr Shultz walked up followed by Herr Hildebrand, and spoke. "What do you think of our little club?" he asked. Herr Hildebrand translated.

"Very nice," answered General Layton, and large enough so no one is crowded"

"This is a very special club for the upper echelon of German society. One can come here, if one's a member, drink, eat, relax, and not be bothered by hand shakers, or anyone needing a favor. I recommended, and the board members approved, that you two be accepted as honorary members of the Club Social," he said handing each of them a membership card, "the club is open for the noon meal and seven days a week for the evening meal with piped in music for listening or dancing. There are also private rooms in the rear, with full service, for small conferences. Please use the club and welcome."

"Thank you very much Herr Shultz," replied General Layton, "this is a great honor. I'll see about setting it up so you and your wife can be an honorary member of our club."

McNeil, not being married, had no trouble finding a dance partner. The German Frau's thought he was a good looking man and one of them seemed to be always available for dancing when the band was playing.

All in all the party went well and it seemed that each had a great time. A gathering such as this allows people to meet and talk with their counterparts and establish a good working relationship which promotes better German American relations.

Since the people attending were all senior people, the two youngest were Herr Hildebrand and Capt. Henry, General Layton's junior aide, everyone seemed to get along well. At least no one got drunk and started an argument. Everyone conducted himself, or herself, in a very well-mannered way.

# MCNEIL

## 7TH ARMY HEADQUARTERS STUTTGART GERMANY

### Chapter 38
### 12 March 1956

Old man winter finally lost his grip on the German country side. The snow on the ground finally melted and as the air warmed up the golf course was in use once again. Even McNeil, who knew little about the game, took it up mainly for the exercise. Though Rose barracks only had a nine hole course it gave the men an opportunity to get exercise.

During McNeil's many trips to the general's quarters he only saw the woman with the long black hair a couple more times. Each time she quickly turned away and left the room when she realized that someone was watching her. McNeil never asked about her and nothing was ever said about her to him.

General Layton was busy going over a new regulation at his desk when his office door opened and Henry came in struggling with two cups of coffee. Just as he reached the desk the phone rang and he almost spilled a cup of coffee in his haste to grab the phone before General Layton could. "Office of the Commanding General, Capt. Davenport speaking. How may I help you?" he answered in the proscribed manner as he set the second cup of coffee down.

"I have a call from General Clark for General Layton."

"Yes sir. One moment sir," replied Henry almost dropping the phone when he heard who the call was from.

"Sir, a call is coming in from General Clark of Seventh army."

"Don't you think I should have the phone so I can speak with him," said General Layton as he looked up at Henry clutching the phone to his chest.

"Yes sir. Sorry sir. Your coffee Sir. Shall I leave the room sir?"

"No. No need to leave Henry. Drink you coffee and relax," replied General Layton reaching for the phone.

"General Layton."

"General Clark here Walter. How are things going over there at Rose barracks?"

376 | R. W. POWERS

"Very well sir. Thank you for asking."

"And your wife, Marie I believe it is, how is she?"

"Marie is doing fine sir. How about your wife, Doris?"

"Doing great. Walter, what I'm calling about is that I have some official unofficial business I need to discuss with you. I know that doesn't make much sense but it would be better if we had a private discussion. Is there any reason you can't get away for a couple of days?"

"No reason I can think of sir."

"Good. An L-23 will be at your airfield at 08:00 tomorrow morning. Bring your wife and don't forget your golf clubs. I'll go a round or two with you on a eighteen hole course."

"Lieutenant Generals actually have time to get out on the golf course?"

"We make the time Walter. See you and your wife tomorrow. Until then." the phone went dead and General Layton placed it back in the cradle. I wonder what that's all about. What is this official unofficial business that he can't discuss over the phone? I guess I'll find out tomorrow.

He picked up the phone again and dialed his quarters. "Mrs. Layton please," he said when the butler answered the phone.

"Hi Walter. What's going on?" Marie asked because he almost never called home unless something was wrong.

"Nothing's wrong dear. I just had an interesting conversation with General Clark. You remember him and his wife Doris?"

"Oh sure. How are they?"

"They are well. What I'm calling about is to let you know we'll be seeing them tomorrow. He's sending a plane to pick us up. Us, as in you and I. Pack for a couple of days. We depart at 08:00 in the morning. I'll see you later this evening. Bye dear."

"Henry, business as usual tomorrow. I have some business to take care of in the morning them we'll pick up Mrs. Layton and head to the airfield. You make yourself useful around headquarters because I want be needing you for the next two days."

Henry was a bit disappointed that he wouldn't be going to Seventh Army where he would meet General Clark.

When the L-23 airplane landed at Stuttgart Army Airfield and taxied up to the control tower where it was directed to park, and after the engines were shut down a staff car approached with the two star flag of a Major General flapping in the breeze. Once the bags, which included a set of golf clubs, were removed from the plane and stowed in the staff car trunk it left the airfield. Thirty minutes later it arrived at Kelly Barracks, and the headquarters of Seventh Army.

Apparently the driver, a staff sergeant had his orders and he went on through the garrison and into the quarter's area stopping at a rather large single story house. The sign on the lawn proclaimed this to be the residence of Lieutenant General Mathew Clark.

When the staff car stopped in front of the house a well-dressed woman came out to meet it. Doris Clark, even though she had to be in her late fifties, did not look her age. She wasn't plump and the only thing that gave away her age was a bit of grey in her hair.

She was very animated and seemed very pleased to have company this morning. "Hello Walter and Marie," she said as they stepped out of the car, "it's good to see you two after such a long time. Welcome to our quarters." she shook Walters hand then hugged Marie since they had known each other for a few years now.

"Sergeant, will you be so kind and put the luggage in the rear bedroom?" asked Mrs. Clark.

"My pleasure ma'am," he replied picking up the bags and entering the house as if he had been here many times before and knew his way around.

After the sergeant went into the quarters Doris spoke again. "Mathew said for me to get you two settled in and offer you drinks. He also said for you, Walter, to get into your golfing clothes. I think he's anxious to get out on the golf course with you. So as soon as you two get freshened up we'll have brunch. Mathew should be here by that time. You know Marie," she said as she started leading the way into the quarters with her arm still around Marie, being a general's wife is very lonely."

"I have often thought that but never voiced it."

"Voice it. Who's going to contradict us? We know," laughed Doris.

After the Layton's were shown their room they were left alone to freshen up. "Just why are we here Walter?" Maria asked.

"I've been wondering about that but as yet I haven't been apprised of that fact. We'll just have to wait and see."

When the Layton's came back into the living room drinks were offered but not of the alcohol type. It was coffee, tea, or lemonade. While they were sipping their selected drinks General Clark came in. He wasn't what one would think of as a general. In a suit he looked as if he should be sitting on a corporate board somewhere. He wore glasses and his hair line was receding. He was a bit on the heavy side from riding a desk. But when he was in uniform and gave orders there was no doubt he was the general. After greeting everyone he went to change into his golf clothes. General Clark did go on to become a vice president of a major insurance company after he retired from the military.

They chatted as they ate the light brunch then it was off to the golf course. General Clark was very animated as the two got set to tee off. It was apparently his first time on the course this year and he was really looking forward to the exercise and fresh air.

It wasn't until they were ready to tee off from the third hole that he finally opened up about the reason Walter had been invited to play golf at Kelly Barracks. "What do you have this Colonel McNeil doing besides being your senior aide Walter?"

"Since he speaks German I use him as my interpreter plus he's the 8th Division German American Relations and Rose Barracks labor relations officer. That keeps him busy."

"Ah yes. I do remember seeing that your incident rate has dropped. Would you contribute that to his efficiency?"

"Absolutely sir."

"Maybe I should have him as the 7th Army German American Relations officer. Just kidding Walter. Tell me, I have heard that General MacArthur had something to do with young Colonel McNeil retaining his rank when he left Korea, anything to that?"

"Absolutely. General MacArthur not only made the request that Colonel McNeil be allowed to retain his earned rank but he favorably indorsed the recommendation for the award of the Congressional Medal of Honor for Colonel McNeil."

"I have heard you say that you have known Colonel McNeil since he was a corporal. Is that your way of saying you have known him a long time or is there more to it?"

"I have literally known him since he was a corporal. Let me tell you something about him that he doesn't know that I know. He was assigned as a squad leader to Baker Company of the 1/5 Infantry Battalion. After the North Koreans crossed the line, and even before really, there was a shortage of almost everything. Young Corporal McNeil would venture out on the battlefield after dark and collect food, weapons, and ammo from the dead North Korean and give it to his men. One time he brought back a captured mortar tube, with ammo, and turned it on the advancing North Koreans. He did whatever it took for him and his men to survive. He has several distinctions general. He is the youngest Captain to command a company in combat and the youngest Lieutenant Colonel to command a battalion in combat. He has never worn gold rank."

"Just what was the circumstance that earned him the medal Walter? I have read some of the material about him but you know how people tend to exaggerate when they are writing letter of accommodations. I would rather hear from someone who was there."

"One would have had to be there to fully realize the problems commanders faced, general. We were short of just about everything when the North Koreans crossed the 38th parallel. In a letter from the Department of the Army we were told to make do with what we had because nothing would be coming our way for a while. We were so short of personnel that in some cases sergeants were acting as company commanders. A thirty day reserve of ammo, vehicles were falling apart from lack of spare parts and due to the lack of fuel the vehicles were restricted from use for anything but necessary and emergency uses.

"On top of all this 8th Army laid a mission on us that required an officer to accomplish it. We had no spare officers so I asked for and received permission to award battle field commissions. The mission was handed to the 1/5 Infantry Battalion commanded by the late Colonel Winters. He saw something in Corporal McNeil that others failed to see and talked him into accepting a commission. He had to do some hard talking because we found out McNeil had been offered a commission before and turned it down because he wanted to do his two years and get back to college. McNeil had the intelligent to realize how desperate the situation was so he held out for 1st Lieutenant rather than accepting 2nd Lieutenant.

"While he was on this classified mission, best I can remember the mission was for sixty days, the paper work for his commission went to D. A. When they found out McNeil had four years of R.O.T.C and some college they made him a regular army captain on active duty. He became the commander of Baker Company 1/5 Infantry Battalion after setting up and running this classified mission.

Walter only stopped talking when one of them were teeing off or on the green. When they finally reached the ninth hole General Clark suggested they get a drink of water and sit a spell on a bench under a tree. Walter continued his story of McNeil.

"The Ongjin Peninsula was a vital piece of land so there was an R O K Infantry battalion tasked to defend the 38th parallel. During the first big North Korean push to take the peninsula the R O K battalion was rolled over. All personal killed and all equipment taken or destroyed. During the second big push my 1/5 Battalion was destroyed by artillery fire. McNeil was the first man on the scene and reported it to me. The late Colonel Winters had stripped his battalion to send men to the line so thankfully there wasn't that many men in the area but the few men there were killed, except for one radio operator. Eighty percent of the tents and other equipment were destroyed. When, then captain, McNeil reported the devastation to me I told him to rebuild a battalion from on hand assets. He never asked questions nor complained. When I was able to get to the peninsula thirty days later I found a functional battalion. Thought short of men, I believe he had only seven or eight men. Because of the continued lack of officers he retained command of Baker Company plus he had the duty of 1/5 Infantry Battalion Commander.

"I found his men in clean uniforms, clean shaven, on the line and alert. He requested that two people he selected be awarded a commission so there would be officers commanding the companies. He also requested that his supply sergeant be made a warrant officer. I found no fault in the requests and so complied with them. According to the regulations, if a man holds a higher position in combat for thirty days he's entitled to the rank that goes with the position. I promoted McNeil to the rank of Lieutenant Colonel.

"He did an outstanding job of defending the Ongjin Peninsula. General, you have to understand the problem there on the peninsula, there were only two ways off. One was to go into North Korea and come back into South Korea but we were restricted from crossing the 38th Parallel. The only other way off the peninsula was by boat. We borrowed a Mike boat from the Navy to supply the 1/5 Infantry Battalion on the peninsula. Everything was moved by the Mike boat, food, ammo, and personnel. There was no way an entire battalion could be extracted from the peninsula so the only option was to fight.

"General, I apologize for being long winded but to fully understand the situation in Korea one would have to know some of the minor details."

"No apology is required Walter. What you are giving me was never put down on paper. I really had no idea of the desperation you people faced over there. I gather from the way you speak of McNeil you think highly of him?"

"I do general. He's a hard charger and one hell of a combat commander and a very good planner. He has accomplished much in the six years he has been on active duty. He rose to the rank of Lieutenant colonel with a year of combat command time, he made it through the Army language school proficient in two languages, he has completed C & G S plus almost a two year tour of pentagon duty. He also just received his masters in Political Science plus he's working on a second masters. Not too much grass grows under his feet."

They were getting ready to tee off from the fourteenth tee when Walter asked the question that had been on his mind since General Clark asked the first question about McNeil. "If I may ask general, why all the questions about McNeil?"

"McNeil, because of the medal, was high profile when he first arrived here but lately he's become low profile. I'm getting tired of receiving inquiries from Army about McNeil that I have to reply to. I think their interest is raised because the recruiting command is pushing for some news of McNeil. That's just my thoughts, nothing concrete on that. Nothing has been heard of McNeil since he arrived in EUROPE. I'm speaking of the media. And as you know he's the only one with the medal in EUROPE at this time."

"I see where you are coming from general. I'm open for suggestions."

"I never interfere with a commander unless he's dead wrong and needs guidance. So this is only a suggestion Walter. Give McNeil a command. That should generate enough media attention to get Army off my back for a while."

"Well, he does have the time in grade, but he's only, I believe twenty nine years old. I have older colonels in line for a command."

"You are a Major General Walter. You can designate whomever you want to command your units."

"I'll certainly do what I can for you general."

"I know you will Walter. Now," he said as he sunk the final ball on the nineteenth hole, "we'll get back to the quarters, shower and change where we'll have diner then just the four of us will play bridge like we did in the old days. Tomorrow morning I have a staff meeting which I would like for you to attend then I'll get you and Marie back to Bad Kreuznach."

That night after they retired he told Marie what this trip was all about. "He is such a nice young man," commented Marie, "with a lot going for him."

"He certainly does have a lot going for him."

"It's a shame he and Connie can't get together."

"Now dear don't you go and try any match making. I do agree he and Connie might make a good pair but let nature take its course. If it's to be it will be."

"So what are you going to do dear, about Charley? If you do what General Clark asked you to do you will lose Charley. Do you think you will ever find someone to take his place?"

"There is always someone to replace a man with, how good Charley's replacement will be is another matter."

It was an hour later before Walter could drop off to sleep. He gave it a lot of thought as to where to assign McNeil and assign him to a command he would because that was the desire of General Clark. He knew Charley was ready for a command because he had brought it up more than once. Where to assign him? Colonel Davie was ready to depart and since Charley was airborne qualified maybe that was the place to assign him?

During the plane ride back to Bad Kreuznach Walter gave the situation more thought. There were two Lieutenant Colonels ready for command but neither had as much time in grade as Charley even though their time in service was greater. Charley was younger than they were but Charley had the medal and combat command time which counted a lot.

# MCNEIL

## 8TH INFANTRY DIVISION
## BAD KREUZNACH GERMANY

**Chapter 39**
**5 April 1956**

Walter gave the situation a lot of thought over the next few days and each time he came to the same conclusion. Ltc. Charley R. McNeil was due a command and with the backing of General Clark he would get one. His last command was five years ago. If the Army needed news about Col. McNeil, the Congressional Medal of Honor holder, then this was a way to do it. Col. Davie would depart in four weeks and a new commander would have to be assigned to the 504th Airborne Infantry Battalion. Even though there were two qualified colonels on hand there was McNeil, though young, just as qualified. The medal would have to be the deciding factor and if those two colonels had a beef they could take it up with General Clark if they didn't care for his decision. He made his decision and had orders cut assigning McNeil as the replacement commander for Col. Davie.

McNeil sat at the table and Frau Olga at the desk and both were engrossed in additions to an existing regulation in reference to the German American relation program. When the intercom buzzed McNeil looked over at it and saw it was the general. "Yes sir," he replied after pushing the button.

"If you aren't tied up right now Charley come to the office."

"On my way sir," replied McNeil as he stood up and straightened his shirt.

He, as usual, knocked at the generals door then entered, closing the door after himself. "Good morning sir."

"Good morning Charley. There's coffee if you like."

"I believe I will sir. May I refill your cup?"

"If you don't mind Charley, then have a seat."

"Some changes are about to take place in the division Charley," said General Layton after McNeil placed the generals cup on the desk and sat down. "You have been my senior aide for six months now. Normally such an assignment is for a year but I'll have to replace you early. I'll look around for a suitable replacement. You will also be replaced as the division German American relations officer. Who would you recommend as you replacement?"

"May I ask what's going on sir?"

"As I just told you, changes are about to take place. Do you have someone in mind as your replacement?"

"Not on such short notice sir. I would have to give it some thought."

"Do that and let me know tomorrow."

"Sir, if these changes are a reflection on my inability then I apologize."

"These changes have nothing to do with your inability Charley. You have done an outstanding job and your records will indicate such."

"Then I don't understand sir? Why am I being replaced and where will I go?"

"As you know Col. Davie will be leaving soon and I need a replacement for him. I have decided the replacement commander will be you Charley."

"Me, Sir? I–I–"

"Charley, are you at a loss for words?"

"It would seem so sir. This comes as a surprise to me. I had just about given up all hope of ever having a command again."

"Never give up hope Charley, I told you that once before. Now this change of command will be very formal with a parade and media and I wouldn't be surprised if General Clark dropped by. You have the medal Charley and anything that happens to you, good or bad, is news. You have a week to get your office in shape then you will, since you have over sixty days leave on record, take a two week leave before taking command of the 504th Airborne Infantry Battalion. Here are the orders Charley," said General Layton passing him several sets of orders.

So much to do and in such a short time, thought McNeil as he looked at the orders that would see him with a command once again. This really comes as a surprise, but a nice surprise.

It took McNeil two days to locate a man who was qualified and willing to take over the position of German Americans Relations officer. Major Gates wasn't as fluent in the German language as McNeil thought a man taking over such a position should be but no one else was qualified, or wanted the job. McNeil was confident that Frau Olga could handle the office by herself but it required an American officer be assigned there. McNeil spent two more days briefing Major Gates then two more days clearing out his desk and packing his bags.

Frau Olga watched the hurried activity for a day before she finally asked what was going on. "I'm being replaced Frau Olga."

"Replaced Charley? May I ask where will you be going?"

McNeil didn't fail to notice that Frau Olga finally called him Charley rather than Colonel as she usually did. "You Frau Olga will remain in your current position and a Major Gates will be assigned in my place. I will be taking command of the 504th Airborne Infantry Battalion right here on Rose Barracks. I'll be near if you ever have a problem."

"It won't be the same around here without you Charley."

"That's very kind of you to say that Frau Olga but that's the way of the military."

There was so much to see in Historical Germany but McNeil knew he would never see all of it in two weeks. He headed south to a place near the foot of the Alps, the Bavarian Alps, a town called Garmisch Partenkirchen. After WW2, and during the occupation by American forces, the town was taken over as a resort center for American troops. Today Special Services still maintains three hotels for American troops where they can stay and eat for very little expense.

He had two weeks of leave so he was in no hurry to get to his destination. He drove slow and broke up the trip by stopping at a small town and staying the night at a Guest House. The food was excellent and so was the beer. After a good night's sleep he continued on. The closer he got to his destination the cooler the mornings and evenings were even thought the sun came out and warmed everything up in the middle of the day. One could see snow on the peaks of the Alps which explained the cool weather.

The hotel, at the Eidelweiss Resort where he stayed in Garmisch, served a good breakfast at a reasonable price, in fact all the meals were good. He did get to several of the local German Cafe's to try the local food and he spent his time sightseeing in the small Bavarian town.

By the seventh day he had made the trip up to the Zugspitze by cable car where he spent a day above the clouds and watched people ski. One could ski at the high resort all year long since the place was so high up the snow seldom melted. He watched an ice show at the Olympic Stadium and tried his luck on ice skates and had the bruises to show for it. The local Casino's, though small, were interesting to visit and the food at the casino café was of the best quality, though high priced.

On this Monday morning, a week after he started his leave, McNeil had a late breakfast then decided to drive into town, park his car and walk. During his stroll he came across a small side walk café with umbrellas over the tables. He ordered cold white wine and sat down to watch the people walking by. He was about half through with his wine when he saw three people, women, who looked very familiar, coming up the sidewalk. As they got closer he recognized two of them and he had seen the third one but didn't really know her. It was the woman with the long black hair, trim body, and dancer legs, whom he had seen at General Layton's quarters. The other two were Jesse Caldwell from Rose Barracks Education Center and Ursula Mueller, the German lady who taught the German language at the education center. The three were slowly strolling along, talking and window shopping. They did not see McNeil sitting at the sidewalk café until he stood up and spoke to them. "Good day ladies. I trust you are enjoying yourselves in this scenic town?"

They were startled to hear the English language spoken and even more startled to see someone familiar speaking it. "What a pleasant surprise. Fancy running into you here Charley," spoke Jesse.

"You ladies look like you could use a cool drink. Please sit and allow me to order you a cold Rhine wine. They serve the best and coldest here."

"Why not. Charley you know Ursula and this is Connie," she said pointing to the lady with the trim body and long black hair he had seen in General Layton's quarters, as they all took a seat at the umbrella covered table. "What brings you to this resort area Charley?"

"How do you do ma'am," he spoke to the very beautiful lady then he turned to get the attention of the waiter. "I suppose everyone needs to get away and recharge one's batteries," he said after placing the order. "I thought this was as good a place as any other. Have you ladies seen any of the sights yet, such as the Zugspitze?"

"We plan on getting up there," answered Ursula, "but right now we are taking a walking tour of the town."

"Good idea. There is so much to see that one might miss something driving around."

The drinks arrived and each took a sip and declared it was the best they had tasted. "You look familiar," spoke the lady named Connie, "haven't I seen you in Dad's quarters? I'm sure I did. You are the one who comes by unannounced and disturbs dad when he's trying to relax. You must have a pet peeve you are trying to get dad to get involved with. I really resent it when people do that to him. Why don't you see him during duty hours rather that at his quarters. Could be you are looking for a free meal while making your pitch."

"Connie!" exclaimed both Jesse and Ursula at the same time.

"I really resent it when people do that to dad. He deserves to be able to relax at home without someone burning his ear about a special project."

"Ladies," said McNeil standing up, the drinks have been paid for so enjoy them. I believe I have been insulted enough. Goodbye." he walked to where he had left his car then drove back to the resort hotel where he was staying.

The three ladies watched him leave then Jesse spoke. "Connie, I realize you haven't been socializing much and maybe I should have introduced Charley differently. He requested that we all call him Charley. He's one of the good guys. He could jump my bones anytime but he treats me like a lady."

"He treats all of us at the education with great respect," added Ursula, "and he keeps my Spoken German classes full so I am assured of a job. Adding to what Jesse said, that big hunk could jump my bones any time."

"How you girls talk," spoke Connie taking a sip of her wine. "One would think he was somebody special."

"He is someone special Connie," spoke Jesse, "but before I tell you just who he is, and I can't believe you don't know already, he just completed his Masters in Political Science and is well on the way to a second masters. He's in the military and what makes him special, other than his good looks and manners, is that he has the medal, the Congressional Medal of Honor."

"That man?" asked Connie, "He's military?" He was sort of good looking and well mannered. But what am I thinking? I just got out of a bad marriage and I'm not ready to get involved. Then why did I start shaking inside when he looked at me?

"Yes that man," spoke Jesse. "What I should have done is introduce him as Lieutenant Colonel Charlie McNeil, the holder of the medal and your fathers senior Aide."

"He's my father's senior aide? I had no idea. So that's why he's at the quarters so much. You don't think he will run and tell dad what I said do you?"

"I don't think Charley will do that even though you did cut him deeply."

"Maybe I should go after him and apologize?" said Connie with a worried look on her face.

"I think you should, apologize that is, but you couldn't catch him," said Jesse. "If you are really serious about apologizing I think we should get back to the hotel and call around and locate the hotel where Charlie is staying. There can't be too many places here that are controlled by the Special services. Maybe we could buy him dinner."

"I'll go along with that," offered Ursula, "let's finish the wine before we leave though. I wouldn't want to see it go to waste."

It took two tries before they located the hotel that McNeil was staying but he had already left. "Well girls," spoke Jesse, "let's have some fun with the time we have left then maybe, Connie, you can catch up with Charley, Col McNeil, back at Rose Barracks."

McNeil went back to his hotel, packed, and checked out as soon as he left the ladies. He should have said something, he realized, but what does one say to a general's daughter, especially one who seems spoiled? He knew she had to be the daughter of General and Mrs. Layton because she said 'dad' and he had not been in any quarters except the generals. Its best I depart from here before I run into her again and possibly say something I'll regret later. Besides, there are other places to see before my leave is up.

He spent two days in Historical Munich visiting the museum and strolling through the parks and drinking the local beer at an outside bar. He left Munich and drove to Stuttgart where he spent two more days sightseeing. The time in each town was both educational and relaxing before he had to get back and take command of a battalion once again. That he was really looking forward to.

# McNeil

## 8TH INFANTRY DIVISION
## ROSE BARRACKS

**Chapter 40**
**28 May 1956**

Lieutenant Colonel McNeil's last act as the senior aide to General Layton was to oversee and MC a party at the club Saturday night where the Burgermeister, his wife, and several other German dignitaries would attend. He would have to mingle and do some translation for those who didn't speak German. There he took Major Carstairs in tow and introduced him as General Layton's new senior aide and his replacement. After tonight he would officially hand over the duties of senior aide.

Monday morning the formal ceremony of passing the guidon from the departing commander to the incoming commander would see McNeil as the commander of the 504th Airborne Infantry Battalion. Commanding Officer, a title he had waited years for.

When Marie asked, one last time she decided, if Connie would accompany them to the club for the Saturday night party Connie surprised her mother by answering 'yes'. She had been trying to catch up with McNeil ever since she returned but with no luck. Maybe she could have a word with him at the club and offer her apology, and besides it was time for her to come out of her shell as the girls at the education center had told her several times. It was time to move on and start a new life. Stop living in the past.

When Marie Layton heard Connie agree to accompany them to the club she couldn't believe it. She found Walter in the den and spoke to him. "Connie hasn't been the same since she went away with those girls from the education center," she said as she sat down.

"Is that good or bad?" asked Walter looking up from the paper he had been reading.

"Definitely good. She even consented to accompany us to the club tonight which is a surprise."

"Maybe that little vacation was all she needed to overcome her bad experience."

"It could very well be Walter."

Connie took extra care that Saturday evening taking a long soaking bath and in doing her hair and labored over several dresses before she finally selected a deep blue evening gown. She had inherited her mother's Spanish facial features and dark hair and her father's blue eyes. The blue gown would complement those eyes. She selected dark blue high heel shoes and tied her long black hair back with a blue ribbon.

As usual Henry would go with the staff car to pick up the general and family while McNeil, dressed in his Mess Dress uniform with all the regalia of an aide in place for the last time, went to the club to make sure everything was ready for the party.

The band was playing soft music when the guests started arriving. General Layton and party was the last to arrive and McNeil met them at the door. "Good evening General and Mrs. Layton," he greeted them, "everyone is here except a few stragglers.

"Charley," spoke Mrs. Layton this is our daughter, Connie."

"Yes ma'am. Very glad to meet you, formally," said McNeil with a bit of ice in his voice.

"What did Charley mean, formally?" asked Marie of Connie after McNeil walked away. She didn't fail to hear the coolness in his voice when he spoke.

"I'll tell you later mother," answered Connie. "Dad," said Connie, "I have heard you speak of Charley but I had no idea who you were talking about. I heard you say one time you had known Charlie since he was a corporal. What is that all about?"

"I'll explain that later Connie," answered her father as he turned to greet Herr Shultz and introduce his family to him.

McNeil stepped up to the mick and got every ones attention by tapping on it. He did his MC duties in both languages, English and German. When he finished he located Major Carstairs and took him around and introduced him to the German dignitaries. Herr Shultz was a bit concerned that McNeil might be leaving the area until McNeil explained that he would be leaving his present duties to take command of a battalion, but he wouldn't be leaving the area. The Burgomaster, Mayor, was somewhat relieved to hear that. He had grown fond of the young Oberstleutnant.

After McNeil made the introductions he danced with Mrs. Shultz and several other ladies. When he came to where Mrs. Layton sat and asked her to dance she declined. "Charley," she asked softly, "would you do me a favor?"

"Certainly ma'am."

"Ask my daughter to dance."

"Yes ma'am," he answered back softly. He turned to Connie who sat at the table alone. He knew there were available men to dance with her but he guessed they were not too anxious to get too close to a general's daughter.

"Miss Connie," he said when he stood beside her, "would you do me the honor of allowing me this dance?"

Connie had kept her eyes on the very handsome man, hoping she wasn't too obvious, as he went about the club doing his duties. She had that strange feeling in the pit of her stomach tonight as she had in Garmisch when she first laid eyes on Charley McNeil; a fluttering that she had never felt before. *Maybe that's why I lashed out at him, fear. It's too soon to get involved with a man after the mess I went through. What has it been, almost two years now? Charley seems so confident, and here I am calling him by his first name, so self-assured. He also looks very nice in that mess dress uniform with all the ribbons and other regalia; narrow waist and wide shoulders.* She had lost sight of Charley and so was startled when she heard her name called and looked to see him standing beside her. "I'm so sorry. My mind was wondering. What did you say?"

"Would you allow me this dance Miss. Connie," he repeated.

The butterflies were really fluttering in her stomach now as she looked up at Charley. She decided this was her chance to make her apology for her past actions, that is, if she didn't trip going to the dance floor. "Yes. I accept the offer Colonel McNeil," she said standing up with Charley pulling back her chair. He put his hand on her warm back to guide her to the dance floor and he could smell the faint fragrance of her perfume; something that reminded him of orange blossoms.

"May I say how lovely you look tonight ma'am?" said Charley as he put his arms around her on the dance floor.

"Thank you and that's very kind of you but would you please stop calling me ma'am. Call me Connie."

"Only if you'll consent and call me Charley."

"Agreed. Ah Charley, I need to speak with you, privately."

"I don't believe we will have any privacy here. What is it you wish to talk about?"

"Later, in private. Will you answer a question for me?" she asked as they moved around the dance floor. They danced quite well together which surprised Connie.

"Certainly. If I can."

"I have heard dad say he has known you since you were a corporal. What does he mean by that?"

"That's a long story and I would probably be biased in telling it. Why don't you ask your dad to tell you about it?"

"I did and he said later. How do you propose for us to have some privacy. I really need to speak with you."

"As I said before, certainly not here. I'll come up with something later," he said as the music stopped and he escorted Connie back to the table. "Thank you very much for the dance Miss. Connie." What's on her mind, wondered McNeil? The last time we met she had a very sharp tongue and now she wants a word in private.

"My pleasure Charley," answered Connie. I hope I can pick up my drink without spilling it, though Connie. I can't believe how effected I am in the presence of that man.

"Thank you," mouthed Marie as she looked at McNeil.

"You two looked very nice on the dance floor dear," said Marie after Charley walked away.

"We do dance well together mother. Listen mother, I told Charley I had to speak with him, in private. I'll tell you all about it later but when we, the girls and I, were in Garmisch, I met him but had no idea who he was and I said some unpleasant things to him. I hope to have the chance to apologize tonight. I won't be leaving here with you and dad."

"Oh. You do have your key, don't you?"

"Yes mother."

"And you will tell me what's going on between the two of you, won't you?"

"Yes mother."

As soon as McNeil felt he had accomplished all his duties he approached the Mayor, Herr Shultz, and spoke to him in German. "Sir, I'll be taking my leave now but I do have a question. You gave the general and I an honorary membership card to your exclusive club. I was wondering if it would be ok to visit the club tonight?"

"Certainly. You have full access to the club at any time. You don't have to ask permission."

"I wasn't sure I would be admitted sir."

"Is there a phone I could use?"

"Yes sir. Right around the corner."

After Herr Shultz made his phone call he returned to where McNeil stood waiting. "I called the club to let them know you would be using it tonight and you will be welcomed."

"Danke . Thank you so much sir."

"Are you taking a young lady with you?"

"As a matter of fact I am."

"Enjoy the privacy and pleasure of our little club Herr Oberstleutnant."

May showers were falling, quite heavily, on the German country side when McNeil stepped out the door of the club. His plan was to get to his quarters and change out of the expensive mess dress uniform before it was soiled and had to be cleaned. Now the uniform would get damp when he ran for his car. He never thought about bringing an umbrella because there was no threat of rain earlier.

At his quarters he quickly undressed and hung up the mess dress uniform. He dressed in a charcoal grey suit and this time he remembered to take an umbrella. It was still raining when he got back to the club so he used the umbrella to get from his car to the club door so he wouldn't get wet and ruin his best suit.

He decided it would be best if he didn't go into the club and mingle again so he stood just inside the door and looked the crowd over until he spied Connie dancing with a young captain. When he knew she was looking his way he made a motion with his hand for her to come to him. She gave just a slight nod of her head that she understood but being the lady that she was she waited until the dance was over and the captain had returned her to her table before she joined McNeil at the door.

"What's going on Charley?" she asked when she joined him.

"You said you wanted to talk, in private, and I have found a place to go. Are you free to leave?"

"Yes. I spoke to mother earlier and told her I wouldn't be going home with her and dad. Let me get my purse and tell mother I'm leaving."

"I'll wait here then."

"Oh God, it's pouring down rain," Connie said when they stepped out the club door several minutes later.

"I brought an umbrella," said McNeil opening it and holding it over their head as he urged her to move to his car which he had parked close to the door. He opened the car door and held the umbrella over her until she was safely in the car and the door closed. He went around and got in the driver's side, putting the damp umbrella in the rear, and started the car.

Connie didn't talk much on the drive but when McNeil stopped in the parking lot of the big building, which really looked like some kind of warehouse with no lights showing, she looked around and spoke. "Just where are we Charley and what is this place, looks like a warehouse? I certainly hope this isn't your idea of a joke."

"Miss Connie, you said you wanted to talk in private. It's obvious we couldn't have any privacy at the club and it's also obvious we couldn't take a stroll under the moonlight with the rain. It's forbidden to take a woman into ones quarters and I didn't think it prudent that we go to the general's quarters, your home."

"So we come here to a dark warehouse on a rainy night. What gives?"

"It is a rainy night but what you see really isn't a warehouse. This is a German social club. Your father and I were made honorary members and I have never had the chance to use the privilege of the club. I wasn't even sure I would be admitted until I spoke with the Mayor tonight, the Burgermeister, Herr Shultz. He made a phone call and assured me we would be welcomed here. This is the only place I could come up with that would assure us any degree of privacy."

"So what is it like inside? It doesn't look like much from the outside."

"I have only been here once and that was when the Mayor hosted a party for the military. From what I saw, which was only the big dining room/ dance floor, it's rather nice inside, quiet and subdued. Definitely warmer and drier inside than in this car. Look, you can sit here in the car if you want but I'm going inside where I'm sure I can get a hot cup of coffee. It's your choice."

"I suppose it would be better inside," Connie finally said.

McNeil held the umbrella over Connie's head until they reached the door and went inside. They came to a locked door with no handles. McNeil did what he had been instructed to do, tap on the door and present the honorary membership card when the peep hole was opened. The card was taken from him and the peep hold closed and thirty seconds went by before a click sounded and the massive door opened.

"Good evening sir and welcome to the Club Social," spoke a man dressed in a tuxedo. "Will you be dining with us or do you wish something more private," he asked in German.

"Some privacy tonight please," answered McNeil in English for Connie's sake.

The man, who was obviously the club Maître D', reached behind him and pushed a button. Almost immediately a very pretty lady dressed in an evening gown and with long blond hair came from the left. There was a short hallway to the right which McNeil knew led to the dining room but the lady came from the left and he had no idea where that hallway led to. "Good evening Herr and Dame. If you will follow me please," she spoke in English and turned and walked back the way she had come. McNeil put his hand on Connie's back to guide her and again he could feel the warmth of her through the evening gown. A feeling came over him, a feeling that he had never experienced before, like a warm glow that warmed his insides. It was a strange feeling that he had never experienced before with any woman.

They followed the young lady as she turned right and stopped at a door with the number two on it. She pushed the door open and motioned for them to enter. The room wasn't all that big but well decorated with rich looking paneling and a thick carpet on the floor. A couch sat before a fireplace with a coffee table in front of it and end tables at each side of it. There was also a very comfortable looking matching easy chair. To the right was a table with eight chairs around it. McNeil guessed that this room could be used for a private meeting for a small group of men.

"Would you care for a fire?" asked the lady.

"Yes, if you please," answered McNeil, "it's rather damp outside."

She squatted down, turned a hidden knob, then struck a match and put it to what looked like a pile of wood but was actually imitation wood for a gas fire. When the fire caught she turned it down low and stood up. "Would the Herr and Dame care for something to drink?"

"I think coffee would go good, plus some cognac. Maybe some pastry?"

"Very well sir. I'll be right back," she said as she went to where a cart on wheels stood behind the door. She pushed the cart out and closed the door.

As he and Connie stood waiting Connie spoke, "What did that woman call me, a Dame?"

"Yes she did and that's a compliment. A dame is a woman of rank, or authority." he didn't tell her that a Dame was also thought of as an elderly lady.

There came a light tap on the door and it was opened and the serving cart was wheeled in. The same lady placed the coffee, silverware, condiments, napkins, and a bottle of Cognac on the coffee table along with a tray of small pastries. She wheeled the cart back behind the door then asked if we would care for some music. "I think that would be nice," answered McNeil

The lady went to the right end of the couch where there was a small console of which he had not noticed. She pressed a button and soft music filled the room from hidden speakers. "Will there be anything else sir?" she asked.

"That will be all and thank you very much," answered McNeil in German.

"If you need anything press button two," she answered in German as she opened the door and left the room, closing it after her.

"Please, sit down Miss Connie," said McNeil as he poured coffee into two cups and passed one to her. "I take mine black, usually, but tonight I will lace it with something a bit stronger to take away the chill of the weather. You may doctor yours as you wish," he said as he sat down in the easy chair which put him a few feet from where Connie sat on the couch.

"This is very nice," spoke a nervous Connie as she looked around, "nothing like I imagined it would be."

"It is nice," answered McNeil as he sipped his coffee and waited. Please, try some of the pastry."

"It does look good but probably full of calories."

"I'm sure. That's why they cut it in very small pieces," he said as he picked up a piece and popped it into his mouth, "very good."

Connie reached over and selected a small piece and nibbled on it. "It is very tasty."

"Miss Connie, you said you needed to speak to me in private, it doesn't get much more private than this. So what's on your mind?"

She chewed on the last bit of the pastry then took a sip of her coffee before she spoke. "When we met in Garmisch, I said some things I shouldn't have said, I wish to apologize for that. If I had known who you were then."

"What does knowing who one is have to do with insults Miss Connie?"

"Nothing really. I shouldn't have spoken in that manner, to you, or in fact to anyone. Again, I apologize."

"Apology accepted and allow me to apologize for not properly introducing myself. But, in fact, I really didn't do the introduction did I?"

"No you didn't. I believe it was Jesse who did the introduction and she never mentioned who you were. She just said Charley. I have heard Dad speak of you as Charley but I didn't, at that time, make the connection. So you and dad have served together before?"

"Yes we did, what now seems a life time ago."

"Korea, perhaps?"

"Could be."

"You don't talk much about yourself do you?"

"I wasn't aware this conversation was supposed to be about me."

"I stand corrected. Sorry."

Connie finally relaxed some, and realized that McNeil was a good listener, so she told all about her experience with men, mainly her ex-husband and how she felt that maybe she had somehow failed in their relationship. She asked about his family and if he had ever been married. He told her he had not stopped long enough to find the right woman and he said his family, mother and father, was no longer with him. He didn't mention that he had a brother and sister who might as well have passed on.

It was near midnight before they finished the coffee and conversation. "I can't remember when I have been so relaxed and talked so much," spoke Connie, "what time is it?" she asked.

"Twenty three thirty," answered McNeil looking at his watch. He walked over and pushed button two on the consol.

"If you are ordering more coffee, none for me," said Connie.

"I suppose these people would like to close up. I'm asking for the bill."

"Oh. You do speak the language very well Charley."

"Thank you Miss Connie," he answered just as a faint knock sounded at the door and it was opened. "We'll be departing now. Would you prepare a bill for me?" he asked in German.

"No charge sir. Herr Shultz said this was on him."

"The service here was excellent so allow me to leave a generous tip," he said as he pulled some Marks from his wallet and placed two hundred Marks on the coffee tray. The lady escorted them from the room and back to where the Maître D' waited." He opened the door and bid them good evening.

The heavy rain earlier had tapered off some but was still falling so McNeil used his umbrella to cover Connie as he helped her get in the car. "This has been a delightful evening Charley," spoke Connie after he left the parking lot and was on the way back to Rose Barracks, "May I call you Charley?"

"Certainly Miss. Connie."

"I'm not sure if I am a Mrs. or a Miss now but it would be much better if you just called me Connie."

"Sorry. Force of habit, Connie it is."

"So, there will be a change of command ceremony Monday and you'll be a battalion Commander."

"That's the plan right now. Will I see you at the parade?"

"If I can get someone to take my class I'll try and be there."

"Class, as in?"

"Didn't I mention that I'm a school teacher here at Rose Barracks?"

"If you did I failed to hear it, sorry."

"I teach the fourth, and sometimes, fifth grade students."

"Is it interesting work?" McNeil asked.

"Sometimes, and sometimes it's very frustrating when kids don't care to learn."

"I'm sure."

It was very formal when McNeil escorted Connie to the quarter's door and they said goodnight. They shook hands.

McNeil had a hard time getting to sleep that night. Thoughts of Connie were on his mind. Never had a woman affected him the way Connie did. Before, with women, it was good conversation, a meal, a dance, then sex with no strings attached. With Connie it was different somehow. Sex was the farthest thing on his mind tonight. They had gotten off to a rocky start in Garmisch but more than made up for it tonight. Will I see her again? How does she feel about me?

It was two AM before McNeil finally drifted off to sleep.

Connie's mom and dad had not come home yet so she prepared herself for bed but instead of going to bed she sat in a chair by the window with the lights off. As she sat there looking out the window and the gently falling rain she tried to analyze her feelings. What happened tonight she asked herself? Why are my insides all jumpy and jittery when I'm near Charley? That has never happened to me before, with any man, not even to the man I married.

*I promised myself I wouldn't get involved again but it seems I have no control over my heart.*

She was still in the chair trying to reason out the strange feelings she felt when she heard her parents enter the quarters. It was some time later when she turned back the covers of the bed and slid under them with thoughts of Charley on her mind as she slowly drifted off to sleep.

It was late Sunday morning when Connie woke up from a restless night of sleep. She decided to not get dressed until she had some coffee in her so she belted the bathrobe around her, combed her long hair, and went to the dining room. She found her mother sitting at the table reading the paper and drinking coffee. "Good morning Mother," Connie greeted her as she filled a cup with coffee and sat down.

"Good morning dear, how did it go last night?"

"It went well mother," she replied taking a sip of the coffee. Connie knew her mother was curious but she refrained from asking questions. "I suppose you are wondering what that was all about last night mother so let me explain. When I met Charley in Garmisch I had no idea who he was and being my usual bitchy self I said things I shouldn't have said. I simply wanted to apologize to him. He took me to a very nice German club where we had coffee and talked. That's all there is to it."

Marie could tell by the look on Connie's face that wasn't all there was to it. Something more happened but she would wait for an explanation.

"Charley is a nice guy isn't he?"

"I'm sorry mother. What did you say?"

"Nothing important dear," replied Marie. *Could it be that what I hoped would happen has happened? Well Walter said for me to not get involved so I'll just wait and see.*

# MCNEIL

## HEADQUARTERS
## 8TH INFANTRY DIVISION
## ROSE BARRACKS

**Chapter 41**
**7 June 1956**

A week later, a Wednesday, after McNeil officially took command of the 504th Airborne Infantry Battalion of the 8th Infantry Division he was in the headquarters building to drop some papers off at the S-1 then he intended to drop by his old office to see Frau Olga and Maj. Gates and ask if there was anything he could do for them. As he left the S-1 and was walking down the hallway he heard someone speak. The voice sounded familiar but the use of words really got to him. "He probably won't even have time to speak to us peons anymore."

McNeil stopped suddenly and turned around to see who had spoken. He intended to have a word with the speaker about what was said because, regardless, of whom it was, officer or enlisted, he always had time to answer questions. He stood almost stunned as he looked at the three men standing in class 'A' uniforms with big smiles on their faces. There was a big guy in the middle Sergeant Major strips on his sleeve with a captain and a staff sergeant on each side of him. "I told you he would never get too big to speak with us," spoke the Sergeant Major as McNeil started walking to them with a smile on his face.

"What are you three doing here, not that I'm not glad to see each of you. Bob," he said reaching for his hand. "I see you still wear those railroad tracks."

"Yes sir I do. It's good to see you also Charley."

"And look at this guy, even bigger than I remember and wearing Sergeant Major strips. Legally I presume. How are you Tiny."

"Very well colonel. Good to see you again sir," replied Sergeant Major Brockman, (Tiny) as he shook hands with McNeil.

"And look at this? Wearing staff sergeant strips no less. How are you Willis?"

"Good colonel and thank you for asking sir," replied Staff Sergeant Willis.

"Curiosity overwhelms me, not that I'm not glad to see each of you, but what are all three of you doing here?"

"We're assigned to the 8th Infantry Division," offered Capt. Johnson, "all three of us. We just arrived and were about to report in when we saw you."

McNeil and the three men had served together in the 5th Infantry Division in Korea. They were old friends. McNeil had been instrumental in getting Corporal Johnson a field commission to 2nd Lieutenant so he could take command of a company which, at the time was commanded by a sergeant. Tiny, SGM Brockman, who at one time was a Private First Class he promoted to Corporal, then staff sergeant, then made him a Master Sergeant and put him in the position of acting Sergeant major of the 1/5th Infantry Battalion. Private First Class Willis was the sole survivor of the devastated 1/5 Infantry Battalion which was wiped out by artillery fire. McNeil rescued him and made him the new 1/5th Infantry Battalion radio operator after promoting him to corporal.

"None of you have assignments yet," asked McNeil.

"We were told we would receive assignments after we arrived," answered Capt. Johnson.

"Come with me please. There is someone who would, I'm sure, like to speak with you and welcome you to the 8thInfantry Division."

McNeil turned and walked down the hall then stopped and knocked on the Commanding General's door of the 8th Infantry Division and entered after he heard the request to enter. "Hello Charley. What can I do for you today/" asked General Layton as he looked up from the paper he was studying to see who had entered his office.

"Could you spare just a moment of you time sir. There are three men outside from the 5th Infantry Division just reporting in. Could you spare the time to welcome them?"

"Three men you say. I had a back channel about some men who may show up here. Sure I have the time to welcome men from the 5th. Please show them in Charley."

When McNeil stepped back out into the hallway Capt. Johnson spoke, "Charley, this is the office of the Commanding General."

"Yes, so?"

"Is he going to take the time to see us?"

"You'll have to see him sooner or later so why not now. I don't know if any of you remember General Layton but he's not as bad as one would think he is. Please follow me gentleman," said McNeil as he opened the door and motioned for the three to precede him. The three men stopped in front of the General's desk, came to attention and saluted. Each man reported and gave his name.

"Gentlemen," said General Layton returning the salutes, stand at ease. It's my pleasure to welcome you to the 8th Infantry Division and Germany. It's an even greater pleasure to welcome someone from a distinguished unit such as the 5th Infantry Division. I have heard that the three of you raised quite a ruckus at the pentagon. Is there anything to that?"

"I take full responsibility for that sir," spoke Capt. Johnson.

"I can't allow you to do that sir," spoke Tiny, "it was partly my fault. Sir, they didn't want to send us here, that is all three of us. We insisted. We knew Colonel McNeil was here and we wanted to serve under him again."

"Sir, if we caused you any problems, I apologize," said Capt. Johnson.

"No problem for me, and as far as I know, since you are here, no problem exists."

"General, may I ask what we will do with these men? I would be more than pleased to have them in the 504th." asked McNeil.

"Is there room for all three of them Charley?"

"I have a company commander about to depart with no replacement and the Battalion Sergeant Major will be leaving soon. I would like to replace the commo sergeant since he doesn't have much knowledge of communications. Possibly I could send him to S-1 for a new assignment."

"That would be removing an unsatisfactory man and shipping him to another unit. What will that accomplish Charley? If the man isn't trained then train him or find him another line of work. You have my permission for these three men to be assigned to the 504th. Again, welcome aboard gentlemen and good luck," said General Layton dismissing the men.

McNeil stopped at the entrance to the S-1 and spoke. "I'll go in with you and make sure the S-1 understands where you are to be assigned, which is VOCG (Vocal Order of the Commanding General). During your in-processing you will be provided transportation and when you get to the education center sign up for the spoken German class. Not to start today or tomorrow but sometime in the near future. You are in Germany for three years so you should be able to at least have a bit of knowledge of the local custom and learn a few words of the language. That is not a suggestion gentlemen, if you get my meaning. Later today, say about ten after twelve, I'll meet you in the snack bar where I'll buy lunch and you can fill me in on what has been happening to you. Now, if you are ready, let's go in."

At ten after the hour when McNeil entered the snack bar and looked around he saw the three men, Bob, Tiny, and Willis sitting where two tables had been pushed together. The extra space was needed because sitting with them were Jesse and Ursula from the education center, plus Connie.

During the change of command ceremony McNeil had a chance to look around and he spied Connie in the reviewing stand sitting beside her mother. He got that warm feeling just knowing she was there.

"You guys certainly didn't waste any time did you," commented McNeil as he stopped behind Connie and put his hand on her shoulder. She reached up and placed her hand on his which didn't go unnoticed, "and from the looks of this cozy little gathering I would guess that no introductions are necessary."

"When these guys stopped by the education center," spoke Jesse, "and made mention that they were friends of yours and that you were buying lunch, we decided to join them."

"I hope that's Ok," said Ursula in German and McNeil answered in the language that it was all right.

"How did your day go so far?" asked Connie.

"Good so far. Since this will cost me my jump pay you'll each have to get your own food. I'm not bringing it to you." said McNeil as he started pulling Connie's chair back to help her up.

After they had food and settled back at the pushed together tables McNeil spoke. "Let's start with Willis since he's the junior man. What have you been up to since Korea and when did you get out of there?"

"They started rotating us about six months after you left sir. I was assigned to the signal school until I got orders to come here."

"He's being modest Charley," spoke up Bob, "when the signal school realized Willis knew as much or more about radios and communications than the instructors they made him an instructor and promoted him."

"Do you have a family Willis?"

"I'm engaged sir."

"How about you Tiny, what have you been up to?"

"Like Willis said, about six months after you left we started getting replacements. I was allowed to keep my stripes and was assigned as a 1st Sgt at Fort Benning. I kept up with my studies by enrolling in night school. Later I was promoted to Sergeant Major and here I am."

"Do you have a family?"

"I'm still running free."

"And you Bob, what have you been up to?"

"I had time to do some heavy thinking before leaving Korea. Since I held my rank in combat and commanded a combat unit I was allowed to retain it. I'm married and the wife and I were talking about starting a family before I went to Korea. I realized I would never have the time to get all the

education and school I would need while on active duty so I requested, and
it was granted, that I be released from active duty and placed in the reserves.
There, using the GI Bill, I was able to get the schooling I needed plus attend
both the primary and advanced Infantry schools for Infantry Officers. Later,
with the concurrence of my wife, I asked to be re-instated on active duty as
a regular Army Officer. Because of my military schools, plus my degree, plus
my combat command time, here I am. The wife and I now have two children,
a boy of five and a girl of four. End of story. How about you Charlie? What
has been happening to you?"

"Before we get to me what was that all about in the General's office?
And by the way, in case you don't know yet, Miss Connie is the daughter of
General Layton. What was that about a ruckus in the pentagon?"

"When a junior NCO, a Senior NCO, and a Company grade office
showed up at the same time at the Pentagon and each asked for the same
assignment, not asked but rather demanded, it got some people a bit shook
up. I seem to recall that it got a general involved. After waiting two days we
three finally got the assignment we asked for. We heard that you were with
the 8th Infantry Division here in Germany so we wanted to join you. It'll be
like old home time with us three together."

"Up to a point Bob. I command an Airborne Infantry Battalion and
that takes up much of my time. I want it understood, here and now, that
just because we are old comrades in arms you don't have access to me as you
once did in combat. We're in a peace time army now, training and planning
for the next war, and hoping that one will not happen. I made the comment
that I commanded an Airborne Infantry Battalion but I didn't notice any
reaction from you."

"Sir," spoke Willis, does that mean that because we are assigned to the
504th that we'll have to take airborne training?"

"It's encouraged but not mandatory. Airborne is now and has always been
voluntary. However, those who are qualified and make the required jumps
each month receive extra pay, jump pay. Keep that in mind."

"Is it true that you got the big Medal Charley?" asked Tiny.

"I did and I have wished many times that I hadn't. The Army likes to
remind me of that fact quite often by putting me on display for the media."

"Which happened Monday of last week," spoke Connie

"What happened Monday?" asked Bob.

"A formal change of command ceremony with plenty of brass and the
media," answered Connie.

"Gentlemen, and ladies, time is marching on and I have duties to get back
to as I'm sure each of you have. We'll have to continue this discussion another
time. Do you ladies have transportation?"

"We came in my car Charley," said Jesse. McNeil had noticed that Tiny kept glancing at Jesse but quickly diverting his eyes when she looked his way.

"And you guys?"

"We're supposed to be picked up here to continue the in-processing." said Bob.

"Don't forget about dinner tonight," Connie reminded him.

"I've got that on my calendar."

The next day the three men reported in to the 504th Airborne infantry Battalion and as it was McNeil's policy to interview and welcome all new arrivals, he had them in his office. "Bob, you'll be taking over Able Company. I'll have the present commander here shortly. Tiny, have you met the current Sergeant Major?"

"Very briefly sir."

"I'll get you with him after I release you here. Willis, you will be the new NCOIC of the battalion commo section. I have already spoken with Capt. Hardy, the OIC, about that and he agrees with me. There may be a bit of conflict but we'll take care of that when and if it happens. Let me say that I'm glad to see the three of you, for many reasons, and I welcome you to the 504th Airborne Infantry Battalion. All I ask is that you do what is expected of you to the best of your ability. Bob, will your family be coming over to join you?"

"They will as soon as I can get quarters."

"If you run into any problems there let me know. Fellows, we are not at war now so I expect each of you to use military curtsey at all times. I'm a stickler for using the chain of command. Have each of you completed the in-processing?"

"As far as I know Char--, sorry, Sir." spoke Bob. What about this jump business? You did say one could get jump pay if one was qualified."

"I did. We have plenty of time to get into that. Tiny, I'll call the current Sergeant Major in and introduce you then unless you have questions I'll turn you over to him for further briefing."

"I have a question sir," said Bob.

"What is it?"

"Did I not hear you say, at the snack bar, that very beautiful lady, Connie, was the daughter of the Commanding General, General Layton?"

"You did. And?"

"Just an observation sir. You do seem to come out on top every time."

"I'm not sure just how to take that Bob but let me say this, a man makes his own road in life, good or bad, keep that in mind. Now, speaking of women, didn't I see someone eyeing a young lady at the snack bar yesterday? Let me tell you Tiny, Jessie is a fine, corn fed, Iowa bred, well-educated woman. I don't think you could find a better one."

"I was just admiring her from afar sir."

"You may be surprised if you started admiring her closer. Let me get some people in here to show you around then I have to get back to work. Again, welcome aboard gentlemen."

The next weekend was jump day for the 504th so the three, Bob, Tiny, and Willis decided to be at the airfield to see what jumping was all about. The first seven men dropped out of the helicopter and with their parachutes open they floated to the ground, McNeil leading, and making it seem effortless. "They get an extra fifty dollars a month for doing that!" commented Bob.

If it was good enough for McNeil then it was good enough for anyone. They all three decided to become jump qualified.

McNeil had found out that he couldn't get his men jump qualified at Bad Tolz, in Germany. The only school, he was told, qualified to certify a man to jump status was the Jump school at Fort Benning Georgia. When he had twenty men signed up he presented the request to division for the men to be sent to Fort Benning. They would be gone almost a month.

That worked out well for Bob, Capt. Johnson, because he was able to get his wife's departure delayed so he could accompany her back to Germany. He had signed for his quarters and was waiting for her and the children.

Sgt Willis had said he was engaged so he asked for a leave after he completed jump school, while he was in the states, so he could get married. His new wife would be joining him in Germany later.

McNeil was in and out of Division Headquarters at least once a week for the staff meetings and to check with Frau Olga to see if she needed any help and it wasn't unusual for General Layton or the chief of staff to request his presence at Division Headquarters quite often. So he was surprised one morning two months after he had taken command of the 504th when Tiny knocked at his door to get his attention. "What is it Tiny?"

"Sir, you are to report to the general in one hour."

"Did they say why?"

"No sir. Just that you are to report to General Laytonat ten hundred hours this morning."

"Then I suppose I should be there then. Anything else for me?"

"No sir."

When McNeil knocked at the door of the Division Chief of Staff's, Col. Steel, office Col. Steel motioned for him to enter. "Good morning sir. I'm to report to the general this morning and I thought I would check in with you to see what it's about."

"Is it that time already?" he asked looking at his watch, "I suppose we better get going then," he replied without answering McNeil's question.

When Col. Steel knocked at the door of the commanding general's office and they both heard 'enter' Col. Steel pushed the door open and motioned for McNeil to precede him. Waiting in the office was the division XO, General Campbell. Maj. Carstairs, General Layton's senior aide, and Capt. Davenport, his junior aide, and a couple of people McNeil didn't recognize. McNeil stopped in front of the desk and rendered a salute, "Sir, Lieutenant Colonel McNeil reporting as ordered."

"Stand at ease Charley," said General Layton, "in fact relax. How about some coffee?"

McNeil had noticed that each man had a cup of coffee in his hand so he wondered just what was going on. There wasn't much formality in the office. "I never turn down a good cup of coffee sir," he replied as Capt. Davenport, who apparently anticipated his answer handed McNeil a cup of coffee.

"Charley," spoke General Layton, "how long have you been a Lieutenant Colonel?"

"About five year's sir."

"Do you realize that makes you have more time in grade than anyone else on active duty, in that grade? That is other than those who have disciplinary action pending or those who have been told to not expect a promotion."

"I really never gave it much thought Sir," replied McNeil.

"Well it's a fact and the Army has decided to do something about it and I really approve of it. Col. Steel will you read the order, just the pertinent paragraph."

"Attention to orders. Special order number 316 from the Department of the Army. Paragraph five. Lieutenant Colonel Charley R. McNeil, serial number 0-637813 is promoted to full Colonel effective this date."

McNeil saw General Layton get up and come from behind his desk with something in his hand. General Campbell, will you assist me?" said General Layton as he started to remove the silver oak leaf from McNeil's collar.

The other men in the room were army photographers which McNeil now saw as they got into position to record the pinning on of the new rank. "I haven't heard you say anything Charley," spoke General Layton.

"I'm flabbergasted sir, stunned. I have grown use to the silver oak leaf and never thought I would replace them."

"Good things do come to those who have patience. Will that do gentlemen?" asked General Layton as he and General Campbell stepped back after removing the silver oak leaves and pinning on the silver eagle to McNeil's collar points.

"That will do general," replied the photographer.

"And you have the press release I dictated?"

"Yes sir, we have it."

"Then I thank you for coming. Gentlemen, I have work to do as I'm sure each of you have. Charley, those new eagles will have to be wet down tonight at the club. Congratulations Charley." said General Layton taking his hand. Before the others left the room each shook McNeil's hand and offered their congratulations. After they had all left the room, even Capt. Davenport, General Layton spoke. "How does it feel Charley?"

"These eagles will take some getting used to sir, but, as I have stated before, I wish I could give back the medal and get on with my career."

"We discussed that Charley and you know that can't happen. Those eagles look good on you and you have earned them and you deserve them. Wear them with pride Charley."

"Yes sir I will."

When McNeil returned to the 504th the first person to notice the new eagles was Tiny who came into McNeil's office with some papers for McNeil's signature. "Well I'll be da–, sorry sir. May I offer my congratulations sir and might I say those eagles look good on you."

"Thank you Tiny."

"Will you be staying here sir? I mean after the promotion?"

"I'm not sure Tiny but it seems inevitable that I will be transferred since this job calls for a lieutenant colonel."

"Don't be too hasty sir. I just received an update to the battalion T O & E. All Battalion command slots are to be up-dated to full colonel positions."

"What's the effective date Tiny?"

"The change read immediately."

"Then I suppose you will have to put up with me for a while yet."

"That's not hard to do sir."

Since their private meeting back in January Connie and McNeil were seeing each other on a regular schedule. McNeil was at the general's quarters at least twice a week to eat.

When it became evident that they couldn't stand to be apart each knew that the love bug had bitten. One evening after they attended a movie McNeil decided to surprise Connie and go to the Club Social for a bit of privacy and a drink. Once they were in one of the private rooms with a fire going, soft music floating in the air and champagne glasses full they sat side by side on the couch. "Connie," said McNeil.

"Yes dear? She answered in a sleepy voice.

"I have a question for you."

"Oh, and what would that be?" she asked raising her head from his shoulder and looking at him.

"I know you have told me of your past life and the trouble you had. I also realize we haven't really know each other a very long but I feel as if we have known each other a lifetime."

"That sounds more like a statement than a question," replied Connie taking a sip of her champagne.

"Bear with me I'm getting there," replied McNeil turning his head to look at her. "Do you think you will ever get married again?"

"I suppose, somewhere in the future, if the right man comes along," Connie replied after giving the question some thought and wondering why such a question from a man who had never been married. "Why do you ask Charley?"

"Again, please bear with me because I'm new at this and I'll probably do it wrong. You know I do love you and we have a lot in common and we seem to want the same things in life. If you answer my question in the negative I'll understand and hope we can still be friends."

Is he getting ready to do what I have hoped he would do for weeks now, propose? How do I answer him? You answer him in the positive because you know you love him also and don't want to think about living without him. "I won't know how to answer until I know what the question is, will I?"

"No you won't. Connie, will you marry me and allow me to love you and try and make you happy for the rest of your life?"

"Try to make me happy? Charley you do make me happy and I feel so comfortable being with you. I love you and the answer is yes to your question. If you had asked me weeks ago the answer would be the same."

"I'm pleased to hear you say that," replied McNeil as he pulled her to him and gave her a gentle kiss. "One other item, would you be opposed to accepting the ring that my mother wore? If not we'll go shopping for the one you do like?" McNeil took the box from his pocket that held the ring his mother had passed on to him.

"That's a beautiful ring Charley," said Connie after she picked up the ring and looked at it. "As long as it's from you I'll accept it and wear it with pride," replied Connie putting the ring on her finger, surprised that it fit so well.

"So what's the next step?" asked McNeil as he watched Connie turn the ring to catch the dim light.

"First we drink a toast here then at a convenient time we tell mom and dad."

That fell in with what McNeil believed was the proper way to do things. Even though Connie accepted his proposal, being a bit old fashion, he wanted to ask her father and mother for their blessing of the union. That happened one evening after Connie invited McNeil to dine with the Layton's late in June.

After the meal General Layton and McNeil retired to the den and they had just splashed some brandy in their coffee and lit up cigars when the door opened and Connie entered arm in arm with her mother. She placed her mother by her dad then came over and put her arm through McNeil's before she spoke. "Mom and dad, Charley and I have something to ask you. Go ahead Charley."

"General Sir, and Mrs. Layton," began McNeil, "I'm sure it's evident that Connie and I have been seeing a lot of each other. We have had many conversations and we are in agreement about what we want out of life. What I'm trying to say sir, and Ma'am, is that Connie and I are in love and I have asked Connie to be my wife and she has accepted. We are here tonight in hopes of receiving your blessing."

Mrs. Layton put her hands to her face and gasped, "this is so sudden."

"Dear you had to know something was going on since they spent so much time together. Connie," said General Layton as he moved to her and placed his hands on her arms, "I realize you have had a rough start in married life–"

"Yes dad and Charley knows all about it."

"Is this really what you want? Is this the man who you wish to spend your life with?"

"Absolutely dad. I love Charley and I have no doubt that he loves me."

"Then you have my blessing," he said as he kissed Connie on her cheek before moving to McNeil. Mrs. Layton came to Connie and wrapped her in her arms. "I'm so happy for you Connie. I think you are getting a good man here."

"I know I am mother."

"Charley," spoke General Layton, "as everyone knows by now, I have known you since you were a corporal and back then you had some rough edges which you have polished some. It's my pleasure to welcome you to the family," he said shaking McNeil's hand."

"Thank you very much sir."

"Charley," spoke Marie, "as Walter knows I have often though you and Connie would make a perfect pair, and now it's going to happen. I'm so happy I think I'm going to cry."

"Here's a tissue mother," said Connie passing her a tissue.

"Thank you dear. And allow me to add, welcome to the family Charley. Have you two set a date yet?"

"We haven't yet ma'am but sometime in the near future; probably next month."

"So soon! Connie we have a thousand things to do. What about a ring?"

"Already taken care of mother," said Connie holding out her hand so the diamonds sparkled, "this was Charley's mothers ring. Isn't it beautiful?"

"It is a beautiful ring, and such a big diamond," replied Marie taking her daughters hand so she could better see the ring better.

"A toast is in order," said General Layton as he started filling brandy glasses.

Colonel Charley R. McNeil and Miss Connie Layton were married at the Rose Barracks post chapel the third week of July 1956. The post photographers and the Stars and Stripes, the Army newspaper, reporters were present to record the occasion. The reception was held at the O-Club and McNeil and Connie honeymooned in the old town of Garmisch where they first met.

When they returned from the honeymoon quarters were waiting for them on Colonel's row where they set up housekeeping.

Captain Johnson's wife and kids arrived and took up residence in the company grade quarters on Rose Barracks. Captain Johnson insisted that McNeil and Connie dine with them one evening in late August. Captain Johnson's wife, Ellen, was a tall woman and very slender with long blond hair. She had a good sense of humor and didn't allow much to faze her. Their two children, four year old Gail and five year old Robert Junior, were bubbly children and a joy to be around.

When McNeil and Connie arrived at the quarters they were met at the door by Bob and his wife and introductions were made.

"I'm so pleased to finally meet you Col McNeil. Bob has spoken so often about you that I feel as if I know you."

"Thank you for having us Mrs. Johnson and Bob and I went through some rough times, in the past, which tends to cement friendships."

"Welcome to our home Mrs. McNeil," said Ellen turning to Connie.

"It's my pleasure to be here Mrs. Johnson."

Sergeant Willis married and finally quarters were available so he could bring his wife to Germany. After his wifeSharon arrived and they were settled in he and his wife had a chance meeting at the Post Exchange with McNeil and they were introduced.

Sergeant Major Brockman and Jessie, from the education center, started dating but so far nothing serious.

# MCNEIL

## 7TH ARMY HEADQUARTERS
## OFFICE OF G-3 COMBAT TRAINING
## KELLYBARRACKS

**Chapter 42**
**10 Nov 1956**

There was a knock at the closed door of the office of Combat Training and it opened and 1st Lieutenant Toby Hancock, Infantry, walked in. He was dressed in a Class 'A' uniform and wearing all the regalia required of an aide-d-camp to a Brigadier General. "Sorry to disturb you sir."

"I'll be the first to let you know if you are disturbing me Toby," said Brigadier General Charley R. McNeil, "what's on your mind."

"Sir, there's a 2nd Lieutenant Morehouse of the 117th Artillery that keeps calling here to speak with you. I keep putting him off but he is persistent."

"He didn't say what he wanted to see me about? The name doesn't ring a bell."

"No sir he didn't."

"Maybe we should see what this 2nd Lieutenant Morehouse has on his mind Toby. If he calls again check my schedule and see when I have the time to speak with him."

"Yes sir."

"Is there anything else Toby?"

"No sir."

"Then I have a lot of work to get done. Are we set up for next week for that trip to Bamberg?"

"Yes sir. Everything is ready."

There is no time in grade requirement for promotion from Lieutenant Colonel to full Colonel and likewise no time in grade requirement from full colonel to general. McNeil had five years as a Lieutenant Colonel and met all the requirements for a promotion. Three months after he took command of the 504thAirborne Infantry Battalion he was promoted to full colonel.

With the blessing of General Layton and Mrs. Layton he and Connie Layton were married in the Rose Barracks post Chapel shortly after he pinned on the silver eagle of a full Colonel rank.

Since he met all the requirements for the rank of full colonel he was promoted to Brigadier General three months later. Orders arrived a month after he pinned on the silver star transferring him to Seventh Army Headquarters at Kelly Barracks near Stuttgart Germany. He was assigned to the G-3 and put in charge of Combat training. Connie was in the family way and expected to give birth in five months.

There was a knock at the door of the G-3 Combat Training and the door opened and in walked Lt. Toby. "Good morning sir."

"Good morning Toby. What have you for me today?" asked McNeil as he looked up from a paper he was studying.

"Lt. Morehouse sir. He called and I set him up with a meeting with you this morning. I left a note for you on your desk."

"I must have missed it."

"If you are busy sir I can have him come back."

"Come back as in he's outside now?"

"Yes sir."

"Show him in Toby and let's see what this lieutenant has on his mind."

"Yes sir."

A few minutes later a young 2ndLieutenant entered the office, stopped in front of the desk and rendered a hand salute, and spoke, "Sir, 2nd Lieutenant Robert Morehouse of the 117th Artillery requests a word with the general."

McNeil took his time looking the young man over but once again failed to call to memory ever having seen this man before. He was a sharp dresser, glossy shined boots and a short haircut. But just who is this man who is so anxious to meet me wondered McNeil as he returned the salute. "Stand at easy Lieutenant Morehouse. Would you care for some coffee?"

"Thank you sir but I don't wish to take up much of your time."

"Then what may I ask are you doing here lieutenant?"

"Sir, I'm here at the request of my mother. I tried to tell her that lieutenants do not take up Generals time but she insisted that I see and speak with you. I apologize for bothering you sir."

"We must obey our mother's wishes lieutenant but just who is your mother? Do I know her?"

"My mother is Barbara Morehouse sir. I believe she is managing some property for you sir."

So this is Bab's little boy all grown up and a 2nd Lieutenant in the Army. She did tell me that he was attending VMI (Virginia Military Institute). I wonder just why she insisted he call upon me. Could it be? No, she would have said something long ago.

"I do remember your mother, with fond memories I might add. As I remember she can be quite persuasive which tells me why you are here. Is she still in the real estate business? I'm sure I would have heard something if she wasn't."

"Yes sir. She is well pleased and the business is thriving. I'm to tell you, from her, best wishes and congratulations on your promotion and she wishes you a long and successful marriage."

Now how did she know about the promotion and marriage? Because I am high profile, it was carried in all the papers. No big surprise there.

"When you speak with your mother again, by phone or letter, tell her I said best wishes in her career and that I received you and we spoke. I suppose I should send a card to her myself."

"I'm sure she would appreciate that sir. She speaks of you often. You gave her the inspiration and provided the moral support she needed to get on with her life, and career."

"If I had anything to do with her decision and career choice then I'm glad."

"Sir, I believe I have fulfilled mothers request and again I apologize for bothering you."

"I'm glad you did stop by lieutenant. I'm pleased to hear about your mother. How are things going with your assignment?"

"Very well sir."

"If you need anything you know where I'm located."

"Thank you very much sir. I'll take my leave now sir and it's been a pleasure to speak with you," said 2nd Lt. Morehouse as he came to attention and saluted.

McNeil returned the salute and Lt. Morehouse did an about face and marched out of the office. Toby, who had sat against the wall and listened, went out with the lieutenant to escort him out of the headquarters building. When he returned he closed the office door and spoke. "That was very interesting sir."

"Yes it was Toby. Toby, being my aide you are privy to much classified information of which you should not pass around. What you just heard, even though is not military classified, should not be repeated. What happened, happened years ago before I met and married my wife. That man's mother, Mrs. Morehouse, was, and is a wonderful person but she had no desire to marry. Enough said."

"I understand sir."

"You'll be departing here in February I believe?"

"Yes sir, the later part of February."

"What I want you to do, very discretely, is find out everything about 2nd Lieutenant Morehouse. Unless he does not wish it he could be your replacement."

"I'll get started right away sir."

The holidays came and went and with them came the cold of winter and snow. Not near as much as last year but enough to make it miserably cold outside. The holidays were not as lonely now as they were in the past because McNeil had someone to share them with. Connie was getting bigger each day and Marie, Mrs. Layton, spent much time at the McNeil's quarters. This would be the first grandchild of the Layton's and both, general and Mrs. Layton, were excited about it. The delivery was expected sometime in April.

## 15 Jan 1957

January through March is the busiest time of the year for field training in Seventh Army and it kept McNeil, and his staff, busy evaluating the combat redness of Seventh Army units. He was out of his office and on the go most of the time during those ninety days.

Transportation was provided for his trips by the Seventh Army Flight Detachment at Stuttgart Army Airfield. Most of the time he traveled in the H-19 helicopter since it was large enough to carry him and Toby plus their baggage and equipment. Most times it took two of the helicopters especially when McNeil traveled with a full staff which consisted of not only his aide but two Captains and four sergeants plus a couple of privates; far too many men for just one helicopter.

The evaluating team had already been out in the field evaluating three different units and they were getting ready to go out again. McNeil allowed his team to have a few days at Kelly Barracks, after all reports were completed, to take care of personal needs and spend time with their families before they had to take to the field again. Of course that was based on when a unit they were evaluating went to the field.

"Toby," called out McNeil to his aide.

"Yes sir?" he answered as he entered the office.

"What's the situation for tomorrow? Has the helicopters been scheduled? Has everyone been notified? What's the weather like?"

"Everyone has been notified sir, and the flight detachment has been alerted. The weather is unknown at this time. I'll have to check with the pilots early tomorrow morning."

"Do it as early as you can so we'll have an idea if it's a go or not."

"I'll take care of it sir."

When General McNeil entered his office early the next morning well before daylight Toby was waiting with two cups of coffee. "Good morning sir."

"Good Morning Toby. Do we have good news?"

"The weather is marginal but the pilot said he thought he could fly around the bad weather but we'll have to refuel in Nurnberg. There's scattered snow and the temperature is in the twenties."

"Have the vehicles stand by and get them loaded as soon as the men arrives. Tell Capt. Stewart to fly with us so we can go over the agenda on the way."

"Yes sir. I'll handle it."

McNeil, no stranger to the cold, had dressed in his long john's this morning. While he drank his coffee and waited for his team he pulled on a pair of wool pants, then over that a pair of field pants. He slid Galoshes over his boots to protect them from the mud plus provide a measure of protection for his feet from the cold. Over his long john top he pulled on a wool shirt then a field jacket with a heavy liner. The gloves he would add later. He had advised his team to dress accordingly.

Daylight was just breaking when they left Kelly Barracks, his staff car leading with him, Toby, and Capt. Stewart in it with a 6x6 following loaded with the other men and baggage.

The two helicopters were ready and the pilots standing by when they reached the airfield. The lead helicopter had a red plate displayed with a white star in it to indicate a Brigadier General, an 0-7, was aboard. As soon as the team had the baggage loaded the pilots started the helicopters and lifted off.

Conversation was impossible in the noisy helicopter but General McNeil and his senior captain, Capt. Stewart, sat side by side and communicated with gestures and notes. Toby was looking out the window at the snow falling on the mountain to their right.

The second helicopter was following the lead one when the pilot saw a puff of dark smoke come out of the right engine air vent. The lead helicopter started a gradual right descending turn heading for the snow storm and the trailing helicopter pilot, Capt. Peters, knew there was a mountain somewhere in the blinding snow.

"838 to 821. You need to do a left one eighty. There might be some rocks in that snow."

"821 to 838. I'm having a bit of a problem here. The engine is dead, I'm auto-rotating. The pilot is unconscious and has the right rudder jammed with his foot plus his body is against the cyclic control. Now would be a good time for you to call an emergency."

"Roger that," replied Capt. Peters as he flipped a small switch which allowed him to communicate on the emergency radio. "All stations and airplanes, H-19 helicopter 821 with an 0-7 aboard has declared an emergency. Anyone copy?"

"Copy," replied Stuttgart control, "understand you are declaring an emergency?"

"Negative. I repeat, I'm trail of a flight of two. Lead, 821, has declared and emergency. Engine out, pilot unconscious and has controls jammed. Helicopter is in an auto-rotating mode headed for a snow storm and a mountain. 821 has an 0-7 aboard."

"Copy 838. What's you location?"

"Ten clicks north east of Crailsheim on a radial of one seventy five."

"838, can you remain in the area?"

"838 can stay on station for another thirty minutes. Fuel and the approaching snow storm is the factor."

"Understand thirty minutes on station?"

"Correct Stuttgart control."

"Stand by."

838 started a right turn away from the approaching snow storm so as to circle in the area. As Capt. Peters started the turn he saw helicopter 821 disappear into the snow. "821 I have lost sight of you."

"I have lost sight of myself. It's a white out and I'm still unable to regain control."

"838 is on station for another thirty minute and the emergency has been called in."

"Thank you 838."

All that came over the radio after that transmission was static. "821, how do you read? Come in 821." There was no answer.

McNeil, who was engrossed in the paper he was reading, heard the sudden quiet when the engine shut down. He looked out the window and all he could see was the white of the snow. He felt the helicopter start descending in a right turn headed for the snow storm. When he looked back inside and up to where the pilot and copilot sat in the cockpit he noticed that the pilot seemed to be slumped down in his seat. A small amount of smoke entered the cabin and about the same time he noticed what looked like blood dripping down on the cabin seat directly under where the pilot was seated.

He sensed that something wasn't quite right so he quickly stuffed the papers back in his attache case and checked to make sure the others were buckled in. As the helicopter continued its right descending turn and got closer to the falling snow McNeil unbuckled his seat belt and stood up going to the cabin door. There was still nothing to see but white.

McNeil slid the cabin door open so he could see better and a blast of cold air entered the cabin which cleared out the smoke. He stood in the door way bracing himself with his hands on the ceiling as he had done so many times getting ready to jump. Suddenly he could see the snow covered mountain coming closer and there were rocks visible. The helicopter didn't slow down and he knew in that instance that they were going to crash. The helicopters forward movement slowed just before impact and McNeil jumped from the helicopter tucking and rolling as if he had just reached ground from a jump. The ground rushed up to meet him just as he heard the helicopter crash into the mountain side a couple hundred feet away.The forward movement of the helicopter plus the wind from the blades caused him to miscalculate. He also forgot about the incline of the snow covered mountain. He landed hard knocking the wind out of him and he was on his back starting to slide down the mountain side head first. He was able to twist his body and roll over onto his stomach but there was nothing to grab onto to slow his forward momentum. He was sliding head first and gaining speed when suddenly a large snow covered rock appeared in front of him. He tried to twist his body but was unable to avoid the rock and his head contacted it first then his left shoulder. His lights went out as he continued to slide further down the side of the mountain.

"838 to Stuttgart control."

"Go ahead 838."

"Be advised that 821 has disappeared into the snow storm and there is no radio contact. 838 is leaving the area now."

"Understand lost contact with 821 and 838 is departing the area. Return to Stuttgart 838."

"Roger. Understand return to Stuttgart."

Pandemonium was in full swing at Stuttgart Army Airfield, or it would seem so to an outsider. But actually everything was going according to plan. The controller had made the correct phone calls when he got the word from helicopter 838 that 821 was down. The president of the accident investigation board, Lieutenant Colonel Green, was notified and he was present in the airfield operations. The flight surgeon was notified who in turn notified the medics to stand by. The airfield commander, Colonel Aniston, was notified and he was also present and conversing with Ltc. Green. Flight crews of helicopters had been alerted and the pilots were in the operations checking on the weather. In fact the weather man had front stage at this time because everyone wanted to know when the snow storm would move from over the area of the last sighting of helicopter 821.

Even though men's lives were at stake, an unknown factor, what made it far worse was the fact that an 0-7, a Brigadier General was on 821. Not just any Brigadier General but one who wore the medal; a Brigadier General who wore the medal and was on the staff of Seventh Army Headquarters under General Clark.

When Col. Aniston had all the information he could gather at this time he went back to his office to make a call he did not want to make. He had to pass the information on to the duty officer at Seventh Army Headquarters.

When the duty officer received the call he quickly made notes then had a clerk typist type them up. As quickly as his hastily scribbled notes were typed up he took the paper and went to locate General Clark's Aide, Brigadier General Peter Gallows. General Gallows read the paper then quickly got to his feet and headed for General Clark's office. He knocked then entered General Clark's office without waiting for an invitation to enter. General Clark was busy studying a paper and he looked up to see who was invading his area. "What's up Pete," he asked when he saw who it was.

"Sorry sir but I though you would want to see this," said General Gallows placing the typed report in front of General Clark.

General Clark picked up the paper, read it, then slowly placed it down on his desk. General Gallows waited patiently as General Clark did some thinking. There is no need to ask if there is more information because if there was it would be in the report. I'm sure everyone at the airfield is doing all that can be done under the circumstances. And then there is General McNeil's wife who is pregnant. She should have someone with her when she hears the news. Also this situation should not be broadcast to the public just yet. "Pete, two things should be done and fast; call Col. Aniston at the airfield and tell him to expedite the search but under no circumstance is he to endanger another flight crew. Also tell him to keep the incident a low profile because of who was on the helicopter. Next place a call to the 8th Infantry Division and when you have General Layton on the phone buzz me."

"I'll get right on it sir," replied General Gallows as he picked up the report and left the office.

Ten minutes later General Clark's intercom buzzed and he punched the button. "Yes"

"Sir, General Layton is on two."

"Thank you Pete," said General Clark as he picked up his phone and pushed the button that was lit up.

"Good Morning Walter."

"Good morning sir. What can the Eighth do for the general today?"

"It's not really a good morning Walter. I'm afraid I have some bad news for you."

"Oh!"

"There is no way to soft peddle this Walter so I'll get right to it. Charley, and his crew, was on the way to Bayreuth early this morning and the helicopter developed a problem. All we know at this time, and we won't know more until the snow storm moves on, is that the helicopter was lost in the snow storm. The reason I'm calling you is because of Charley's wife, your daughter. I'm worried of what might happen when she hears the bad news, especially if she is by herself."

"General I can have a convoy of trucks and men on the road within the hour if you have the location?"

"Sorry Walter. We do have a general location but it's too dangerous for vehicles in that area until the storm passes. Helicopter crews are standing by to go as soon as the storm passes. My idea was to send a plane for you and Marie so you could be with Connie when she hears of the situation, or maybe it would be a good idea if you broke the news to her. How soon can you be ready to travel?"

"How soon can the plane get here sir?"

"I wanted to wait and see if you and I were thinking along the same lines before I dispatched the plane. Now that I see we are I would guess it will be at your location within the hour, weather permitting. Call me when you get here Walter."

"Yes sir. Certainly Sir. Thank you for calling me sir."

# McNeil

## Kelly Barracks
## Quarters 47

## Chapter 43
## 15 Jan 57

Connie McNeil had just finished tidying up the quarters when she heard a car pull up and stop. She was in her sixth month of pregnancy so she couldn't move as fast as she once could. She went to a window to see who it was and was surprised to see both her father and mother step out of the staff car with baggage. She opened the door as they came up the walk. "Well, isn't this a nice surprise. Hi Mom and Dad," she said going to each and hugging them. "Please, come on inside where it's warmer. What brings you out in this weather?" she asked as she closed the door behind them.

Neither said a word but Connie caught the look they exchanged. "Somebody want to tell me what is going on before I start guessing and get it wrong?"

"How are you feeling dear?" asked her mother.

"I was feeling fine until just now. Not that you aren't welcome anytime but why an unannounced visit?"

"Can we at least drop this luggage and sit down?" asked her dad.

"Oh, I'm sorry. Sure, just drop the luggage anywhere and let's go into the living room," said Connie leading the way and taking a seat on the couch.

"Connie," said her dad, you're right. There is a special reason for this unannounced visit. There is no easy way to say this. Connie, Charley is missing."

"What do you mean dad, Charley is missing? How? When?"

"Please stay calm dear," said her mother as she moved closer and put her arms around her daughter."

"It's hard to stay calm when something like this is sprung on me. Talk to me dad."

"All we know at this time is that the helicopter Charley and part of his team was on disappeared into a snow storm and radio communication

419

was lost. We won't know more until the storm passes. I offered to send in troops but General Clark, who called me and sent his plane to bring me and your mother here, said that all that could be done is being done. We are all waiting for the storm to pass so helicopters with men can get into the area and determine just what happened."

"I'll make some coffee," offered Marie, "I think we could all use some and a splash of brandy might go good."

"I think that's a good idea," said General Layton, "and while you are doing that I'll call General Clark and find out if he has any news."

"Coffee is fine mother but you know I'm not supposed to drink alcohol."

"Under the circumstances," spoke General Layton, "I don't think a small shot of brandy will harm you or the baby. I'm going to have one myself right after I speak to General Clark."

While Marie was in the kitchen preparing the coffee, and after Walter spoke to General Clark, the doorbell rang and Walter went to see who was at the door. "Hello General Gallows," he said when he opened the door and saw who rang the doorbell, "won't you come in?"

"I don't mean to intrude sir but General Clark sends his compliments and best wishes."

"Please tell him I said thanks."

"Is there anything I can do sir?"

"Nothing at this time. Do you have some new information?"

"The latest is that the storm is slowly moving north and the helicopters will try to fly around to the rear of it. They took off ten minutes ago with medics and part of the accident investigation team. Hopefully we'll have an update soon."

"Thank you general and you will keep me posted?"

"Yes sir. Please relate to General McNeil's wife mine and General Clark's compliments and if there is anything we can do please don't hesitate to call."

"Thank you and please thank General Clark for me. We are about to have a bit of coffee, fortified. Would you care to join us?"

"Under different circumstances I would be glad to but I best get back to headquarters sir."

"I understand general. Call anytime if there is a change."

"Yes sir."

"Who was that dad?" asked Connie when he came back into the living room.

"That was General Clark's aide, General Gallows. He and General Clark send's their compliments and if we need anything we have but to call."

"That's nice of them but right now all I need is some good news."

"He did say the storm is slowly moving north and the helicopters have departed to try and get behind it. Let's hope they are successful and can get men on the ground to find out what happened."

"Ah, here comes the coffee," said Walter sitting down near the fire.

"Anything new Walter?" asked Marie as she poured the coffee..

"There's nothing new until the helicopters, which were finally able to get off the ground, reach the crash site dear."

Walter and Marie were finally able to convince Connie that one shot of brandy wouldn't be harmful. As they sat and drank the brandy laced coffee they talked about the past and the future. About things they seemed to never get around to during a normal visit. The waiting was the hardest part and an hour had passed when the doorbell sounded again. "I'll get it," spoke General Layton as he got up to answer it.

"I'll come with you dad," said Connie as she slowly got up off the couch, "I need to move around anyway.

"I might as well tag along also," spoke Marie as she put her arms around her daughter and walked her to the door arriving just as Walter opened the door to find General Gallows standing there.

"Won't you come in General?" asked General Layton holding the door open.

"Just for a moment, I'm just here to pass on the latest information Sir," he replied as he looked at the two women present. Good morning Ladies." "I had hoped to speak to you alone sir," said General Gallows turning back to General Layton."

"We're talking about my husband here General Gallows. Whatever you have to say I'll hear about it later so please go ahead," said Connie very forcefully.

"Well, if you're sure."

"I'm sure general, replied Connie.

"The rescue team has reached the wreck which is about half way up the side of the mountain. The helicopter is totaled. Inside the team found four people, all deceased."

"Oh my God," called out Connie as she turned to her mother and laid her head on her shoulder.

"Ma'am," spoke General Gallows, "none of the four was General McNeil."

"What? Did you hear that mother? Charley wasn't in the helicopter—. Wait a minute," said Connie as it dawned on her, "if Charley isn't in the helicopter then where is he?"

"At this time we have no idea Ma'am. The teams are still searching through the snow around the crash site."

"Mom," spoke Connie very softly to her mother as the two turned to go back into the house but General Gallows and Walter heard her, "I have a very strong feeling that Charley is going to be ok."

General Layton looked at General Gallows and shrugged his shoulders. "Thank you for stopping by General Gallows. Please come again with any news."

"Sorry to be the bearer of sad news sir," replied General Gallows as he turned and walked out the door. General Layton closed the door and joined his daughter and wife in the living room.

"Dad, Mom," spoke Connie when they were all seated again, "Charley and I have, I don't know what one would call it, maybe a strong connection. I know in my heart that he is ok and will come back to me, to us. He may be missing but---"

"Hang onto that thought," said her Dad, "Charley has always been a hard charger, but a survivor." I only hope, for my daughter's sake, that he is a survivor, just one more time, but the chances are pretty slim. But if he wasn't found in the wrecked helicopter where is he? Or should I say, where is his body?

Even though it's been only a few years it seems a life time that I have known Charley McNeil.

Now here he is missing and presumed dead and I have a pregnant daughter who will give birth to a child without a father; a child who will never know what a fine man his father was, except by word of mouth.

What kind of a world will it be without Charley McNeil in it?

The men who comprise the United States Military forces are your friends and neighbors. They have been called forth to preserve the freedom that many people take for granted. Many of these men will make the supreme sacrifice.

R. W. Powers, a widower, resides in his home state of Florida.

He is a retired military veteran who was awarded the Bronze Star and Air Medal for service in Vietnam.

# WATCH FOR
# MCNEIL TOO

He heard voices in the other room and then people in some kind of uniforms entered the room where he was lying in bed. Just who they were he had no idea but a tag on their uniforms read U S Army. Who and what is U S Army? Where are Frau and Herr Guthrie who have taken care of me? Why aren't they here now?

When he was finally able to regain conscience he had no idea where he was at or what had happened that caused him to be out in the cold and blowing snow. He stood up and brushed the snow off his clothes and almost fell when a spell of dizziness caused him to sit back down. He had trouble moving his left arm and there was great pain when he tried to move it. He was finely able to stand up again and not having any idea where he was he staggered down the mountain side and started walking. Sometime later he saw lights and a small house appeared through the falling snow. He had to hold onto the wall as he knocked on the door. His head hurt and his shoulder felt as if it was on fire but he had no idea why that was so. Finally the door was opened and a woman stood there with her mouth open. "Mein Gott," she exclaimed as she stood looking at the man with blood on the side of his head.

When he next opened his eyes he was undressed and lying in a warm bed, apparently inside the house. He had no recollection of events after the house door was opened. His head was bandaged and his left shoulder was in some kind of sling. He recalled the times the woman and sometimes a man came in to the room with warm food. Always the woman asked who he was and why he was out in the snow. He had no answers. The woman introduced herself as Frau Guthrie and the man as her husband Herr Guthrie and she kept asking for his name. She did ask if the name on his shirt was his name. He couldn't answer truthfully because he didn't know. They called him McNeil so he had to assume that was his name.

He had no idea how long he was in the house with the two people caring for him. His head ached and his shoulder was in constant pain.

When the men in some kind of uniform entered the room one man spoke and called him general. Is that my name, McNeil General?

"We're here to help you General," said the man who seemed to be in charge. "We'll get you checked over and out of here to a place where you can be treated properly. How does the head feel?"

"Very painful," he answered wondering why Frau and Herr Guthrie spoke to him in a different language yet he could understand both languages.

"If you will take these two pills they will ease that pain somewhat," said the man holding out two white pills and a glass of water.

"Just who are you and why are you here," asked the man refusing to take the pills because he had no idea of what was going on and who these people were that came in out of the cold.

"I'm Doctor Everett and we have been looking for you for several days now General. I assure you the pills won't harm you and they will ease that head pain."

The man who had no idea who he was or who these strange looking men were reluctantly took the pills and swallowed them.

"We can't do much for you here General so we will have to move you. I'm going to give you a shot that will put you to sleep so that any pain from moving you won't be felt by you." A man handed the doctor a cotton swab then a needle.


When he woke up he found himself in a different room with the drapes drawn and he was lying in a bed. He felt his head and discovered it was bandaged. His left shoulder and arm was in a sling. There was little pain from either now. There was no noise and he had no idea where he was. He looked around and discovered he had a needle in his good arm which was attached to a bottle on a stand. Some kind of liquid was slowly dripping through a tube and into his arm. The room was warm and with no pain he drifted off to sleep.

Voices work him and when the room door opened a distinguished looking man entered followed by a dark haired lady. Behind them came a pregnant woman who looked so much like the elderly lady.

"I do believe he is awake," spoke the man, "Welcome back to the world Charley."

He called me Charley. That's three different names I have been called. Just what is my name and where am I. Who are these people who seem to know me yet I have no idea who they are.

As he watched the three people the pregnant lady wiped tears from her eyes and came to the bed and wrapped her arms around him. "I'm so relieved that you are ok Charley," she said.

"Who are you," he asked.

The lady suddenly pulled back with a surprised look on her face.

"Don't you remember me Charley?" she asked.